Child of Aetos

Ian Saunderson

Published in 2008 by YouWriteOn.com

Copyright © Ian Saunderson

First Edition

The author asserts the moral right under the Copyright, Designs and Patents Act 1988 to be identified as the author of this work.

All rights reserved. No part of this publication may be reproduced, stored in a retrieval system, or transmitted, in any form or by any means without the prior written consent of the author, nor be otherwise circulated in any form of binding or cover other than that in which it is published and without a similar condition being imposed on the subsequent purchaser.

Published by YouwriteOn.com

Chapter 1 – *Bolton, October 15, 1651*

"Be Thou my refuge in this time of trouble." Psalms ix. 9.

A crimson pool on the boards of the scaffold dripped through the wood to the dry earth below. A black mongrel ran up and licked the blood. With a strange display of compassion for the executed man, a soldier kicked it and the dog scampered away. The Earl of Derby's body lay on the platform, head parted from torso. The executioner, a smile on his lips, lifted the head to the crowd which let forth a groan. In the mid afternoon sun, the dead face displayed a calmness it had lacked the last few days.

    Paul Morrow looked down at his shirt and touched some of the droplets of blood that had splattered him. He smelt the coppery blood of the earl and the shit of the soldiers' horses; evoking memories of battlefields. Paul suppressed the impulse to retch and looked up, taking in his surroundings again. He saw Parliamentarian soldiers striding around the market place, hitting out at people. Some of these people were now staunching their own wounds with linen handkerchiefs they had brought to dip in the Earl of Derby's blood.

    Paul was holding the earl's speech and signet ring. He rubbed the shape of the eagle, "aetos" in the centre of the ring and this familiar symbol reassured him.

    The earl's chaplain, Mr. Greenhalgh, vomited. From his position on the scaffold he directed his spew onto some of the soldiers on the market square below. The onlookers laughed, revelling in the soldiers' discomfort. The Parliamentarian officer, Captain Smith was talking to the sergeant of the earl's escort and pointing at Paul. Paul knew with James dead on the scaffold, the soldiers now wanted his papers.

    Taking advantage of the commotion around Mr. Greenhalgh, he descended from the scaffold and pushed past a soldier at the bottom of the steps. The crowd was between him and the main company of soldiers. Using the body of people as a shield he ran to Daniel, waiting outside the Man and Scythe inn.

    'We've got to get away,' said Paul.

    'No, Paul. I can't go. I promised James I'd do him one last service. I'll go to Ormskirk with Charles and Mr. Greenhalgh to see him buried. It's you they want and those papers.'

    'Don't provoke them,' said Paul. 'Leave as soon as you can and take care of Charles.'

'Here take my sword,' Daniel replied, unbuckling his scabbard belt. 'Go. God be with you.'

Paul mounted his horse and drew the sword, dropping the scabbard in his haste. He spurred his horse on, aiming to escape out of Bolton by the Preston road over the moors. In the market square, people were screaming and rushing in all directions, trying to get out of the way of the soldiers; the soldiers bellowing at them to clear a path.

His horse was pressed in by the frightened mob. Paul turned to see a cavalryman bearing down on him, sword outstretched. He parried and felt a sharp pain in his shoulder as he deflected the blow. In desperation he thrust out his blade and slashed the trooper's thigh. The throng had finally scattered and he urged his horse on. He had left his assailant behind, but heard the sound of other horses pursuing him down the cobbled street. The air was thick with sweat and the sound of his ragged breath. Paul kicked his heels into the horse's flanks and galloped until he reached Smithhills Hall. He dared glance over his shoulder and winced with the pain as he did so. Two men were chasing him, but their horses were losing ground.

Seeing an orchard to the side of the road he steered his horse towards it, using it as cover as he headed off at a right angle to the road. He put his hand to the wound. Warm, sticky blood greeted his fingers and although it did not seem deep, his shoulder throbbed and he felt giddy.

After a few more miles he began to slip in and out of consciousness. He grasped the neck of his horse to stay upright. Some time later he woke on hearing muffled voices. It was now dark all around and a cold mist swirled about. The reins of the horse were taken and the beast stopped. A man and a woman helped Paul down from the saddle; he stumbled and fell, losing consciousness.

***

He awoke to find himself lying in a bed, sunlight streaking through the small shuttered window. Paul was not sure how long he had been asleep, though his bladder told him he had just woken in time. His shoulder still pounded and on trying to stand his legs did not seem to work. He collapsed onto the chamber pot by the bed. The blissful relief was interrupted as he heard footsteps approaching the door.

'Wait,' he shouted as the door latch began to lift. Whoever it was stopped and knocked. Paul righted himself and with his dignity restored said, 'Come in.'

A woman entered the room with a bowl and a pitcher of water on a tray.

'Awake at last,' she said smiling. 'Thought you were going t' sleep all day.' Putting the tray down on a chest at the foot of the bed she continued, 'Expect you'll want to wash. But before you do, drink this. It'll help with the pain.'

As she spoke Paul looked at her more closely. She was about fifty years old, small and squat, dressed in simple clothes. She had broad arms and her large strong hands held out a cup for him.

He took the drink from her. In it was a dark, foul smelling liquid. 'What is it?' he asked.

'Burdock in hot water. Doesn't taste right good, but it'll help.'

Paul downed the liquid, grimacing. It was bitter, but thankfully there was not very much to drink. He sat back down on the bed and noticed his satchel lying open on the floor, its contents visible. Paul saw she was looking in the direction of his gaze.

'We had a look in it to see who you are. With that wound we were worried you'd die. By God's grace the wound were clean. I had much worse to deal with after Cromwell's butchery at Preston. You'll need a few days rest, but after that you'll be fine. Name's Mary by the way.'

Paul's initial fear that the letter, books and papers in his satchel would lead to his betrayal was eased by her words. 'It's not safe for you to shelter me; I should leave,' he said looking at her face for any sign she agreed, hoping she wouldn't. 'They'll come looking for me, and it would be bad for you if they found me here.'

'Don't fret about that. You'll be safe. We've got a few priest holes you can hide in. The Earl of Derby was a good friend t' Catholic gentlemen, so I'm happy to shelter you from the roundheads.'

She looked Paul in the eye and asked, 'Were you there at his execution?'

'Lamentably, I was. The earl was a noble man, honourable to the end. Even on the scaffold he spoke of forgiveness for his enemies.' Paul paused, recalling the horrific scene of the day before. Mary was silent, her eyes encouraging him to carry on. 'I've lost a true and gracious friend.'

'But, why did the soldiers attack you?' she asked.

'They attacked the crowd out of fear,' replied Paul. He was being truthful, but did not want to reveal that the Parliamentarians wanted to capture him because of the earl's papers.

'My final duty for him is to take a letter to his wife, Charlotte,' he continued. 'She's still on the Isle of Man and may not even know of his death.' An image of his own family, sheltering on the Isle came into Paul's mind, rekindling the longing in his heart.

'Poor woman,' Mary replied. 'How many of us have suffered these past ten years?' she said. 'Anyroads, you'll still be tired no doubt. When you're rested we can talk more.'

'Are you sure it's safe for me to stay here? I mean safe for you?'

'Don't you worry. We're not scared of a few soldiers.'

Chapter 2 – *Lathom House, November 1625*

"Some men have in readiness so many tales and stories as there is nothing they would insinuate but they can wrap it into a tale which seemeth both to keep themselves more in guard, and to make others carry it with more pleasure." Private Devotions of James Stanley.

I am Paul Morrow, a man now held in contempt by many I once counted as my true friends. To them I will always be the man who betrayed the Stanleys. Certainly the countess never forgave me. That's why we had to leave Lancashire and come down to London, where my wife has family. But it was not really a betrayal; I was only doing as James asked me. Besides my desire to fight had died with James, so how could I watch others suffer? I am sorry; these must seem like the ramblings of an old man. I must do as the old earl taught me and apply some method to this history. It all seems a long time ago, and we have a Stuart on the throne again. So much bloodshed, so many sacrifices. Was all of it worth it?

I entered the service of the Stanleys in the year the first King Charles came to the throne. It was a cold, damp autumn morning as I rode the final miles to Lathom House. Mist rose from the fields and seeped into my bones. I drew my cloak tightly around my shoulders. I could make out a large tower from a distance and knew from the talk of the inn keeper the night before that this was the Eagle Tower, planted in the middle of the house itself.

It was impossible to get a full view of the house as there was hilly, forested ground in front of me. Then I rounded the summit and there, spread out before me, was the most formidable castle I had ever seen. The Eagle Tower rose up out of the mist; a hard, square sandstone keep, proclaiming the power of the Earl of Derby.

In comparison to Hoghton Tower near Preston where I had spent several years, it was larger and looked to be impregnable. Its aspect resembled the palm of a man's hand, the castle in a hollow in the centre with ascending ground all around. There was a circular wall, as tall as three men, with crenellated battlements. In front of the wall was a wide moat, with a bridge across it leading to a gateway that had two guard towers on top. Interspersed around the wall were further towers.

I rode up to the gate where my way was blocked by a guard. He thrust his halberd towards me and shouted. 'Stop. Who are you and what is your business here?'

'Paul Morrow,' I replied, 'come to serve the earl as estate clerk.'

I dismounted and walked through the gate and under the portcullis. I handed over my letter of introduction, doubting whether the fellow could read it, but knowing he would recognise the seal of the Earl of Derby.

The guard saw the seal and took a step back, lowering his halberd.

'John,' he called out to a lad who was sitting on a wall eating some bread. 'Stable this gentleman's horse and then take him up to the steward.'

I walked into the court where maids were about their morning chores, fetching water, gathering eggs from the hen coops. Stable lads were grooming horses and preparing them for a morning ride. I looked up at the house with another inner wall protecting it. John led me through a gate in the inner wall and then into the house itself. After mounting several flights of a spiral staircase, we entered a small antechamber.

Here a man was seated at a desk covered with papers. He was in the middle of eating and looked up as we approached, brushing some crumbs out of his beard.

'This is the steward,' whispered the boy who had brought me up from the gatehouse.

'Sir, I've brought Paul Morrow to see you. He says he is the new estate clerk.' With that the boy turned and left the room.

The steward got up, looming over me as he stood up to his full height. 'Break your fast with me,' he said indicating bread, cheese and a pitcher of beer with a wave of his arm.

'Thank you, that is most kind.' I was hungry after the early morning ride and the food looked very appealing.

'Where are you from?' he enquired.

'From Hoghton, near Preston,' I replied, biting into a chunk of bread.

'I'm a Wigan man myself, though I've lived here at Lathom for the past nine years. I've only been to Preston a few times. The earl does not have much business up there.'

I nodded and took a mouthful of beer. It was cold and refreshing.

'I don't know the name Morrow. None in the household to my knowledge. Have you come from Hoghton Tower?' he asked.

'Yes, I was in the service of Sir Richard Hoghton. He took me into his household about five years ago when my aunt found it too difficult to keep me.'

'You're an orphan then?'

I looked down. 'My parents died when I was eight.'

The steward ruffled a few papers on his desk. 'The earl will explain most of your duties, but you will work for me one day a week on the household accounts. I have ledgers that need copying, and there are new ones to be written.'

Brusquely he told me what money would be mine after food and lodging had been deducted and then a servant was called to show me to my sleeping area.

The lad was about my own age of seventeen. He was lanky and walked as if he had not fully grown into his body.

'Mornin'. My name's Bootle. I'll show you the ropes. Don't worry about the steward. Thinks he's something special that one. Just do your work and you'll be right. Best person round here is Meg in the kitchen. Stay on the right side of her and she'll see you're fed proper.'

Bootle led me down through a series of rooms, initially quite large until we were away from the main chambers. Then the rooms became smaller and windowless, flames from torches providing minimal light. Shadows flickered behind us as we walked, and my nostrils took in the stale smells of the old castle. Eventually we stopped at a door which he opened.

'You'll be sharing this room with me. It's a bit damp because of the moat, but
the bedding's good. Put down your things and come back with me. You've to wait on the earl now, but it could be a long time before you see him. His actors are here again and there's nothing he likes more than talking to them about their latest plays.'

I was nervous as we walked back up to the main chambers. I knew I came with a good reference from Sir Richard Hoghton, but I was not acquainted with anyone of such prominence.

There were shouts up ahead in the main hall and I wondered how there could be so much noise in the presence of the earl. The doors were open and I saw a group of men dressed in half armour and holding spears and swords. Surely the place could not be under attack?

'Don't worry,' said Bootle smiling as he saw my unease, 'it's just the earl and his Derby Players. They are practising a play. Stand over there and watch.'

For a few minutes I watched the actors as they rehearsed. Behind them, on the other side of the room was a group of men. They were sat together and watching the actors. I continued to observe and then one of the men stood up and applauded, causing the players to step aside. He praised them for their efforts and they left the room. For the first time I was able to get a good look at the earl. I knew him to be in his sixties, but he looked at least ten years younger. He was dressed in the fashion of the late court, with a ruff around his neck and his breeches ended above his knees. He wore a full facial beard after the practice of the late King James, rather than the moustache, adopted by men recently returned from the Grand Tour. His hair was short and mostly grey, though there was a dark tone to it, suggesting it had once been black.

The earl approached and I took out my letter of introduction. For a man of his age his movement was quick and energetic. A seal hanging on a gold chain around his neck bobbed up and down with each step. As he came towards me I bowed low.

'Pleased to make your acquaintance Mr. Morrow.' The earl offered his hand.

As I shook it, he leant forward and patted me on the shoulder. 'Did you like that?' he asked, smiling. 'They are in good form, but not as good as when they played at Hoghton with Will Shakespeare himself leading them. How we miss him.'

'Yes I enjoyed the short piece I saw, my lord.'

The earl fingered the seal hanging from his neck. 'They are performing tonight, so you will be able to see it all then. Now, you have a good clear hand I trust, as I write some plays myself and I prefer to dictate rather than write it all down.'

'Yes, certainly,' I replied. 'And I can copy manuscripts too, should you require.'

'Excellent. Well then, I expect you are tired after your journey. Tell me how is
Sir Richard? I felt very sorry for his incarceration. Hosting a king on a royal progress is always expensive, but laying a red carpet, half a mile long all the way down the hill from the gatehouse!' said the earl, chuckling. 'No wonder he landed himself in debt!'

I did not share the earl's amusement and thought it wise to steer the conversation in another direction. 'Sir Richard is well my lord.' I took a letter out of my pouch. 'He asked me to deliver this to you.'

I had written the letter for Sir Richard and so I knew the contents. The main purpose was to ask William for his advice about more actively enforcing the Recusancy laws against Catholics, in line with the latest instructions from the King's secretary. This caused Sir Richard some consternation, for it was well known that as part of the negotiations prior to the marriage of King Charles with Henrietta Maria of France, the French had asked for a suspension of the penal laws.

I knew from Sir Richard that the earl, although Protestant, pursued a policy of peaceful coexistence with his many Catholic neighbours. In Lancashire many people, gentry and commoners, still held to the old religion. Some said it was due to the distance from London and the remoteness of the region. However, there were areas where Protestantism was strong, places like Stockport and Bolton, where merchants and cloth makers held sway, the influence of the great landowners and the gentry being very limited in the towns. Here the church ministers and also the lecturers appointed by the town corporations, were active in preaching the Gospel of Protestantism.

The earl took the letter, broke the seal and began to read. As he did so, he ran a finger through his beard, and a concerned look came over his face. Abruptly he stopped reading, saying he would finish it later in his chamber. He went out of the hall by another door which I presumed led to his private rooms.

I took myself to be dismissed. Looking up at the walls as I made my way to the door, my eyes were drawn to a tapestry of a battle scene, with coats of arms above the knights engaged in the fighting. It had to be Bosworth. Richard III was lying dead in the foreground. Two prominent figures were standing nearby, a Stanley offering the crown to Henry Tudor.

I wondered if the guard at the gatehouse would let me onto the walls. I made my way out of the Eagle Tower and back across the courtyard to the gatehouse.

The guard recognized me and nodded a greeting as I approached. I was grateful to him for I knew no-one at Lathom.

'The earl takes youths into his household and men too, but I can't work out where you fit. How old are you?'

'Seventeen,' I replied.

'Old enough for service. What is it you're here to do?'

'I'm to be a secretary for the earl. I've been tutored with Sir Gilbert Hoghton's son, Richard and have been secretary to Sir Richard Hoghton for the last year.'

'A scholar, ay. Well the earl will like that. See the tower over there?' he indicated a tower to our right on the curtain wall. 'That's the Private Tower, where he has all his books. His library is full of them.'

I tried not to smile. What else did he think a library was for? I was about to ask if I could go into the gatehouse and up onto the walls when I saw Bootle crossing the courtyard. He waved to me and came over.

'Do you want me to show you around?' he said. 'How about a tour of the Eagle Tower or do you want to see the chapel?'

'I would like to see the earl's library. Is that possible? I don't think I'll be allowed in there on my own.'

'If you are going to be the earl's secretary then you'll need to know where his library is. Come with me,' said Bootle, starting to walk towards the tower.

I took my leave from the guard and followed Bootle. The Private Tower was large and square with a door close to the curtain wall. We entered and Bootle immediately scurried up a spiral staircase on the right. Nobody stopped us, but then I assumed Bootle was well known and had the run of most of the castle. After a short climb we reached the first floor. The staircase continued upwards, but Bootle opened the door in front of us.

A musty smell of old books, mingled with the aroma of scented candles greeted us. Bootle was blocking my vision, but what I could see excited me, a table in the middle of the room covered with papers and books, and at the far side of the room books piled high on shelves which seemed to reach the ceiling. Following Bootle inside, I saw more bookcases lining all the walls.

'The earl must have been amassing this collection all his life,' I marvelled.

'Oh, he's always having new books sent from London, or Amsterdam, or Paris. You can find all sorts here. I can only read the English ones, but the earl can read French, Latin and Greek too.'

I walked over to the desk and read the titles of the books lying there. I saw a copy of 'Lives of the Twelve Caesars' by Suetonius. Next I picked up 'Mr. William Shakespeare's Comedies, Histories and

Tragedies'. I did not recognize the names of the next few I looked at. Then one caught my eye, Machiavelli 'The Prince'. I tried to recall why this was familiar to me and then I remembered. Sir Richard Hoghton had talked about it giving guidance to a ruler about how to govern. He did not possess a copy and so I had not read it. Perhaps I would be able to read it here.

My browsing was interrupted by Bootle. 'Have you seen enough? The earl keeps some of his own documents in the library and we really should have his permission to be in here alone.'

I was surprised Bootle had not told me this before, although spotting some papers lying on the desk, I saw it could be true. I put Machiavelli's book down, wondering when I would be able to ask the earl if I could read it.

***

That evening, Bootle took me back to the Great Hall to dine. Nearly all the household was assembled by the time we arrived and we found a couple of places on one of the benches at the far end of the room. We sat and waited for the earl and his family to take their places on the high table. A few minutes later all chattering stopped as the earl entered the hall from his chambers and took his place. I assumed the elderly woman on the earl's left was his wife, Elizabeth de Vere. I caught a glimpse of a handsome man of similar age to me, seated on the earl's right; his son perhaps.

Once the earl had started to eat, the kitchen lads brought out our food in trays. One was set down near to me and I got a whiff of stew, causing my stomach to rumble.

Bootle laughed and pointed to the platter. 'Have you tried these? They're potatoes. The cook mixes them in with bits of lamb and cooks it as a stew. Grab a plateful.'

I took hold of my spoon and scooped out a helping into my wooden dish. I had not eaten these before. They were floury white and seemed to have been cut into pieces. As I set them in my dish a lamb bone was revealed.

'Good,' I mumbled with a mouthful of the warm food in my mouth. I held the bone with my left hand and cut off the meat with my knife.

'The Derby Players will be on after we've supped,' said Bootle. 'We'll have to stay and watch.'

'I'd like that.' I helped myself to some beer from a large tankard. Over on the high table the earl and his family were eating a variety of game birds and slicing cuts off a hog roast.

Once we had finished eating, the platters and bowls were taken away and under the instruction of the steward, we pushed the tables back against the wall. Some sat on the benches, others on the tables as we waited for the actors to appear.

The troop made their way out into the space in the hall. They moved a few people back and picked up some bones that had been discarded onto the floor. Then they walked out of the hall.

'That were good,' said somebody from behind me. A few people laughed. The earl looked over and frowned.

'Shut yoursel' up,' hissed the steward. 'Remember, Earl William likes his players and pays them handsomely.' The crowd settled down and we waited.

A single actor ran back into the hall. He was short and wiry. Holding a small crown in place with his hand, he made a low bow to the earl and the high table. Then he walked to the centre of the room, stood motionless for a few moments and then began to speak.

During the evening as we watched the play, I thought of its significance to the Stanleys. No doubt Earl William enjoyed seeing his forebear portrayed as a Kingmaker. It was a play unlikely to be performed a great deal on the public stage. The theme of deposing a king, albeit a cynical exploiter like Richard III was not popular with our new royal house. Charles, having just come to the throne did not want his subjects thinking rebellion could be justified, no matter how evil the King.

***

The next day I learnt the reason for the earl's sudden exit when I had handed him Sir Richard's letter. I was summoned to attend on him in his private chamber. A man was seated by the fire with some papers spread out over a small table. I took him to be about eighteen. He had similar features to the earl, but wore his dark hair long and had a thin moustache rather than a full beard. Despite the coldness of the day he wore a white linen shirt, black breeches, black stockings and black shoes. The clothes though simple were well tailored and immaculate. He seemed at ease in the company of the earl.

'Mr. Morrow, this is my son, James the Lord Strange,' said the earl.

Lord Strange acknowledged my arrival with a nod. I bowed in front of him.

The earl looked at his son, and continued. 'We have need of your services. James will be setting out for Lord Morley's house to seize weapons which could be used in a Catholic rising.' He paused briefly at this point and his son shifted his position on his chair.

'This is on the orders of Conway, the King's Secretary. He does not think us diligent enough in enforcing the penal laws in our counties. We have no doubt as to the loyalty of Lord Morley. His great grandmother was a Stanley. Still, we have to be seen to be carrying out the royal policies, even if we do not agree with them.'

As I listened, I imagined they wanted me to accompany Lord Strange as a scribe in order to make a record of any weapons found in the search.

The earl continued, 'Lord Morley may know you from your service at Hoghton, but so that he knows your warning to be genuine, you are to give him this and tell him one word, "aetos".'

The earl handed me a small ring. On it was a small design of a Greek eagle, "aetos", a bird I knew to be a symbol of the Stanley family.

'You are to set off at once for Hornby Castle and tell Lord Morley that a search is to be made of his house. James will follow the next day. That will give enough time for Henry to remove any weapons from the house. So as to avoid any suspicion you are to travel on your own and come back to Lathom before James returns.'

Perspiration trickled on my brow. The earl continued, 'If you are intercepted then you are not known to us and are acting on your own.'

With that he took a letter from the table and put it on the fire. I saw it was my letter of introduction. I stared at the parchment as it browned at the edges and then burst into flames, burning bright.

The earl and his son were both watching me for my reaction. I groped for words. 'Err…, it will be an honour to perform this service for you.'

'Excellent,' exclaimed Lord Strange as he got to his feet. He came over and extended his hand for me to shake. 'Excellent, excellent,' he repeated. 'Go to the stables now. You'll find your horse saddled and ready for you. If anyone asks, tell them you have letters to deliver to Knowsley and will be gone for several days.'

I was stunned and stood there mute. I knew Lord Morley lived near Lancaster, but no more than that. 'How do I get to Hornby Castle?'

'Go up to Lancaster and then follow the Lune valley,' the earl replied. 'After about seven miles you'll come to a split in the river. Follow the right fork, which is the river Wenning. It'll take you to the castle.'

My mind raced, but I understood enough to know how to get there. Fiddling with the earl's ring in my fingers, I bowed to him and Lord Strange before leaving the room.

***

The request gave me a feeling of great trepidation. I recalled listening to the sermons of the minister in Lancaster. Was it not true that the Pope is the Anti-Christ? To be caught helping Catholics could be fatal. Just a few years before I was born a group had attempted to kill King James in the Gunpowder Plot. Persecutions of Catholics had followed, and I did not want to be caught up in any treason. Despite worrying about what I had been asked to do, I did not feel I could question the earl and Lord Strange on this.

I expected the journey to be uneventful, but it would take several days, which gave me ample time to fret about the task. I decided to call in on my old schoolmaster at the grammar school in Lancaster and ask his advice. Arriving in the town as the watch was preparing to shut the town gates, I made my way up to the school. Ann, the housekeeper opened the door when I rapped on the knocker of the master's house.

'Paul, is that you?' she asked. 'Come in here so I can take a good look at you.'

I entered the hallway, a warm fire inviting me in. Light came from candles set into sconces on the wall.

'A man now, I see. Nout but a boy when you left us to go to Hoghton,' she said smiling. 'What brings you here?'

'I need to ask some advice of the master.'

'He'll be taking his supper soon. I'll see if I can stretch it out to feed you too.'

'That is very kind. I don't want to be any trouble.'

'You'll be wanting a bed tonight,' she replied. 'I'll fix up a mattress in the school room. Now come with me; I'll take you through.'

I followed the soberly dressed Ann to the master's rooms, passing the chair she used to make us sit on if we felt ill. We found the master in his study. He put down the book he had been reading and came over to greet me.

'Well, if it isn't Mr. Morrow,' he said, pumping my hand. 'Very pleased to see you again. Here, come and sit down.'

'Supper will be in ten minutes,' said Ann. 'I'll set a plate for Paul.'

I fidgeted in the chair, waiting until Ann left the room. The master watched her close the door and then continued. 'Lovely woman, but she often makes me think I married her! Now Paul, I sense you have something on your mind. Tell me.'

I explained how the earl had asked me to take a verbal warning to Lord Morley about the impending search of his house for weapons. 'Look, here is the ring he gave me to convince Lord Morley.'

'You are in a quandary, aren't you?' he replied, balancing the ring on his palm as he looked at it. 'If you are caught with this, then its link back to the Stanleys could be dangerous for you. How you will explain your possession of it without betraying your mission?'

'I don't know, and I fear the Stanleys would denounce me as a thief to protect themselves. But if I don't do this for them, then I have no future in their household. And I cannot go back to Hoghton as they would soon discover me there.'

'Do you think they want you to be caught?'

'Well the earl seems kind enough, more interested in his books and plays than politics. I don't think he means me any harm. I'm not so sure about Lord Strange. He seems more aloof and I'm not sure if I trust him.'

'The earl is an experienced man. He's been running his family affairs for nearly thirty years since his brother died. He keeps the peace with a lot of Catholic gentry, so no doubt he turns a blind eye to what they do in private. I wouldn't be surprised if he gives them warning before any searches.'

'So do you think it'll be safe for me to do this?'

'Now Paul, I can't tell you if this will be safe. What I can say is, you probably don't have any choice if you want to remain in their household. You could run off to London. You could join the navy. I think we will have wars enough to fight with Buckingham's influence over the young King. However, I know you are a sensitive scholar; I can't see you at war or on the streets of London. You could do well with the Stanleys. They always have need of intelligent servants. Just keep your eyes open and think of this as a test.'

Ann called us through to supper. While we ate she asked all sorts of questions. They flooded over me. 'Is Lord Strange going to be married soon? Is his mother ill?' I answered as best I could, but for every answer I gave she had another question.

After we finished eating I left them and went off to bed. As I unrolled my mattress on the cold schoolroom floor, memories of my schooling came back to me. One of Sophocles' expressions sprang to mind, *"there is a scorpion under every stone"*. I had no money and little hope of being employed anywhere else. It seemed I had to go through with it.

***

The noise of my horse disturbed birds feeding on blackberries in the hedgerow of the Lune valley. Having travelled about six or seven miles I reached the point where the Wenning joined the river. I dismounted to give my horse a rest and followed the tributary east towards Hornby. Kicking crisp autumn leaves out of my path, I thought about the task ahead.

After a while I remounted, thinking it would create a better impression arriving on horseback. I could see a small village nestling around the large tower of a castle. I was stopped before I even got to the village. A lone sentry was posted on the bridge.

'Halt. What brings you here stranger?' he said in a surly tone. No doubt his mood was affected by his solitary duty.

'I have business with Lord Morley,' I replied. 'I bring a message from the Earl of Derby.'

'Follow the road up to the castle and ask to see the steward,' he said, pointing up the road.

At the gate the guards steered me into the guardroom, but would let me go no further. I repeated that I had a message to deliver to their lord.

'Wait here for the steward. He will decide if you can see Lord Morley.'

As I waited I turned the Stanley's ring over and over in my fingers. What if Lord Morley did not believe my message? By the precautions he took it seemed he was a suspicious man. After what seemed an age, but in truth was probably no more than a quarter of an hour, a man entered the guardroom. He was short and strutted over like a cockerel.

'I hear you have a message for my lord. Hand it over and I'll take it to him,' he said curtly.

'It is a verbal message,' I replied.

He looked at me and was momentarily struck dumb. A few heartbeats later he asked, 'What is so important it can't be written down?'

'I don't wish to offend you, but my instructions are to explain that to Lord Morley.'

'Very well,' he said, studying me. 'But first you are to remove your sword.'

'As you wish,' I replied and unbuckled my sword belt, laying it on a table.

'This way,' said the steward, strutting out.

I followed him out of the guardroom, past the guards and across a courtyard. We climbed a staircase and came to a second floor. We passed through a doorway into a small antechamber, then entered the lord's chamber. It was far smaller than the chamber at Lathom. Fine tapestries of hunting scenes in rich red and green hues draped the walls. I smelt recently snuffed incense candles. At the far end of the room a man was seated in a raised chair, just as the earl sat in his presence chamber at Lathom. I hesitated, waiting for a signal from the steward.

'Approach,' boomed a voice from the dais.

I walked up alongside the steward, matching his pace. We stopped in front of Lord Morley.

'This man brings a message from the Earl of Derby,' said the steward. 'It's not written down and he says it is for you only to hear.'

'You may speak in front of my steward,' replied Lord Morley. 'I have few secrets from him.'

But I wager there are some you only share with your priest at confession, I thought, realizing the scent of incense meant the priest was probably close by.

'As you wish my lord,' I said. 'This will seem an odd message, but I have been sent to warn you that Lord Strange will arrive tomorrow with a warrant to search your house for arms and priests. It is the Earl of Derby himself who has sent me to warn you.'

The steward stole a glance at his master.

'We have nothing to hide,' said Lord Morley. 'We are loyal subjects of His Majesty. If I did have something to hide why would I believe you?'

'I have no written instruction my lord as the earl did not want any risk of the warning being traced back to him.' I brought out the ring that had been clenched in my hand and said, 'He asked me to show you this so you would know I speak the truth.'

'A ring. How does that show you are telling the truth?' spat the steward.

'William would never send me an unknown messenger with just a ring,' said Lord Morley. 'Take this madman away.'

The steward seized my arms and began to drag me towards the door. The guard on the door started over to help him.

'Aetos,' I blurted, remembering what William had instructed me to say when I showed the ring. 'Aetos,' I repeated as the second man wrenched my arm up my back, sending a stabbing pain through my body.

'Hold. What is it you said?' asked Lord Morley. The guard spun me round to face his lord.

'Aetos. The earl told me to say this as I showed you the ring.'

'And why this word then?' asked Lord Morley.

'It means eagle, which is a symbol of the Stanley family,' I replied. I looked into his face and the lines around his eyes fell away. The tension began to slip from me too as my arm was released from the guard's vice of a hold.

Turning to his steward, Lord Morley said, 'Have our muskets moved to a safer place.'

The steward and the guard left the room, leaving me with Lord Morley.

'Are you of the faith too?' he asked, looking me firmly in the eye.

'No, I am a Protestant of the Anglican Church.'

'Well, you must find the actions of the earl strange?'

'It's my duty to serve him, not question him.'

'Quite. Quite.' Lord Morley's eyes released me from their stare. 'I must apologize for my steward. I trust you are not hurt?'

'No, I am fine,' I said, stretching my arm out behind me.

'Thank you for delivering the message. You must go now.'

I took my leave from him and headed back out to the courtyard. Muskets were being loaded onto a cart. About three dozen of them were piled up and then a mound of straw was placed on top. The carter was an old man and he slowly climbed up behind the horse. Then he hurried the horse into action and set off down the track.

I followed the cart, then passed it. The driver looked up at me and grinned, revealing just a single tooth. I laughed, pleased to have carried out my task successfully, and my heart felt a lot lighter as I made my way back to Lathom House.

**

Lord Strange returned to Lathom a few days after me. I received a summons to see him the next morning.

'You have done well, Paul. My father decided to test you to see how you would respond to unusual orders. Having spoken to Lord Morley, I think you carried out the task dutifully.'

'Thank you my lord,' I replied.

'Our actions towards our Catholic neighbours might seem unusual. The Catholic gentry of the county are loyal to the Stanley family, and as we are loyal to the King, then by extension the Catholic gentry are also loyal to him. The King's ministers do not appreciate this.' Here he paused and looked at me to make sure I understood what he was saying. 'Hence the instruction of Conway to actively enforce the penal laws and disarm Catholics. Conway fears the Catholics might use the opportunity of the death of the King to rise before Charles's authority is well established.'

'And you do not see men like Lord Morley as a threat, my lord?'

'No, but we have to be seen to be enforcing the laws. But I won't prevent the Catholic gentry from protecting themselves and their estates. I am not the keeper of a man's conscience; that it between him and God.'

Chapter 3 – *Brindle, October 18, 1651*

"Mine eyes, mine eyes, run down with water, because the Comforter which should relieve my soul is far from me; my Children are desolate because the enemy prevailed." Lamentations i. 16.

Paul's wound was healing, but Mary did not think it was safe to travel. Dragoons were patrolling west of Preston, cutting off that route to the coast and the Isle of Man. This, in turn, prevented Paul from delivering James's letter to Charlotte. By now she might have learnt of his death and he thought the letter would give her some comfort. He resolved to wait another day then set out, hoping to find unguarded roads to the east of Preston. He would make for Salmsbury Hall, then travel north with Lancaster as his goal. Here he hoped to find a ship bound for the Isle of Man.

His thoughts were interrupted by an urgent rap on his door. It opened. 'There are soldiers in the village at Brindle. They are looking for one of Derby's men, who fled after the execution,' said Mary, a little breathlessly.

'Eh…, how soon before they come here?'

'There are a few other farms closer to the village they will probably search first. But we need to get you hidden. We have a priest hole that's never been found.'

'But what about my horse?'

'We can pass him off as one of ours. He is unsaddled and in the field with our horses. He looks a little grander than a farm hoss, I grant you. If they ask, I can tell them my man has been extravagant of late. Now grab your things and come with me.'

Paul stepped into his boots and picked up his satchel and sword. He followed Mary into the kitchen, thinking she was going to take him out of the farmhouse to hide in a barn. She stopped in front of the large open fireplace, where a low fire was burning, potage simmering in an iron pan suspended above the heat.

'Over here,' she said, beginning to move the pans and cooking utensils hanging on one side of the fireplace.

Paul looked at Mary, puzzled.

'Crouch down,' she said. 'Slide yoursel' round the fire to the back of the fireplace. Then go into the corner. See how the chimney breast opens up at the back?'

Holding his sword and satchel close to his chest, Paul squeezed around the fire. His wounded shoulder grazed the wall and he flinched at the pain. He saw a small recess in the side of the fireplace, but it was sealed with an iron panel. The heat from the fire was making him sweat.

'Once I've pulled the bars out from this side you can lean on the panel and push it out of the way,' Mary said. 'Get yoursel' through. You won't have much space, so put your things at the far end and then turn round and push the panel back. I'll put the pots and pans back in place. Then I'll build up the fire. The heat stops anyone from looking too close.'

Paul wondered how small the hidden space was on the other side of the panel. It did look to be a good sized fireplace, which encouraged him. 'Can I take in something to drink?' he asked.

'You'll find a flagon of small beer in there with a reed straw in it, so you can drink without too much noise,' she replied. 'And I put a loaf in there this morning. Right, you can push now.'

Paul leant his shoulder against the panel. It gave way and he dropped his satchel and sword to his feet, and got his hands around the sides of the panel and pushed it away. The panel was warm but not too hot to touch. He bent down and shuffled himself through the gap. Peering into the darkness he saw a rat scurry out of his way. As his eyes got accustomed to the dark he took in the surroundings. The space was taller than the panel, so he was able to fully stand up. On a small recess in the wall on the left he saw the beer and the bread. He picked up his sword and satchel and put them to the back.

'Push the panel back into place,' Mary said, her voice muffled. 'Don't worry about air. Above the panel there is a small passage which lets in air from the chimney breast.'

As he gripped the panel to move it back into place, Paul caught sight of this small tunnel above his head.

Mary's voice began to trail off as she gave him one last instruction. 'I'll tap on the panel when the soldiers arrive. Then you must be as silent as the grave.'

Paul heard Mary putting more logs on the fire and wondered how hot it would get in his hiding place. He set the panel back into place and heard the bars go back in. Settling himself as comfortably as he could, he sat down and waited. Sweat dripped down his back and his stomach tensed in fear. He felt he needed the privy. The Parliamentarians wanted the contents of his satchel; the speech the earl had tried to make at his execution, and more than that, the letter Paul had been entrusted to take to Charlotte.

What would they do with him? Arrest and a trial was the best he could hope for. At worst they might string him up from the nearest tree; the last ten years had seen many such deaths in England. He was no more encouraged by the prospect of a trial, if it only served to legalize murder, as he had witnessed with the earl.

Chapter 4 – *Lathom House, January 1626*

"Most gracious God! Fountain of all good! I praise Thee for Thy bountie in having given me a wife soe much according to my heart." Private Devotions of James Stanley.

My next few months at Lathom were spent in preparations for the marriage of James to Charlotte de la Trémouille. James was now twenty years of age, and over the previous two years the earl had been active in seeking a marriage partner for him. I was spending more and more time working directly for Earl William who was dictating an account of his travels on the Grand Tour as a young man. He too seemed to have been pleased by how I had carried out my duty with the business over Lord Morley's weapons.

One day while working with the earl I asked him how Charlotte de la Trémouille had been chosen as a bride.

The earl smiled and his eyes, the colour of old oak, sparkled just as they did when he recounted an amusing incident in his youth. 'Well, we are related to all the major families of this realm. It is time we married into a noble house from abroad, just as the late King James did when he married Elizabeth to the King of Bohemia.'

I knew he did not mind my curiosity and continued, 'I understand there is some relation to the House of Orange?'

The earl replied, like a schoolmaster instructing his pupil. 'Yes, on her mother's side. Charlotte's late father was French, Claude Duke of Trémouille, and her mother is Charlotte Brabantine of Nassau, a daughter of William Prince of Orange.'

'Ah, Prince William who fought the Spanish.'

'Exactly. Now Paul, I understand the steward has done you a disservice. I hear you are sharing a room with one of the grooms. As a gentleman you are entitled to much better. I will see to it that you are moved right away.'

'My lord you are most kind, but there is no need. Bootle has been agreeable company and he has helped me to settle in here. Indeed he has recently left for Knowsley and so the room is my own. I am quite happy to remain there.'

The earl continued with some more dictation. He had reached a most interesting point in his adventures and was eager to set it all down on paper. After an hour or so he said, 'Enough work for today.

Tell me have you read Tacitus or Plutarch? I would like someone new to converse with now James is busy managing our affairs. I would like your opinion of these.' Earl William handed me two books. 'They are translated from the Latin for ease of reading.'

'No my Lord, I have not read them, but I would be pleased to.' I knew these to be accounts of the Roman Republic, and after the evening meal I began to read Plutarch's "Lives".

***

The marriage between James and Charlotte de la Trémouille was to take place in the Noordeinde Palace in The Hague. I was excited to be travelling abroad for the first time, but anxious about going to a country at war. The earl and his son were not overly worried. They had received letters from Charlotte's family informing them that the war was confined to sieges of fortified towns like Maestricht, over a hundred miles from The Hague. Charlotte's uncle Maurice, Stadtholder until his death the previous year had proved to be the master of the Spanish in military campaigns. Maurice's younger brother, Frederick Henry had succeeded him without any major difficulty and was now Stadtholder in five of the seven provinces.

We rode out to Liverpool to embark on a boat to take us across to the United Provinces. The party comprised James, the earl and his wife Elizabeth, their chaplain and about a dozen other household retainers, including myself. In addition there were maids and various male servants and a small number of these were armed to provide an escort for the earl. We made our way down to the dock to embark on one of the earl's own ships; for he had several, used for commerce and communication with his lands on the Isle of Man.

As we arrived some fishermen were landing the morning's catch. Gulls soared overhead looking for a chance to swoop down and snatch a meal from the quay side. To stop this some small boys were throwing stones at any gull that tried to land. Some women were gutting a basket of mackerel, chatting to each other as they worked. I caught a smell of the fish guts and turned my head away to try to avoid the stench. Here I saw a man who caught my eye and he smiled at my discomfort. He had a full beard with streaks of white, and large gold earrings.

'Mornin' my lord,' he said to the earl.

'It's a fine morning for sailing,' replied the earl. 'Is the ship ready to leave?'

'A few more provisions to load, but first we need to get you on board. We'll be ready for this afternoon's tide.'

'That's the captain,' James said to me. 'They say he's been a sailor so long he can only walk straight on land when he's drunk. But he's sober when he's at sea and he is a good sailor.'

We dismounted from our horses and walked over a gangplank onto the ship. Our baggage was brought on behind us and stowed away below deck.

'Come, let us go and eat,' said the earl. 'I always find the best way to start a sea voyage is with a good meal. You don't know when you'll eat well again,' he said winking at me.

This was my first encounter with a ship and it was a terrible experience. I was sick for the first couple of days until my body got used to the motion of the vessel. Although I was to sail on many more occasions in the next twenty-five years, it was always the same. I would be sick for the first few days then find my sea legs. This time I had the prospect of the United Provinces to console me, for I had never travelled outside Lancashire before. There was also the spectacle of the wedding to look forward to. Frederick Henry the Stadtholder would be there, and some of the servants were saying the King and Queen of Bohemia would attend. Their presence would indicate King Charles's approval of this union. I had Plutarch's "Lives" and two works by Tacitus, "The Histories" and "The Annals", to read. Towards the end of our journey, the earl sought me out while we were walking on deck.

'How goes it with Tacitus?' he asked, raising an eyebrow.

'Well, my lord. The books have helped me pass the time on our voyage. I have enjoyed learning about the history of Rome.'

'What have you learnt from studying them?'

'Tacitus was certainly no admirer of the Roman Emperors. He believed in the virtues of the Roman Republic, before the age of the Emperors,' I replied, pleased with my learning.

'Does this teach you anything about politics of our time?'

I was struggling here, for while I had been absorbed by the history, I had not taken great meaning from the writings of Tacitus. 'No, my lord. I confess I find few parallels. We live in a monarchy; our King Charles being God's anointed on this earth. Tacitus held the Roman

Emperors to be corrupt and sometimes vile men, but this is not the case with our sovereign.'

The earl stopped walking and turned to face me, his expression serious. 'Well in The Hague you may meet some men who will tell you that Tacitus justifies the Dutch revolt against their King. I think the words of Tacitus are "a desire to resist oppression is implanted in the nature of man". They argue it is justifiable by the laws of nature to resist oppression in whatever form. It is a dangerous argument and one which must be refuted if it is heard in England.'

Chapter 5 – *Brindle, October 18, 1651*

"My Lord, my Strength! I beseech Thee save me from the malice of my Enemies." Private Devotions of James Stanley.

Paul's legs were starting to ache and his buttocks were numb. He shifted his position as best he could. His eyes were now adjusted to the darkness. He could see he was not the first person to have hidden here; the etching of a five bar gate in the brickwork gave him the unwelcome feeling he might be there for days.

He heard somebody enter the kitchen. There was a knock on the panel giving him his signal to be quiet. The soldiers must be close by. Paul tensed in the gloom, suddenly aware of the sound of his quickening breaths. He could hear Mary at work in the kitchen, no doubt wanting to make as much noise as possible. Paul had his arms drawn up to his chest, almost hugging himself, the thump of his heartbeat against his fingers.

A few moments later he was aware of other people in the kitchen. Their voices sounded as if he was under water, so he strained to understand them.

'He must have come your way.' Paul could make out a well spoken man, probably an officer.

'If he did, I've not seen 'im,' replied Mary, her voice calm and unhesitant. 'Escaping from Bolton, you say. Can't see why he would come this way. It's not as if we're on the road to anywhere.'

'No, but a good place to hide,' interrupted the man. 'We know this area is full of papists. You'll have him hidden no doubt, in one of those stinking priest holes.'

'We are faithful to the true religion,' replied Mary. 'Ask the vicar. We attend his services.'

'No doubt you do, but I'll bet you have your own services too,' he answered. 'What's that cooking on the fire?'

'Some potage for lunch,' said Mary.

'Well, I'll have it while my men search your house,' he said in an affable tone. 'If they don't find anything we'll be on our way. If they find him, then you know the punishment for harbouring traitors.'

'They can look all they like, they'll find nowt,' replied Mary. 'Now let me get you a bowl and some bread.'

Paul wondered at her nerve. She was about to serve lunch to this soldier who would burn her house if the hiding place was discovered. He saw the sense in having the priest hole in the kitchen. Being the focal point of the house meant the room was likely to be overlooked in a search. The smell of the soup reminded Paul of his own hunger. Further away he could hear the soldiers banging on the wattle and daub walls and then the sound of their footsteps on the wooden stairs as they went up to the bedrooms. Soon they would enter the room he had been sleeping in and he tried to recall if there was anything there to betray his presence. He was glad he had gathered up his sword and satchel. The signet ring with the emblem of the eagle was on his finger. He could not think of anything he had left in the room. Still he felt uneasy. Would they be able to tell that the bed had been slept in last night?

Through the air vent, Paul heard more sounds from upstairs; men moving about and pushing furniture out of the way. A loud crash signified they had toppled something over, a bureau perhaps. Paul imagined them leaving it lying where it had fallen, clothes strewn out across the floor. He hoped they would not loot the house. Above all he prayed they did not find him. For a few dreadful minutes everything went quiet. Then Paul heard the soldiers' boots on the kitchen flags.

'Come quickly sir, we've found a priest hole,' said one of the men. Paul heard the men leave the room. Mary followed; her tread lighter on the stairs. Paul's heart froze and he instinctively grabbed his sword. He strained to hear what was happening upstairs.

'Let me see in there,' said the officer. A few heartbeats later, 'there's nobody here,' he continued. 'I knew you were a papist,' he shouted. 'So where is he?'

'Now, you've got it all wrong,' replied Mary's voice. 'We're not papists. This hiding hole hasn't been used for years. Look at the dust on your breeches. We used to let the children play in it. Look my daughter's old doll is in there. She wasn't quite ready to get rid of it, so she asked if she could put it in. That must have been five years ago. Married now she is; with a bairn of her own.'

The officer barked an order. 'Search the outbuildings. If we find him; then burn this house.'

Chapter 6 – *The Hague, June 1626*

"With respect to choosing a wife; if your estate be good, match near home and at leisure; but if weak or encumbered, marry afar off and quickly." James Stanley's letters to Lord Strange.

The next day we docked in The Hague. Immediately I noticed a difference in the buildings. They were not single or even double storied; instead they had at least three, and sometimes four or even five, floors. This was no doubt the result of commerce; the wealth of the Dutch merchants who traded throughout the world displayed in their houses. There were some in England who held the Dutch as the model to be copied in terms of trade and also religion. Certainly, my initial impressions of the results it brought were favourable. The second thing to strike me was the number of windmills. There was one at Lathom for making flour. The Dutch either had a lot of corn to grind or they were also using them for something else.

It seemed there were a few difficulties to resolve before the marriage could proceed. James had already been to the Dutch Court in The Hague to see if Charlotte was a suitable marriage partner. The rumour in the Derby household was he had needed to borrow money to buy new clothes, before being presented at the Court. Money still seemed to be a problem. Earl William had been involved in litigation for many years with the wife of his late brother Ferdinando. This had been costly and had resulted in the loss of many of the hereditary Stanley estates.

Both the earl and James were determined to obtain a large dowry from the marriage with Charlotte. A huge sum of £24,000 had been agreed. I knew from working on the accounts books that the earl's annual income from his estates was something around £5,000.

James had asked me to draw up a document, which indicated in the event of his death Charlotte would have an annual allowance of £1,000 to live on. However, Charlotte's family believed her standing entitled her to a larger amount. So I was told to draft a second document in which the allowance was doubled to £2,000 a year.

I had finished the document and taken it to James. He was pacing up and down the room with his hands clasped behind his back. His father was also in the room, seated by the window.

'That woman is insufferable. First she disagrees over the dowager allowance for Charlotte, and now she challenges English law! She does not accept that should I die before Charlotte then the remainder of the dowry will be passed on to my relatives. Am I to be married or not?'

The woman James was bemoaning was Charlotte's mother, the Duchesse de la Trémouille. Widowed and a firm defender of her family's interests, she had proved quite intractable during the marriage negotiations.

The earl continued to stare out of the window as if the answer to the quandary lay out there. After a pause he turned to speak to James. 'It vexes me, but the only way around this might be to accept the dowry in instalments. That way she can stop paying should you die before Charlotte.'

'Father, it is as if she is trying to belittle us. What demand will she impose next?'

'I think this is her last demand. Remember, she has invested time and expense in these negotiations too. If they were to collapse now, she would be as humiliated as us. She has had difficulty obtaining a partner for her daughter. A marriage in France to a man of her rank is almost impossible due to their religion. How old is she now, twenty-six?'

'In danger of being an unmarried spinster,' said James.

'Yes,' said the earl. 'I think we suggest instalments that are favourable to us and she will have to accept. Paul, I will write out our terms for the payment of the dowry and then you will take them together with the document detailing the new dowager allowance.'

I took the documents to the Duchess, though I was denied the opportunity to meet her as they were taken from me by one of her servants. I was told to wait for a reply. It was agonizing, made worse by the fact that after a couple of hours I began to feel hungry and thirsty. This was worsened when I smelt roasted poultry; then saw a group of servants bringing through a fine lunch of roast chicken, cold hams, bread and fruit. The Duchess and her entourage consumed the lunch and still I waited. I had to pace up and down to prevent stiffness in my legs. Finally, late in the afternoon, a servant emerged with a sealed letter. I hurried back to the earl and James.

James tore part of the paper as he quickly broke the seal on the letter. His eyes scanned down the page and we waited silently as he read. Eventually he looked up. 'She agrees, though her French is a little too flowery for me to grasp all the nuances. I cannot tell if she accepts with good grace or not. Here father, you read it and see what you make of it.'

The earl read through it and began to chuckle. 'What a woman. She deigns to accept our offer, making it clear she only does so as a gracious host, to prevent our embarrassment. Not a mention of the embarrassment she would suffer if the marriage fell through. James, you can be married. Try not to let the wrangling of the last few days affect your attitude to your bride. She is an innocent in all this, so do not hold it against her.'

***

With the agreements concluded the preparations for the wedding continued. Additional wedding guests were expected and when the King and Queen of Bohemia arrived, I was told to give up my comfortable lodging in the Noordeinde Palace. Several of us were now to be lodged at a cost in some of the merchant's houses.

On the day of the wedding we assembled at the palace, mingling with nobility from several countries. In the palace's chapel the couple made their vows in front of a gathering of clergy which included the earl's chaplain. I was not important enough to be admitted into the chapel so took a stroll around the palace. I followed a group of servants taking bread on polished pewter platters into a dining chamber. There were silver platters at the head of the table in the places of honour. Here alongside James, Charlotte and Earl William would sit the King and Queen of Bohemia, Stadtholder Frederick Henry, Charlotte's mother, and kinsmen of the Stanley's. White linen cloths were draped across the tables and large piles of fresh fruit sat like mountains in golden dishes. Flagons of wine waited for the guests. I left the room wondering if there would be anything for me to eat.

I entered the main chamber just as James and Charlotte were coming back from the chapel. It was my first opportunity to see James's new bride. She could not be described as a real beauty, being quite short and matronly. As I watched her talking to James she seldom smiled. I did not know if she was pleased by her marriage partner or disappointed in him, but even an unhappy bride usually smiles at her wedding. Her sullen appearance gave the impression of haughtiness, as if she were superior. I knew her to be a Calvinist by religion and I took it she counted herself as one of the godly elect.

A table had been placed in the centre of the room and James and Charlotte now approached it. Here they would place their names on the marriage document, which would seal the issues of the dowry more than the vows, spoken in front of the ministers. James sat and signed his name on the document before handing the quill to Charlotte. Again she did not smile. The quill was passed to Earl William and then to Charlotte's mother. Just when I thought everyone had had their turn I noticed a scuffle between two grandly attired gentlemen. Both of them were making for the table and each seemed intent on getting there before the other. As arms and elbows intertwined, a hat was knocked off and fell to the floor.

One of the gentlemen spoke in French. 'As the English ambassador to The Hague I should sign first.' He had now arrived in front of the table and put out his hand to receive the quill from Charlotte's mother. She looked at him without any sign of emotion on her face and waited for the second gentleman to arrive.

'Here, I shall give it to the French ambassador,' she said with a sly smile and handed the quill to the second gentleman. He made a low, graceful bow before taking the quill and signing his name with a flourish.

The English ambassador shot an evil look at the Frenchman and put his hand to the hilt of his sword. He was starting to withdraw the weapon when the earl stood up.

'There is to be no fighting at my son's wedding,' he warned, his voice ice cold. 'Put away your sword.'

For a couple of heartbeats the ambassador stood still and then with a smile he let go of the sword hilt, letting it fall back into the scabbard.

'I apologize for any offence I have caused. Let me be the first to congratulate your son on his marriage.' He made a low bow in front of James and Charlotte. As he stood up one of his aides handed him his hat which he placed back on his head, glaring at the French ambassador as he did so. With a scraping of chairs and an embarrassed cough from James, the wedding party stood up. They seemed unsure what to do next until a servant ushered them towards the dining chamber. I sought out Jan Oudijk, the Dutch merchant I had been lodging with. In our previous brief conversations we had spoken in French as I had no Dutch. Once again I addressed him in French. To my surprise Jan replied in English.

'I was a soldier before I was a merchant, a translator in the Earl of Essex's army during the first war with Spain. This is a good day, one of the Stadholder's family marrying an English nobleman. May it be a good sign for our two countries to be united against Spain.'

'You are doing well enough without our help,' I replied. 'Which was the town you astounded the Spanish by taking, surrounded as it was by a marsh?'

'Utrecht. Yes, that was a major success and broke the Spanish morale as they did not think the town could be taken. We used windmills to drain the water out of the marsh.'

'So you use science in your war. The Protestant struggle against the Catholic King of Spain and the papacy must be the other reason for your success?'

'Religion is an important factor, but to me what has united the six provinces has been the feeling we do not want to be ruled and taxed by a foreign king. John Calvin instructs us that the magistrate may call upon the people to rebel against the sovereign. We can then stop his foreign taxes and enjoy the benefits of our trade and the wealth it brings.'

'Is it not against the laws of God to fight against your anointed sovereign?' I asked. 'I can understand a religious war against Catholicism, but what gives you the right to challenge a king for reasons of trade and wealth?'

'You are still young Mr. Morrow, and have ideals about the rights and wrongs of the world. Look at the people who fight against Spain. Yes, you see idealists who fight for religion or for what you might call Republicanism, but far more are interested in what they can get for themselves. Those who are motivated by ideals provide the legitimacy to those who have more base motives.'

I interrupted him for I thought his views were cynical. 'You have a low opinion of men, many of whom have died for what they believe.'

'You can say that, but I have been there during the wars and studied the men who led the fight against the Spanish. I do not doubt the sincerity of those who are committed in their beliefs, but I question the sincerity of some of those around them.'

'You have interesting views. I doubt I will be able to challenge them, for England is a settled nation and I do not fear rebellions in her lands.'

'For your sake I hope you are right, but I do not think everything is peaceful in your country. You are at war with Spain again and does the King not have trouble with the Parliament as it does not want to pay for war?'

'Lord Strange has said as much. Last year he went to Parliament for the first time. He said there was a lot of mistrust of Buckingham and criticism of his conduct of the war with Spain. Very little was granted in subsidies by the Parliament.'

'This news is bad. Lack of money will hinder England in the struggle against Spain. Now, enough of these serious matters of politics and religion. Let's drink to the health of the young couple and a toast to the continued friendship between our two nations.'

We were on route for more wine when I saw a young boy causing havoc amongst the guests. He had a sword and a wooden horse's head on a pole. He was running up and down bumping into people and slashing out with his toy sword. Now the boy was coming at us and before I could get out of the way he was upon us and engaging in mock combat.

'*Pak aan Spaanse hond,*' he said as he bashed my legs with his sword.

I was about to cuff him about the ear when Jan said to me. 'I'll take care of him.'

'*Zoals u wilt Prince Rupert. Dit is een engelsman, een vriend van ons. Ik denk dat jij alle spanjaarden hier hebt vermoord. Vertrek en neem wat rust.*'

The lad now spoke to me in English. 'Pleased to make your acquaintance, Sir,' and he bowed gracefully before turning round and running off.

'Who was that?' I asked.

'Prince Rupert, known as Devil Rupert to his family. I told him he had killed enough Spaniards for today, and that you were an Englishman and therefore an ally.'

'Ah, so he's a prince. I wondered why nobody stopped him,' I replied.

'And related to Charlotte too; so you may see more of him. Because of the war in the Palatinate he's living at the Court of Orange. Apparently Charlotte is very fond of him.'

'Well I hope James and Charlotte aren't planning to take him back to England. My legs are black and blue where he hit me. He's the makings of a soldier.'

With that we resumed our celebrations until the wine ran out.

Over the course of the next few days the earl and James did not have much cause for my services. With the departure of most of the wedding guests, I was once again lodged in the Noordeinde palace. One of my few duties was to fetch warm water for James. One morning when I entered the kitchen, I saw a young woman with an empty pitcher at her feet, and a servant tending a pan of water over the fire. I could see there was only going to be enough water to fill one pitcher. I looked again at the woman. She had a round face bordered with dark hair, pulled back tightly from her forehead. Dark ringlets of hair hung down below her ears and bounced on the short lace mantle on top of her shoulders. Her clothes were sober black, of good quality and very clean. Apart from the lace mantle which was very fine, the only item of value she wore was a large jet brooch. I remembered seeing her near Charlotte at the wedding, and assumed she was fetching water for her mistress.

'Mademoiselle, I fear there is not sufficient water for us both. I am in a quandary as to what to do. Do we serve the Lord Strange first, as he is the husband? Or would he prefer this opportunity to be chivalrous and satisfy his wife's needs before his own?'

She responded in perfect English. 'Sir, I think the Lady Charlotte has precedence. This is her family's palace and your lord is only a guest here. I will take this water. If you wait there will soon be some more.'

I was a little surprised at this answer. I had not expected her to be so resolute, but I was not overly concerned. James would be amused at this incident and in truth I knew he would expect his wife to receive the first water. Still I thought I could tease her a little. 'Mademoiselle, of course you are right. I shall stay here and wait for the next pitcher of water. Please tell me your name as the Lord Strange will be desirous to know the identity of the lady who took his water.'

'My name is Louise Bardin, but it is not his water.' She had not understood the jest and picking up her pitcher in one hand she gathered her skirts in the other, turned around and without another word bustled out of the room.

Although this had been an unusual introduction, something in her manner attracted me to her. I resolved to seek her out as soon as I could.

I was able to meet her again the next afternoon. From my window I saw her walking in the garden. I left the palace and followed the path she had taken. I approached her, my feet crunching on the gravel. She turned to see who was following her.

'So it is the master of the water pitcher,' she said smiling.

I smiled too. 'As the Stanleys have brought very few servants, I have been required to perform such duties during our stay here. Back in England I will no longer be master of the water pitcher.'

As we talked I studied her face. Her dark brown eyes were large which made me feel like she was absorbing me as she held my eye. I felt the look to be too intense and glanced away, looking down the avenue and pointing.

'If you are you walking down to the trees, I will join you.'

'It will be pleasant to have your company,' she replied.

'How does an English woman come to be in the service of Lady Charlotte?'

'My father is a Huguenot. He left France to avoid the troubles and settled in London. He married an English girl and I was brought up to speak both languages. Lady Charlotte took me into her service when it seemed likely that she would wed an English lord. Her English is good and improving all the time, but she wanted someone who can converse in both languages so she is never at a disadvantage.'

'What does Lady Charlotte think of her new husband?' I said.

'He is a most attentive and considerate man. She thinks they will have an agreeable marriage. She is eager to journey to England and see where she is to live.'

'She will not be disappointed. Lathom House is truly a wonderful place. There is also Knowsley which is a fine building, more modern in style.' I paused, considering how to frame a question I had not dared to ask James. Louise looked at me intently, sensing I had something else to say.

'Is it true that Charlotte's mother is returning with us to England? I asked.'

'It is. She wants to help her daughter settle in and see she is accorded the status at Lathom due to one of her birth.'

More like she wants to tell the earl how to manage his household, I thought. This was not a happy prospect. The thought of the Duchess sharing a roof with James and the earl gave me a feeling of unease. Adding to that my sea-sickness, I dreaded the return sea voyage to England.

Chapter 7 – *Brindle, October 18, 1651*

For half an hour Paul huddled apprehensively in the priest hole. He resolved to fight if they found him. Then he thought of Mary and reasoned it would be better for her if he surrendered. He heard someone enter the kitchen.

'It's all right, they've gone away.' He recognized Mary's voice as she continued. 'Well apart from two they've left behind to watch. You think they'd know better than to hide in the wood under a rookery. As soon as the birds took to the sky, I knew what they were up to. Here, let me get the bars out and then you can push away the panel.'

Blinking in the daylight, Paul edged his way around the fire. He saw Mary holding onto the table, her hands shaking.

'Thieving soldiers', she said. 'They've taken a ham, fresh butter and eggs. Still, at least they didn't take the horses.'

'I'll go now,' said Paul.

'Yes, that'll be right. Your wound is healing well and you're strong again. You can get away at the back of the house.'

'I'll need to saddle my horse,' Paul interrupted.

'Of course you will,' replied Mary, making for the door to the back of the house.

Outside, Paul instinctively gripped his sword as he looked around. Mary told him to wait in the barn while she fetched his horse. While he waited, he lifted his sword and tried out his arm. The muscles in his shoulder were sore, but with effort he was able to work through his sword drill.

Mary entered the barn leading his horse and Paul put his sword into his belt. Pleased to see his mare, he went over and stroked her muzzle.

'I'll saddle her up and then be on my way. Thank you for all you have done for me. The Stanleys will hear of this and will be grateful.'

'Just doing my Christian duty,' interrupted Mary. 'Now get yoursel' away. Stay below the sky line and make for the church spire you can see over there. Keep out of the village and you should be right. Those troops are billeted in Hoghton too. So don't go through there neither.'

***

Nearly a quarter of an hour later, thinking about how he was going to get over to the Isle of Man, Paul was riding towards the church at Brindle. He knew he would have to skirt around the village to avoid the soldiers lodged there. Passing the village on the eastern side would take him close to Hoghton, so about half a mile short of Brindle he decided to head west. He was pleased to be on the move again and glad he was no longer putting Mary in danger. A movement to his right interrupted his thoughts. He looked again. Two dismounted dragoons were shouting at him to ride over. Paul pretended he had not seen them and continued, hoping they would let him carry on. Turning his head slightly he could see they were mounting up. He touched his horse's flanks with his spurs and called on her to gallop. Their shouts echoed in his ears as he rode hard.

Chapter 8 – *Northwich, late 1626*

Back in England we did not have the excitement of a wedding to look forward to, but the newly weds seemed happy enough. James and Charlotte were content in each other's company and frequently took themselves off for walks in the grounds. Despite the earlier protracted negotiations over the wedding settlement they looked very much like a young couple truly in love. The atmosphere at Lathom was uplifted by their happiness and not even the presence of Madame de Trémouille could stifle it.

James could not be away from politics and the government of the locality for long and was soon brought back down to earth by a new policy of the King. Starved of funds by Parliament, King Charles's lawyers had recommended he levy a forced loan. It was the duty of the earl as Lord Lieutenant of Lancashire and Cheshire to see that the money was collected in these two counties. I was given the responsibility of helping to raise the money due from their manor in the Northwich hundred of Cheshire.

During my time in the town I lodged with the Stanleys' steward. He had rooms in their courthouse on the town square. The prominent citizens of Northwich had to present themselves in the courthouse, and it was my job to assess their wealth to see if they had to make a contribution. A Ralph Bradshaw who lived in the town came before us. He was accompanied by a man of about twenty. He was dressed in the clothes of a gentleman and initially his countenance did not suggest any trouble. However, as we spoke he became quite severe, immediately seizing the initiative.

'I am Mr. John Bradshaw, a kinsman of Ralph Bradshaw. I am a lawyer and do not recognize this loan. It was not passed as a statute of Parliament and as such I hold it illegal. I have told Ralph to refuse to pay.'

'You can hold what opinion you like, but if he is obliged to make a loan and refuses to pay then he could end up in gaol. At the very least he will spend some time in the cells below the courthouse while we decide what to do with him. Now, Ralph Bradshaw declare your income and we will see if you have any loan to make.'

Ralph Bradshaw was not dressed as a gentleman and when he spoke I realized he would not have to make a loan. 'Sir, I have no income from land or property and I work as a labourer for Roger Pavor in the town.'

'Well Ralph Bradshaw there is no need for you to be here. Only gentlemen of sufficient means are asked to make the loan. I would have expected your kinsman to know this, and I am afraid he has wasted his time here today. Good day to you both. You may go.'

As they both got up to leave, John Bradshaw shot me a malevolent glance and seemed to be about to say something more, but whatever thoughts he had, no words came from his lips.

***

Once my work was complete in Northwich I returned to Lathom. Here I found the earl in his study surrounded by papers and books. James was also present.

'Paul, it is time for me to leave the management of affairs to James and retire to the house at Bidston. Elizabeth found the journey to The Hague extremely tiring and has taken ill. I want to take her away from the hubbub of Lathom.'

Although he did not say it, I feared he felt they did not have long left together. I was asked to help draw up a submission for letters patent, which would surrender his post as Chamberlain of Chester in favour of a new grant conferring the office upon both William and James. The intention was that William would leave James to exercise the office, but he would continue to support him and offer guidance.

'There shouldn't be a problem in obtaining the royal approval, but I have heard John Bradshaw, a lawyer wants the office.'

As it was unlikely there could be two lawyers in our locality with the same name, I recounted my meeting with him in Northwich.

'I have made enquiries about this man,' said James. 'It seems he attended Brasenose College, Oxford and thereafter was admitted to Gray's Inn to be trained in the law. I do not fear him, for he has no influence at Court. However, we should watch him, to be sure he does not prove a nuisance to our interests. One should always be wary of lawyers, especially those who quote the law to serve their own purposes.'

'I hope you don't count me in that group of self-interested lawyers?' asked William with a smile. 'Remember I was at Gray's Inn myself.'

'No, father of course I don't.' Turning to me he asked, 'Paul, what did you think of John Bradshaw?'

'He had a high regard for the law and I thought he was very eager to make an impression, though he did not have much concern for who he might offend in the process. I found him a little naive. He could prove intractable as an opponent.'

Chapter 9 – *Brindle, October 18, 1651*

Paul rode his horse hard for his life depended on it. He had doubted he would be able to bluff his way past the two dragoons. By taking flight he had settled it. The dragoons now knew he was a fugitive and probably the man they had been told to watch out for. He had to outrun them or find somewhere to hide. Knowing he had a good start on them and that his mare was going to be faster than their cavalry mounts, he searched his memory of this countryside around Hoghton. Many years ago he had hunted around here with the Hoghton family. To the south of Brindle he remembered moors that led onto the Pennines. The moors would be too open and offer no cover, but he remembered some nearby wooded areas and decided to make for these.

Taking a look over his shoulder, he was pleased to see he was getting away from his pursuers. His horse seemed to relish the gallop after her recent inactivity and snorted in pleasure as she pulled away. After a few miles of hard riding he looked back again and could no longer see the two dragoons. He coaxed his mare to slow down and settled her into a walk. To his right a large wood opened up, but he looked past it to a smaller group of trees, about a quarter of a mile away. He walked his mare up to the trees, making for a bramble bush. Loosening the linen kerchief around his neck, he reached out and draped it onto the thorns of the bramble, making it look as if he had brushed against it as he left the road. He then rode into the wood for about twenty yards, before turning left and following parallel to the road for another fifty. He turned left again, and cautiously approached the edge of the wood. There was still no sign of the dragoons. He left the wood and cantered the short distance to the other trees. He took his horse in a short distance and tied her reins to a tree. After giving her a pat on the neck to calm her, he walked back to the edge of the wood and crouched down, watching back down the road.

Paul was beginning to wonder if the two dragoons had given up the chase when he saw a group of about twenty cavalry approaching. He crouched lower and his hand went to his sword hilt. He had no hope of fighting his way out so he had to stay hidden. One of the dragoons stopped and pointed at the wood where Paul had left his kerchief. The whole troop stopped. After a few moments about half of the soldiers entered the wood, the other soldiers rode on, drawing closer. Paul backed away from the edge of the wood and mounted his horse. He steered her deeper into the wood away from his pursuers. Doubling back the way he had come, he reached the far side of the wood and then headed back towards Brindle.

This time Paul would not try to go north of Brindle. Instead when he was about a mile short of the village, he turned west and headed for Leyland. He had now decided to go to Liverpool in search of a ship to take him over to the Isle of Man. His heart was heavy with the thought of what he must do there. He had promised James he would deliver his last letter to Charlotte, but that was not a burden to him. It was what he had promised James he would do once on the island that tormented him.

Chapter 10 – *Lathom and London, 1627*

A horseman tore along the road up to Lathom, along which Louise and I were walking on a cold, crisp March afternoon. I recognized the rider as one of the servants from Bidston Hall.

'It's a message from the earl,' I said to Louise. 'Let's get back to the house to hear the news.'

On entering the courtyard beyond the gatehouse, the messenger announced he had to see Lord Strange immediately. He would say no more, and waited silently, shuffling from one foot to another as the steward was fetched to take him through to see James. The breath from his horse's nostrils formed a light mist around its head. The animal snorted while it stood recovering.

'What could it be that can only be spoken of to James?' asked Louise.

'I'm not sure, but I think it could be bad news.'

'Lady Elizabeth,' said Louise.

'Let's go to the grand hall and wait to be called,' I said.

A short while later James and Charlotte entered the hall. By the look on their faces the news was grave.

'My father sends news that my mother died yesterday. She passed away peacefully after they had shared a supper together. She had gradually been getting weaker since they went to Bidston.'

'We must go to him,' said Charlotte. 'Louise, see to it that clothes are packed for me. Paul, you see to a carriage and an escort. We will set out tomorrow morning at first light.' James turned to leave the room. Charlotte grabbed his hand and went with him. I looked at Louise and without a word we set off to make the arrangements.

A sombre party set out the next morning. James rode in the carriage with Charlotte and the rest of us were on horseback. Louise often went riding with Charlotte and looked confident, mounted side-saddle on a bay. Out of respect to James there was little conversation on the journey. I thought of my own parents, both dead for ten years, victims of a plague that had afflicted our manor. I had then lived with my aunt who had cared for me well enough, but had enough children of her own to ever have any time for me.

We crossed the Mersey by the bridge at Warrington. Night was falling by the time we reached Bidston. James and Charlotte went straight in to see the earl, leaving Louise and me to organize the unloading of the coach.

I did not see the earl for two days. He remained in his chambers and would not come out to see anyone, permitting only James and Charlotte to see him. James was concerned that a miasma had caused his father's illness and state of melancholy. The earl turned away the physician each time he was summoned by James. He only began to improve after the funeral, and several days after the burial of his wife, he summoned me.

'Paul, it is time James returned to Court. He is a similar age to King Charles and I believe the son has more likelihood than the father of gaining influence at Court. Charlotte shares the same nationality as the Queen, which could be valuable; though as Queen Henrietta Maria is a Catholic I doubt she will receive a Calvinist into her inner circle.'

This news about my new role gave me mixed feelings. It was an exciting prospect to be going to London, but I wondered if Louise would go as well.

'Don't worry; Louise will be going too. You won't have to be parted from her.' He smiled at me then continued, 'we have an interest in purchasing some land in the Delamere Forest which is being deforested. Charlotte's dowry has not started to come through, so we need to continue to augment our revenues. The best way to achieve this is to become a suitor to the Duke of Buckingham. The duke is a favourite of King Charles and the web of patronage he controls is the key to getting control of this land in Delamere. You are to accompany James. He may need my advice from time to time, and we trust you to act as a messenger between us.'

James was not keen to leave his father and it was actually a few months before we set out for London. By then James was assured about the earl and arrangements had been made to ensure the estate at Lathom was well managed in James's absence. The Stanleys' residence in London was Derby House in Canon Row, Westminster, and I accompanied James, Charlotte and several servants to the house in the early summer of 1627. Louise was happy to be going to London, for it would give her an opportunity to see her family.

On the journey down we were frequently in each other's company. During one of our conversations I remarked that Charlotte had looked unwell for the last few days.

Louise confided in me. 'I don't know if I should tell you this, but my Lady Charlotte thinks she is with child. She has felt sick the last few mornings. She finds the journey uncomfortable, with all the jostling of the carriage on the road. Despite this she is happy, for she has been worried about her dowry. She does not want to be a burden to her husband and it has embarrassed her that no funds have come through from France. She feels giving James a child will go some way to making amends.'

'James has not mentioned this and I will have to wait until he tells me. He will be pleased by the prospect of an heir.'

'You men and your heirs. All that Charlotte wishes for at the moment is an end to the sickness. She is very eager to get to London.'

***

The initial negotiating and bargaining over the land in Delamere took place between James and the Duke of Buckingham's party without the duke who was in France trying to aid the Huguenots at La Rochelle. He had taken a fleet of ships and about 8,000 men. However, in all accounts we heard he was not faring well and indeed he was back in England by October without any victory to report.

Upon the duke's return to England, James sought to pursue the matter of the Delamere land. Matters were not progressing as quickly as he wished and so James invited the duke to dine with him and Charlotte.

Prior to Buckingham's arrival, James took me aside to discuss how he would press his case. 'We must be wary of the duke. He has King Charles's ear and the young King trusts him and all he does. Although Buckingham was also a favourite of King James, the old King was wise enough not to be solely influenced by Buckingham's council. The other Lords still had good access to the King and felt able to argue their concerns. Charles does not listen to any other minister.'

I looked forward to the opportunity to meet the duke. His rise from a minor gentleman to the King's first minister was a matter of some interest. There were many at Court resentful of his success, and he had made several enemies along the way.

Reports of the duke's handsome looks had not been exaggerated. It was said King James had thought Buckingham possessed the face of an angel. It was even rumoured he had shared the late King's bed. If this was true, then he had a relationship of a different sort with King Charles, like an elder brother more confident in the world than the shy and reserved Charles.

We sat down to eat and the first few topics of conversation were polite and conventional. Then the duke changed tone.

'How is your father? Does he still write plays? Not a very noble profession for an earl, penning plays for the entertainment of the common sort.' I saw one of the reasons for the duke's success at Court, mocking others, so his own position remained elevated.

'Now James, if you are to be successful in this venture over the land in Delamere you will need to demonstrate your loyalty to the King. You can do this in one of two ways. You could equip ships and men to serve in our war against the French King or you could make a contribution through me. Using my offices and my expertise, I will see this money is used to finance the war.'

James did not seem to want to drawn into an immediate decision. 'I thank you for your kind offer and will reflect on your words. What sort of sum would ensure that his Majesty's army and navy are well provided for?'

'A figure of £10,000 would be sufficient for a man of your means,' replied the duke. 'Now let us end this discussion of money. I find it a vulgar subject. Mr. Morrow what do you think of our reversal in the French war?'

I was surprised he wanted to talk about this. Everyone in the country who had an opinion believed the war was a failure and that the duke was responsible. I sought a cautious course. 'My Lord, I know little of such great affairs of state. As a humble gentleman, I always find war to be an expensive business.'

'It is my belief that war can finance war. To the victor the spoils, as in the age of Alexander. He left Greece with a small army and conquered the Persian Empire. We too can achieve greatness. You can play a part. I need captains for the army, intelligent men who can exercise command.'

I could not see how the duke could have arrived at so rapid a decision on my skills. I took it as an intended slight to James and his father. 'My Lord, I am very happy in the service of the earl and his son. While they continue to favour me I can think of no more worthy a role. I trust you will not be offended, but I must decline your offer.'

'James, I commend you for such loyalty in your household. We will talk again about this Mr. Morrow.'

James was getting irritated by this and Charlotte sensed it. I knew she opposed the war for it was preventing portions of her dowry coming from France. She sought to unsettle the duke. 'My Lord Buckingham, in the matter of the French war, I think you have miscalculated. This kingdom is not strong enough to seriously harm the King of France. This war is your folly and will be your downfall.'

'My Lady talks as if she wishes to play a part in this downfall. I had not counted the Stanleys amongst my enemies. I see I shall have to tread carefully. Now what do I have to fear from you?' he said looking at James. Then his mouth began to curl upwards as he phrased his riposte, 'perhaps the earl will attack me with a poisoned pen.'

False laughter came from James and Charlotte. James sought a more conciliatory tone and asked the after the health of the duke's wife who was expecting their second child.

'She is flourishing and this time I hope she will give me an heir. Lady Charlotte, I see you are also with child. I hope you give birth to a son and then your husband will have the comfort to know his line will surely continue.'

Chapter 11 – *Liverpool, October 19, 1651*

Paul approached one of the gates into Liverpool and saw a cart ahead taking vegetables in for the market. At the gate two soldiers stood together watching the road. Paul gradually increased the pace of his horse, so he was partly hidden by the cart when he passed the soldiers. They paid him no attention. Having ridden through the night, he was tired and just wanted to find an inn. But sleep would have to come later. First of all he needed to find a ship sailing for the Isle of Man.

Mounting the crest of a hill he looked down to the port. He was surprised to count only three ships at anchor. Paul steered his horse through the narrow lanes running down to the river. At the first ship he called out to one of the sailors on board and asked where she was headed.

'Just in from Ireland,' the sailor replied. 'Got some shore leave now before we sail back next week.'

Paul shouted over his thanks and moved along to the second ship. He could not see anyone on the deck, so he rode towards the third ship.

Two men were on the dock side carrying barrels onto the vessel. As they walked back to the barrels Paul jumped down from his horse and called over to them. 'Where are you headed?' he asked, studying the two sailors. One of them was no more than a boy and struggling with the task. He looked grateful for the chance to take a breath.

The one closest to Paul looked him up and down and then spoke. 'We've been ordered down to Chester to meet up with a fleet sailing for the Isle of Man,' he replied. 'Looks like they're going to attack the island at last.'

'Aye, it's about time,' Paul agreed, hiding his own feelings about this news. 'When do you sail for the Isle then?'

'We've been told to get to Chester in three days. Then we'll take on soldiers and 'ead over with Colonel Duckenfield.'

'God speed to you,' replied Paul. 'Do you know where that ship is headed?' he asked pointing back to the ship he had just passed.

'That one is going straight to the Isle of Man. They say it's carrying a messenger with a letter to the Lady Derby, calling on her to surrender.'

'It must be sailing soon, then,' Paul replied.

'This afternoon on the tide. Why are you so interested?'

Paul knew he would arouse suspicions wanting to sail to the Isle so soon after the death of James and he had prepared an explanation.
'I've got letters of my own to take to the Lady Derby. My master was owed money by the earl, but with him dead now I'm being sent to get it from her.'

'You'd better be quick,' laughed the sailor. 'Once they capture the Isle, the Parliament will 'ave their claws in 'er. She'll be lucky if she has ten pounds t' pay for 'er husband's funeral.'

'I can't say I care about her,' Paul lied. 'But my master in London will have my hide if I go back to him empty handed. Who do I see about getting on that ship?'

'Try the inn over there,' replied the sailor nodding towards a tavern on the quayside. 'The captain has spent most of his time there since he docked.'

Calling his thanks over his shoulder, Paul led his horse over to the inn.

***

It took Paul's eyes a few moments to see properly in the gloom of the tavern. He made his way over to a table where a man was serving beer from a barrel. Paul paid him a few coins for a tankard to rid himself of the taste of dust from the road. He turned around and looked for the captain. Then his heart froze. Seated at the table in the window was a man with a full white beard and large gold hoops in his ears. His eyes were firmly fixed on Paul and must have watched his progress across the room.

Paul did not know what to do. This was the captain who had first carried him over to the Isle of Man all those years before. He had last seen him a year earlier on the Isle. Would the man speak to him as a friend or denounce him to his enemies? Praying for a welcome reception, Paul crossed the room.

Chapter 12 – *London and Lathom, 1628*

Preparations were being made for Charlotte's confinement. A midwife, Mademoiselle de Beaulieu had come over from France. James was getting anxious for his wife and one evening after we had eaten, I sought to ease his worries.

'Don't fret over Charlotte. She is healthy and strong. She has a very experienced midwife to guide her through the labour. God willing, she will deliver a healthy child.'

James frowned. 'I tell myself these things too, but I cannot stop worrying. Despite our problems over the dowry we have become very close and I do not know what I would do should the Lord take her.'

As we spoke there was a loud knock at the door and Louise entered, her brows furrowed and her mouth set tight. 'Charlotte is in labour. It is not well advanced, so it will be some time yet. I will come back when there is more news.'

'So we wait, like two birds trussed up for market,' mused James. He stood up and began to pace up and down. After a while he spoke again. 'With my own concerns I had quite forgotten I wanted to ask you about Louise. She would be a suitable wife for you. Had you thought about marrying her?'

'My Lord, I am not so forward as to have thought this. We are both new to your household. If we stay in your service for a few more years, I will have the security to be able to ask her.'

'Don't worry about that. You are both valued servants. Indeed Charlotte speaks with affection of Louise. You can make a home within our household.'

'Thank you my Lord. This is wonderful news.' Thinking again about Charlotte I continued. 'Let's play a hand of cards to occupy our minds.'

After countless hands of every game I could think of, the door burst open again. It was Louise, her face flushed with excitement. 'My Lord, you have a healthy son. Charlotte is well, though extremely tired. She wants you to come through to see them.'

James jumped up from his chair and rushed out of the room. Louise remained and talked with joy about the child. 'He has dark hair and he gave such a cry when he was born; he is sure to be a healthy child. Mademoiselle de Beaulieu would not let me hold him, but I'm sure Charlotte will when I go back. They do not want to swaddle the baby, saying it's not the French way. It seems they like him be able to move his arms and legs. I have never heard such a thing, but Mademoiselle de Beaulieu holds sway over Charlotte.'

I next saw James the following morning. The worry had left his face, replaced by a contented grin. He had called me to take a letter north to Earl William to give him the good news. 'We are calling the boy Charles after the King,' he explained. 'We plan to return to Lathom for the baptism in two months time when Charlotte can travel. My father will make all the arrangements with the Bishop of Chester.'

***

Waiting for Louise to come up to Lathom with James and Charlotte was tiresome. I even wrote to her once, but never posted the letter; my thoughts looked foolish when expressed on paper. I did not know if she felt anything for me. Evidently she enjoyed my company, but I did not know if there was anything more. I had no wealth or status to attract her. She would not have a large dowry, but she was pretty and intelligent, so she would have no shortage of suitors.

Eventually the wait was over. In the middle of March, James brought his wife and child into the courtyard at Lathom. Charlotte alighted from the carriage. She looked ecstatic holding the baby in her arms. Louise was behind her and she was scanning the crowd, looking for someone. She stopped when she saw me and came over smiling.

'I did not know if you would be here or at Bidston with Earl William,' she said.

My heart missed a beat and I returned her smile. 'The earl came over to be here when James arrived,' I replied. 'I have been helping him to sort out some of his papers. How is the baby?'

'Young Charles is healthy and always hungry. Charlotte had to get him a second wet-nurse. One was not enough,' said Louise with a laugh. 'I'll have to go now, there's so much to do for one so small. I'll see you later, when we have settled Charlotte back in.'

***

After a long deliberation and with the counsel of his father, James decided to continue to play suitor to the Duke of Buckingham for the land in Delamere. The main reason for the delay was James's distaste for what was little more than a blatant request for a bribe. If James handed over £10,000 to the duke it was likely only a fraction of it would enter the war chest. Most would be swallowed up by the duke's own voluminous pockets, for his extravagance was legendary. Indeed £10,000 was a vast sum; equivalent to twice the annual value of rents due to the earl from his lands. I travelled down to London with James and a small party of retainers. Charlotte and baby Charles remained at Lathom.

Upon arriving in London we learnt the duke was at Portsmouth supervising the preparations for another expedition to aid the Huguenots at La Rochelle on the Île de Ré. I was given a letter to deliver which indicated James was willing to make a contribution of £5,000 towards the financing of the French war. James instructed me to deliver the letter in person to the duke and to await a reply before returning to London.

The docks at Portsmouth were crammed with men and supplies. It did not seem possible that they could all be loaded onto the ships berthed in the port. The oppressive heat of the August sun added to the feeling of enclosure, and with some difficulty I made my way to the Greyhound, the house of Captain John Mason, the duke's paymaster. The duke had commandeered the house as his headquarters.

Once inside, I sought out the duke. I was not sure if I would be able to gain an audience, but fortunately he was getting ready to leave as I arrived, which meant we met in the open area of the main downstairs room. He recognized me instantly and called me to come over.

'Mr. Morrow, have you come to fight the French?' The preparations for the war seemed to excite him and he appeared to have little awareness of his surroundings as he greeted me. He had the aura of tirelessness granted to those who have gone beyond the normal level of fatigue.

'No, my Lord. I bring a letter from Lord Strange.' I used James's title for the letter was addressed from him and not Earl William.

'Give it to me,' he ordered. 'I shall read it on my return.' Without looking at it he pushed the letter into a pocket inside his doublet. He evidently had more important things on his mind. 'Come with me Mr. Morrow. I want to show you our fine fleet, ready to give the King of France a bloody nose.' He was moving towards the door as he spoke and I followed him.

The duke issued orders in all directions. He seemed concerned with the smallest detail as if he did not have enough confidence in his captains to discharge their duties. He received several surly looks from the men and I presumed his overbearing manner was unpopular. Having completed the tour the duke and his retinue returned to the tavern. Back inside the duke led me to a room that seemed to be set aside for his use and closed the door so we could have privacy. He sat down and slumped into the chair, his body betraying his tiredness. There were deep black rings under his eyes.

'I hope it is good news you bring me,' he sighed, taking out the letter. 'Many of the soldiers have not been paid for months and they are mutinous. I've had to threaten them with my sword to drive them back to their ships. Money from the Stanleys will enable me to pay the arrears and restore good order in the army.'

He looked up from the letter with a smile. 'Excellent, you shall have your reply tomorrow. I had not expected the full sum. £5,000 is sufficient,' and with that I was dismissed to find my own lodging in the town.

***

I returned early next morning to the Greyhound. A party of supplicants had already gathered and I joined them to wait for the duke. A few of the men were chatting about the issues they wanted to put before him, most of them being about arrears of pay. I studied my neighbour as like me he was silent and I wondered why. His dress was that of a gentleman but the clothes were old and worn. He was holding his left hand to the centre of his body and I could see the left sleeve had been sewn to repair a tear in the fabric.

Eventually the duke emerged. He did not appear to have seen me and went over to address a gentleman by the door. 'Good morning Sir Thomas,' said the duke as he bowed to his acquaintance. 'An excellent morning. A night's sleep has eased all my worries like a sea mist lifting over the fleet.'

Sir Thomas bowed in reply and at that moment my neighbour moved out of the crowd and passed close to the duke who cried out in pain. The stranger dropped a blood stained knife which clattered on the floor. For an instant there was complete silence as everyone froze in the horror of the scene. The stranger stood still, looking at the duke who fell to his knees. 'I am wounded by,' the duke's bewildered eyes looked up at his assailant, 'by Felton. Seize him.' This was easily accomplished for the man made no effort to flee.

Felton flinched as if he expected one of the duke's men to run him through with a rapier, but instead they grabbed his arms and held him.

Four other men lifted the duke by his arms and legs and carried him back through to his room. As they lifted him up he cried out in pain. There was a pool of blood where he had been lying; the wound looked very deep. Sir Thomas sent for a doctor and then went through to the duke, shutting the door on the room. Felton was manhandled away to be confined while he awaited his fate. Excited chatter filled the room. I overheard that Felton was known to have been refused promotion by the duke on several occasions.

I was shocked by what I had just witnessed. I confess I did not like Buckingham, but to see him cut down left me feeling sick. Then my mind turned back to the letter I had given the duke. What would happen if the duke died and the letter was found amongst his papers? In all likelihood someone coming across it would see it as a bribe and such a revelation would damage the Stanleys. I would have to try to retrieve it. But how was I going to do this? The letter was in the room with the duke's body and I would not be allowed in. I decided it would be best to wait until dark, but was worried I would not be able to gain entry to the house after nightfall. Outside, I scouted around to see if it would be possible to get in by a ground floor window, but all the windows seemed secure. I went round to the back of the house and opened the door. It led into the kitchen and had a key on the inside. There was nobody in sight. Quickly I grabbed the key and shut the door. The key might not be missed in all the confusion and even if it were, they might not have any other way to lock the door.

I spent the rest of the day wandering about summoning courage for what I had to do. The news about the attack on the duke had spread all around the town like fire through a thatched roof, a slow crackle at first and then a deafening roar as the word spread further. The wound had indeed been fatal. As a soldier, Felton would have instinctively sought out a major organ. Nothing could be done to save the duke and he had died soon afterwards.

***

In the dead of night I found myself outside the Greyhound. I was still turning the events of the morning over in my mind. Why should I risk myself to retrieve a document which would implicate the Stanleys rather than me? I thought of the earl, an affable, intelligent man who was prepared to use his learning and knowledge to help me understand the affairs of the world. I thought of James, newly wed with a young child. Both men treated me with respect and I realized I would risk my own safety for them.

There was nobody else in the street. I listened, but apart from some noise from an inn over the way it was quiet. Slowly I walked round to the back of the house, my senses heightened in the dark and by the feeling of danger. I seemed to be making an awful lot of noise and I wondered why nobody called out to challenge me. At last I reached the door. I listened again and when I felt it was safe to do so I tried the latch and pushed. The door opened with a creak and again I thought somebody must surely cry out. Nobody was there to do so. I stepped into the kitchen and waited a few moments for my eyes to make sense of the room. Once I had my bearings I moved over to the door which led into the main room. Cautiously I opened the door and passed into the next room. The embers of a fire still burnt in the hearth, giving me some light to guide my way. It was a smaller room off this one where the duke had been taken. Slowly I edged my way across the room. Reaching the far door I stopped and took a deep breath. I don't think I had allowed myself to breathe until that point. I tried the door. Unlocked. Good. At that moment I heard a sound behind me. Someone was coming down the stairs.

I opened the door, got into the room and quickly shut it behind me. I stood rooted to the spot not wanting to move any more in case a noise gave me away. I listened to the footsteps coming down the stairs. They began to move across the room. Had I been heard? Gradually the footsteps moved across the room. They weren't coming my way. I heard sounds in the kitchen and in my head I saw an image of water being poured from a pitcher. Someone needed a drink. I waited and after a few minutes heard the footsteps again. Whoever had woken up was now back on their way upstairs. When I could no longer hear anything I allowed myself to move. My legs were stiff from standing completely still. I walked it off as I moved around the room looking for the duke's papers.

There was no sign of the duke's body. I took out the small tinder box I always carried and lit a candle, sufficient to provide enough light to look through the papers piled on the desk and on the floor. They must have been moved when the duke's body was laid on the table.

Some of the letters had blood on them and an attempt had been made to wash down the table. To compose myself, I took a mouthful of air, but it had an unpleasant stale, metallic taste. The letter I sought was not there. Then I caught a glimpse of a doublet lying on the floor. It must have been discarded when they were trying to save Buckingham's life. I reached inside and my fingers located a letter. I felt the seal on the side. I made out the shape of an eagle, the Stanley seal. I pushed it into the inside of my doublet and stood up, getting ready to leave the room. I blew out the candle and headed for the door.

My eyes had not yet adjusted to the darkness and I crashed into the edge of the table. This dislodged several items including another candleholder, which clattered to the floor. Quickly, I headed out of the room and back across to the kitchen. I heard noises upstairs. This time I had disturbed someone. I ran through the kitchen and out of the house. My pursuer was coming down the stairs and shouting to raise the rest of the household. Above me someone was opening a window. I saw a flash of light and heard the crack from a pistol. Without thinking I ducked and then broke into a run. I twisted and turned down various streets to evade the shadows behind me. I felt as if I had run for an hour before the sounds of pursuit tapered out behind me. Exhausted I made my way warily to my lodging.

***

Towards the end of the next day I arrived back at Canon Row. I had not been able to rest for I wanted to reach James before the news from Portsmouth got to London. The excitement of the night before kept me going for most of the way, but by the time I reached the city I felt myself nodding off as my horse walked the last few miles to Derby House.

I gained admittance to see James immediately. He was already aware of the fate of Buckingham and looked anxious.

'Paul, are our plans undone?' he asked. 'Did you see the duke and give him the letter?'

'My Lord, I did indeed see the duke and passed the letter over to him. I had found him in a rather melancholy mood. Your letter lifted his spirits, but before he could act upon it he was killed by Felton.' James shot me a look betraying his worry and I continued, hurrying to get the words out. 'Later I retrieved the letter from the duke's room, so there is no danger to you.' I told him the full details of my adventure and handed over the letter.

James wanted the advice of his father now Buckingham was dead. New factions would be stirring at Court which meant James could not leave London at this time. Indeed to leave now could imply James had played a part in the assassination. So I was sent back to Chester to seek the opinion of Earl William. One of the Stanley's servants, George Brereton was sent with me as an escort. George had several duties in the household, one of them being an assistant to the gamekeeper and he was noted as an excellent shot with the fowling pieces.

George was a quiet man, keeping his thoughts to himself, except for when we passed a large forest which prompted him to comment longingly on the good game for the pot in there.

Coming close to the end of our journey we spent a night in Northwich, about half a day's ride from Chester. Entering the inn, I picked up a sense of excitement from the conversation of the drinkers. I asked for a room for the night, as we had decided at the outset it would be safer to share. I eavesdropped on the conversation, the talking being done by a man close by who stood with a pot of beer in his hand. He had the attention of everyone in the room and we turned to listen.

'Yes, that's what I said. A papist priest has been caught near Preston and taken to Lancaster Castle. They say one of his own betrayed him to the justices. He tried to get away but was seized on the road.'

'They'll hang him for sure,' said one of the other drinkers. 'Traitors the lot of 'em. They'd sell us out to the devil,' he said spitting on the floor.

'Traitors that's true', replied the innkeeper. 'The penalty for a traitor is hanging, drawing and quartering. We've not had one of those for years. There'll be a big crowd in Lancaster if he's found guilty. The inns will do good business. They always do when there's a hanging.'

I noticed George had left the room. I stayed a little longer listening to accounts of hangings they'd seen. After a while the gruesome talk began to disgust me, fuelled as it was by beer and bravado. I went up to our room. As I went in George pushed something looking like a bracelet into his bag. His brow was taut with worry.

I couldn't imagine the talk of a hanging bothering George. A man used to gutting and skinning animals wouldn't be upset by descriptions of hanging, no matter how graphic. Then I thought about the beads he had concealed.

'George, are you a Catholic?'

He looked at me warily.

'You have nothing to fear from me,' I continued. 'I'll not denounce you.'

'Ay, I know that. I've heard what you did for Lord Morley, and don't worry I'll not repeat that to anyone I don't trust. Yes, I am Catholic,' he continued. 'What's more I'll know the priest likely as not, as there aren't many. I get myself off to see one every few months, saying I've gone to see my mother near Blackburn. It's not true what they say about the priests, you know,' he said looking at me. 'They don't incite rebellion; they just practice the old religion and minister for those in their care. They are better priests than some of those that sit in the parish churches. What's more they are prepared to die for their faith. I don't see many others willing to do that.'

'But there haven't been any priests hung for years. Surely he'll be set free?'

'It all depends upon whether he stands by his faith. If he renounces, then he'll probably be spared. If he doesn't then they'll hang him,' said George sighing.

'Let's talk to Earl William tomorrow,' I replied. 'He will no doubt know more about what has happened.'

We resolved to make a very early start the next morning and settled down to what proved to be a fitful night's sleep. Once on the road, George was anxious to get to Chester to see the earl, and he pressed his horse hard to cover the final miles.

Earl William was taking his ease in the library when we arrived. George did not come in to see him, as he did not have ready access to the earl. I handed over the papers I had carried and the earl quickly read through them.

'Were you really present at the assassination of the Duke of Buckingham?' he asked.

'Indeed I was my Lord. I was standing right next to Felton before he stabbed the duke. Nobody could have prevented it; he moved so quickly.'

I was beginning to follow the earl's way of thinking. His mind moved from the facts to their consequences. 'He might have been unpopular but without him, King Charles might now stumble,' he said, drawing his fingers through his beard. 'James must stay at Court to see if there are any opportunities in the King's service. Tell me, what day was the assassination?'

'August 23rd,' I said. 'The next day I relayed the news to James in London. I had waited in Portsmouth to retrieve a document from Buckingham. In it James promised £5,000 to Buckingham to help finance war against France.'

Earl William raised his eyebrows. 'That was commendable and you have my heartfelt gratitude, as no doubt you have my son's.'

'I hear a Catholic priest is in Lancaster gaol waiting to be tried.'

'That is correct, but I think you heard old news. Edmund Arrowsmith was seized over a week ago near Brindle. His trial was swift and a couple of days after being arrested he was hung, after the usual fashion for priests. In fact, he died on the same day as Buckingham. He refused to recant his faith and before his execution was heard to ask the crowd to convert to the Catholic faith.'

'Why was he prosecuted?' I asked. 'Catholics have mostly been left in peace these past ten years.'

'Until now that is. King Charles is young and does not have enough belief in himself to set his own policies. Therefore he has relied heavily on the Duke of Buckingham. It is Buckingham who took us to war with the French as well as the Spanish. The toleration given to Catholics as part of the marriage to the French princess is no longer the policy. Buckingham set the tone and the local magistrates have followed it. Some no doubt will be pleased to persecute Catholics; others may do it with a troubled conscience.'

'My Lord, do you see the irony here? Buckingham was assassinated on the same day that a Catholic priest hung because of his policies.' I took my leave from the earl and went back to talk to George.

'It's bad news, George.' We went outside for some privacy. 'The priest, Edmund Arrowsmith, has already been convicted and hanged.'

'I feared as much,' George replied. 'They've been keener to root us out in the last year or so. Before that a blind eye was turned. As long as we were seen in the parish church on Sundays and Holy days, then we were left to carry out our own services in private. Now we'll have to be even more careful.' He thanked me and walked away.

***

I took the opportunity while in Chester to visit the market, as it was one of the finest in the north. I had need of a new belt and there would be tanners selling their goods on the market. Chester was an impressive city with its cathedral and city walls. Men and goods bound for Ireland often sailed from the port and there were many prosperous merchants within the town. As I walked along the streets, it struck me the town houses were not as grand as some of those I had seen in The Hague. On the market square I saw all the usual stalls and traders. A group of people was gathered at one end of the square, in front of a man dressed in drab black clothes. He looked like a preacher. Interested to hear what he was saying I joined the crowd.

'Brethren, I urge you to seek the path our Lord Jesus Christ has shown us. He came amongst us, became flesh and shared our labours and our trials. He died that we might be saved. It says in Psalms, "put not your trust in princes, they will all fail; the men perish, and their thoughts perish". You must live a good and holy life, avoiding the temptations of Satan. The rich do not live a good life.' A few people murmured assent, knowingly. The preacher continued. 'It is better to be a poor man and a rich Christian, than a rich man and a poor Christian. Look around you, there is temptation all around,' he paused to let his words rest on the ears of the crowd. 'Satan is at work in this market. Don't the traders cheat you with short measures? The Bible tells us in Proverbs, "The Lord abhors dishonest scales, but accurate weights are his delight". Look there, at the whores eager to rob a sinful man of his money. Now is the time to repent and follow the Lord's way, for we are coming near to the end of the world.' He looked around the people, trying to draw them in. 'Jesus Christ will rise and come amongst us.'

The Stanleys would certainly want to know more about this man who seemed to be preaching rebellion. In need of some refreshment I headed for the inn. The landlord served me with a mug of beer and told me the preacher's name was Henry Marshall and he was often in the city on market days. 'He's a Puritan, that one. Gaol has not mended 'im of his ways. Neither did the beatings he got from the market traders, not pleased at being called dishonest.'

When I got back to the house of Earl William I found him amongst a pile of papers in his study. Since his retirement from public life he spent most of his time writing. He was currently working on a play about his travels to the court of Navarre as a young man. I'd learnt from the earl that he'd fought a duel during his time in Spain. It was hard to imagine this bookish man as a passionate youth, ready to risk his life over a quarrel.

'What news from the town Paul?' asked the earl, as he looked up and saw me.

'I saw Marshall, a Puritan preacher on the market square. His words were designed to turn the common man against his masters and he drew quite a large crowd.'

'He has been preaching such a message for a couple of years. At first he was ignored and regarded as a fool, but recently people have begun to go just to hear him. On the market he is just a nuisance, but he is known to preach to men higher in the social order. That is where the real danger is. The rabble are not a threat on their own, they need to be lead. He is known to preach in Northwich where funds for a preacher were collected by some of the townspeople. It is an open meeting as they claim to have no fear about doing the Lord's work.' The earl thought for a moment and then continued. 'Perhaps if you were to attend one of these meetings you could learn who we need to watch. James has a responsibility to maintain order in the city and while he is at Court, I have agreed to carry out these duties for him.'

'I'll willingly carry out such a task my Lord. Truthfully I am interested to learn more about Marshall and his followers. I'll have to find some more plain and sober clothes as my current dress is too rich for their taste.'

Two days later I set out for Northwich. Being a Thursday there was a good chance I would be able to hear him preach at Friday prayer. On my previous visits to the town I had stayed in the Swan Inn or with the Stanleys' Steward. This time the earl advised that as innkeepers, and for that matter the Steward, are keen to know the business of their guests, it would be better if I lodged in one of the family's properties in the town. As well as owning several wich-houses used in the production of salt, the Stanleys possessed a large shop on the market square and I was told I would be able to stay there for a few days.

The journey of roughly twenty miles was easily accomplished by horse. On reaching the edge of the town I dismounted, for I would be more visible riding my horse than leading it. I crossed the bridge over the Weaver as people from the nearby villages were heading out of the town after visiting the market. I reached the end of the bridge nearing the Stanleys' courthouse. The Stanleys' Steward lived here and I had met him when in the town to collect the forced loan two years earlier.

I did not want to run into him on this visit, as he would surely recognize me and then my chance of hearing one of Marshall's sermons incognito would be lost. Passing the courthouse without incident, I crossed the market place and went to the back of the Stanleys' shop where there was a small courtyard for deliveries and stabling. I tethered my horse and then entered the shop by the back door. This was the living area and a woman was preparing a meal. I explained who I was and that I needed to stay for a couple of nights. However, if anyone asked about me I was to be a gentleman travelling to London in need of a few days rest. I was shown to a chamber above the living hall, accessed by a ladder. Here I would be able to sleep without disturbance.

'Has Marshall, the preacher ever been to St. Helen's church at Witton?' I asked the shopkeeper as he sat down to breakfast of bread with cold bacon and a bowl of milk.

'Marshall, yes he's often here,' the man replied, looking up from his food. 'He's on good terms with Richard Mather the curate and Richard Piggot, master of the grammar school. Both of them are of the godly Puritan sort, talking about redemption through Jesus Christ and the sinfulness of all those that's not one of them. They won't have anything that seems like the old religion. They've removed the rood screen and painted all the walls white, covering up the pictures of the saints. They'll not burn candles in the church unless they're made to. That's a bad business for Richard Wright the candle maker, he has had to turn to labouring to make a living.'

'I've a mind to go and hear him and see who else goes along.'

'Go along this morning to the service, likely as not Marshall will be there. He was preaching on the market square yesterday until the steward came over and threatened to put him in the prison.'

I decided to walk to the church as arrival on horseback would mark me out as a gentleman and curiosity would arise. There were a good number of people in the church as I entered. With attendance only compulsory on Sunday's and Holy Days, I took them as a core of godly Puritans, eager to hear the Lord's word whenever they could. It was quiet, without the usual grumblings that were heard in most churches on Sundays as the congregations gathered.

The service was unlike any I had ever attended. After he had welcomed the congregation the curate called upon Marshall to preach a sermon. Just as he had done at Chester, he railed against the sinfulness of man and called on us to look to Jesus Christ for our salvation. Mutterings of assent greeted every sentence.

After the service I made my way slowly out of the church. I avoided looking anyone in the eye for fear they would come and question me as a stranger to their church. I passed by a group of gentlemen talking outside the porch door with the curate and Marshall. Nearby a boy was holding the reins of their horses. I recognised one of the men as John Bradshaw. He had an air of seriousness about him and during the conversation he looked down as if weighing a grave matter in his mind. Here then was John Bradshaw amongst the godly. This was an interesting association and I resolved to learn more.

Rather than ride straight back to Chester I decided to stay until Sunday in order to attend the next service. During the course of the day on Saturday I thought through the beliefs of the Puritans. I sympathised with their complaints that many of the clergy were ignorant and unable to cater for the needs of their flock. It was true the congregations were outwardly Protestant in that they attended church services, but like the Puritans I doubted their beliefs were truly Protestant. Indeed many of them were still Catholic. Personally I did not hold with the Catholic beliefs about the intercession of the priest and all the Catholic saints, but I also felt the Puritan belief in Predestination left no room for a man to work towards his own salvation through good works.

The service on Sunday was more in line with the format stipulated in the Book of Common Prayer. The curate was wearing a surplice which he had lacked on Friday. It seemed Richard Mather knew the regular Sunday congregation could not all be counted amongst the elect, and therefore he carried out a service more in line with the teachings of the established church. John Bradshaw and Richard Piggot were both in church, sitting together near the front. At the end of the service I found myself heading in the same direction as Bradshaw and Piggot.

Once on the market square in Northwich they went over towards the Swan. I continued to follow them. As we got close to the inn I saw a thick set man stagger out of the door. Although no beer was meant to be served on the Lord's Day, he appeared to be drunk and must have missed the Sunday service. John Bradshaw had also seen him and looked aghast at the man's behaviour. He was attempting to mount a horse, but was finding it difficult to put his foot into the stirrup. Eventually his foot found enough purchase and he swung himself onto the horse. However, in his inebriated state he carried on over the back of the horse, ending up face down on the square.

Bradshaw evidently knew the man and rounded on him. 'That is God's judgment on you for sacrilege on the Sabbath. I will give your name to the curate and you will be in the Consistory Court to account for your profanity.'

'Do what you like,' was all the man could utter as he struggled to get up.

After those words Bradshaw and Piggot went into the inn, no doubt to harangue the innkeeper for selling alcohol on a Sunday. I knew they would be suspicious if I followed, so I returned to my room in the town. It would be difficult to learn any more without revealing my motives, so I resolved to head back to Chester the next morning.

'You have done well, Paul,' remarked the earl when I spoke with him next. 'This is valuable intelligence. We must continue to be aware of the activities of Bradshaw and his acquaintances. It concerns me that Richard Mather is taking the church at Northwich along the Puritan road. As a rule Puritans challenge the established order, for their nature is to be self-assured in their own beliefs. While James is at Court, I will keep my eye on this. I'm afraid you will have to be on the road to London again with my letter of reply to James.'

Chapter 13 – *Liverpool, October 19, 1651*

With so many strangers in the tavern, Paul decided to approach Captain Bartlet at the table as if he did not know him. He walked over, his eyes trailing in the dust and old rushes on the floor. Three years ago the man had still been in the service of the Stanleys, but Paul could not believe that he still served the family. The captain watched Paul from his small, intelligent eyes as he came near.

'Good day to you, sir,' Paul began, noticing a flicker of a smile cross the captain's face. 'Are you the captain of the ship sailing for the Isle of Man today?'

'Aye, that's me,' replied Bartlet. 'Have you got business there?' he continued.

'Yes, I have,' replied Paul. 'How much for passage for me and a horse?' he asked.

'A shilling for the pair of you,' answered the captain. 'We leave at two o'clock to catch this afternoon's tide. Come with me now and we'll get your horse aboard.' Bartlet stood and put a few coins on the table. Paul drained his tankard of beer and set it down beside the captain's, wondering how many he had drunk. Did the man still drink huge amounts while ashore?

Paul followed Bartlet out onto the quayside. Out of the hearing of the tavern the captain spoke again, with no hint of drunkenness in his voice. 'It's good to see you Paul. I can't believe the earl is dead. They say he went to the Lord readily,' pausing for Paul to comment.

'Indeed he did,' nodded Paul.

'And I also hear there is a fugitive with a price on his head, who escaped from the execution?'

Paul turned to unfasten his horse's rein from the post that had held her. Had he got so far to be betrayed now? He paused, considering whether to leap onto her back and ride away.

'Easy there, I don't want their Judas gold,' whispered Bartlet. 'I just wanted to know if it is you, or is there someone else hiding nearby who you want to get away?'

'No, it is me,' replied Paul. 'There is only me.'

'Let's get you onboard then, out of sight of prying eyes.' The captain set off towards his ship. With a look around the quay, Paul followed him.

Captain Bartlet shouted over two deckhands who had now appeared and were trying to look busy. 'Get this horse on board,' he ordered. 'And fetch some fodder for it. We're putting to sea today, so get to it.' The two sailors looked at each other quizzically and then set about their task. Paul went below with the captain to his cabin.

'Will Charlotte fight, do you think?' he asked Bartlet.

'I've not seen her for a few years, but if I know her, she will fight,' he replied.

'But it's hopeless,' Paul bemoaned. 'The Parliament is master of England and Scotland. How can Charlotte hold out on one tiny island, now they have decided it's time to finish her?'

'She can't expect to win, but I think she will fight for the memory of her husband and her honour,' answered the captain.

'Aye and she would take us all down with her,' Paul retorted. 'That is something I can't allow to happen.'

Chapter 14 – *London, 1629*

When I next saw James in London he was bouncing baby Charles on his knee. The child was now a year old and squealing with delight. In response James smiled and bounced the boy higher.

'Paul, meet Sir Charles, a gallant knight who is riding far in search of adventure and heroic deeds.'

'Is he the Sir Charles told of in legend?' I replied joining in with the game.

'The very same. Today he is on a quest in for fame and glory. He does not know where he is going so he lets his horse choose the way,' said James as he half dropped Charles to one side. 'Now tell me what news from my father? Is he in good health?'

'Indeed he is my Lord. He sends you his greetings and this letter.'

Reading through the letter, James nodded in agreement. 'As ever my father offers sound advice. I had already resolved to remain at Court for I hope to be given the honour of being made a Knight of the Garter. Charles is in need of new friends and I think I can be good company for him. Did you know he sent Charlotte a jewelled bracelet? And look at these,' he said, pointing at a pair of exquisitely worked silver cups. 'Aren't they beautiful?' his eyebrow arched.

'Truly they are,' I replied lifting one in my hand, my fingers five stubby reflections in the metal.

'Charles sent them for my son,' continued James. 'I know it will be difficult to make a close friendship with the King for he keeps a tight group around him. To see if I can take pleasure in one of his pastimes I have begun to read some of Ben Jonson's work, for Charles enjoys his plays.'

'Your father will be pleased for your interest in the theatre.'

'Perhaps I should be asking him to write something especially for Charles. Though I doubt he will find the time. He is as anxious as me to restore our family's fortunes since the legal wrangling with the Dowager Countess. However, political works to glorify the Sovereign are not really his forte. No, he will play his part in a different way. Thank you for your service these past weeks. Now you may have some time of your own. I believe one of my wife's maids is anxious to see you again.'

With that I was free to go and seek out Louise. It was true I had not seen her for weeks and I felt a sense of excitement as I thought about her. Would she still be keen to see me, I wondered. James had implied she would be, so I took comfort in that.

'So you're back from your travels,' were the first words Louise greeted me with. 'I'm surprised you can find any time for us, with all your important missions up and down the country. Are you staying long this time?'

I stammered my reply. 'At present my Lord has no more plans for me. I have time of my own. If you are able, perhaps we could take a walk to the river this afternoon?'

'I'll have to see if my lady is as generous as your lord.' Then she smiled, revealing dimpled cheeks, and jumped into my arms. 'Of course, let's go straight away.'

'What has been happening while I've been away?' I asked as we walked together.

'Charlotte is expecting her third child. This time they don't see the need to fetch a midwife from France. Baby Charles is growing all the time, but Charlotte finds him difficult to cope with as she is tired due to her pregnancy. He spends most of the time with his nurse. Young Charlotte is unwell, but it is not expected that the Almighty will take her.'

'I heard Charlotte's brother has renounced the Protestant faith. Tell me, is it true?'

'Yes, and Charlotte is very saddened by this. It seems her brother felt this was the only way to escape the political wilderness. Soon afterwards the Duke received a post as Commander of the French light cavalry from Cardinal Richelieu.'

'I need to go and congratulate Charlotte on her good news. Can I see you again this evening?'

'I'll look forward to it. See you at dinner.'

It was wonderful to be with Louise again. I knew she felt the same. Earl William and James seemed to take delight in teasing me for my uncertainty about her feelings, as if everyone but me knew that God had matched us. I decided to ask Louise that evening if she would marry me. Of course if she agreed, I would have to go to see her father. I thought about how he would see me as a marriage partner for his daughter. I had now been in the Stanley household for four years and had a good prospect of continued employment. It was known that I was a trusted member of the household and, because of the confidences they had shared with me, I did not think the earl or James had any thought of dismissing me. While not wealthy, I had saved some money, enough to support a family if God blessed our union with children.

After dinner I drew Louise to a quiet corner. Her eyes viewed me quizzically, but there was a flicker of a smile on her face. My mouth was dry and I had a sudden fear she would say no.

We sat on some cushions in a window seat off the hall. I took her hand in mine and looked into her dark eyes. Now I could hold her gaze, confident in my love for her. 'Will you marry me?'

'Most certainly I will, Paul! I thought you would never ask.' Her eyes shone and she leant forward and kissed me.

'I must go and see your father. Will he agree?'

'I'll come with you, and when he knows I am truly happy, he won't be able to disagree.'

I felt overjoyed and I needed to tell someone that Louise had agreed to marry me. 'We also ought to ask the permission of James and Charlotte,' I said.

'Yes, we must,' agreed Louise. With her hand still in mine we walked over to the high table. They watched us as we approached. Charlotte was smiling.

'We have some news,' I began.

'You're going to get married,' interrupted Charlotte.

'But how did you know?' I replied.

'I can see it on your faces, and when does my lady-in-waiting hold a gentleman's hand in public?' Charlotte's broad smile indicated her approval.

'This is excellent news,' offered James. Turning to a kitchen boy he said. 'Take away these ale pots and get some glasses. Send for a bottle of French wine from the cellar. We shall toast the happy couple.'

'That is very kind James, but I still have to get the permission of Louise's father,' I said.

'But why should he object? His daughter will be wedding the secretary of Lord Strange. If he has any objections tell him he's to speak to me. Now tell me, would you like to be married here or at Lathom? Perhaps Louise would like to be married in the London church she attended as a girl?'

'My lord, I would be very happy to be married here in London with my family.'

'And I have no family except in your household, so London it is,' I said.

***

As if matching our mood, the smell of spring was in the air when we set of the next morning through Derby Gate to see Louise's father. After the cold of the winter it felt wonderful to feel the warmth of the sun again. We had both been given the day to ourselves for Charlotte suggested it would be a good idea to spend the day with Louise's family. Louise's mother and father lived in Cheapside, a couple of miles east along the Thames and we decided to walk, for horses were useless in the crowded, narrow streets. I wanted to use the walk to ask Louise more about where she had grown up.

'Didn't you say your family live in Bread Street? The earl told me he used to send a servant to the inn there, to fetch Will Shakespeare over to Derby House.'

'We would never enter such a licentious house. It's not a place for honest, respectable people.' Her tone was abrupt and I instantly wished I'd not mentioned the inn.

'I'm sorry. I did not mean to suggest your family would have anything to do with such a place. I was simply curious because the earl had spoken of it. Let's not quarrel, today of all days.'

Turning towards me she smiled and replied. 'No, let's not quarrel for that would be a bad start. I didn't mean to bite. It's just that my father hates the place.'

'I'll make sure I don't talk about it with him then,' I replied laughing.

We wound our way through the crowds which got busier the closer we got to Cheapside. These were the streets which fed the cities of Westminster and London. We passed through a poultry market with chickens being chased by small boys who were supposed to have tied them up. The odour of the chickens mingled with the sweat I could smell on the people in the crowd. Then I caught the comforting smell of baking bread.

'Here we are,' said Louise, 'Bread Street.'

We walked down the aptly named street. Their house was on the end of a row of two story town houses, mirrored on the other side by another row. Washing flapped above our heads, pegged to lines strung between the houses across the street. I carefully avoided walking in the human detritus which pooled in the middle of the street. I caught sight of the Mermaid Inn, but thought it wise not to say anything. I could also see a church and wondered if this was where Louise wished us to marry. We walked up to the door which Louise tried; finding it unlocked she entered and I followed, removing my hat as I stepped over the threshold.

'Papa, Mama,' called Louise. The room we had entered was empty. There was a fire burning in the hearth with a half empty pan of porridge suspended above it. The table looked like it had recently hosted breakfast, with a partly eaten loaf sitting in the middle. A fine lace tablecloth covered the table. Besides this luxury, the room was simply furnished with little apart from the table and some chairs, but the floor was of expensive black and white tiles, unusual for this type of house. The walls looked to have been recently whitewashed and a large, plain, black wooden cross hung above the fireplace.

There were sounds of someone moving in the room at the back and a woman came through the door. On seeing us her face grew into a large smile. 'Louise,' she cried and came over and threw her arms around her. This had to be Louise's mother, a little shorter than her daughter, but of the same build and with the same dark hair, mostly hidden under a white headscarf.

'This must be Mr. Morrow,' she said as she stepped away from Louise and turned towards me. She was still smiling as she looked me up and down, which I took as a good sign. 'I'm Anne, Louise's mother.'

'I'm very pleased to make your acquaintance,' I said with a low bow.

Turning back to Louise, she continued. 'Your father will want to see you. He's at his workshop, teaching a new girl to make lace.'

'Paul would like to see him, as he has something to ask,' said Louise, her face beaming with unsuppressed joy.

'And what could this be?' Although Anne asked the question, her tone suggested she already knew.

'I've come to ask for his permission to marry your daughter.'

For a couple of heartbeats, Anne looked into my eyes. She had the same penetrating stare as her daughter. 'If you are the man my daughter has chosen to marry, then I would be delighted. But her father has always planned for her to marry Philippe Garnier.'

'But Philippe is nothing more than a childhood playmate,' replied Louise.

'Yes, but he is the son of another Huguenot and your father has always wanted you to marry a Frenchman. He's always wanted this. You had better approach him carefully.'

'We'll go and speak to him. When he knows of my wish to marry Paul, I'm sure he will relent,' replied Louise. 'I will be back later.'

Louise moved towards the door and I followed. 'I wish you a good morning,' I said to Anne.

Out on the street I almost had to trot to keep pace with Louise. I mulled over what we had learnt from Anne. So Louise's father had already planned a wedding match for her. How resolute would he be? From what Louise had told me, she was his favourite child, but would this be enough to make him change his mind?

The shop he worked out of was not far away and soon we were standing outside. I looked into the small window in which some pretty pieces of lace were on display. Hung above the door was a sign which proudly stated, "Georges Bardin, lace-maker to the King".

'That's impressive,' I said to Louise, pointing with a nod of my head. 'Does the King buy a lot of lace from your father?'

'Enough for him to keep taking more girls on. He must have four working for him now.'

I followed Louise through the door into a workshop, with lace strewn everywhere. There was finished lace on display, fine cuffs and collars for gentlemen's shirts, ruffs, doilies, nightdresses for babies, and for those who could afford them exquisite bedspreads and tablecloths. As we entered a man and two girls looked up at us from the lace they were examining together.

'Papa,' said Louise as she reached out to hug her father. He stood up and embraced her.

They stood apart and Louise introduced me. 'This is Paul Morrow, secretary to the Earl of Derby.'

'I'm very pleased to meet you, Monsieur Morrow,' he said as he offered me his hand. The fingers were long and thin and his grip was firm. It felt as if he was crushing my fingers in his embrace. He held my hand, preventing me from backing away and his eyes bored deep down into me as if searching for my soul.

'Is the earl wanting to buy some lace?' he said smiling and finally released my hand. I wondered if he too had guessed why I had come to see him

'No,' I replied. 'Your lace looks to be of excellent quality, but the earl has not sent me here to buy any. It's another matter I wish to discuss with you.'

'Very well, then we will go to my room.' He gestured to a door and walked over to it. Louise remained where she stood, and as I followed her father I heard her starting a conversation with the lace makers.

I felt more nervous than I had done when I had been searching through the Duke of Buckingham's papers on that fateful day in Portsmouth. My mouth had gone dry and as if to compensate my palms were dripping with sweat.

Louise's father sat down behind a desk piled high with ledgers and indicated I should sit on a bench under the window. He picked up a pipe from the table and rummaged in his pocket for some tobacco.

'Well, Monsieur Morrow, what is this important matter you must discuss with me?'

I watched him pressing the tobacco into the pipe as I began to reply. His eyes were focused on the pipe rather than me, which calmed my anxiety. 'I've worked as secretary to the Earl of Derby for four years and have known your daughter, Louise for three of these. While she has been in the earl's household we have grown close. So much so that I would like to take her as my wife. I've come here today to ask you if will consent to our marriage.'

He looked up, and once more his eyes engaged in their quest for my soul.

'Is that so,' he asked. 'And why should I agree? I don't know you and have no idea if you are suitable for my daughter. I'm good at my trade and my business is growing. My daughter will bring a good dowry. Why should it go to you?'

Immediately I replied, 'I don't care for her dowry. It is Louise I care about and would want to marry her with no dowry. As to whether I am suitable, Lord Strange is willing to provide a testimony of my good character.'

'Ah, you have the earl's son on your side. What then of the Lady Charlotte, what does she think about this?'

I realized Charlotte's opinion as another French Huguenot might carry more weight with him than James's. 'She has given Louise her blessing.'

'So it seems only I stand in the way. I wish to talk with Louise about this. Let's bring her in.'

He opened the door and called for Louise to join us. She broke off her conversation and looked enquiringly at her father. As she entered the room her eyes questioned me, searching for a sign. I could neither nod nor shake my head for I did not know where I stood. Louise's brow furrowed as she realized her father had not yet agreed.

'I expect you know the reason for Monsieur Morrow's visit?' he said addressing Louise. He made it sound as if we were engaged in a conspiracy.

'Yes, Papa. Isn't it wonderful? I'm so happy. Tell me that you'll agree.'

'*Doucement, doucement.* I want to get to know Paul a little better and I wish to talk this over with your mother. There is also Jacques Garnier to consider. He's always expected you would marry his son, though some of Philippe's recent behaviour has made me question this. Stay and have a meal with us. Come let's go home now and see your mother.'

Before we could leave, Louise's father had to give some instructions to his lace makers. He explained he was going home and they were to close up the shop at the end of the day. It seemed one of them lived upstairs, which given that Louise's family did not live on the premises was a sensible arrangement, for Louise's father would not need to worry about the safekeeping of his shop.

Back out on the street, Louise took hold of my hand as we walked. She did not seem to be taking this as a major setback. Once back in Bread Street she saw me looking at the church.

'That's not where I want to get married. We go to the French church on Threadneedle Street.'

Her father smiled at her. 'That's my Louise. Once you've decided on something, nothing's going to stop you. Does your mother know?'

'Yes, we've told her. She seemed to have guessed before Paul said anything.'

'That's your mother, good intuition. No doubt she'll have been preparing a meal, for she'll expect me to go home with news like this.'

A pleasant smell of cooking greeted us when we returned. I saw a large covered pot suspended over the hearth. There were sprigs of rosemary and some bay leaves on the table, and Anne was clearing up some peelings, orange carrot and red potato.

'Poule au pot,' said Louise. 'Paul you will love this, it is a French dish that my father taught mother.'

'But she still can't do it as well as me,' grinned Louise's father. 'Come; now let us drink some French wine while we wait for this to cook. The vintner near St. Mary's Colechurch sells me a fine Bordeaux, though at five times the price I used to buy it in France.' He jaunted off towards a cover leading to the cellar and disappeared in search of the wine.

Louise walked over to a dresser and took down four glass goblets. Her father returned with two dusty bottles of wine, setting one down by the fire. 'Here, I've been saving this. I think now is a good time to drink it.' He uncorked the bottle and the wine glugged invitingly into the goblets. Raising his own goblet he continued, 'Paul, you must now call me Georges.'

I raised my goblet in return and then tilted it to my lips. The cool red wine hit my mouth and I swallowed it sooner than I intended.

'No, no Paul. As the wine is a little cold you must keep it in your mouth to warm it up. Then you can enjoy the taste.'

I took another mouthful and this time I let the wine roll around, between my teeth and over my tongue. The wine warmed as I did so, and when it touched the back of my mouth the taste was so intense that I coughed as I swallowed it.

Georges laughed and clapped me on the shoulder. It seemed as if he was warming to me as we shared this French wine ritual. I stole a glance at Louise who was now smiling.

Georges went around recharging our glasses. He seemed to relish his role as host. Next he uncorked the second bottle and placed it back down by the hearth.

'Well, Ann what do you think about this man marrying our daughter?'

'If this is what Louise wants then I'm happy for her,' Ann replied. 'She is a sensible woman and able to make her own decisions in life.'

'I agree with you on that,' said Georges. 'I also think that if someone else makes this decision for her, then it is likely to be the wrong choice.'

Louise was now beaming. She put down her goblet and came over to her father and hugged him. Although he had not said it outright, he had all but consented to our wishes.

***

The next morning I was having an early breakfast with James as he was taking me on a day's hunting with the King. I was telling him how Louise's father had agreed to our marriage, when our meal was cut short by a piercing shriek from Charlotte's chamber which echoed around the house. James fearing a reverse in the infant's recovery ran through to his wife. With some trepidation I followed him, not wishing to pry, but feeling I should offer support. As we approached her chamber Charlotte burst out.

'The stupid English girl has killed my baby. I knew we should have sent for Mademoiselle de Beaulieu.' She fell into the arms of her husband, sobbing uncontrollably.

I went to find Louise to ask her to check the baby. When I found her, she told me the baby was indeed dead. The child's nurse was bereft. She had admitted she had taken the baby into her bed to keep it warm. She now confessed she had done this for the past three nights and it had broken the child's fever.

'She must have rolled onto the baby and suffocated it,' surmised Louise. 'She would not have meant to harm the child. I will go and comfort Charlotte. You must speak to James. He may be angry, but the poor girl did not mean this to happen.'

When Louise went back into Charlotte's chamber James took his leave of her and went to his own room. There he sent for a messenger to take his apologies to the King, for he would not be able to attend the hunt today. Then he crumpled into a chair, his face drained of any colour. He stared into space and then began to speak as if in prayer.

'I bow before the Lord in all humility, acknowledging in Him a power to save and to kill; to do what He likes best, and no-one must ask Him why. Nothing in this world comes to pass without His council or without His Providence, or without a good cause why. Now that I consider, it is good that He has humbled me. He knows what is good for us, better than we know ourselves.'

'Indeed it is the Lord's will,' I replied. 'Shall I fetch your chaplain?'

'Yes please do. More for Charlotte's sake than mine.'

I left the room, marvelling at the strength of James's faith. He had been confronted by the most sorrowful news, but his trust in the Lord had not been shaken.

Chapter 15 – *Isle of Man, October 19, 1651*

Paul sat alone in his cabin looking at the letter James had told him to deliver to Charlotte. James had written it himself and sealed it without giving it to Paul to read. Paul fretted that James's written word might not convey a clear enough message. He turned it over in his hands and looked at the seal, an eagle. At the time, numb with emotion, Paul had hardly noticed how James had used his signet ring to bind the letter fast. Now an idea occurred to him. He had James's signet ring in his money pouch, given to him by the earl on the scaffold. He could open the letter, read it and seal it again without anyone else knowing. Reassuring himself he was only doing this to be sure Charlotte would understand what James wanted her to do, Paul put the letter down on the table and walked over to the door. There was no way to lock it, so he jammed a chair under the handle. Guiltily, he sloped back to the desk and picked up the letter again. Carefully, he broke the seal with a pocket knife and pulled the ribbon away before unfolding the paper. He took out the ring and began to fiddle with it in his fingers. With a deep breath he began to read.

"Chester, October 13, 1651

> *My dear Heart, I have heretofore sent you comfortable lines, but, alas, I have now no word of comfort, saving to our last and best refuge, which is Almighty God, to whose will we must submit; and when we consider how he hath disposed of these nations and the government thereof, we have no more to do but to lay our hands upon our mouths, judging ourselves, and acknowledging our sins, joined with others, to have been the cause of these miseries, and to call on Him with tears for mercy.*

> *The governor of this place, Colonel Duckenfield, is general of the forces which are going now against the Isle of Man, and however you might do for the present, in time it would be grievous and troublesome to resist, especially those that at this hour command three nations; wherefore my advice, notwithstanding my*

great affection to that place is, that you would make conditions for yourself, children, servants, and people there, and such as came over with me, to the end you may go to some place of rest where you may not be concerned in war; and taking thought of your poor children, you may in some sort provide for them; then prepare yourself to come to your friends above, in that blessed place where bliss is, and no mingling of opinions.

I conjure you, my dearest heart, by all those graces which God hath given you, that you exercise your patience in this great and strange trial. If harm come to you, then I am dead indeed, and until then I shall live in you, who are truly the best part of myself. When there is no such as I in being, then look upon yourself and my poor children, then take comfort, and God will bless you.

I acknowledge the great goodness of God to have given me such a wife as you: so great an honour to my family, so excellent a companion to me, so pious, so much of all that can be said of good, I must confess it impossible to say enough thereof. I ask God pardon with all my soul, that I have not been enough thankful for so great a benefit, and when I have done anything at any time that might justly offend you, with joined hands I also ask your pardon.

I have no more to say to you at this time, than my prayers for the Almighty's blessing to you, my dear Mall, and Ned, and Billy.

Amen. Sweet Jesus.

DERBY."

    Paul rocked back on his chair. Why had he doubted James? The letter was clear enough; no more unnecessary fighting for a cause that was lost. He refolded the letter and placed the ribbon in place again. Dragging the candle across the desk he then held the wax above the candle to soften it. Just before the wax got hot enough to drip he put it down on the table and resealed it. Leaving the letter on the table he went to retrieve the chair from the door. He pulled it over to the desk and then sat on it, placing his head in his hands.

***

'We've sighted the Isle,' said Captain Bartlet, entering the cabin without a knock. 'In a few hours we'll drop anchor in Derbyhaven and you'll be able to get up to Castle Rushen.'

'Thank you captain,' replied Paul, a knot of anxiety in his throat. He was not sure if he would be able to do this, but he knew he had to try.

Once onshore he did not even wait for his horse to be unloaded, but walked briskly up to the fort at the point. Despite himself he was pleased to see that the fort was still properly garrisoned. He explained to the sergeant in charge who he was and that he had letters from the earl for Lady Derby. He asked to borrow one of the two horses kept at the fort for sending messages back to Castle Rushen. The sergeant was reluctant at first, but Paul explained he would let the man have his own horse once it was unloaded. He would then arrange for someone to ride out to swap the two animals.

All the best mounts had gone over to Lancashire with James earlier in the year and Paul had to bully this one into a canter. As he rode, he rehearsed what he had to say to Charlotte. He reassured himself that his satchel was still firmly fastened over his shoulder and galloped on, his mouth moving silently as if in prayer.

Chapter 16 – *London, 1631*

"Court friendship is a cable that in storms is ever cut." Private Devotions of James Stanley.

James was ecstatic. He had received an invitation from the King to play in a performance of Jonson's "Love's triumph through Callipolis". James felt he was finally being admitted into Charles's inner circle. His one reservation was that he saw the name of Sir Charles Cavendish on the list of players. Cavendish was the brother of the Earl of Newcastle and this made James uneasy; he did not feel comfortable in the company of the earl, who he felt tried to belittle him in the eyes of the King.

I was allowed to attend, for James would need an attendant to help with the costume. James's excitement was infectious and I felt a little giddy as we entered the Palace of Whitehall. Several members of the court looked down their noses as we entered. I knew they felt James to be an outsider. Despite his rank and his fine house in Canon Row he was regarded with suspicion. He was not an obsequious courtier and there were several at court who saw this as a sign he felt superior to them, and some of them even held that, with his blood line, he felt superior to the King himself.

We entered the room reserved for the players and James was immediately greeted by Sir Charles Cavendish.

'Has his Majesty has invited you to dance today? I don't suppose you've learnt your part?' Cavendish asked sneering.

'Indeed I know my part well sir, and I am looking forward to the masque,' James replied.

'He knows his part. Or, should I say a Stanley knows his place. I shall have to tell my brother,' mocked Cavendish.

I saw James' cheeks flush but he managed to ignore this petty slight and proceeded to get ready. A few minutes later there was a commotion.

'His Majesty is coming. Quick is everyone ready?'

Fortunately James was now fully attired and he took his turn in line to greet the King.

The King stopped at Cavendish who was at the head of the line. He paused and the concentration required to speak without a stammer was evident as he mentally composed his words.

'Gentlemen, I am pleased to see you all here today. I have assembled an interesting group of masquers, for I know the rivalries at Court. I do not want your differences to spoil my entertainment. James, it is your first time with us. I expect you to be well prepared for your role of Secure Love. Myself, I take the part of Heroic Love. To your places so we can begin.'

I did not particularly enjoy the masque. The allegory was not subtle and it seemed to be nothing more than a means for Charles and Henrietta Maria to demonstrate their love for each other. James performed his role well, dancing with grace and dexterity. As the piece concluded, Charles addressed the group once more.

'Bravo, well played. Let this signify the harmony of my court. Put aside your factions and unite in love for your King.'

He then came closer to James and spoke quietly, so only James and I could catch the words. 'James, I hope you understand the intent of my words. This petty rivalry with Newcastle must end if you are to be held highly at my Court.'

'Majesty, I will do nothing that will harm my reputation in your eyes. I wish to continue to receive your grace and good favour.'

'Excellent, then we're agreed. Let's speak no more of this.' Then adopting a louder voice for the benefit of the wider group he continued. 'Come and join me now for supper. I am sure you are all in need of refreshment.'

After we had all feasted on quails and roast pheasant followed by venison, King Charles announced he would take his leave of James and the other courtiers.

Bowed down on one knee as Charles left the room, James whispered, 'Come, let's get back to Canon Row. I have had enough of Cavendish's company for today.' In the carriage back to Derby House, James sat in uncharacteristic silence, no doubt reliving the conversations with the King in his head.

***

A few weeks later James received an invitation from the King to join him for a day's deer-coursing at Greenwich. As he was getting attired for the day in his dressing room, he gave me my instructions.

'Get my keeper to get the deerhounds ready,' James instructed me. 'And make sure they're not fed this morning; I want them hungry and fast. Have them put in the carriage. I don't want them tired out before they get there.' James unlocked one of the drawers in his bureau and took out a velvet bag of coins. 'This should be an excellent day's sport. I'll take one hundred pounds to cover my bets.'

We crossed the Thames by bridge and rode along the far bank to Greenwich, the pampered hounds following us in the carriage. We entered the royal park at a trot. Sun glistened off the white walls of the 'Queen's House', the palace begun by James I for his consort and completed by his son for Queen Henrietta Maria.

Once we arrived the four hounds were taken by their keeper to the 'slipper', the man who held the two dogs before releasing them after the deer. We walked over to the wooden grandstand at the end of the mile long course, where several men were already waiting. The seats on the top row were reserved for the King, and James led me up to a pair of seats just in front of the gentlemen who had already gathered. A whiff of pipe tobacco greeted us before we shook hands with the group of courtiers who were talking animatedly about the coming sport. I looked down at the course the hounds would chase the deer along; it narrowed at the end just below us. From our vantage point we would be able to see which dog was the closest before the deer escaped over a wide ditch that the hounds could not jump.

Soon afterwards the King's party approached. I noticed the Earl of Newcastle to the right of the King. The two of them were engaged in conversation and Charles turned his head and laughed at some comment from Newcastle. I looked across at James; his face visibly fell as he recognised Newcastle.

'Well gentlemen, are we in for a good day's sport?' asked Charles looking around the grandstand. A murmur of assent greeted him, to which he smiled briefly. 'Who will help us start and put a hound up against one of mine?'

'Let me have the honour Your Majesty,' replied Newcastle. 'Though I doubt my hounds can match yours for quality.'

The two dogs were taken over to the slipper. He placed a double collar over their necks, and holding them ready he looked up at the King. Charles flourished a white handkerchief from the end of his sleeve and handed it to a page. 'Take this down and give it to the deer keeper. Tell him he is to use it to start the hounds.'

The slipper walked the two dogs a mile down to the starting point, which gave the King and his Lords ample time to lay their bets. Newcastle was demonstrating his wealth for he could not allow his dog to beat the King's. Possibly sensing this, the King kindly limited his wager to £5 which Newcastle had to match. He would not take any bets from the other lords and nobody wanted to bet against the King's hound.

The chatter around me was broken by a horn sounding at the starting post. I craned my neck to catch sight of the deer and the pursuing hounds. After about one minute I saw them racing towards us, the two hounds level about fifty yards behind their quarry. A cheer went up around the grandstand. As they came up to us the King's hound started to pull away from Newcastle's. The deer flashed past us; a red-brown blur, the pounding of its hooves echoing off the grandstand. It jumped the first ditch, closely followed by the King's dog. Again it leapt at the second ditch, easily making it to the other side. Gamely the King's hound tried to follow it, but it could not clear the ditch. Whimpering and looking bewildered the dog climbed back out.

'Bravo,' shouted the King clapping his hands. 'He's a fine animal, one of my best. Now Newcastle, do you have another hound to race?'

'I do your Majesty, but I fear my dogs are no match for yours,' he fawned.

'This time you shall race against somebody else.' The King looked around his assembled courtiers. 'Ah, Lord Strange do you have your hounds with you today?'

'Yes indeed, your Majesty.'

'Well, put your best one up against Newcastle's. I'm sure he has saved his best hound,' said the King with a wry smile. 'I'll have £5 on Newcastle's.'

'I'll put £10 on the dog myself,' Newcastle replied.

I knew James would want me to take a record of all the bets, and picked up a stylus and some wax tablets that had been placed in the grandstand for that purpose. The other lords were excitedly calling their own wagers and I had trouble keeping up with them. After a few hectic minutes I had distributed half a dozen tablets.

'Well gentlemen,' said the King. 'I think we are easily past the £20 wager, so this will be a fleshing course. First hound to try to bring the stag down wins the wager.'

An enthusiastic murmur of consent went round the grandstand. 'Gentlemen, get your squires to ready your horses,' continued the King. 'We'll follow them into the woods.'

The starting horn sounded again and soon the stag was in sight, his proud antlers cutting through the air as he ran. Trailing behind came the two hounds; Newcastle's dog was just in front.

'Go on Achilles,' urged James. 'He's got stamina, so if he can stay in the race at the start he should outrun any other hound.' The stag passed in front of us, closely followed by the two dogs.

'To the horses,' shouted the King. We all hurried down the steps of the grandstand and clambered onto our horses, being careful to ensure the King was first to be mounted and away after the hounds. Charles directed his mount at a wooden fence that was being moved out of the way by the keepers.

The hounds were still in sight and we sped after them into the woods. Achilles had made up the ground and the two dogs were now about fifty yards behind the deer, which was twisting and turning through the trees. I had to weave my way through the wood, ducking under low branches as we gained on the deer. James was riding to my right with Newcastle on the other side of him.

A shout went up from the King as Achilles put on a spurt and closed in on his prey. The stag sensed the danger and changed direction, heading off left towards a denser part of the wood. We all turned our horses to follow. To my side I heard James cry out in alarm and I turned to see what had happened. Newcastle was just alongside him, his brows resolved in deep concentration. Surely Newcastle would veer away; if he continued that course his horse would crash into James. Newcastle did not deviate and James, his eyes staring at Newcastle in panic, wheeled his horse further left to avoid the impact. As he did so he collided with a bough and fell to the floor. With a frantic pull on the reins I slowed my horse and turned back to aid James; the other riders passing around me.

James was staggering to his feet as I pulled up in front of him.

'Arrogant Devil,' he spat, holding onto my saddle for support. 'He really did mean to unhorse me. You saw?' he asked, his lips pursed in anger.

'Yes, I truly think he intended that,' I replied. 'Are you all right? You took an awful fall.'

'I'll have a bruised arse tomorrow, but nothing broken,' he replied.

'Here take my horse. You might be able to rejoin the chase.'

'No, we'll walk up together,' James replied.

We came upon the King who was patting Achilles, the hound having being dragged off the dead stag. Most of the other courtiers were dismounted alongside him, Newcastle amongst them.

'James, where have you been?' asked the King.

'Perhaps my Lord Newcastle can explain,' James replied. 'He seems to have wanted to stop me from seeing the kill.'

'What are you saying, my Lord,' Newcastle's brows rose in mock innocence.

'You deliberately unhorsed me.'

'Just the excitement of the chase.'

'No Sir, you sought to unhorse me,' repeated James, his voice rising with anger.

'Sir, I am not a liar and if you repeat your accusation I will have to challenge you,' threatened Newcastle, his hand moving to his sword.

'G….gentlemen,' stammered the King. 'E….nough of this. James, if you feel you have been wronged by Newcastle then be sated by the victory of your hound. He brought the stag down cleanly and you win the purse.'

'I will take his money,' James replied. 'That will be apology enough. Paul, gather in my winnings.'

On the ride back James was silent at first, uncomfortable in his saddle. As we neared the bridge back across the Thames he confided in me. 'I have lost my patience with the Court. I am neither a good politician nor a good courtier. I cannot play their games of intrigue and favouritism. And Newcastle,' he sighed and looked at me. 'At every turn he outwits me and does me down in the eyes of the King. See today how I was wronged, but the King didn't see it.'

'But your hound won and I collected nearly one hundred pounds from the gentlemen,' I replied trying to cheer his humour.

'That's not the point,' he replied and then slumped back into silence. After a long uncomfortable pause he resumed. 'The Queen, although French and although she has some common interests with my wife, remains a Catholic and she cannot tolerate my wife's Calvinism, so I have no ally there. It is time I went back to Lathom. My father has retired from the management of our estates and I am needed there,' he sighed. 'I am reminded of Scipio Africanus when he was accused by the tribunes of Rome. He determined to go home to the country, far from all ambition and envy.'

Chapter 17 – *Isle of Man, October 20, 1651*

Putting thoughts about his own wife and children aside, Paul went straight to see Charlotte.

'What news do you have for me,' Charlotte asked anxiously.

'It is the gravest news my Lady,' replied Paul, struggling with the emotion in his voice. 'James was beheaded at Bolton on the 15th of October. '

'Lord protect us,' Charlotte stammered. She sat down and then continued. 'I had heard rumours and sent Mr. Broyden across to Anglesey for news, but until you told me I kept a vestige of hope. Were you there?'

Paul nodded, scarcely able to speak. 'I have a letter from James for you,' he said after a while. 'He gave it to me just before the execution.'

Charlotte took the letter and began to read through it. Tears fell from her eyes as they tried to follow the words on the paper. 'Ah, my sweet darling,' she whispered. 'Taken away so cruelly.'

'It was a noble death, my Lady. He prayed for forgiveness for his enemies.'

'They don't deserve it. May their souls rot in Hell,' she said bitterly.

Paul gave her a few moments to take in the news before resuming. 'Parliament is sending an army to seize the island. We must surrender to them and avoid any more deaths.'

'I'll not surrender, not after this,' Charlotte replied adamantly. 'I don't care if I live or die now. I won't see James again on this earth, and dying means I will be reunited with him.'

'You mustn't speak so,' Paul replied. 'You have your children to take care of. Who will look after them if you are dead?'

Charlotte looked at Paul for a moment before replying. 'You are right. I have the children and I must do what I can to protect them. But I will still fight.'

***

Paul begged to take his leave of Charlotte in order to seek out Louise. He found her in their chambers. They embraced as if they were clinging to the wreckage of a storm. When the calm returned they stood apart.

'How are Alice and the boys?' asked Paul.

'Oh, the boys, they are almost wild; forever at the beach. Alice is well and growing all the time.'

'I will go and see them, but first I must tell you about James.' Paul retold his tale to Louise who listened throughout, nodding now and then.

'Despite all she has suffered, she still wants to fight,' said Paul.

'Maybe she will reconsider tomorrow,' replied Louise with more hope than conviction.

'No, she is stubborn; she won't surrender now James is dead. She would have surrendered the isle to save him, but it is too late for that.'

'Will you help her?' asked Louise.

'My honour would compel me to aid her, but I have one last duty to perform for James. You must tell no-one. James asked me to see to it that Charlotte does not fight. I don't know how I will stop her, but I must try.'

Chapter 18 – *Lancashire, 1639*

Although it was the middle of winter the militia had to be mustered. With his attempts to impose the English prayer book on Scotland, Charles had roused a hornet's nest. War had not yet broken out, but the two nations were preparing for it. As part of the efforts to assemble an army to march against the Scots, a Captain Anthony Thelwall had been sent from London by the King's secretary, Windebank to determine the state of the militia in Lancashire and Cheshire. James called me to him to dictate instructions for two musters, one at Preston Moor and one at Knutsford. Once he had listed the names of the parishes that were to send men to the musters, I remarked this was not a complete levy.

'That's right Paul,' replied James. 'I don't want Windebank or the King knowing how many men my counties can provide. Better to hold back a good number of our men. If we reveal them all, the King will ask for some for the war against the Scots. Then I will have the expense of providing them with arms and equipment, and obtaining stores for the campaign. No, we will hold two musters when it fact we could hold three, and we will exclude a good number of men from the two that we do hold.'

I rode with James and Captain Thelwall to the muster of the Lancashire militia at Preston. I had been present at several of the annual musters during the previous years. The men always grumbled at being called out to them. They would feel even worse about it being called out in the depths of winter. We lodged with Sir Gilbert Hoghton, the son of the man I had briefly acted as secretary to before entering the service of the Stanleys.

The morning of the muster was cold and damp. It had rained overnight and it felt as if more rain was due during the day. Sir Gilbert Hoghton and three of his sons, Richard, George and Roger, were waiting for us in the courtyard. When I had last seen them more than ten years ago there were still boys; now they were young men. I looked at them in turn and remembered their characters; Richard the eldest, a serious boy who seldom smiled; George more carefree and always playing tricks on his brothers; and lastly Roger, impetuous and forever getting into scrapes. Mounted on his horse at the gate of Hoghton Tower, James addressed Sir Gilbert and Captain Thelwall.

'This rain will restrict us in the practice of the musket, for the powder will be damp. I suggest we concentrate on the pike today. We can also have the horse practice some manoeuvres.'

'Agreed,' said Captain Thelwall. 'The men soon learn how to prime and fire a musket. They have more trouble with the pike manoeuvres.'

On the moor we met Major Brown, a professional soldier appointed by James to work with the Lancashire trained band.

'Good morning Major Brown. It isn't a good day for this. We should keep the men occupied so they do not suffer too much from the cold,' said James.

'Indeed my Lord,' replied Major Brown. 'I have organized the pikemen into three companies of fifty men. This is the right number to drill together, for in battle they would be formed into a full company with an equal number of musketeers. I have the pikemen ready to drill, and the musketeers are sorting the arms and equipment so that we can take an inventory. I judge it too damp today to do much useful practice with the muskets.'

'My opinion too,' said James. 'Captain Thelwall, do you wish to supervise the inventory or do you want to watch the pike drill, or perhaps the horse practice?'

'I will watch the men drill and move about between all arms if I may. I want to judge how well trained the men are as well as how well provided for.'

We watched the pikemen as they began their manoeuvres. Each company was drawn up in five rows of ten men. From the other musters I had attended I knew the three positions for the pike; first position with the pike elevated between the vertical and the horizontal; second position with the pike braced on the shoulder and held out on the horizontal; and third position, similar to first but with the pike butted up to the right foot ready to receive enemy cavalry. Major Brown commenced with first position used by the front ranks when marching to the attack. The three companies looked competent with this manoeuvre. Next he progressed to second position, used by the rear ranks when marching to the attack. This would allow the sixteen foot long pikes of the rear ranks to extend beyond the front rank to engage the enemy. At the change of position some of the younger, less experienced men were slower than the rest to adopt the correct stance.

'Faster than that. Right, I see we will have to practice it again. First position,' bellowed Major Brown. Once the pikes had moved back to first position he bawled out again. 'Fourth and fifth ranks move to second position.'

This almost looked comical. Some of the pikemen did not know which rank they were in and pikes began moving in a haphazard manner from first to second position, and then some moved back to first as men in the first two rows realized they had not been supposed to change position.

James looked around to Captain Thelwall and Sir Gilbert Hoghton. His face bore a look of mild consternation. 'Gentlemen, I suggest we ride over to review the horse. I hope they are more practised than the pike.'

As we rode over to the horse, something about their composition seemed wrong. At around one hundred there seemed to be about the right number for this Lancashire muster. But where was Sir Thomas Tyldesley, usually so prominent in the front rank. Then it struck me. I couldn't see any of the known Catholic gentlemen here. James must have excluded them from the muster as officially they were not allowed to bear arms.

Sir Gilbert then commenced the horse practice by splitting the men into two troops. They were to attempt the Dutch style of attack. Each troop was split into six ranks and then advanced to an appointed marker. Upon reaching the agreed spot the first rank fired their pistols. Despite the limited number of men the noise from their volley was loud enough to startle birds from nearby trees. Small tufts of smoke rose from the men's guns. Then instead of firing a second pistol as would be the normal practice, the first rank retired and the second rank came forward to fire.

James remarked to Captain Thelwall, 'We do not have sufficient pistols to arm all the men. In order to allow as many as possible to practise we have given the pistols out one to a man.'

'A sensible decision, for it is the manoeuvre that is difficult to master, not the firing of a pistol,' replied Thelwall.

Now it was the turn of the second rank to fire. They did so and then retired. This was repeated until the fourth rank came forward. They did not have pistols, but practised the manoeuvre and pretended to fire. The fourth rank did not move back with the ease of the earlier ranks. Most of these men were wearing a buff-coat rather than breast and backplate armour. Their line became disorganized and one or two stragglers were slow to retire to the main body. The fifth and sixth ranks were even worse. I noticed some of these men were wearing breast and backplate and mounted on good horses with expensive shabraques and horse equipment, but they did not look like nor ride like the gentlemen that their attire suggested.

'Lord Stanley,' began Thelwall. 'A large number of the horse are competent riders and able to carry out manoeuvres. However, there are some who seem to lack the necessary skills. I advise that in future you mount the sons of gentlemen and freeholders, for these will been experienced horsemen.'

I looked again at the men in the fifth and sixth ranks. Some of these were no doubt the tenants of the Catholic gentlemen like Sir Thomas Tyldesley, sent in their place with their horses and equipment.

'Now can we go and see the inventory of arms and equipment?' asked Thelwall.

'Most certainly we can,' replied James and he turned his horse and kicked him into a trot.

We met Major Brown again by the men who had been sorting the weapons and armour. 'A shortage of corselets to protect the pikemen and a shortage of bandoleers for the musketeers is my summary of the inventory. We have a sufficient number of muskets and good provisions of powder in several towns like Chester and Manchester.'

'We have made enquiries about buying equipment in the locality and also sent to London for some,' said James. 'However, as I expected there is nothing to be had locally, and what there was in London has all gone into equipping the soldiers for the Scot's war.'

'Indeed, that is the case,' replied Thelwall. 'The London armouries are working hard at the moment, but they cannot make enough corselets for all those who are asking for them. Try again in a few months and you may have more success. Gentlemen, thank you for your diligence. I will report to Secretary Windebank that I find the county very willing to serve the King according to its ability.'

Chapter 19 – *Isle of Man, October 21, 1651*

Paul needed to know how strong Charlotte's garrisons were on the Isle. The castles at Douglas and Peel were incidental; it was Castle Rushen that mattered. If it fell to Parliament, Charlotte's will would crumble. What he had seen since arriving back told him the morale of the garrison was low. Indeed as all resistance to Parliament in England had been crushed, they had little hope of a victorious outcome. But the castle was strong and in a good state of repair. If there were sufficient provisions it could withstand a long siege and Charlotte still resolved to fight.

In Sir Philip Musgrave she had an experienced soldier as commander of the castle's garrison. Paul remembered him as the man who had captured Carlisle from Parliament in 1648, and he wondered if Musgrave still had the stomach for a fight. Perhaps he could be persuaded to handover the Isle?

Paul set off on a circuit of the castle. There were several pieces of artillery situated in strategic places on the walls, mostly minions and falcons with several heavier sakers. The men were watchful but subdued. None of them engaged him in the banter as he was used to. Perhaps it was because they did not know him, but Paul felt it was because they did not want a fight. However, a fight they would have to have, unless he could change Charlotte's mind or find some other way to avoid unnecessary bloodshed.

'Here comes Musgrave,' said one of the men as Paul was walking past them. Paul turned and saw the castle's commander, slowly climbing the steps to the battlements. Taut lines in his face matched the weariness in his gait.

'Can you see anything?' he asked a little out of breath, as he reached the top.

'No sir, all quiet out there,' said the man nodding out to the bay.

'I want to know the minute you see any ships out to sea.' Turning to Paul he continued, 'Mr. Morrow, the hero of Lathom isn't it? Walk with me. I have something to ask you.'

Paul followed Sir Philip back down the steps. 'Will you take a glass of wine with me?' he asked.

'Yes, certainly,' Paul replied.

'We are a bit cramped at Rushen. My room for what it is; is through here.'

Paul followed Sir Philip into a small room. 'Shut the door,' said Sir Philip.

He did so and as he turned round he saw Sir Philip taking the stopper out of a bottle. 'I've only got good stuff left as we can't get anything on the Isle. A glass of Malmsey,' he said pouring the wine into a glass.

'Thank you,' said Paul, wondering what Sir Philip wanted to talk to him about. The taste was sweet on his tongue as he waited for Sir Philip to speak.

'Now Paul, is it true a fleet is on its way here to take the Isle?'

'Yes, it is and it will be here soon.'

'A day, a month; makes no difference. We won't get any stronger. With King Charles in flight after Worcester, we have no hope. Charlotte knows it too, but she seems to have lost her reason with James's death.'

'So we die here for our honour?'

'I don't see any other course, do you?'

'We could try to secure honourable terms for surrender,' replied Paul.

'And how would we do that? I don't think Charlotte will want to bargain for our lives.'

'But we could speak to them?'

'How? If we were to go out there and speak to them, Charlotte would put us in irons as soon as we came back.'

Paul took another sip of wine and spoke no more. An idea was forming in his mind. Sir Philip was right, they could not go and speak to the enemy, but he knew a man who would be able to send someone to meet with them, William Christian, the island's governor.

Chapter 20 – *London, 1641*

"So, beginning in Parliament to show a thirsty desire of human blood, they first accused the Earl of Stratford; and, his Majesty giving way unto a fair trial against him, the people made bad use thereof. For, like wolves that, after their first tasting of man's blood, grow bold, and rather mad of more, so do they." History and Antiquities of the Isle of Man, by James Stanley.

The King called a Parliament in 1640. In fact he called two. After eleven years of personal rule, he needed it to raise money to fight his war with the Scots. But Parliament wasn't going to give Charles money until he addressed their grievances. All the expedients Charles had used in the 1630s to rule without Parliament were pulled down. On the whole James supported this. I remember he told me he had voted to remove the unpopular Star Chamber and the Council of the North. Indeed James even supported the campaign to have regular Parliaments, ensuring the King would no longer be able to rule on his own. What turned James against the reformers were the methods they used to remove the Earl of Strafford. They made him a scapegoat for all the ills of Charles's rule in the 1630s and even accused him of plotting to bring an army over from Ireland to crush the opposition to the King.

***

While James attended the Parliament we were all staying at Derby House. The trial of Strafford had been proceeding for several weeks, but there was not sufficient evidence to convict him. Now his enemies were trying a different tack; they had introduced a Bill of Attainder which simply meant Parliament could vote him guilty.

As James was preparing to set out for the House of Lords we heard a lot of noise outside. 'Pym has whipped up the prentice boys to cow the waverers into submission. These are troubled times Paul. Pym might not be able to keep the prentice boys in check, and if that happens I fear for our safety. Come with me to the Parliament today and put on your sword. I don't think the rank of gentlemen is a sufficient protection at the moment.'

Charlotte came into the room, her brow furrowed. She approached James and grabbed his hand.

'James, take care at the Parliament today. People will be watching what you do. If you support Strafford have a special regard for your safety as you come home. There is a mob out there and I fear its leaders will turn it on those who defy their plan.'

'Don't worry my love. I think the spilling of one man's blood will satiate them for the moment. Besides, I'm taking Paul with me. They will not challenge us in the open. On my conscience I cannot vote for this Bill of Attainder. Where are we if we vote to execute a man on Parliament's whim? Pym is a client of the Earl of Bedford. I think they are pushing the King so he will give them an office in his government. It's a dangerous game they play, and I fear they have pushed too far.'

Outside the house we joined the tail of the mob, as it was also headed for Parliament. Most of the Prentice Boys here looked harmless enough, just taking the chance to leave their trades for a day. Once we had arrived at the Palace of Westminster we had to pass through to the front of the crowd. As we got closer to the front we began to get jostled.

'Lads, here comes a fancy lord. Let him pass for he has an important duty today. Vote for the death of Strafford and then the King can have good council from his ministers.'

Sensibly the earl made no reply. 'Paul, return to Canon Row now. Meet me here when the business is done. I will send a messenger for you.'

I spent the day with Charlotte. She could not be still and moved from window to window to watch the crowd. 'Was it safe for a lord to walk in the open when you went to Parliament?' she asked me.

'Yes, there wasn't any ill feeling towards us. The mob is excited and they have an expectation that if the bill to remove Strafford passes both houses, then everything will be all right. But if the King does not agree to the bill then there will be an impasse.'

'The behaviour of the King concerns me. He has never courted the affection of the great lords like my husband, preferring instead councillors with opinions similar to his own. Thus, in their turn the great lords have no great affection for the King. Instead they serve him from a sense of duty and not love. In a time of crisis they may desert him, for duty does not bind many men when their own interests are concerned.'

'Do you think love binds men to their King?'

'Yes I do, and that is how a king should rule, by the love of his subjects and not by ideas about divine right, and not by surrounding himself by like-minded councillors.'

The messenger came to fetch me late in the afternoon.

'The Lord Strange requests you go to meet him at the House of Lords. He says the day's business is done and that he needs you now.'

I set off for Parliament immediately. The mob seemed merry and nobody barred my way. As I came up to the Parliament I saw James amongst a group engaged in conversation.

I approached James and he peeled off to meet me. He spoke to me in a whisper.

'A sad day's business. The Bill has passed. Now Strafford's fate lies in the hands of his Majesty. I would like to think he would be loyal to his minister, but I fear he will sacrifice him. Pym has roused the rabble and I believe Charles is afraid. He hates chaos and disorder. He thinks that by giving in now and allowing Strafford to be executed his troubles will pass and order will be restored.'

Two days later James despatched me to learn if there was any news concerning Strafford's fate. I immediately sought out a broadsheet seller. I read the sheet and there in print before me was the intelligence James sought; the King had agreed to the act against Strafford. The loyal servant was to die as a scapegoat for the King's troubles.

***

Days passed into weeks as the summer approached. The air was still and listless, as if before a storm. James continued to attend the Lords, but each day he came home more troubled than the last, as the reformers moved beyond curbing the King's excesses to imposing limitations on his royal prerogative. He had long since withdrawn his support and was part of a group of lords who sought to curb any further restrictions on the King's power. King Charles himself was in Scotland. His enemies said he was scheming with Scottish nobles in order to defeat the Covenanters, thereby allowing him to bring the English army to London to intimidate Parliament.

Summer passed into autumn as October began, but the weather was still hot and muggy. It was as if the heavens sensed the mood of man. Then, in November, the storm broke.

Louise had been in the kitchen and she came to see me with a look of concern on her knitted brow. 'Paul, the kitchen talk is that there is rebellion in Ireland. The Catholics have risen and are massacring the Protestant settlers. Women raped and babies mutilated and killed. They say thousands are dead. Some say that they will cross to England and join with the Catholics here to rise up against the Protestant religion.'

'This is horrible news, if it is true. James is at the House of Lords today. I will speak with him when he comes back to see what he has learnt about this.'

I did not get to see James until after dinner. He was slumped in a chair and his brow was furrowed.

'The talk has all been about Ireland today. There are reports of a great rising by Catholics who are murdering the Protestants. If the accounts are true then I fear for the outcome in that Kingdom. But I am more worried that this might spread to our counties. They lie closest to Ireland with frequent commerce by sea bringing people to the ports every week. We also have many who hold to the old faith. I trust the loyalty of those who are my kin and most of the Catholic gentry, but there are some who might use the current troubles to foment unrest. I can't have one ear to the North and the other here in Westminster. I need to return to Lathom to learn for myself the truth about the news from Ireland and to make sure there is no unrest in our counties.'

'Will you take Charlotte with you? It will soon be the time for her confinement.'

'She does not want to stay here on her own. This will be her ninth child and she tells me it should not be born for another month. I worry about her travelling at such a time, but in truth I do not want to be without her and I would fear for her if she remained in London.'

***

The household packed hastily the next day. Valuables were locked away, as James feared his house might be ransacked by the mob if the situation continued to deteriorate. Boards were put on the downstairs windows. When we went out to our carriages it was with a feeling of trepidation, for we did not know when we would be coming back.

The inns on the roads north were busy as many other lords had also decided to return to their estates. Some were alienated by the increasing radicalism in London; others were in fear of what they might find on their estates.

One morning, near the end of our journey, as we prepared to set out from the Stanley manor at Northwich, James called me aside for a private counsel.

'I need to go immediately to Lathom, but I want you to go to my father at Bidston for he will have the latest news about Ireland and will know if there is any serious unrest in Lancashire or Cheshire. Don't stay long for I want this intelligence as soon as possible.'

I made my farewell to Louise and set off for Bidston. When I arrived there I went straight in to see the earl. I had not seen him for more than a year, and as he greeted me there was the familiar warmth in his smile, but as we embraced his touch was cold and weak. He was frail and immediately sat down by the fire.

'Ah, Paul so pleased to see you again. I wish we met in happier circumstances, but I fear we are about to enter troubled times. You have heard no doubt of the revolt in Ireland and the fate of so many of the settlers?'

'Yes, the news soon reached London. Can it be true that thousands are murdered and many in such hideous ways?'

'It is true that many are dead, murdered or starved on the roads when they were turned out from their land. But be wary of accounts that say thousands. How many common men can count more than their fingers? Disposed settlers have come over from Ireland and I have had some of them brought here, had them fed and then spoken to them. Some of them have seen no killing or death at all; they fled as the first survivors of the revolt came to their villages. Those who did suffer the revolt first hand do have accounts of death and some have wounds to show they were there. Here, put another log on the fire for me will you.'

I did as he asked and he carried on. 'It is true there have been many deaths and the Catholics have taken up arms in revolt, but I sense there are those in London who have made much of the revolt for their own aims. They need to maintain the tension and keep pressure on the King. That way he will be forced to give in to their desire to limit his power or grant them office in his government.'

'James wishes to know if there has been any unrest here. Have any of the Catholics been encouraged to rise, spurred on by the news from Ireland?'

'No, but tell James he would do well to disarm the Catholic gentry. Some of them could be tempted to come out in arms, especially if the situation in our kingdom continues to worsen. At the very least they might not feel they have to hide their beliefs any more, and that would only cause trouble if they antagonize the godly sort. Tell James his first duty is to preserve the peace of our counties. He needs to tread carefully between the different interests. Some may need to be cowed; some may need to be courted. I leave it to James to decide which is which.'

Following James's instruction I set out for Lathom at first light the next morning. George Brereton was at Bidston for he often couriered letters for the earl. I took him with me for there were rumours of landless men preying on travellers.

'Difficult times for those who hold to the old faith,' I remarked to George as we rode.

'Indeed they are. The Puritans believe their prophecies to be coming true. They see us as the agents of the Antichrist, seditious and scheming to rise up and return England to the Catholic faith. Yes, there are some hotheads who might plot and dream, but they have little support from the rest of us.'

'But what about Ireland? Aren't the rebels trying to destroy Protestantism and return the country to Rome?'

'We're not going to rise up here and kill you all in your beds, if that's what you are worried about,' he laughed. 'Here we are the minority. In Ireland the Catholics are in the majority, but many have been turned out of their lands by the Protestants. It may be that some settlers have been killed, but I've also heard of some Protestant gentry being protected by their Catholic servants when the mob came. I would do the same for the earl and Lord Strange. They are good masters. They do not prosecute us and are tolerant of our beliefs. Some of the Puritans now accuse James of being a Catholic himself.'

'Surely you don't believe that?' I replied quite startled, for while James did not belong to the godly sort, there were no outward signs of him being a Catholic.

'No, I don't believe it, and I don't think his lady would allow it,' George said with a wry smile.

We arrived at Lathom without incident. I went immediately to see James and pass on the advice from his father. When I entered James's chamber I found him pacing from one end to the other.

Unsure what was troubling him I began, 'I have news from your father.'

'Later, later,' he interrupted. 'Charlotte is in labour. The baby has come early, its time brought forward by the journey from London.'

This time I knew exactly how James felt. After nine years of marriage and no children Louise had thought herself to be barren. But finally she had conceived and last year she gave birth to a son, who we had christened James after Lord Strange. The child was healthy and we rejoiced in him.

'I'm sure she will be all right. She knows more about childbirth than the midwife. I know you can't help being anxious, but put your trust in the Lord and He will deliver to you a healthy child and He will protect Charlotte in her labour.'

'You're right,' James replied. 'Go send for my chaplain. I will pray with him.'

The blessings of our Lord were granted to James and Charlotte for she was safely delivered of a boy, who was named William after his grand-father. Due to the troubles in the kingdom in the next ten years, James was not to see much of his last born, save for the happy intervals in the Isle of Man when he was able to live in relative peace with his family and friends.

Chapter 21 – *The North, 1642*

"It hath been the will of God that in the year 1642 (wherin a general plague of madness possessed the minds of most men in Christendom, of which the dominions of the King in Great Britain have most reason to be sensible) his subjects there, by so long a peace being unacquainted with the miserable effects of war, grew weary of their good condition, and stirred their hearts unto a rebellion against the most virtuous, pious, and clement prince that ever England had." History and Antiquities of the Isle of Man, by James Stanley.

It was a time for all of us to search our consciences. The King and Parliament were moving closer to war, but which side should James take? The household could talk of nothing else. One morning I was in the company of Bootle, as we returned from an early hunt with James.

'Paul, you are in the confidence of James. Will he side with King or Parliament?'

I paused for a moment to consider my response. 'I believe James's first desire is to keep the peace in his counties. He is like a father with two quarrelsome boys; he wants to prevent one from striking the other. For just as any sibling quarrel can soon get out of hand, James believes that should these two parties come to blows then it will escalate to a bloody conflict to the great harm of the Kingdom.'

'But if it should come to war, will James chose the King or Parliament?'

'What would you have him do?' I replied.

'I would have him serve the Parliament. Theirs is a righteous, godly cause. The King surrounds himself with papists who give him bad council. Only the Parliament can defend the Protestant religion. Look at Ireland and see how the papists have risen up and murdered the Protestants. The same will happen here if we do not follow Parliament.'

'But what will Parliament do? Will it tell the King what he can and can't do?'

'The King should return to London. While he is in York, Parliament fears he will plot with the army officers or the Scots and march to London to make them bow down. If he were in London the King could make peace with his Parliament.'

'I do not see the King returning to London. He fears his capital. After his failure to arrest Pym he lost any remaining support in the city.'

'Then maybe it will come to war. By my conscience, I would have to leave the service of James if he chose the King.'

'For my part I will serve James whichever side he chooses.'

'Then God forbid that we should be at war with each other,' replied Bootle.

***

Several weeks later James revealed to me his intention of going to see the King at York.

'I want to find out if he is resolved on war. I'll pledge my loyalty and offer as much assistance as my estates allow. I don't want war, and with God's will it can still be avoided. But if it comes to it, then I believe we need to strike hard and fast and defeat the King's enemies before the conflict spreads through the country.'

We set out as a group of twenty horsemen. Once we had left the Stanley estates the villagers were wary of us and retreated indoors on our approach. With all the bad news from Ireland, it may have been some of them took us for Catholics under arms, or it may have been that with the good sense of country people, they knew to seek shelter in the face of armed strangers.

Arriving at York, we sought to enter the city by the Bootham Bar. This proved difficult as the city watch were vigilant and stopping groups of armed men.

'Who are you and what is your business in the city?' the captain of the watch demanded of Sir Thomas Tyldesley who was riding at the head of the column.

'Loyal subjects of his Majesty, come to pledge their allegiance.'

'And what proof can you give of your loyalty?' replied the captain.

'Here is Lord Strange, heir to the Earl of Derby. You will not find a more loyal subject in all the north.' Sir Thomas turned and indicated James with a wave of his arm. James rode up to the captain.

'Good day to you sir, but how am I to know that you are the Lord Strange?'

'Here, I have my signet ring and a letter which matches the seal.'

The captain looked at the ring and quickly read the letter. 'You may pass. I wish you luck in finding lodgings. The city is crowded with strangers.'

***

James was granted an audience with the King a few days later. On the ride out to the Archbishop of York's palace, we discussed the deteriorating situation.

The King was playing bowls when we approached. Although we should have found him at his ease in this pursuit, his face looked tired, and much more lined than when I had last seem him twelve years ago. He looked us over as we got near and on recognizing James, smiled and walked over to greet him.

'Dear James, it has been too long. See how my loyal cousins come at my time of need,' he observed to the attendants close by.

James smiled awkwardly at this unusual affection. 'Your Majesty, I come with some loyal men of the north to pledge our allegiance.'

'Walk with me and bring your two companions with you,' replied the King. We walked towards the river, where it was clear we could not be overheard.

'Who are your two men?' asked the King.

'Sir Thomas Tyldesley,' replied James, and indicating me continued, 'This gentleman is Paul Morrow, my secretary.'

'The first is tall and strong, a good fighter I warrant. The second looks more of a scholar than a fighter. But tell me, will you both fight for me if I need you to?'

Sir Thomas replied immediately. 'I would lay down my life for you, your Majesty.'

'Ah, reckless and brave too? But tell me, aren't you from a Catholic family, Sir Thomas?'

'I am my Lord, and I pay for my allegiance to the old faith in the Recusancy fines I have to pay.'

Charles looked at him, considering his reply. 'It will hurt my cause to have known Catholics associated with it. I'm going to issue a proclamation to state that I will have no Catholics in my army. However, I'll not be able to control all my local commanders, so you can continue to serve by being part of James's forces.'

'We are all keen to fight the Parliament,' replied Sir Thomas. I can never forgive the death of Father Ambrose last year. It still makes me sick to think of a Protestant vicar leading a mob to seize the good father while he celebrated Mass.'

'I am sorry for that,' replied the King. 'I truly wish I had stood up to Parliament sooner.' Turning towards me he continued, 'Your secretary ponders over my question, a sign of a scholar. He no doubt weighs my every word, looking for hidden meanings. Sir, it is simple. Would you fight for me?'

'I will fight for my Lord and as I believe he will fight for you, then I can answer yes.'

The King chuckled. 'A loyal servant. And James, can I count on your support?'

'Indeed you can your Majesty. Do you have plans to raise an army?'

'Newcastle urges me to raise the royal standard in York, but I think we have already brought in all the loyal men of Yorkshire. I am looking for somewhere else to raise it, where it can bring in most men.'

'Then raise your standard at Warrington,' replied James. 'I can summon the Lancashire and Cheshire trained bands there. I guarantee to raise three regiments of foot and some troops of cavalry. It'll also give you the opportunity to muster the men of North Wales. Together with the men you already have about you, this will be a sizeable force. From there we should march on London, recruiting as we go. This will give us an army to match anything the Parliament can raise, and we will be able to beat them in open battle.'

'I like your plan James, but how will you arm your men?'

'My influence in Chester is good enough to secure the city magazine. Also I plan to seize those of Liverpool, Lancaster and Manchester.'

'Good, good. I will adopt your plan and raise my standard at Warrington. Go now and secure the town so that we won't be opposed. We will be with you in a couple of weeks.'

***

Invigorated by pride and purpose, James made good the first part of his plan and secured the arms and ammunition held in Liverpool and Lancaster. Acting quickly, he did not encounter any opposition. In July we rode to Manchester where James knew there was a more organized group of Parliament's supporters. A meeting had been arranged between James and the Parliamentary commissioners. On the outskirts of the town, James called us to halt.

'Most of you will wait outside the town. I do not want to provoke any hostility by taking a large body of armed men into Manchester. Sir Richard Molyneux, Sir Gilbert Hoghton, Sir Thomas Tyldesley and Paul Morrow will accompany me together with twelve men of my escort.'

As we rode along the streets towards the appointed place of our meeting with Parliament's commissioners, I noticed a number of men milling about the town. They stared at us as we rode, and I felt their eyes on my back as we passed them. Coming into the town square there was a large group before the town hall. A murmur went through the crowd and then one man cried out, 'God save the Parliament.' His shout was picked up by others. As we dismounted from our horses it had reached a chant.

Those at the front of the crowd jostled us as we passed, and a few blocked our path. Sir Thomas affronted by this open defiance spat out a warning, 'Get out of our way,' and placed a hand on the hilt of his sword menacingly.

James intervened, 'We have not come to fight, but to talk with the commissioners. Let us through and we will be about our business.'

Reluctantly the men shuffled out of the way, and we proceeded into the building. I cast my eyes around, recognising many gentlemen who had availed themselves of James's hospitality over the years. Here was Lord Wharton, who had been appointed as Parliament's Lord Lieutenant for Lancashire when James refused the post. I saw Alexander Rigby the Member of Parliament for Wigan. Then in the corner engaged in conversation with Richard Shuttleworth, I spotted John Bradshaw.

Lord Wharton assumed seniority amongst the Parliamentarians and addressed James, 'Lord Strange, it is good to see you again. I wish we met in happier circumstances, but I am hopeful we can find an accommodation. I must tell you that if you have come to seize the arms in the town's arsenal, you will be sorely disappointed. We intend to keep these arms for the defence of the town. What we would like to discuss is how we can avoid conflict in our own county, should the King and Parliament come to war.'

'I also wish to avoid conflict,' replied James. 'But if my King does come to war with his own Parliament, then I am honour bound to assist him.'

'We hear that you have been trying to raise men for the King by means of the Commission of Array. You must stop this as it is not recognized by Parliament.'

'I do not care whether it is recognized by Parliament or not. I am obeying the order of the King.'

John Bradshaw pushed himself forward. 'My Lord, the statute for the Commission of Array has not been endorsed by Parliament for over one hundred years. As such it is illegal. You are on dangerous ground if you continue with this.'

'Again, I say I am obeying the orders of my King, as is my duty. I defy any man to stop me.'

Lord Wharton attempted reconciliation, 'James, come through and dine with us and we can talk more amicably.'

We got up to walk through to the dining area. I noticed a couple of the Parliamentary commissioners leave the room. James had noticed too, and with a quick toss of his head indicated I was to follow them.

In the hallway the two men were issuing instructions to a third. I strained to overhear what they were saying.

'Call out the trained band. We must show them we are not defenceless and will not be intimidated.'

With that they saw me and broke off their conversation. 'Have you lost your way?' one of them asked me. 'We are dining through here.' The two men approached me, with such speed I had to turn and walk in front of them to avoid being knocked over.

I sought an opportunity to talk to James as soon as possible. 'It seems they intend to call out the trained band while we dine. They want to demonstrate that they won't be overawed.'

The dinner passed by unremarkably. James and Lord Wharton attempted to agree to a neutrality pact if either the King or Parliament openly declared war on the other. However, they could not agree on what to do with the arsenal in Manchester. Lord Wharton wished to keep it. James, on weaker ground as Lord Wharton already had possession of it, suggested it be kept locked up and guarded by a group of gentlemen chosen by each side.

On leaving the building it was evidently a different crowd to before. Many of them were armed with the weapons of the trained band, muskets, pikes and swords. They had also spent the time drinking and animated by ale, they were more hostile than earlier. We tried to pass through, but our way was blocked. The ringleader was once more abusive and directed his venom at Sir Thomas Tyldesley.

'Not so mighty now are we?'

'Hold you tongue. I warn you, I can still cut you through.'

'Try it then.' And with that the oaf drew his sword and lunged at Sir Thomas.

To his misfortune, he had chosen the wrong man. Sir Thomas was a noted swordsman. In an instant he stepped back to avoid the initial strike. At the same time he drew his own sword and with a rapid thrust he pierced his assailant. The attacker crumbled to his knees and with wide questioning eyes looked up at his killer. Sir Thomas looked from him to the crowd, wary of another attack. He was right to do so, for another man had drawn a pistol and levelled it at him. Sir Thomas dived to the right as the man fired. His bullet sailed harmlessly into the wall behind.

To his credit, Lord Wharton stepped forward and interposed himself between his own men and Sir Thomas. 'Enough of this. These men are here under my protection. They are to come to no harm. Step aside and let them pass.'

With a murmur of discontent the crowd parted. No doubt they had been subdued by the fate of their colleague and a group of them were cradling him on the floor where he had fallen. James's escort rapidly surrounded him and Sir Thomas, offering their own bodies as protection as we made our way back to our horses.

'Did you have to kill him?' asked James.

'You saw it. He meant my death. It was pure instinct. When I counterattacked, I made sure he could do me no more harm,' replied Sir Thomas.

'That may be, but I doubt our dispute with the Parliamentarians can be patched up now. We must return to Lathom.'

***

We rode back in silence; each of us mulling over the events in Manchester. It was nightfall when we arrived, and the advance riders had to rouse the guard to let us in. I made my way to our room. Louise was already asleep, but awoke when I entered. I looked over to Henry's bed in the corner.

'Don't worry, he's fast asleep. I thought you'd be away for a few more days.'

'It didn't go as planned. Sir Thomas killed one of Parliament's supporters in self-defence, and we had to leave without the arms from Manchester.'

'If both sides have weapons then there is more likelihood of war,' replied Louise.

'You are right. I don't think war can be avoided now.'

'Why is it that men always resort to violence to resolve their disputes? There will be many widows and orphans by the end of this war. As ever, it is those the men leave behind that suffer the most.'

'It is my duty to defend my Lord and my King. I do not want war either, but unless the King wishes to be a King in name only, the Parliamentarians have forced him into one.'

James evidently thought the same, for the next morning he assembled his men to drill. During the next few weeks as we waited for further news, he drilled the men each day. I spent hours at sword practice. I reasoned that if I was going to have to fight, I'd better get good at it. Riders were sent out with messages to the gentry in the county to try to determine on which side their allegiances lay. Most were staying neutral and not declaring for either side, but many of the Catholic gentry like Sir Thomas Tyldesley and Sir Gilbert Hoghton were known to side with the King. On the other side, many of those whose sympathy lay with the Parliament were known Presbyterians like Richard Shuttleworth of Gawthorpe Hall.

One morning James asked me to bring in the accounts books.

'I intend to keep my promise to the King and raise three regiments of foot. They will be commanded by my good friends and neighbours Sir Gilbert Gerard, his nephew Charles, and Sir Richard Molyneux. We have some arms and equipment for them, but will need more. I need your help to determine how I will pay for it.'

James's careful management of the family estates over the last decade had given him a surplus, which he was able to put towards equipping the soldiers. However, little ready money was then left. James was putting the King's interests above his own.

Amidst these preparations for war, James received a message from the King. Despite his declaration to James that he would raise the royal standard at Warrington, the King now intended to do so at Nottingham and the date was set for 22nd August. James was requested to attend, and to bring his regiments with him.

'Once again the King is influenced by his courtiers and they have turned his mind. Let my master be happy, though I be miserable; and if they consult well for him, I shall not be much concerned what becomes of me. My wife, my children, my family and country are very dear to me; but if my prince and my religion are safe, I shall bless even my enemies.'

'But will you attend the King at Nottingham?' I replied.

'How can I leave my counties when there is a nest of Parliamentarians in Manchester? No, I shall have to stay here and steady the county.'

***

Parliament's reply to the skirmish in Manchester was to impeach James for attempting to subvert the fundamental laws and government of the Kingdom of England, and the rights and liberties and the very being of Parliaments. As they phrased it, James was accused of maliciously, rebelliously and traitorously inciting the people to make war against the King, Parliament and Kingdom. James's party was accused of killing Richard Percival in Manchester and also a Lynen Webster in Lancaster. Behind their rhetoric which did not make sense even to the most fervent in its cause, the Parliament was trying to present James as a dangerous usurper and aimed to weaken his support by stating any who aided him were also likely to face charges of treason.

When this tactic did not weaken his support, Parliament sent a messenger to speak with James. The messenger had a document which he handed over to my Lord, but he evidently knew the contents for he began to speak as James was reading the message.

He had a high voice. As he spoke, he stuck his head up in the air as if to indicate his message was of such import and dignity that it could not be rebuffed.

'Parliament is offering you the Lord Lieutenancy of Lancashire as enjoyed by your illustrious ancestors. This is an appointment worthy of you. The King is being misled by evil councillors who are only allowing Catholics access to him. The aim of Parliament is to remove these councillors from the King and restore harmony to the realm.'

James heard the man out, but I could tell by his pacing and his tight lipped face, that he was indignant. As the messenger finished he replied, 'Pray tell the gentlemen at Manchester and let them tell the gentlemen at London, that when they have heard that I have turned traitor, then I will listen to their propositions: but till then, if I receive any other papers of this nature it shall be at the peril of him who brings it.' The messenger's head dropped and he scampered out of the room.

***

We were riding to Manchester. We were riding to war. The King had thrown down the gauntlet by raising his standard. Proclamations were then issued from both sides, as each sought to gather supporters together. As James had said before, he could not march to the King until he had removed the Parliamentarians from Manchester. This is what we now prepared to do. Most of us had not fought before and I had an uneasy stomach as we rode. I wondered if I would survive this encounter and realized even if I did, some of my friends might not.

I rode over to Sir Thomas Tyldesley. We were in the vanguard looking out for enemy outposts. 'Sir Thomas, I am concerned for James. I'm sure the Parliamentarians will single him out and try to kill him. You are a skilled swordsman. Will you stay by his side and do what you can to protect him?'

'That's my intention, Paul. I will take a special care for James's safety, but I am counting on you to be there too. I need someone to watch my back.'

'I'll be glad to do so. I only hope your impetuosity doesn't get us both into trouble,' smiling as I said this.

As I spoke there was a shout from the front of the front of the group. 'Enemy pickets ahead.' On the brow of a hill there looked to be about half a dozen men who were now running toward a group of horses. Sir Thomas shouted, 'After them. We don't want them to raise the alarm.'

We kicked on and crested the hill. Some of the enemy were in such a panic, they had not managed to mount their horses. They now stood meekly, not wanting to fight but unsure what we would do to them.

'Hold them and let's round up the rest,' ordered Sir Thomas.

A couple of the men remained behind while the rest of us raced after the two fleeing Parliamentarians. Their horses were fresh, while ours had already covered a good distance that morning. They were getting away. Sir Thomas realized the pursuit was futile and called a halt. We reigned in our mounts and watched the two fellows head towards the town. As I looked I could see the Parliamentarians had prepared the town in a state of defence. It was not an ancient fortress like York, protected by strong walls, but earth ramparts had been built to slow down any attacker and soldiers were clearly visible.

'Now they know we are coming this is going to be harder,' I said, and we turned to ride back to our prisoners.

'Let's see what they can tell us,' said Sir Thomas.

They were still cowed and shuffled about, probably embarrassed to have been captured so easily. Here was our enemy. They were Lancastrians like me. The only difference between us was whether we believed the King or the Parliament to be in the right. Could I kill them when the time came to fight?

'How many soldiers are in the town?' asked Sir Thomas.

One of them spoke up. He looked the surliest of the bunch and had elected himself as spokesman. 'We don't know Sir. We've been on watch here for three days.'

'Well, then how many men have gone past you while you've been here?'

'Couldn't say Sir, probably hundreds.'

It was difficult to know whether to believe him. He could be deliberately exaggerating their numbers to make them seem stronger than they actually were.

'Tie their hands and bring them with us. We'll report back to James,' said Sir Thomas ending the interrogation.

***

James was not disappointed by the news. 'I didn't expect to be able to surprise the town. Approaching from Salford means Manchester is defended by the river, and no doubt the bridge will be well defended . We have about four thousand men. That should be enough to storm the town if we can find a way in. Sir Thomas and Paul, take a scouting party and find me another crossing of the Irwell. Then we can approach the town from the other side and avoid a bloody battle over a bridge.'

We assembled our men and set off at once. We headed upstream of the Irwell. When we had gone a few miles, we found our goal, an unguarded bridge. We crossed with the intention of probing deeper, but we had gone less than half a mile when we ran across a large enemy force, no doubt recently dispatched to seize the crossing.

They were about fifty yards from us and looked to be twice our number, too many to fight. Sir Thomas had reached the same conclusion, 'Turn about and retire to the bridge. We can make a stand there.'

As we turned there were pistol cracks as the enemy patrol let off a few shots. Fortunately we were too far away for this to cause us any harm, but it was a frightening moment to be under fire. Upon reaching the bridge Sir Thomas ordered the men across.

'Paul, you and I are going to show them how the King's men fight. Draw your sword and hold close to me. The two of us can hold this bridge.'

We waited. Time passed slowly. I watched the Parliamentarians approach. They moved at normal speed, but my mind was working slowly. I clasped my sword. I adjusted my helmet. My legs felt hollow. I shifted in the saddle. I wanted to run.

'Easy lad. They'll be here soon. Don't grip your sword so tightly; you'll not be able to use it.'

The enemy came on. They stopped at the far side, deciding what to do. Then two of them drew their swords and filed onto the bridge. I steadied myself to meet my opponent. I only had an instant to study him, but my senses must have been heightened for I absorbed every detail of his face. It was pock marked and unshaven. His eyes were large and dark. As I looked into them he struck. It was a rapid downward blow and instinctively I parried. I felt his strength in my arm. He had the upper hand and struck again. Again I parried. Seeking some way to unsettle him, I freed my foot from the stirrup and kicked out at his horse. The beast drew back in alarm side-on, presenting me with an opportunity to attack the man's left side. Now having to defend himself across his body, his reach was restricted. I aimed a blow at his left shoulder. He parried. Aware he was now vulnerable, he tried to turn his mount. There was a roar from Sir Thomas. He had unhorsed his foe. This noise momentarily distracted my enemy and I aimed a blow at the top of his left leg, below his breastplate. The sword struck through his buff coat and into his flesh. He screamed and turned his horse about and fled back across the bridge.

I drew a deep breath. It could not have lasted for more than a couple of minutes, but my arm already felt tired. I rested my sword across the saddle.

'Here come the next two,' said Sir Thomas. 'You've done well, but don't let them get the first blow in.'

This time I avoided looking at the man's face. Instead I watched his sword arm. As he began to raise it above his head, I kicked my horse and moving forward struck at his sword arm. I caught him on the elbow and he dropped his sword. The fellow then retired, leaving his companion alone. I looked to see how I could intervene, but it did not look as if Sir Thomas needed any help. He was pressing the fellow back, forcing him to retire under the speed and force of his attack. Then a blow to his shoulder put the foe out of the fight and he turned about and sought the safety of his companions.

They had had enough of gentlemanly combat on the bridge. Now they dismounted and drew their carbines. They advanced into range and prepared to fire.

'Time to go,' said Sir Thomas. 'We can't defend ourselves against bullets.' We turned about and trotted back across the bridge. They discharged their first shots. I felt something strike me on my backplate, but it did not hurt. Fortunately nothing hit our horses, for if we lost a mount we would have great difficulty getting away.

'But they'll capture the bridge,' I said to Sir Thomas.

'We're not strong enough to stop it. Look more dragoons are arriving to reinforce them.'

This was my first experience of war. Nobody had been killed, but I felt I had been bloodied. We had wounded four of the enemy, but had not been able to hold the bridge.

James was not pleased with the news when we returned. 'We are too weak to split our forces. So we are forced into a head on attack across the Salford Bridge. But first I'm going to ask them to surrender the town. Even now we might be able to avoid war.'

We rode up to Salford Bridge under the protection of a white cloth fixed to a cut down pike. A group rode across from the other side. As they approached I spotted Alexander Rigby. I did not recognize the others.

'I have come to offer the town an honourable surrender,' said James. 'Any man who wishes to leave will not be harmed and townsmen who wish to stay must be disarmed, but they will be free to continue their life here. The town's munitions must be handed over to me.'

'And what if we are not prepared to surrender on these terms?' replied Alexander Rigby.

'We have enough cannon to bombard the town into submission. If you do not surrender we will commence firing at noon. The fate of the townspeople is in your hands.'

'I will go and confer with my brother officers, but I think they too are resolved to fight. The fate of the people is not in my gift. What happens to them is the will of God.'

Noon came without any reply from the Parliamentarians. Our guns had been trundled into position facing the enemy on the opposite bank. Now they were primed and ready to fire. James was pacing up and down, staring across the river. He turned round to us.

'So, it has come to this, war with men who were our friends and neighbours. May God forgive me. Make ready to fire.'

The gunners stood ready with their tapers in anticipation.

James brought his arm down and roared, 'Fire, fire the guns.'

A salvo was unleashed. Smoke billowed out from the mouths of the cannon and an instant later their deadly impact was felt on the other side. They brought down bits of wall or thudded into the earthworks; though some fell short and splashed into the river.

'Captain Standish, get your men ready to make an attack across the bridge,' ordered James.

This brought a company of pikemen forward. The aim was to rush the bridge while the Parliamentarians were still dazed by the bombardment. They marched forward, a drummer beating a steady rhythm and Captain Standish barked out words of encouragement.

The Parliamentarians were ready with pikes bristling in anticipation as our men went across the bridge. They also had muskets trained on the bridge from nearby houses and their fire thinned out our ranks as the men advanced. Then we were on the enemy with a huge roar as pikes clashed and the two groups of men began a deadly embrace. They jostled each other, both sides trying to push the other back. A second group of our men raced up and threw themselves into the rear of their colleagues, aiming to use their weight to push the first ranks through the enemy's line.

We watched the two groups battle it out. The walking wounded from each side were making their way to the rear, some of them walking with an arm round another man's shoulder for mutual support. It seemed the Parliamentarians were getting the upper hand, for our men were slowly being pushed back. They battled on for a good while longer, but eventually they were back on our side of the river. A shout from a Parliamentarian officer recalled his men across the bridge and to deter our men from following the musketeers began to fire again.

Captain Standish rallied his men and took stock of his casualties. The men were too exhausted for another attack. We would have to try again tomorrow.

***

The next morning our guns began another bombardment. This one lasted longer aiming to weaken the enemy's resolve. Captain Standish was talking to Sir Thomas Tyldesley. 'It is too cramped on the bridge to use the pike. I'm going to get the men to cut their pikes in half so they will be able to wield them easier.'

'Make sure they all have swords too, for these are better at close quarters. Keep the ranks compact and try to force a gap in the enemy line. When you have a gap push your men into it and break them.'

The guns were petering out, dangerously hot from their exertions and they needed to be allowed time to cool down.

'God be with you,' said James as Captain Standish readied his pistols and prepared to advance with his men.

'And with you my Lord. I will win this bridge before the day is done.'

Again the Parliamentarians fired onto the bridge as our men advanced. This time they kept their ranks thinned to make themselves a poor target. As they got close to the enemy the order came to close ranks. Once more the two groups of pikemen hurled themselves upon each other like two stags butting.

Captain Standish could be seen in the front rank. He discharged both his pistols dropping two of the enemy in front of him. He drew his sword and then jumped into the gap, lashing out in all directions. His bravery gave our men heart and they charged in after him. The Parliamentarians began to buckle under the ferocity of the attack and they slowly retreated back across the bridge. Then all of a sudden they broke. A huge cheer came up from our men. They stood to catch their breath as the foe routed before them.

I watched and the enemy pikemen peeled off to either side of the bridge. This looked like an orderly retreat not a disorganised rout. Then I saw a formed body of musketmen in the open space on the other side of the bridge. I began to shout a warning, but too late.

Captain Standish had already seen the danger and urged his men into another charge before they were cut down by the musket fire.

James also appreciated the danger and ordered Sir Thomas to cross the bridge with a second body of infantry.

The musket volley tore into the ranks of our men, knocking about half of them down and out of the fight. Captain Standish tried to rally the survivors, but then another musketeer fired and our brave captain grasped his hand to his throat where the ball had struck him. He tumbled forward onto his knees. Two of his men grabbed him by the arms and turned to bring him back. Sir Thomas's men were moving through the ranks of our first company, but were loosing their order and cohesion as they did so.

Sir Thomas prepared to charge the enemy, but the musketeers had retreated behind barricades at the head of the street which were manned by more pikemen. He pressed his men forward and they broke onto the enemy wall.

Captain Standish had been brought back by his men and was propped up by one of them. Blood was gurgling in his throat. His eyes were rolling. James bent down beside him and clasped his hand.

'My friend, have I done this to you? May the Lord spare you.'

Captain Standish opened his eyes and looked into the face of James. The eyes were dark and staring. His face was the colour of a winding sheet. It was clear to us all that he would not be spared. His head rolled to the side, the eyes fixed.

We had lost a valiant man. I looked over to what had been the cause of his death, the Parliamentarians nestled behind their defences. Sir Thomas was pressing them hard, but he did not seem to be making any headway. He was also losing men and those who remained were losing heart. He sensed that their morale was about to break and he ordered them to retreat.

James was distressed over the death of Captain Standish, but not too disheartened about the failure to capture the town. 'We have them hemmed in and we have time. They will break. We just need to press them hard.'

Although we were not to know it, we did not have all the time we needed. For a couple more days we bombarded and attacked. It seemed they were weakening. Then we received some news that stopped the siege. The Earl had died. It was as if the affable old man could no longer live in this world, with his friends and neighbours torn apart by hostility. He had represented a time of peace and prosperity.

Now his counties were about to be divided irrevocably by chaos and carnage. James ordered all forces to retreat back to Lathom. He needed time to bury his father.

***

On the ride back I realized how much I was looking forward to seeing Louise and Henry again. I had seen a lot of death in the last few weeks and this had heightened my love for them. I felt sad that I had not had chance to take my leave of the Earl, but then I thought that James must be feeling such regret more acutely.

Back at Lathom our women were waiting to meet us. James got down from his horse and embraced Charlotte. I followed him and hugged Louise and Henry close to me, feeling reassurance as I did so.

Later, alone with Louise I asked her what she knew of the Earl's last days.

'He was at Bidston with his servants. He took to his bed, but would not send for James, fearful of ruining his chances of capturing Manchester. But I have heard that at the very end he asked for a Catholic priest to hear his confession.'

'Who did you hear that from?' I replied.

'From Charlotte, who learnt it from the Earl's old steward. She is frightened it's true and it could mean that James's own faith is inclined to Rome. Charlotte has reason to fear a conversion to Catholicism, for that is what her own brother did.'

'But I think his reasons were more political than religious. He was never going to get on at the court of the Catholic French King, unless he renounced his faith.'

'What if our King is secretly a Catholic? Certainly some believe it to be true. If it were the case wouldn't James have more royal favour if he also converted?'

'James is not so shallow. He is a man of firm beliefs and principles. I do not see any signs that he holds to the old religion. Look at his chaplain, Samuel Rutter a man firmly of the Protestant faith. Look at how his children are being brought up, in the doctrine and practice of the Protestant church. Have you ever seen any secret visits to Lathom by Catholic priests? Look at how conversant James is with scripture. Does he not quote the Bible as often as any Puritan? James is no Catholic.'

'Why then does he surround himself with Catholics like Sir Thomas Tyldesley?' replied Louise.

'I do not think he sees them as Catholics. More important to him is that they are traditional friends and retainers of the Stanley family.'

'That may be true, but it creates the belief that he is secretly a Catholic, and it can do him no good in these times.'

***

There were no signs of Catholic rites at the funeral held in the church at Ormskirk. Samuel Rutter conducted a solemn and dignified service from the Prayer Book, befitting Earl William. Practically the entire household attended, save some left behind to guard Lathom. As he had always been a sociable man, he would have noticed some of his friends were missing, friends who had declared for Parliament and therefore had to stay away.

James, who had effectively been head of the family since his father had retired to Bidston, was now the Earl in title too. I expected his first act would be to take his men back to Manchester to resume the siege, but he received an order from the King to join him at Shrewsbury with his troops.

When this order was relayed to the men there was some disquiet in the ranks. They did not like the fact that they were leaving their county, for it meant leaving their families undefended. I also felt uneasy about leaving Louise and Henry, but at least I had the comfort of knowing they were in Lathom, which had a small garrison to defend its formidable walls.

On the march to Shrewsbury I rode with James and we discussed the King's order.

'I worry that our going to Shrewsbury exposes Lancashire and Cheshire to the Parliamentarians. They will have time to gather men and train them, and so can only get stronger. On the other hand the King is taking my advice to gather his supporters together, presumably for a march on London to strike at the head of the Parliamentarian body. If we separate the head from the body, the other parts will soon whither and die.'

'It requires a resolute mind and unity of purpose. I hope the King's councillors are united on this,' I replied.

James had asked me to compile a list of men who were serving as captains in his little army. It was after I had made my way around all the troops and companies I realized Bootle was missing. He had been with us at Manchester and I had seen him at Earl William's funeral. He must have taken the opportunity to abscond while we were all at Lathom, preparing to leave. I remembered his words to me, that his conscience would have him serve Parliament. He had chosen his path. For the sake of our friendship I hoped our paths would not cross while we were on opposite sides in this struggle.

Our southward march was not opposed by any enemy forces. We were quite a sizeable force, too large for small local forces to tackle us. As we approached Shrewsbury we were challenged by a group of scouts.

'Who goes there?' asked the captain of the troop.

'The Earl of Derby,' replied James. 'Please lead us to the camp and show us where my men can rest.'

James was summoned to see the King as soon as his men had pitched their first tents. He took me, Sir Thomas Tyldesley and the three commanders of his regiments along with him.

We were allowed in to see the King and the first thing I noticed about him was that he seemed agitated. He was pacing up and down his hands behind his back, as if he was trying to resolve some inner dilemma.

'James, I was sorry to learn of the death of your father. At least he died peacefully. I fear many of us will be taken before our time if we cannot defeat Parliament quickly.'

'Are you resolved to march on London?' asked James.

'Yes, I am. A quick strike at the rat's nest should settle this business. What's more I need your troops in my army, but I also want you to return home and secure Chester and the route to Ireland. I may still have need of men from our army there.'

'But my Lord, that will deprive me of my men. It is as if you do not trust me. Who is it at the court who turns you against me?'

'James, I do not intend a slight against you. My affairs are troubled and my enemies are getting stronger every day. Newcastle will stay in the north and defend our interests there. You will be able to apply to him for arms and troops.'

'Your Majesty this is an indignity. I can only conclude my enemies at court mistake me for the First Earl of Derby. I am no Kingmaker. You do not need to fear where my loyalty lies on the battlefield. I will not turn traitor and betray you, turning my men on your army. Who is the source of this calumny? I will wipe this slander from his lips with the point of my sword.'

'My Lord, I repeat I mean no slight against you. I will give you a warrant that you can send to Newcastle for the troops and arms that you have lent me. If your advice proves true and I can defeat the Parliament by a swift march on London, then you will have no need of these men. Return to Lathom and keep open the road to Ireland.'

'Your Majesty, I have discharged a good conscience in this, and my honour is safe in spite of the worst detractors. I will go back to Lathom and raise more men for the defence of my counties. May God protect you, and may the justice of your cause bring the victory that will scatter these rebels.'

James turned and we left the room. I noticed a smirk on the face of one of the King's attendants. He no doubt was one of the Earl's detractors, pleased to see the result of his intrigue.

***

We rode hard to be back in the North before our enemies could exploit our absence. Most of the Earl's captains returned with us, for the King had chosen to put his own men in charge of James's regiments. This had caused some resentment among the men and James had needed to speak with the junior officers to persuade them to serve under their new commanders.

On the ride back James told me of his plan to raise a new force. He would collect money from the hundreds of Lancashire based on their Ship Money assessments. He was confident that this would give him sufficient funds for new foot regiments. He could always count on his retainers and the local loyal gentry to furnish him with cavalry.

We spent the winter raising the money, recruiting new men and trying to equip them. James sent over to the Isle of Man where there were arms and equipment in Castle Rushen. Despite this the men were poorly equipped and were no better than militia, no where near as good as the troops who had been taken by the King.

We had heard the King had come close to defeating the Parliament's army at the battle of Edgehill, but he did not carry the day and the battle ended in stalemate. By good manoeuvre, the King's nephew Prince Rupert got the King's army in front the Parliament's army on the way back to London, but Parliament called out the

London Trained Bands and they blocked Rupert's path. The King returned to Oxford to winter his forces.

Chapter 22 – *Lancashire, 1643*

"The right hand of God is glorious in power; the right hand of God hath dashed my Enemies in pieces". Exodus xv.6

Towards the end of winter James was more optimistic about success and he explained his strategy for the coming campaign.

'My problem is defending what we hold with too few experienced troops. Most of the infantry are "Clubmen" and aptly named because of their lack of arms and training. So I have decided to mount some of the best soldiers I have as dragoons. I will form them into two regiments, one under Sir Gilbert Hoghton and one under Sir Thomas Tyldesley. As dragoons they will be able to move quickly to defend our main strongholds, Lathom, Warrington and Wigan.'

'Will you attack the enemy at all, or remain at the mercy of his plans?' I asked.

'No, I intend to take some of the towns held by Parliament. First we will attack Bolton, for it is a hotbed of Puritanism and if we can capture it their morale will be dented.'

Sir Gilbert's manor at Hoghton was chosen as the place to come together before attacking Bolton. However, we were never to reach the town. At a place called Chowbent we came across a large body of young men blocking our path. They resembled the Prentice Boys of London, nail makers, weavers and wheelwrights, together with farm labourers. I was riding close to James who remarked.

'This is no army facing us; these are tradesmen and farm hands armed with the tools of their trade. Look there; do you see there are two ministers close to their mounted men?'

'This has had a reputation as an area of Puritanism. I think we face an enemy who believe God is on their side,' replied Sir Gilbert.

'God takes no part in this,' retorted James. 'What we are engaged in now is the work of man. Prepare to attack.'

We engaged the enemy, but rather than break in front of us as we had anticipated, they stood firm and by their weight of numbers they pushed us back through Leigh. It was if each of them fought with the strength of two men. James gave the order to disengage and retire. Once there was some distance between us and their main body, their small number of mounted men who had pursued us became isolated from the rest and we attacked them, causing many casualties.

This was a small success for us, but it did not hide the fact that our advance on Bolton had been repulsed. Leaving a small company of foot with Sir Gilbert in Hoghton Tower, James retreated back to Lathom.

***

A few weeks later while in conference with his officers; James received a strange report that a Spanish galleon had grounded in the north of the county near Rossall Point.

'If it really is a Spanish galleon, then there should be a store of muskets on board. We might also be able to salvage the ship's guns. Let's ride up there quickly before the Parliamentarians get their hands on the ship. Sir Thomas, we will take your dragoons.'

The troop was assembled and we set off. As we got near we learnt from locals that a group of men had already boarded the ship. Anticipating them to be Parliamentarians, we proceeded cautiously. Leaving the dragoons out of sight, James, Sir Tomas and I rode on to reconnoitre. As we got close to Rossall Point we could see the galleon grounded in the mouth of the river Wyre. There were a few men on the river bank, and two rowing boats seemed to be ferrying to shore what had been salvaged off the ship.

James formulated his plan. 'We wait for these rowing boats to come to shore, then we ride in and capture them. Once we have taken the boats, we row out and seize the galleon. I only count six men on deck, so will be able to overpower them.'

'I think a ruse will work better here than force,' suggested Sir Thomas. Let me take Paul and a couple of dragoons. We'll ride up to ask them about the ship and once we are close to them we'll draw our pistols. If we can do it well enough, then their fellows on the galleon won't know what has happened.'

'I like your idea,' replied James. 'Once you've got the rowing boats, I'll bring a few men on foot to join you. If your plan fails, I'll ride in with the dragoons.'

Sir Thomas called two sergeants to him. 'Cover your pistol with your blanket and pretend we are local gentry out to take a look at the galleon.'

We rode up to the men who did not seem to recognize us as a threat.

'Hey lads, what have you got here?' asked Sir Thomas when we were getting close to them.

'The Santa Anna, a Spanish galleon. Colonel Doddington thinks it must have been bringing arms to the Earl of Derby and his papists. Anyway we're getting the arms now.'

'Is that so,' replied Sir Thomas. As he spoke he pushed back his blanket and drew his pistols. 'Easy there lads, move over there and drop your weapons. Take off your helmets and buff coats.'

The two sergeants dismounted and bound the hands of the hapless Parliamentarians. They marched them away as James arrived on foot with half a dozen dragoons.

'Nicely done, Sir Thomas,' said James. 'Now let's put on their buff coats and helmets so we look like them.'

We got into the rowing boats and took to the oars. We rode out in silence, watching the deck of the galleon for any sign that our actions on the shore had been spotted. It seemed they hadn't, and I gave a short thanks to God under my breath.

I was in the first boat with James and Sir Thomas. James instructed the dragoons in our boat to board the ship first. 'We'll not pass as soldiers and I might be recognized, so you need to get up there and disarm the men on deck. Keep your weapons away until you are close to them. Try not to fire your pistols, or it might bring more up on deck from below.'

The galleon loomed over us as our boat drew up alongside. We tied on to some netting and the three dragoons started to climb. I followed them, with Sir Thomas and James behind me. My legs felt like lead and I found it difficult to keep my footing and stumbled a few times. Time seemed to stand still. I just wanted to get to the top and get on with it.

Again we possessed the element of surprise. I clambered over the top of the rail and onto the deck. I looked around to assess the situation. The dragoons ahead of me were walking over to the men on deck. I followed them. Behind me, Sir Thomas and James were keeping out of sight.

I watched the faces of the men in front of me. They looked at us. All was calm. Then suddenly I saw one of the men reach for his sword.

'Alarm, alarm,' he cried. His comrades drew their swords and we drew ours in reply. Behind me I heard a thump, probably James or Sir Thomas landing on the deck.

Fearing the arrival of more boarders the enemy rushed us and we had to parry. There were four of us to their five and I found myself facing two men. There was only enough room for one of them to attack me, but I knew if I dispatched the first I would immediately have to face a fresh opponent. Fortunately the fellow did not seem to be particularly skilled with the sword. After a short while of thrust and counterthrust, he left an opening in his defence and I lunged. My sword pierced his buff coat. I had aimed a little too high and caught his lowest rib. I felt the impact jar my wrist and angled my sword down. A pitiful groan escaped his mouth and he slumped forward. Quickly I withdrew my sword and stepped aside. In the heat of the fight it did not shock me to think I had probably taken a life.

Before engaging my second opponent, I took in what was happening beside me. One of our men was down and Sir Thomas was moving into the melee. Our other two dragoons were holding their own. My new opponent attacked savagely with wide eyes and repeated blows. His anger gave him extra strength and I slowly conceded ground. As I backed away he came after me, bringing him out into the open. James stepped up, his sword drawn and spoke calmly to my foe.

'I'll not fight you at a disadvantage. Paul, step back and I will take your place.'

I was about to tell James not to endanger himself when a hard strike by my opponent took the sword out of my hands. Now I was grateful to James who moved into the fight. I could see he had been taught to duel with a rapier, as he projected his left arm back behind his body for balance and fought side on. He clearly had some skill and soon he was pressing forward. Then he made several quick attacks and on the third he caught the fellow on the side of the neck before he could parry. He dropped his sword and clasped both hands to his neck, reeling backwards as he did so.

I looked around. The fight was about over. Sir Thomas had killed his man and the other two now dropped their swords and asked for quarter. James granted it and told them to tend to their comrades.

'You look to our wounded man,' said James to one of the dragoons. 'Sir Thomas, Paul and I will take a look around the ship.'

'See that pile of arms over there?' I asked. 'Do you think they have already disarmed the Spaniards?'

Sir Thomas led the way and picked up one of the swords. 'Toledo steel. See how fine it looks. Have you got the Spaniards locked up?' he asked the Parliamentarians.

They looked at him sullenly and did not reply.

'Looks like we'll have to find out ourselves then,' said Sir Thomas moving towards the bridge. 'It will be cramped below deck so get your pistols ready.'

Sir Thomas slowly opened the door on the bridge. I was right behind him, a pistol in one hand and my sword in the other. I still felt the excitement of what Sir Thomas had called battle lust.

We went to the captain's cabin. I had not expected such a harmonious scene. A couple of gentlemen were seated at the captain's table sharing a decanter of wine. By their clothes, I took one to be the Spanish captain, the other an Englishman. They looked up, startled by our entrance.

'Gentlemen, I am the Earl of Derby and you two are now my prisoners. Who are you?'

'I am Colonel Doddington,' replied the Englishman. 'This is, or was my prisoner, Alfonso the captain of this Spanish galleon.'

'Delighted to make your acquaintance,' chuckled the captain. 'This is the second time I am a prisoner today. The English are very strange.'

'As my prisoner you will be escorted off this ship. Your men must also leave. I intend to fire her and render her unserviceable as a man of war. First we will salvage anything that we can easily carry away by horse.'

James was concerned there might be other Parliamentarian forces close by, intending to re-float the ship. As we were a small mounted force with no sailing men amongst us, we could not hope to do the same ourselves.

As it turned out most of the crew had already been taken off the ship by Colonel Doddington and were now being marched to Lancaster to be placed in the gaol. A dragoon sergeant and two dragoons were detached to escort the rest of the crew to Lathom. Captain Alfonso and Colonel Doddington were each found a horse and would ride with us. Before we could set off we had to set fire to the galleon.

A barrel of pitch stored on board was broken open and the contents spread over the deck and up the sails. James was disappointed that we could not remove the ship's guns, but we did not have any means to get them to shore. Even if we had, he was fearful of being attacked by a larger enemy force who would wrest them from us.

We watched from the shore as the firing party set light to the pitch. The flames soon took hold of the sails, and as they burned free from their supports they wafted like sheets drying in the wind.

On the ride back to Lathom, I sought out Colonel Doddington for I wished to ask him about the remarks made by his men.

'One of your soldiers seemed to think that the Spanish galleon was here by some design of the Earl, to furnish him with arms. Do you seriously believe the Earl would be in league with the Spanish?'

'Of course I don't, but it was useful to tell my men this in order to build up a feeling of distrust of the Earl. My men are Lancastrians who will have to fight other Lancastrians in this war. An Earl of Derby has been the leader of this county all their lifetime and all the time of their fathers and grandfathers before them. It would be easier if we were fighting the Scots or the Welsh. The only way to make the Earl appear different is to associate him with the Catholics in his ranks like Sir Thomas Tyldesley.'

'So by making us appear different you will find it easier to fight us,' I replied summing up his argument. 'How then do we identify you as different?'

'You call us rebels and traitors against the King. You call us Puritans although most of us profess the standard doctrines of the Church. You see, your leaders play the same game.'

'But you *are* in rebellion against your King.'

'We do not wish to remove him from the throne or put another in his place. We want to bring him back to government with Parliament, as only Parliament can protect the liberties of the subjects.'

'You claim to want to bring the King back to govern with Parliament, but what will you do if you defeat him and he refuses your terms?'

'I hope the King if defeated, can be brought to his senses for the good of his people.'

'I am loyal to my King and would give my life for him, but I do not believe for one minute he will accept any more terms from Parliament. He believes himself to be God's anointed sovereign and man cannot undo what God has made.' With that I kicked my horse into a gallop and made for the head of our column.

***

A few days later we received news at Lathom that the Parliamentarians had managed to salvage the guns from the Santa Anna and had taken them to Lancaster. James had been in correspondence with Sir John Girlington in York for the loan of some troops for the spring campaign. A messenger was dispatched asking Sir John to meet up with James outside Lancaster on March 16th. James had decided to make Lancaster his first objective for the campaign and marched there with his own force of six hundred foot and four hundred horse.

Our forces were augmented on the march, and we rested near Lancaster with Lord Morley at Hornby Castle. I recalled my first visit here nearly twenty years earlier when I had been sent to warn Lord Morley that his house was to be searched for arms. With the addition of Lord Morley's men, James's army had doubled since we set out from Lathom.

Soon we were joined by the troops from York. They only numbered six hundred, but were well equipped and trained. James called his officers together to discuss the plan of attack.

'Our aim is to seize the town and the cannon from the Santa Anna. No doubt the enemy will take refuge in the castle. Now, if we have the Spanish guns we might be able to bombard and storm the castle. But I do not want to delay here in a siege. My next aim is to retake Preston. I want a few quick successes to hearten our men and discourage the enemy. Then we march on Manchester. Our position will be much improved if we can oust the Parliamentarian garrison and capture the town's arsenal.'

'What are we to do if we capture a town?' asked Sir Richard Molyneux. 'Do we allow the men to plunder or do we forbid it?' His voice gave more weight to the option of plunder, suggesting that this was the one he favoured. He had the impetuosity of youth and although he was betrothed to James's daughter, Henrietta Maria his relationship with James seemed difficult.

'Lancaster can be plundered for it has given no support to the King,' replied James. 'Preston has been loyal and I still count on the support of many men in the town. If we capture Preston there is to be no looting.'

***

Our march to Lancaster was unopposed. Miles before the town we saw the castle keep, square and cold in the distance. Our scouts returned, reporting that the town was poorly defended. With the town closing its gates after James's summons to surrender, he decided upon a simultaneous attack. Three assaults would be led by Sir Richard Molyneux, Sir John Girlington and Sir Thomas; each commander leading their own troops. If a breach was made James would exploit it with the reserve.

I was in Sir Thomas's column and it was our task to capture one of the city's gates.

'How should we do it, Paul?' Sir Thomas asked. 'A mad rush at the gate; or look for another way in?'

'They'll expect an attack on the gate. While the men find something for a battering ram, let's look and see if we can find another route in.'

We skirted around the walls close to the gate. A lean-to pigsty with a solid looking thatched roof had been built against the outside of the wall. Despite the onset of hostilities, nobody had thought to knock it down. Now if we could balance some short ladders on top, it offered us a chance to climb to the top of the wall.

On rejoining his men, Sir Thomas despatched a dozen of them to fetch some ladders from the small supply company James had brought along. While we waited for them to return, Sir Thomas picked out his best men for the assault on the wall. A diversionary attack would be made on the city gate by the remainder of his force. Some sporadic musket firing had broken out, with both sides trying to pick off any exposed troops. Finally, the ladders arrived and we made our way to the wall using some cottages for cover. The final yards were in the open and we made dash across to the wall. Three of us clambered up onto the roof of the pigsty. I was concerned that we might bring it crashing down but it held, for now.

I turned round and hauled up a ladder from one of the men behind. I set it down as firmly as I could I began to climb up, my sword in my right hand. At the top I peered over. There was nobody in sight, so I jumped down onto the walkway. Sir Thomas landed beside me. I looked down to see how the others were doing. The roof of the pigsty was collapsing under the weight. Two of the men behind us managed to make it to the top of the wall; the third fell back as the roof fell away. That left five of us on top of the wall.

Cautiously we advanced towards the gate. About twenty yards from our goal the enemy spotted us. They got off a few musket shots before we hit them. Fearlessly, Sir Thomas plunged in and had felled one of them before I had even got into contact.

It seemed to be over before it had even begun. We soon overpowered the guards on the gate. Perhaps they thought their cause was already lost, not realizing that only five men had breached the defences. We opened up the gate and our men flooded in, fanning out down the city's streets.

Shortly afterwards James came in with the reserves.

'You have delivered the city to me with the minimum of casualties. Well done to you both. The rest of the city's garrison will hole up in the castle, leaving our men free to loot. Let's restrain the hotheads and limit their excesses.'

'Amen to that,' replied Sir Thomas. 'Our victory does not make us butchers.'

Despite the visible presence of James and his captains in the city, it was turned over to plunder. Either to wipe out their deeds or just out of malice, some of our men set fire to houses in the city. After a few hours it became too dangerous to remain on the burning streets and we retired out of the city back to our camp.

The following morning we re-entered the city, walking amongst smouldering buildings. Bewildered inhabitants of the city looked at us with downcast glances, most of them avoiding eye contact. I did not feel proud of what we had done, but this was war and the people of Lancaster had resisted the forces of the King and given aid to the rebels. I hoped I would never see the same fate befall my loved ones.

We scouted around the castle, but James decided it was too strong to attack. There were also reports that a relieving force was on its way and he did not want to be caught in a trap. Orders were given for our small army to get ready to march. We were going to slip south to Preston.

***

We were morose on the ride, turning the events that had occurred at Lancaster over in our minds. I looked over at James. He had a sullen countenance and I rode with him, seeking to raise his spirits. My best efforts could not improve his humour.

'I appreciate what you are trying to do Paul,' he said. 'My mood is dark and your words cannot lighten it. My county is tearing itself apart. Look what we are reduced to. We are now burning our own towns. What other shameful acts will we be forced to do before this war is over?'

'You have to be resolute, James. We are fighting rebels who would have our King as a mere puppet. Then where would we be?'

'Adrift in a sea of faction as the rebels fought amongst themselves for dominance,' replied James. 'The only winner in that situation would be the man who commanded the most soldiers. I know we must stick to our cause no matter how painful it is, but all the same it grieves me.'

We were interrupted by a call down the column that the front riders had caught sight of two horsemen making towards us. As they came close I recognized one of them as Roger Hoghton.

'Good day to you, my Lord,' said Roger addressing James. 'I come direct from Preston where I have been talking to men loyal to the King. I have agreed a plan with them to let you into the town, bypassing the Parliamentary garrison.'

'Excellent,' replied James. 'If we can gain entry into the town under the noses of the Parliamentarians, then we may be able to compel them to surrender. Tell me, do we do this by day, or do we use the cover of darkness?'

'It is best done at night, my Lord. I will send my servant back into the town to let our party know we will arrive tonight, and I will stay with you and take you to the door where we can enter the town.'

'Where will we enter the town?' asked James.

'On the west side there is a small gate that leads into the town. It is used by the townsfolk to get to their vegetable plots. Our friends will open it for us,' replied Roger.

'Well, to hide our intentions we will make camp to the north of Preston and send out a scouting party to the east of the town. Sir Thomas, please select your best fifty men. Roger knows the town so he will lead them. As you and Paul are proving to be valuable soldiers you will both go with him.'

We spent the afternoon discussing the plan of attack with Roger. Once inside the town we would make for the northern gate and capture it, opening the doors to let in the rest of our army.

Towards evening I took a walk around our camp. There was nervous preparation by the men as they cleaned and re-cleaned their weapons.

'It's only three days since the new moon, so we will have darkness to hide our attack,' said one of the sergeants.

'From what I hear the garrison is so small they cannot patrol the whole perimeter of the town. There might not even be anyone looking out for us where we are breaking in, I answered.'

Later I recalled my bullish words half way across a field of winter vegetables. Either side of me men were picking their way down rows of carrots, cabbages and madde neaps. One of the lads sliced through a cabbage with his sword and was about to slice through another.

'Save your arm for the fight,' I hissed at him. My true motive was to preserve the winter crop of the townspeople. If a few more of the lads aped his example they would strip the field bare in minutes. I knew the people of Preston from my time at Hoghton. They were honest people and I felt a pang of pity for them, lest they lose their food.

Roger led us up to the gate. He tried it, but it was barred on the inside. Then he cupped his hands around his mouth and let out what sounded like an owl's screech. A few moments later we heard noises on the other side of the door as the bar was removed.

The grinning face of his servant greeted us.

'Have you seen the town watch?' Roger asked him.

'Yes, they are not far from here. But there are not many of them. Hurry inside and we can surprise them.'

We came across the watch on the market square, huddled round a brazier keeping warm. They saw us coming and readied themselves to fight. Roger sheathed his sword and walked over to them calmly.

'There are fifty of us to your five. We can do this the easy way or the hard way. Put down your arms and I will accept your surrender. If you don't you are sure to die. What is it to be?'

A clatter of swords hitting the cobbles gave us the answer.

Roger studied the five men in front of him. 'You'll do,' he said to one of them. The man he had addressed was over six feet tall and had a badly pock marked face with a grossly misshapen nose. 'Your face must be well known in this town. You are to lead us to the gate so we can get close enough to the guards without arousing suspicion. If you give us away I'll shoot you in the back. Sir Thomas and Paul, will you come with me? We'll have to leave the others here until we seize the gate.'

We both agreed to Roger's plan and the three of us set off behind the unfortunate watchman, headed for the northern gate.

'Tell them we've come to check if there is any movement from outside the town and to see what they want for supper,' Roger instructed our captive.

'How goes it Jack?' the watchman asked as we came upon the guards on the gate.

'All quiet. I don't think those Cavaliers have got much fight in their bellies,' replied one of the guards.

'Don't they?' queried Roger as he stepped out from behind his prisoner, pistol visible in his hand. Sir Thomas and I raced past him to tackle the other members of the guard. We found them in the guardhouse warming themselves by the fire. We were upon them before they had time to draw their weapons.

Roger entered the guardroom behind his two prisoners. 'Let's lock them in here,' I suggested, indicating a small gaol used to house anyone unruly found on the streets after curfew. We bungled them all in and then set to opening the gate.

Our men had been waiting for the gate to open and they dashed across from their positions and into the town. James was in the front rank and sought us out. By the broad smile on his face I could tell he was delighted.

'Any casualties?' he asked.

'None at all,' I replied. 'No body harmed on either side.'

'That is a mercy,' said James. He quoted Palms, 'whenever I call upon Thee, my enemies shall be put to flight; this I know for God is on my side.'

***

After the capture of Preston, it was James's intention to march with Lord Molyneux to attack Manchester once more. However, he was once again thwarted when the King sent a summons to Lord Molyneux with orders to bring his six hundred foot and four hundred horse to Oxford. With weaker forces James abandoned his plan to seize Manchester and instead decided to probe into the Parliamentarian stronghold in the east of the county. He would do this by a move up the Ribble valley, entering the hundred of Blackburn from the north.

At the same time he wished to secure Clitheroe and the routes into Yorkshire, to deny the Parliamentarians any succour from that county, and to follow up on the promise that he could have further support from the King's forces holding York. The Queen was in York with many of the soldiers of the Earl of Newcastle. James was not on the best of terms with either the Queen or Newcastle, but hoped they could find common cause with him and allow him to have troops, arms and ammunition to keep Lancashire secure for the King.

The main body of the army spent the night just short of Whalley, while the earl and his staff, including Sir Gilbert Hoghton, Sir Thomas Tyldesley and Lord Molyneux spent the night at Sir Robert Sherburne's seat, Mitton Hall, a place of some strategic value as it overlooked a crossing of the river Ribble. The next day we prepared to set off for Padiham and Burnley. The earl sent a troop of horse to the east with orders to secure Clitheroe if it was not garrisoned and to report back to him if it was. The earl's small army had swelled following the success at Preston and the march up the Ribble. I joined him in the morning with his officers as he reviewed their line of march and issued orders for the day.

'They seem confident enough my Lord,' volunteered Sir Thomas Tyldesley.

'Aye, it's the prospect of more success that buoys them,' replied the earl. 'What worries me is the Clubmen we have attracted since Preston. No training. No proper weapons, and no discipline. But still, they make us look more imposing as long as the enemy don't get close enough to see them face to face.'

Lord Molyneux interjected. 'They've been retiring in the face of us for days, drawing us closer to their strongholds. They'll probably hole up in another town.'

'If only we could get them in the field, we could crush them in a single day,' replied James.

'Indeed my Lord, Amen to that,' answered Sir Thomas Tyldesley. 'But I think they will make a stand soon. Shuttleworth isn't going to let us march into Gawthorpe Hall. He'll try to stop us before then.'

'You take the vanguard and scout ahead, Sir Thomas. We'll follow with the main body with riders on the flanks. It's hilly around here and the Parliamentarians could easily hide their forces and then fall on our line of retreat.'

I was with Sir Thomas as the vanguard came to a crossing of Sabden Brook. The only easy way across was by a small bridge and the vanguard had to cross in a file only six men wide. Once they got across they started to deploy on the far bank. They were forming up when was a tremendous clatter from some hilly ground to the left on the bridge. The staccato sound was confirmed as musket fire as some of the men fell to the ground and others clutched wounds. Another volley came from Parliamentarian musketeers who had been hidden behind the ridge. It was deadly and coming in the flank put our men into great confusion. A third volley hit us before the men had really been able to form up in order. A troop of enemy horse came from over the ridge and rode to our front, blocking the road. To the right the brook bent round again so we had no room to manoeuvre on that flank. Sir Thomas tried to rally the troops who were faltering. He was on horseback and used the body of his animal to block the men's retreat.

'Stand and fight you cowards, you'll not run from this field.' But too many men had lost their nerve and they swarmed around Sir Thomas and me. Another volley was about to come, and they did not want to stand to face it.

Sir Thomas turned his horse and said, 'we can't fight them on our own, let's try and rally them on the other side of the bridge.'

To their credit some of the more experienced soldiers had stopped on the other side and were trying to form up. They were hampered by those who wanted to retreat further, and when the retreating men came upon the main body they caused panic in their ranks too. James had been right to be concerned about the quality of the clubmen, for witnessing the retreat of experienced soldiers, they lost heart. They had not been in any type of action before and this small skirmish was enough to unnerve them. They began to run away.

The body of Parliamentarian cavalry sensed a total rout and had moved forward, preparing to cross the bridge. Sir Thomas steadied his men and the vanguard became the rearguard. He ordered the musketeers to fire a volley which halted the Parliamentarian advance. Our musketeers then retreated twenty paces with the pikes covering the manoeuvre. When the musketeers reloaded, the pikemen retreated back to them. After another volley it appeared the Parliamentarians now thought better about pursuit. However, our advance towards Padiham had been halted and we retreated back towards Whalley.

That night as we made camp, James and his commanders were in a foul mood. During the retreat we had lost about one quarter of our men. James posted double the amount of sentries and ordered no fires to be lit, in case they betrayed our location to the enemy. The extra sentries might have been to prevent further desertion, but by morning we had lost another quarter of our original force. Our only option was to retreat back to Lathom and try to hold onto what we had gained so far in the campaign.

***

I was returning my horse to the stables at Lathom after a morning's exercise. A groom was wiping the sweat off a horse's flanks, but he was not one of the local lads.

'Are you here with messages?' I asked.

'I'm here with my master, Sir William Davenant. He has come to see the Earl of Derby with some news from the King. More than that I don't know, but my master was in an awful hurry to get here. He practically ran these horses into the ground.'

This could only be bad news. Davenant was part of Newcastle's circle and one of the Court faction hostile to James.

I went to the main hall to see if Davenant was waiting for an audience with James. However, when I got there he had just been admitted through to James's private chamber. I followed him through.

'Paul, you remember Sir William Davenant. He is here with important news from the King.'

'Yes that's right my Lord. We have received reports that the Scottish Presbyterian allies of Parliament are planning to seize the Isle of Man. This will be harmful to the King's interests, as it gives them a foothold for further raids into the North West. It will also threaten our communications with Ireland, and if the Parliament were able to station some ships on the Isle they would prevent the King's troops coming over from Ireland.'

'So the King would like me to reinforce my garrison on the Isle?' asked James.

'More than that. The situation is so perilous his Majesty desires you go there in person.'

'What!' shouted James, 'he wants me to abandon Lancashire and my estates here to the mercy of my enemies?'

'The Earl of Newcastle has assured the King he can spare forces to defend Lancashire. Lord Goring will bring troops over in a few weeks time. In the meantime you are advised to furnish Lathom with provisions in case of siege, and then sail to the Isle of Man.'

'This is complete ignominy. To flee like a stag before the hunt. No, I should stay here to fight. If I had sufficient troops I could recapture what we have lost.'

'These are the orders from the King, my Lord James,' replied Davenant, fawning concern.

'Aye, but who gave him the idea I wonder? Your master, Newcastle I expect.'

'My Lord Newcastle is in York and the King is in Oxford. How could he offer his counsel?'

'Through the Queen, for is she still not in York with Newcastle? If Newcastle has the ear of the Queen, then he has the ear of the King, for he dotes on her and will do as she suggests.'

A sly smile from Davenant betrayed him, but he continued to dissemble. 'I'm sure his Majesty is his own man and does not need the advice of his wife. Here, I have the order signed in the King's own hand.' He took out the paper and handed it to James.

James read the letter. 'Banished, that's what it amounts to. I shall not quarrel with my sovereign and will go with good grace, but it grieves my heart to leave Lathom vulnerable to my enemies. Well, Sir William, will you dine with us tonight or are you eager to return to your master?'

'I would gladly have accepted your hospitality, but my instructions are to return as soon as I had given you the King's letter. Good day to you my Lord, and God's speed to the Isle of Man.'

The mood was sombre after Davenant had left the room. Eventually James broke the silence. 'We'll have to make our preparations. Paul, I want you to come with me. We'll have to leave our loved ones here. It seems cowardly to run to the Isle of Man and leave them in danger, but what can I do? I have orders from the King.'

***

The preparations for Lathom were easily enough made. Provisions were laid in and some sheep and pigs were brought inside the walls to provide fresh meat if there was a siege. James appointed several captains to aid Charlotte in the defence of the castle. What was difficult was making preparations to take my leave of Louise and Henry.

'We will be all right,' Louise assured me. 'The castle is strong enough to hold out against attack and we have food enough to last years.'

'But I feel so helpless leaving you here.'

'It is your duty to be with James, as it is mine to be with Charlotte. If Lathom were to fall I would be treated with respect as one of Charlotte's ladies in waiting. No harm will come to me, and I will keep Henry out of trouble.'

***

'Land ahoy,' shouted the lookout from the crow's nest. It was a little while longer before we saw the Island. When we did it loomed up out of the sea; a welcome sight for me. Gulls circled and cried out above. I no longer cared about the salty taste of the sea on my lips; my feet would be on solid ground in a few hours.

James and I were on deck with Captain Bartlet who commanded the 'Elizabeth'. We were passing a bay where several ships sat at anchor.

'That's Derbyhaven,' said Captain Bartlet. 'It's the best anchorage on the Island. We're going to pass round this headland and then go into the bay at Castle Rushen.'

'Is that a fort?' queried James, pointing to a building at the side of the bay.

'Yes, a round tower, built in the time of old King Henry in case of raids by the French.'

'It looks sound enough,' replied James. 'I want a garrison in there again.'

'A good idea my Lord, for it commands the bay. With Parliament's control of the navy, we've been concerned that they would send a force to seize the Isle.'

We continued to look at the fort as the ship rounded the headland. Then we had a more impressive sight to feast upon, the fortification of Castle Rushen. It was more compact than Lathom, and no doubt a lot more cramped inside. What made it remarkable was the way it nestled up against the sea, with ships at anchor next to the walls.

'A formidable refuge,' said James. 'I'm pleased to see it.'

'And you have the castle at Peel on the east of the Island, too,' replied Captain Bartlet. 'It sits on its own island. When the tide is in, it can only be reached by boat.'

'It pleases me to know I have strong castles, but it I didn't want to sulk here on this Island. The Isle itself is protection enough as it is so remote from the mainland. No, I hope for some intelligence from Lancashire to indicate when I can return. Until then I'll get to know my dominion here and make it into a bolt hole. With God's grace, we'll not have to use it.'

***

'My Lord, the timing of your coming is very fortunate.' We were in the presence chamber of Castle Rushen. Captain John Greenhalgh the earl's governor of the island was speaking. It was the first time I had met him and I studied him as he related recent events. I saw a mature man in his forties, and despite a prominent nose, he had a handsome if somewhat portly face. He had the more the air of a gentleman than a soldier. From what he said, he seemed to be a thoughtful man, a man who would assess the options rather than plunge directly into action.

'The common people have become infected with the sedition of London,' John continued. 'They demand a change to the laws or new ones. In truth they don't know what they want, but they know what they don't want. They say they will pay no tithes and want no bishop.'

'This is grave news indeed,' replied James. 'How have you sought to control them, with the dove or with the staff?'

'Initially I did use the staff and tried to gaol a man who had refused to pay tithes, but the knaves rescued him. Then I asked them to set down their grievances in writing. I spoke kind words and assured them that I would write to you with their complaints. I made it known that no laws could be changed without your approval.'

'Good, you have done the right thing. There is no prince powerful enough to resist if the common people take up against him; his Majesty knows this only too well. We will hold a meeting with the people to let them state their grievances. Let us see if we can split them. Do we know the names of the ringleaders?'

'Yes, my Lord. The Christian family, powerful landowners on the Isle are chiefly behind this. Edward Christian and his brother, William are the main rabble rousers.'

'Well let's see if we can catch these two birds. Organise a meeting at Castle Rushen. I can try to overawe them with my English soldiers. Let it be known throughout the Isle, I will hear the petitions from each parish.'

On the appointed day a platform for James and his governor was erected outside the Castle on the market place. James would dispense his justice from on high. He sought to impose his authority by all means possible. Soldiers were visible on the walls of the castle and even Queen Elizabeth's clock; visible on the castle wall behind James, seemed to add gravitas to the proceedings.

I could sense the excitement amongst the crowd. Men were grouped in clusters and talking amongst themselves. Some pointed at James and at the soldiers on the walls. Pie sellers were taking advantage of the large gathering to sell their wares. Children ran about, evading calls from their mothers to be still and silent. Seeing them at play brought thoughts to mind of my younger children Charles and Alice, brother and sister to Henry. I wondered how long it would be before I saw them again, and then my thoughts were interrupted as James rose to address the crowd.

'Thank you for coming here today with your petitions from the parishes. I have come over to this island, thankful that there is a place blessed to be free of the sedition that has so affected the mainland. It is my sincere wish that we can avoid the tumults which have blighted England and Scotland, and that this Isle can be a faithful servant of our most noble and clement King.'

James paused to let his words sit upon the crowd, before continuing. 'I count myself amongst friends here, and invite you to honestly tell me what troubles you. Come forward and present your petitions to the court.'

A little subdued, this being the first occasion the Manx people had met James, the petitioners came forward in a manner that almost seemed contrite. Certainly there was no open hostility, and no bold proclamations that they would pay no more tithes, words that had previously been declared in front of the governor.

'I thank you for these,' he said indicating the petitions by a wave of his arm. 'I will not do them justice if I try to answer them now. No, I must read them and consider all in good time. I will summon the officers spiritual and temporal with the twenty four men of Keyes and four good men of every parish to meet at Peel Castle. Go home to your parishes and tell your people that your Lord will consider your grievances fairly, for he has the best interests of the Commonwealth at heart.'

With some murmuring the crowd began to disperse and we made our way back inside the castle.

'That was well handled my Lord,' I said to James once we were through the first gate.

'That was just the first move. Christian did not say a word.' Turning to Captain Greenhalgh, he continued. 'We need some informers to find out what his plans are and how they will behave when we meet at Peel. I hope you know some men who can be persuaded to ferret out some intelligence. Double what you normally pay them, but don't let anyone else know we are doing this. I want this information kept from my other officers here on the Isle.'

***

Gulls circled overhead, squawking their challenge to us as we made our way into Peel Castle. We were spending the night here before the meeting of the Keys. While Castle Rushen was compact, Peel Castle was elongated so that it occupied the whole of the island it sat on.

Over the evening meal, James made plans for the following day. Captain Greenhalgh had recommended that John Canning, a native of the Isle should be involved in the discussions for he knew the Manx people.

James asked Canning, 'How do you think we should deal with the people tomorrow?'

'My Lord, you should overawe them with your authority. Do not permit them to prattle on, for their words of grievance only belittle your office. Silence them and give orders to arrest the ringleaders yourself, so they know to fear you.'

James did not look up from his food. 'Thank you, Mr. Canning. I'll think about this.'

Later after most of the Earl's council had left, James continued the discussion with me and Captain Greenhalgh.

'I am resolved to give the people liberty of speech. I would rather they would speak till they were out of breath, for they will feel better for it. They can't harm me with words, and if I cut them short they will resent me. Canning gave me poor advice and he knows it. Have him sent back to Castle Rushen on some pretence. I don't want officers around me tomorrow who I can't trust. Good night gentlemen. I think we shall have some wrangling tomorrow. Let us be prepared for it.'

James's foresight proved to be true, for we did indeed have some wrangling at the meeting. With the men of Keys, the Deemsters and the bishop and his ministers present the meeting took on the appearance of a court. James was mindful of this and showed respect to the officers of the Isle. He sat patiently as the petitioners presented their grievances again. Some of them spoke in the native tongue of the Isle, so James had to have this translated. At the end of the petitions James rose in reply.

'As at Castle Rushen, I thank you for your honesty. I remain resolved to address these grievances so we may continue to enjoy peace on this Isle as befitting loyal subjects of his Majesty. I will look into, and decide on every grievance. In return I ask you to abide by any order I gave in answer to them. To assist me in this I will appoint a select jury of twelve men from the Keys and twelve men from the parishes of the Isle. They are to examine claims of abuses against my prerogative, the laws of the island or the good of the Commonwealth.'

So far the meeting was proceeding according to the plan drawn up by James. He was presenting himself as a just and sympathetic Lord, willing to examine their issues. In fact he had outmanoeuvred them by drawing up this jury to look into the grievances. The jury had no power and James was confident that it was too large to come back with any proposals.

Just as the meeting was drawing to a close, Edward Christian rose to speak. 'We have not heard among these petitions the just grievances the people have regarding the tenure of the land. Nor have we heard anything about the clergy's abuses like the shameful practice of taking money to write out a will.'

Shouts of 'aye' greeted these words. To prevent the meeting from getting out of control, Captain Greenhalgh shouted above the noise.

'It is not the time to introduce any new matters. We have concluded the day and settled all business for the good of our Lord and the country.'

James now rose from his seat. 'I am the only advocate you need and will study these issues to find a resolution. If anyone says other than this you are to treat him as an enemy of yourselves, just as he is an enemy to me. Our talking is concluded. This court will rise.'

Back in the Lord's chambers inside the castle we reflected on how the day had gone.

'Christian is weak now. We must follow up on this. Have some agitators arrested as a lesson to the others. Paul, I want you to take a lead in rounding them up.'

'Yes, James but I will need the support of the governor,' I replied.

'You have it,' assured Captain Greenhalgh.

So the next morning as the sun came up over the sea, I rode out from Peel Castle accompanied by a sergeant of the garrison and two troopers. We were headed for Sulby where one of the agitators lived. I had no qualms about arresting this man for I regarded them all as dangerous.

The sergeant was a native of the Isle and I was keen to talk to him in order to learn more about the feelings of the Manx people.

'Is there a lot of support for these grievances amongst the people?' I asked him.

'It all depends who you talk to. There's many on the Isle who complain about the governor and the clergy. They hear news of the troubles across and this stirs the bold among them to action. Some see the arrival of the Earl as good, for they trust his words to address their concerns.'

I kept quiet at this point, for I did not think I could trust the sergeant and the troopers with my knowledge of James's intentions.

Our approach to Sulby had been observed by a scruffy boy who ran up the lane announcing our arrival to the village. He was followed by several dogs and their barks mingled with his cries. The noise from the boy and the dogs brought several people to their doors.

The sergeant knew William Carrett's house. I dismounted and went to the door with him. After waiting a short while with no response to my knock, I was about to wrap on the door again when it was opened by a youth. He looked to be an older version of the lookout boy, and I assumed he was a brother. He spoke words in Manx so I did not follow, but I understood their tone and they were not pleasant.

'Speak English, not Manx,' interrupted the sergeant.

'We are looking for William Carrett. Is he here?' I said.

'What do you want with him?' The youth looked past me to the soldiers, and then back to me.

'That is between him and me. It does not concern you.'

As I said this I saw the pupils of his eyes enlarge, warning he was about to strike. An instant later he was on me, pummelling me with his fists. I grasped his arms and pushed them away so he could not strike me. Then the sergeant bundled him to the ground.

'Shall we take him with us too?' puffed the sergeant as he restrained the boy.

'No, I'll not put him in gaol for this. He was only doing this to protect his father.'

'Indeed he was,' replied a voice from the doorway. A man emerged out of the house. 'What do you want with me?'

'It's gaol for you, for your part in the recent unrest,' I replied.

'Is this part of the Lord's new government of the Isle, to imprison men who speak the truth?'

'I am not here to argue with you about the policies of the earl. You're coming with us. Do I have to get my men to shackle you like a common criminal, or will you get your horse and ride back with us to Peel?'

'I will get my pony for I am but a poor farmer, and have no fine horse to ride' he replied with a hint of insolence. 'Let my son go, for he will have to take care of the family with me away.'

Turning to his son he said, 'Go find your mother and tell her where I have gone. Tell her not to worry. I'll be home soon.'

'Let the boy go sergeant,' I said.

'Don't go assaulting the Lord's men again, or you'll find yourself in gaol next time,' said the sergeant as he let the boy go, clapping him around the head as he did so.

At the unspoken bidding of their masters, the dogs chased us down the lane snapping at the heels of our horses. I did not feel troubled by what I had done. This man was a malignant and deserved to be locked up.

Chapter 23 – *Isle of Man and Lathom, 1644*

Servants cleared the pewter plates and drinking cups from the dinner table. Captain Greenhalgh, James and I retired to James's private chamber.

'The news is bad from Lancashire. The entire county except Lathom House and Greenhalgh Castle is in the hands of Parliament,' said James. 'Charlotte is defending Lathom with the garrison, but she is now besieged. Paul, I want you to go over and see how long they can hold out. I'll send messengers to York to seek help from there. Once I've finished preparations for the defence of the Isle, I'll come over and see if we can break the siege of Lathom.'

The war had stifled trade with the Isle of Man, and I had to wait a few days before boarding a ship. I was travelling as a merchant with the pretence of buying cloth in Liverpool. Once on dry land I would buy a horse, slip out of the town and head for Lathom. I felt vulnerable and kept to myself during the journey. I watched my fellow passengers with suspicion, as if they knew I was one of the earl's men and would offer me up to the Parliamentarians once we docked.

My worries proved unfounded and I was able to make my way out of Liverpool without being stopped. This was an important town for the Parliament as it was the only port they had on the western coast. They were now better able to disrupt our communications and supplies from the Isle of Man and Ireland. Accordingly, new defences were being constructed for the town, large earth ramparts in the shape of the letter 'v'. I rode past men and women sweating to build these earthworks. It was a sad sight, for it demonstrated how weak our position was.

***

It is not easy to get into a castle that is surrounded by your enemies. The Parliamentarians were building siege works around Lathom and I could not approach it without being seen from their lines. I spent several uncomfortable days in a ditch watching for an opportunity. At the end of the day I would slip past the besiegers and beg shelter and food from one of the nearby tenant farmers, most of them still loyal to the earl.

In the ditch there was little to do but watch and think. My thoughts were often of my family, who I had not seen for nearly a year. Messages had got through to me on the Isle of Man. Alice had taken a fever in the winter, but had recovered. Charles was a healthy boy with dark hair like his mother. Henry was always playing pretend wars with the other boys at Lathom. He was ten years old now and did not understand why he could not be a proper soldier. So close to them, and they did not know I was here. If I made a reckless attempt to get to them I could be killed. I struggled with my impatience, but was getting increasingly desperate.

Deputations kept on going into the castle. No doubt they were trying to get Charlotte to surrender. By the agitated gestures of the negotiators as they came out, she was not willing to accept their terms.

On the morning of the fourth day I was spying out a route that would get me close to the castle walls. If I could not get past the sentries during the day, then I reasoned I would have more chance by night. I was looking towards the main gate when to my surprise it opened. Perhaps it was another deputation, but this thought was soon dismissed when I saw armed musketeers issuing from the castle. More and more kept appearing. This was a sally from the besieged garrison. Here was my opportunity to get in.

I had great difficulty keeping still as I watched them march up to the siege trench. I wanted to run up to them, but they would probably mistake me for an enemy and shoot. There looked to be about one hundred of them and they kept a good order as they marched. They must have caused great panic amongst the ranks of the besiegers or perhaps there were no officers to issue any orders, for no shots came from the enemy as our men advanced. When they got near to the siege trench they poured a fierce volley into the Parliamentarian ranks, causing many casualties. Those of the enemy that were still able, fled in panic.

Next I caught sight of William Kay leading the small troop of Lathom's horse. They pursued the fleeing besiegers and cut them down before they could escape. Here was my chance. I broke from my cover and ran towards William. I hoped he would recognize me before I was shot down by one of our men.

As I got close I called out, 'William don't shoot. It's Paul.'

I saw the look of recognition on his face and he shouted to his men, 'hold your fire. He's one of us.'

'Climb up behind me,' he said, as I stood in front of him grinning like the village idiot.

'Thank you William,' I replied once I sat behind him.

'It's Captain Kay now. I command the garrison's troop of horse. Right, back to the castle boys,' he said as he kicked his horse into action.

'Dada, Dada,' shouted Henry as we rode through the gate. He was up on the gatehouse, no doubt he had been watching the sortie from there. Henry ran down the stairs into the yard. By then I was waiting for him and hugged him in my arms as he ran into me.

'Did you beat them Dada? I saw them running away from our soldiers. Will they leave now?'

'Steady, steady. Yes we beat them today, but I don't think they are going away. Now take me to your mother and your brother and sister.'

'It's wonderful to have you back and in one piece too,' said Louise as we embraced.

'It's wonderful to be back, but I wish we weren't in the middle of a siege.'

The tension flowed out of me as we clung to each other. The moment was broken when Louise said, 'You stink. Have you been hiding in a dung heap?'

'Almost,' I said. 'I've not washed since I left the Isle of Man and I've been living in a ditch for three days.'

We looked into each others eyes and laughed. I was home.

Much later once all messages had been delivered, the dirt of the journey washed from my body and excited children put to bed, Louise and I were finally alone. We did not need to talk. Our bodies spoke to each other. I had been faithful to my wedding vows for nearly a year. Our lovemaking was intense yet gentle, as if it was our first time together. Afterwards I lay in Louise's arms. I felt safe there. I always felt safe there, whatever the vicissitudes of life.

Next day we interrogated the prisoners. So far the besiegers had not progressed very well with their earthworks, for our men shot at them from the towers causing frequent casualties. The prisoners confessed the plan was to starve the castle into submission. This news pleased us for we were well furnished with supplies and living in our normal quarters. On the other hand the besiegers were living in tents in a field camp. To make sure we disrupted their sleep we decided to conduct regular night sorties.

After suffering nearly a week of these sorties, the besiegers renewed their efforts to build mounts for their siege guns. Towards the end of the week, I awoke to the sound of guns. I dressed in a hurry and went out to see what was going on. During the night the Parliamentarians had brought up a siege gun and they had fired some shots of the wall to try to make a breach. This had not succeeded. A group of officers and some women who had come to witness the spectacle could be seen grouped together.

Having failed with the walls, the gunners now turned their attention to the battlements. In truth this was probably more to entertain the onlookers for it would do us no harm.

That afternoon a messenger came over under a white flag. He was admitted into the castle and taken to see Charlotte. The messenger was Jackson, a zealous chaplain of Rigby the leader of the Parliamentarian besiegers.

'Sir Thomas Fairfax sends you a letter he has lately received from your husband,' said the messenger as he handed over a paper to Charlotte.

Charlotte took the letter and read through it. The whole room of men was silent as she read. 'It seems that out of concern for our safety, my husband has requested a free passage for me and my children. He does not know how well we stand here. I will not desert this house or surrender it, unless it be the will of God that I should do so. Go back to Rigby with my answer.'

Once the messenger had safely been escorted away, Charlotte spoke to me,

'Paul, you are to go to Chester with a message for James. You are to tell him we have the upper hand and there is no danger of the house being stormed. We have ample provisions to survive a long siege. If he can gather even the smallest relief force I think these cowards would run at the sight of him.'

'You are leaving us again so soon?' was all Louise could say when I told her the news.

'What can I do? James and Charlotte trust me, and I am getting skilled in playing the messenger. Hopefully I will be back again in a few days, and if God is willing James will have mustered a relief force. Then we will chase Rigby and his sanctimonious band away.'

'Did Charlotte tell you that the hand of Bradshaw is behind this? He has stirred up the Puritan ministers in their pulpits. They are claiming that Charlotte is the whore of Babylon, and Lathom is the Tower of Babel that will be cast down.'

'They will need to trust in God to bring them success, for they show no signs of being able to bring the walls down through their own labours.'

Later that day another sortie was made to enable me to slip out. I had been given a fast horse from James's stable and while the besiegers' attention was focused on our musketeers I rode out down an unguarded lane.

***

A day later I was in Chester. It was garrisoned by the only remaining Royalist field army in the North West, if indeed it could be considered an army. As I made for the Stanley's town house I passed through the market square. This time there were no ranting Puritans to be seen. Instead there were street entertainers and dice tables; no doubt there were whores to be found close by if you looked. All the things a bored soldier needs.

'How are Charlotte and my girls?' queried James as he paced around the room. He was clearly anxious to see them. 'I can't persuade Lord Byron to give me enough men to march to relieve Lathom. He has his orders from the King to hold Chester at all costs and he claims he can't spare any men at all. Neither can I get any help from York. I've had no replies to my letters to the Queen and now find out that the Queen and Newcastle have problems of their own. It seems the Scots Covenanter army has joined up with the Earl of Manchester's Parliamentary army in Yorkshire.'

'So we are unlikely to get any help at all,' I replied, thinking that Newcastle's rivalry with James was also behind this.

'The only hope is from the south, and the King is unlikely to send an army to help me,' said James.

'No, but he might send one to aid his Queen now that she is hard pressed,' I replied. 'Lathom can hold out for months, especially as our enemy haven't made any serious attempts to deploy siege guns. If the King sends an army north, then there is a good chance the Parliamentarians will gather all their forces together and abandon the siege.'

'It's all we can hope for,' answered James. 'Go back to Lathom and tell Charlotte to hold out. I will pray to our Lord for her deliverance.'

On my ride back to Lathom I passed by Lathom Park chapel. I spied a notice nailed to the door.

'To all Ministers and Parsons in Lancashire, well-wishers to our success against Lathom House, these.'

As I read, I grew angry at these men who called on the people of the county to commend their cause to God. The commanders of the rebels had signed their names at the bottom of the paper, Ashton and Moor. The hypocrites claimed to be fighting in God's name to bring peace to the county. I leant over and tore the paper from the door and shoved it inside my doublet. Wary of being seen, I kicked my horse into a trot and rode to a nearby farm. As I approached the farm I saw soldiers moving outside and realized some of the rebels must be billeting here. I would have to ride further away to leave my horse. Today was Saturday and my prearranged return to Lathom had been set for the Sunday, for while the pious rebels were at prayer there were fewer pickets on guard.

I rode on to a farm that was too far away from Lathom to be used to billet any soldiers. To save me from a long walk, the farmer offered to ride with me back to Lathom. Leading my horse by the reins he parted with the words, 'God save the King and the Earl of Derby.'

My way back into Lathom was through a postern gate. First of all I had to pass through the enemy's siege works. As expected, most of the rebels were away at prayer and I slipped through unobserved. I could see that the besieging guns had done more damage to the walls and began to get worried for my family. I felt great relief when I saw Henry watching on the walls. He called down for the gate to be opened.

Once inside I asked him, 'Are your mother, brother and sister safe?'

'Yes, Dada,' he replied. 'Everyone is safe.'

With my worries eased I went to make my report to Charlotte. She dismissed all save Major Farmer, the commander of the garrison.

Once they had gone, Charlotte greeted me. She gave me a weak smile and I could see lines of worry in her face. 'It is good to see you again Paul. By God's grace you are back safely with us.'

I was still elated to be back and replied flippantly. 'Their sentries are so poor I could have got a regiment passed them.'

'If you were able to get a regiment in then we would defeat these rebels,' snarled Major Farmer. He was a Scottish professional soldier, somewhat dour and always one for plain speaking.

'Now William, go easy with him. He has risked his life again to bring us a message from James.' Turning back to me Charlotte said, 'Forgive him Paul. Our morale is starting to suffer from the battering of the enemy's cannon. What news is there from James? Is he able to come to relieve us?'

'I'm afraid that he isn't. Lord Byron can't spare any troops from the Chester garrison. Our forces in Yorkshire are hard pressed and unable to help. The only hope is if the King sends an army from the south to aid the Queen.'

'Well we shall have to hold out as long as we are able,' replied Charlotte. Looking at Major Farmer she continued, 'we need to do something about these guns, especially the mortar piece.'

'I will organize a sortie to spike their guns, answered the Major. 'It is better for the morale of the men if they are active instead of sitting here at the mercy of the enemy.'

***

The men were nervous as they waited to sally out. I spotted George Brereton, the Catholic gamekeeper making his way up the steps to the battlements. He was carrying a fowling piece. To lighten the mood I called up to him.

'Where are you off to with that? This is no time to be going hunting.'

'I hunt Roundheads these days,' he replied grinning. 'I've bagged a brace already and I'm having a wager with the other gamekeepers to see who can get the most.'

'As long as you don't shoot me,' I retorted, trying to hide any sound of fear in my voice.

We knew their routine, so we were waiting for them to change their guard. The soldiers going off duty were always keener to move than those relieving them. Their officers did not enforce proper discipline and as a result the siege works were poorly defended during the change over. I rehearsed in my mind what I had to do. I had volunteered to join a group led by Captain Radcliffe, tasked with poisoning the enemy's guns. To do this we first of all had to clear the rebels from their batteries. Then we would hammer spikes into the firing vents of the cannon. By sealing their lips we would save ourselves from their salvos.

The sound of the postern gate being opened interrupted my thoughts and I prepared to move out. A last nervous check of my sword belt and then I was off, following Captain Radcliffe out of the gate. There was a good deal of ground to cover before we reached the siege works, and my legs felt heavy as I pounded across the turf. I saw one of the enemy about to raise the alarm. Then he was hit by a shot and dropped into the trench out of sight. I was grateful that George was such a good marksman.

Then we were upon them and fighting hand to hand. It was desperate and confused. I had beaten two of the enemy down and then glanced around to see how we were doing. My stomach dropped. Three of us were isolated with Captain Radcliffe, and the rebels were closing in on us. Radcliffe fought like a demon and we began to push them back. We did not grant anyone quarter and put them all to the sword. It was savage, but we could not keep prisoners in the castle. Earlier in the siege, Charlotte had released some prisoners and in return some of our party were meant to be released as an honourable exchange. However, Rigby kept faith with neither man nor God, and none of our friends were given their liberty. In fighting like this we cleared two batteries and then paused as we had no-one else to fight.

'Right spike the guns,' said Radcliffe. 'I'll keep watch.'

Before I set to the guns, I looked back at the Eagle Tower as I knew Captain Fox was observing the enemy from there and would send us a signal if we had to retreat. His flag was still, so we would have time to do our work.

I took the hammer from my belt as one of our men untied a sack from his back and spread a variety of different sized spikes and nails on the ground. Picking up a couple of spikes, I made my way over to the nearest gun and hammered one into the cannon's firing vent. We worked quickly, expecting a counter by the rebels that would force us to retreat. Our worries were unfounded and we had ample time to complete the spiking of the guns. We even had enough time to collect up the discarded muskets of the enemy and carry them back to the castle.

Entering the castle back through the postern gate we were greeted by whoops of joy from Henry, who must have slipped away from Louise to watch the sortie from the battlements. George called down to me. 'It's all right I've been keeping an eye on him.'

'Thank you, and is it you we have to thank for felling the sentry before he raised the alarm?'

'Yes, that was me. I got a few more besides so I'm still in front in our wager.'

Charlotte and Louise were in the courtyard. Louise looked anxious and I knew the reason.

'Don't fret over Henry,' I assured her. 'He is safe enough, up on the battlements with George. Their guns aren't going to fire for a while, so we should have some peace.'

'This is good news,' replied Charlotte. 'I'd like to see the look on Rigby's face when he learns what we've done to his cannons.'

***

The fire was burning low in the hearth when Louise and I returned to our chamber. The children were all fast asleep. As I checked on Henry he called out and pushed with his arms; no doubt dreaming he was fighting the rebels.

'This is no place for children,' Louise whispered. 'I should have sent them to Knowsley when I had the chance.'

'You weren't to know that Rigby and Bradshaw would show such malice in besieging the castle. Still, they haven't breached the walls yet, and I haven't given up hope that James will find some way to relieve us.'

My voice must have lacked conviction for Louise retorted. 'You don't believe that. What's going to happen to our poor children, caught up in this war that they don't understand? Will the rebels butcher them like the Protestant settlers in Ireland?'

'It'll not come to that. If they breach the walls they will call on Charlotte to surrender. I doubt she will, but she will arrange for safe passage for women and children. Even Rigby must have enough decency to allow that.'

A crash of cannon ball on stone broke into our conversation. It sounded very close, but apart from some soot wafting down from the chimney breast it did no damage. My boast that we would be spared any further torment from their guns had proved to be untrue.

I turned back to Louise. Silent tears were rolling down her cheeks and dripping from her chin which had begun to quiver. I moved over to her and cradled her in my arms. She leant her head on my chest and sobbed. 'My children, my children.'

I steered her over to the bed and we lay down. I hugged her in my arms until she found sleep. I could not sleep; her anxiety had brought mine to the fore. Up until now I had been able to suppress it, caught up as I was in the battle against the siege.

Carefully I rose from the bed, gently allowing Louise's head to settle on the pillow. With the light of the dying fire, I looked down at her face, observing the lines around her eyes. These had deepened in the last few weeks, spreading out like tide marks on a sandy beach. I looked at the children all sleeping peacefully in their bed, totally unaware of the danger we faced.

I needed to clear my head of the dark thoughts that were brooding there, so I made my way up to the battlements. As soon as I stepped outside, the fresh night air woke my numbed senses as if I had plunged my head into a bowl of cold water. I took in my surroundings and was aware that I was not alone. A figure in a hooded cloak was looking out over the battlements towards our enemy.

Afraid of startling him, I approached noisily and when I was within a few yards I spoke.

'They seem agitated. Our assault today must have worried them.'

The figure turned to greet me. To my surprise it was Charlotte.

'Paul, couldn't you sleep either? Look at how they run about in the dark chasing shadows. They think we are still out there. Every crackle from the camp fire sends them running for cover. But despite this I have a heavy heart. I do not think James will be able to relieve us. I remember the fine regiments James raised at the start of the war and how these were taken from him by the King. If they were here now we would not have to suffer this outrage from that virulent Puritan, Rigby.'

'Indeed that is true, but we do not have those men and Rigby remains out there, intent on our ruin.'

'I feel so powerless,' replied Charlotte. 'What can I do?'

'You must continue to do what you have been doing. Remain defiant in the face of the enemy. Doing so gives great heart to the men. They dare not show any fear while you appear so brave. Your example is worth a hundred more men in the garrison. I remember Earl William telling me when Queen Elizabeth was faced by the Spanish Armada she used her position as a woman to spur her captains on. They would rather die than fail to defend her. You must do the same.'

'You are right. This is what I must continue to do.'

'Tell me, if they breach the walls and prepare for an assault will you parley to allow the women and children to leave?'

'Yes, I will. But I'll not leave. While there is a breath of air in my body I will defend this castle.'

***

Rigby continued to fire his guns for the next five days. It was the mortar piece we feared most, especially when they used it to fire grenados.

On the morning of the fifth day, I was searching the walls for Henry who had slipped off. It was not safe for him to be up there during a bombardment. George was up there, looking for any of the enemy foolish enough to leave the protection of their barricades.

'Watch yourself,' was his greeting. 'They are firing their muskets at the battlements today.'

From my vantage point I could see them preparing the mortar. Shortly afterwards they fired it, and a stone ball came hurtling towards my position. I dived down, praying it would fall short. I braced myself for the impact, but nothing happened. An instant later there was a thud as the stone landed in the courtyard below.

The ball did no damage, but this was the first time they had succeeded in firing over our walls. I looked over at the enemy gunners to see if they realized the significance of their last shot. It seemed they had for their captain was urging them to ready the mortar for firing. I hoped they would not send over a grenade, for on landing it would spray out its small explosive charges in all directions, causing death or dreadful injury to anyone near.

There were a couple of soldiers in the courtyard below. They looked bewildered, no doubt grateful that the last shot had spared them.

'Clear the courtyard and fetch water. The next shot could be a fire grenado.'

'George, can you bring down their captain?'

'I've not got a good enough shot at him. If he leaves his cover I'll try.'

We watched for what seemed an age. I wondered where Henry had got to and felt sick with fear.

Then our waiting was over. They fired the mortar again and a few moments later there was another thud as a grenado buried itself in the earth of the courtyard.

Earth exploded upwards as the grenado spewed out its charges. Instinctively I ducked and closed my eyes. A few moments later I opened them again to see dust swirling round in the courtyard below. The dust settled and I could see glass had been blown out of the stone frames and some clay walls had crumbled. Worse than this there was a smouldering fire on a thatched roof.

Screams from below indicated that people were in the building. The soldiers I had sent for water had not yet returned. I ran down the steps and into the courtyard. By now the fire had taken hold and the roof was ablaze.

My stomach lurched when I heard the screams again. They were women's screams and one of them sounded like Louise. I raced to the door and pushed it open, looking inside with dread. Louise came running at me, her arms above her head in protection. Burning thatch fell from the ceiling onto her and she stumbled.

Running into the smoky room I grabbed her by the arms and pulled her out and across the courtyard as far from the fire as possible. As I sat her down another woman slumped onto the floor beside her.

'My hands,' screamed Louise.

Her hands had been scorched by the burning straw, and they were red raw. I reached out to touch them, but Louise pulled them away.

'Go and get me some lard to put on them. Get the cooks to soften it. I'll follow you.'

'Were any of the children with you in the building?' I asked.

'No, there was only a serving woman in there, and as you can see she got out.'

I helped Louise to her feet and then ran to the kitchens. She shuffled behind me, teeth gritted against the pain.

At first the cooks did not understand why I wanted lard, but once I had explained they softened some by the fire and put it in a large wooden bowl.

'Put on the lard and then wrap her hands in clean linen,' advised one of the cooks. 'Then you'll have to leave it for several weeks.'

'Can you come and help me? A maid has also burnt her hands, and I can only help one person at a time.'

'Of course,' replied the cook. I recognized her now as Sally, the daughter of Meg who had been the cook when I first came to Lathom.

'Don't worry,' Sally continued. 'We get lots of burns in the kitchen, maids scalding themselves with boiling water, serving lads falling asleep while turning the roast at the fire. Lard and linen always works.'

Half way back to the courtyard, we found Louise and the serving maid sitting down on a low wall.

'I'll put on the lard,' said Sally. 'You go and fetch some linen.'

'There's clean bed linen in the chest at the foot of our bed,' instructed Louise. 'Fetch a sheet and you can tear it up into bandages.'

I was pleased to have something else to do, for I was distressed by the sight of Louise's hands. She was clearly in a lot of pain, and probably wanted me out of the way while the lard was applied.

Later when I returned with the linen sheet, Sally was holding a cup to Louise's mouth. Sweat beads were sitting on her forehead and Louise gulped the liquid down.

Sally now took the linen from me, and using a small kitchen knife from her apron, she cut the cloth and then tore it into strips.

'This'll hurt.' Then she gently wrapped the strips around Louise's hands until all the flesh was covered. 'Go and rest. I'll see to Mary now.'

Helping Louise to her feet, I realized with some guilt that I had not spared a thought for the serving maid. 'Who will take care of her?' I asked.

'She'll be looked after by the other kitchen maids,' replied Sally. 'Get your wife to bed. She needs to lie down now.'

Putting my arms under hers, I lifted Louise to her feet. I put my arm around her shoulder and she leant on me as we made our way to our room. Once back there I helped her onto the bed. She lay back with a sigh.

'Go and fetch the children. I really need to see them now,' she whispered.

'Will you be all right on your own?' I asked.

'Yes, I need to rest, but I want to see them. I thought I was going to die in there.'

'Lie back and try to sleep. I'll go and find them.'

***

Locating Charles and Alice would be easy enough. Like the rest of the children in the household, they were schooled each morning by the earl's chaplain, Samuel Rutter. Anticipating that Henry would be on the walls, I decided to search him out first.

Up on the walls I came across George, a self-satisfied grin reaching from ear to ear.

'I got that captain like you asked me,' he beamed. 'He wanted to take a good look where the shot was falling. Last thing he ever saw. I brought him down good and proper.'

'Well done. That's some consolation for the harm he has done to Louise. Her hands are all burnt. She could have been killed. I'm looking for Henry, as she wants to see him.'

'Over there on the Chapel Tower. I'll wave him over.'

George beckoned Henry to come over and like a dutiful lap dog he responded.

As Henry approached us I was searching for the right words. I did not want to worry him, but I needed to tell him his mother had been hurt. Before I could speak, George blurted out.

'It's your mother, Henry. Been hurt by that mortar shot. She'll be all right, but you are to go and see her now.'

'Come on Henry,' I added. 'We'll fetch your brother and sister on the way.'

I shepherded the children into our room. Louise was asleep, her bandaged hands resting on top of the sheet. Alice and Charles ran up to the bed. Henry ambled in, looking unsure what to do.

Louise opened her eyes and smiled weakly at the children. She saw the look of concern on their faces. 'It's all right. My hands are a little sore, but apart from that I am fine. Come and lie on the bed with me and I'll rest.'

I watched them settle down and saw the comfort Louise took from their presence. I could not settle so I went to watch the enemy from the walls.

***

We were given some respite for the next few days up to Easter. Perhaps Rigby and his Puritan ministers were praying for the Lord to aid them in their malicious work. On the day following the one we marked as the day of our Lord's crucifixion, Rigby resumed his salvos and concentrated his efforts on a postern-tower. We more than made up for the damage they did to the tower when George shot the cannonier. After this their salvos were less effective for their new cannonier did not have the skill of his predecessor.

On the day after we celebrated the resurrection of our Lord, we suffered the first major damage to the castle. Rigby had ordered his gunners to concentrate their fire on the Eagle Tower. There was no great strategy behind this as the Eagle Tower served as the castle's keep, and lay in the middle of the castle. Damaging it would not give them a way in, and we took it as a sign of frustration, brought on by their failure to breach the outer walls.

During this bombardment I was attending a council of war being held by Charlotte and her officers. We were sat in the great chamber discussing how we could continue to disrupt the enemy.

'I can stomach the cannon, but I have no heart for the mortar piece,' Charlotte admitted.

'It is the same with the men,' replied Major Farmer. 'I have had to lodge them in upper rooms in the castle, protected by clay walls, for they fear death from the mortar.'

'Can't we make another sortie and spike the mortar?' asked Charlotte.

'A spiked gun can be repaired,' answered Major Farmer.

'Well, can't we block the mouth of the mortar with wood?' retorted Charlotte.

'The mouth of the mortar is too wide; it is more than a foot across. Any attempt we make to seal it will quickly be put right.'

'Why don't we capture the mortar then?' I suggested. 'Better to bring it back into the castle than damage it and leave it for them to repair.'

Major Farmer turned to look at me, every inch of his face displaying a professional soldier's scorn at my idea. 'And how do you expect to be able to do that?'

'I'm not sure,' I blurted. 'But there has to be a way. Let me think.'

I began to think of ways to capture the mortar and the council of war progressed; their voices a blur to me.

I was brought round by a huge explosion very close by. Everyone jumped to their feet, but seemed too stunned to do any more. I ran out into the corridor to see how much damage had been done.

'They've caused a breach in the tower,' cried a soldier running towards me. 'A staircase has collapsed bringing down a large part of the wall.'

I went back to the council of war to tell them what had happened.

'Well, Bradshaw and Rigby will be pleased by this,' said Charlotte. 'I know Bradshaw sees me as the whore of Babylon and Lathom as the Tower of Babel. Major Farmer, remind me of the verse from the Book of Jeremiah that Bradshaw profaned recently when he was agitating in Wigan.'

Major Farmer, a strong Presbyterian spoke without raising his eyes from the table. 'Put yourselves in array against Babylon round about: all ye that bend the bow, shoot at her, spare no arrows: for she hath sinned against the Lord.'

When he had finished a silence descended on the room. Charlotte bit her lip and smoothed out the folds in the lap of her dress. I could not believe that anyone could take Bradshaw's words to be true, but his recourse to the Bible did unnerve me.

Charlotte got up and declared the council of war to be over. She retreated into her rooms. We remained skulking in the council chamber.

'Still thinking about capturing the mortar?' scoffed Major Farmer.

Before I could frame my reply a huge explosion roared into the chamber, knocking us back with its violence. Charlotte came running back from her rooms.

'Their shots have broken into my chamber, but I will not leave this house. I will not leave it while there is a single building left to cover my head.'

Her brave words stirred us from our shock. As one body we let out a cheer. Adapting the familiar cry of the Stanley household, I roared out, 'God save the Countess of Derby and the King.'

Everyone around me took up the cry and Charlotte stood in front of us. A single tear ran down her cheek and fell onto the string of pearls she wore around her neck. For a few seconds it glistened on top of one of the pearls. Then it disappeared, transient like her own fragility.

***

The next day was relatively calm and I spent most of the day thinking about how to capture the mortar. Louise was recovering well from her wounds, and had begun to attend on Charlotte again. We had not spoken any more about her fears for the children and I brooded in the silence.

In the afternoon I was watching from one of the towers when I saw Henry and Charles come out into the courtyard to play. Henry was pulling his drag behind him and I knew they were going to use it to slide down the sward at the foot of the Eagle Tower. This was one of their favourite games, and I let my mind wander as I observed them. Henry took the first turn, sitting on the drag and whooping with joy as he hurtled down the grassy bank. When he reached the bottom he stood up, and grinning all the while, he hauled the drag back up to the top of the slope where Charles was waiting expectantly.

Then a realization struck me. We could put the mortar onto a drag and pull it back into the castle. We had made several drags before the siege in order to move stone around the castle should we need to repair any damage to the walls. A few horses hitched up to the drag should be strong enough to move the mortar. I decided to go and put my idea to Major Farmer. I felt pleased with myself, remembering how he had baulked at my suggestion the day before.

I found him in the guardhouse where he was about to set off on an inspection of our sentries. I joined him and we climbed the staircase up to the battlements. At the top we paused to look for any signs of enemy activity.

'I have worked out how we can capture the mortar piece.'

To my surprise Major Farmer looked at me in anticipation, not scorn. 'Since you raised this idea yesterday I've thought of nothing else. Tell me your plan.'

I outlined my idea to him and he listened attentively as I spoke.

'No horses,' he said. 'They will be difficult to control if they are shot at. We will have to use men to pull the drag. I will ask the countess if we can use some of the house's servants.'

'Look,' he said pointing at the mortar piece. 'They have dug a ditch in front of it for defence. First of all we will need to fill it in.'

'And we will need ropes to lift the mortar onto the drag,' I replied.

'I'll make the preparations,' continued Major Farmer. 'We will make the sortie the day after next.'

***

The following day we were getting everything ready. Three drags were lined up in the courtyard, for we had decided to try to capture some of the other guns as well. We were organizing the men tasked with capturing the guns into three teams when we heard the sound a drummer from the enemy's siege works. I looked up to George who was in his usual place on the battlements.

'Messenger is coming,' he called down. 'Just one man.'

The messenger would have to pass through the courtyard on his way to deliver the message to Charlotte. 'Quick, get the drags out of sight,' I shouted to the three teams. 'And then make yourselves scarce.'

The men began to haul the drags out of the courtyard. I heard the beating of the drummer as he got closer to the castle. I ran into the guard tower. 'Keep him waiting at the gate, until we get those drags out of sight,' I ordered the sentries.

I was relieved we did not have to keep the messenger waiting long. I stood watching him through an arrow slit, as the drawbridge was lowered and the first portcullis was raised. The messenger came over the drawbridge and stopped in front of the second portcullis. I stared at him in disbelief. It was Bootle, my former friend who had disappeared from the household at the outbreak of the war. How could he dare show his face here? Bootle put the drum down on the ground and waited for the first portcullis to be dropped. A sentry began to wind out the rope and the portcullis descended slowly, trapping Bootle in the passage.

One of the sentries was about to raise the second portcullis, but I put up my hand to stop him.

'Let him stew there a bit,' I called over to the sentry, knowing Bootle would be able to hear me through the arrow slits.

I watched him shuffle from foot to foot, and he looked up apprehensively to where he knew my voice was coming from.

'What do you want here, turncoat?' I shouted down.

'I have been sent by Colonel Rigby with a final summons to the countess to surrender. I asked to deliver the message out of respect to my former friendships in this house. Rigby intends to raise the house to the ground if he captures it, and I wish to avoid senseless bloodshed here. I think there is more chance that the countess will believe me than a stranger.'

'Let him in,' I instructed the sentry.

I walked down to meet him. I had a strange feeling in the pit of my stomach. It was if someone I had known was dead, but here he was standing in front of me. He had the gall to smile as I approached.

'Well, Paul we meet again in strange circumstances. This war has turned father against son, brother against brother and friend against friend. Because of our friendship I asked to bring this message. I beg you to try to convince Charlotte to yield. Rigby has summoned her to surrender the house, goods, arms and everyone in it, and submit to the mercy of the Parliament. He demands an answer before two o'clock tomorrow.'

I had listened patiently to Bootle up to this point, but now I felt anger welling up inside me. 'For the sake of our friendship you say. But you are the man who deserted his master and his friends, sneaking away like a thief in the night. You've some nerve to come back here. For the sake of our former friendship, I hope Charlotte does not have you hung up at the gates.'

This seemed to unsettle him and he lapsed into silence as we made our way up to the council chamber.

Charlotte was expecting him. Someone else must have recognized Bootle and told her that he was the messenger. She stood at the far side of the council chamber, her mouth set in a grimace of defiance. Around her were grouped the captains of her garrison. Captain Kay stood with his hand on the pommel of his sword and glared at Bootle. I entered the chamber and went to stand by Major Farmer. I did not want to stay next to Bootle in case he thought I was offering him support.

Charlotte asked, 'Tell me why I shouldn't just throw your message straight onto the fire.'

'My Lady, it is out of concern for you and all who dwell in your household that I have come here to implore you to surrender up the house. Colonel Rigby is adamant, if you do not surrender, he will raise the castle. Here is his message,' he said as he handed it over to Charlotte.

Charlotte broke the seal and unfolded the paper. She read through it silently and as she did so a frown came over her face; her eyes becoming wide as she stared at the paper. Taking a deep breath, she looked up at Bootle and said to him.

'A due reward for your pains is to be hung at the gates, but you are nothing but the foolish instrument of a traitor. Carry this answer back to Rigby,' and she began to tear the paper up in front of him, letting the pieces drop onto the table. 'Tell that insolent rebel he shall not have my people, house nor goods. When our strength and provisions are spent, we shall have a fire more merciful than his. Then if God's providence does not prevent it, my goods and house will burn in his sight; and also myself, my children and my soldiers, rather than fall into his hands. This will seal our loyalty to my Lord, to the King and also to our religion.'

As she finished speaking she put her hands on the table to support herself. Her captains began to cheer and Captain Kay spoke out, 'We will die for his majesty and your honour. God save the King.'

Bootle had been looking down at the floor while Charlotte spoke. He now lifted up his face, his eyes glaring angrily. 'I will take this back as your answer. Rigby will still give you until 2 o'clock tomorrow to come to your senses. If you don't, then may God have mercy on your soul for what you are about to bring upon yourself.' As his words hung upon the air, he looked around the room as if searching for someone. When his eyes fell upon mine they narrowed in hostility, every ounce of our former friendship had gone. Then with a final glance at everyone in the room, he turned on his heel and left without a further word.

'What insolence!' exclaimed Charlotte. 'Well they shall have their answer before two o'clock tomorrow. Gentlemen, back to your posts.'

***

With my stomach churning as it always did before a fight, I made my way to the courtyard at four o'clock the next morning. I had not slept well and the crisp morning air cleared my head as I joined the group under Captain Chisenhall and Captain Fox, tasked with capturing the mortar. I had been given command of the servants who would lift the mortar onto the drag and bring it back into the castle. I passed among them giving encouraging words, patting a shoulder here and there; hoping my own fear was well hidden. Captain Rawsthorne was in charge of the sally gate on the eastern side of the castle, and as these gates were opened I looked up onto the battlements for the reassuring presence of George. He was not there. I looked around and saw him standing next to Captain Fox.

'George, what makes you leave your safe place on the walls?' I asked, smiling as I approached him.

'I thought it was time I did some proper fighting. If I can get close enough, we might be able to take care of Rigby,' he continued patting his fowling piece.

'Don't you take any unnecessary risks,' I replied. Then we were moving out through the gates. All talking stopped and we moved as quietly as we could, aiming to use the darkness to get close to the enemy. Every sound was accentuated as we groped through the darkness, scabbards clattering, pikes banging together, but nothing as loud as the drag as it was bumped across the ground, scraping over rocks and stones.

Captain Chisenhall turned towards me, 'Paul, the drag is too noisy. Wait here until you hear us engage battle, then come up.'

I nodded and raised my arm to signal to the men pulling the drag that we were to stop. We waited as our soldiers passed out of sight. I strained my eyes in the darkness, trying to follow their advance. It seemed like an hour, but was probably more like a quarter of an hour, before I heard musket shots coming from near the fort where the enemy had their great guns.

'Right lads, time to move,' I said and we set off towards the fighting. Day was dawning and in the early morning light I could see Captain Chisenhall's men storming the gun battery. They were having the best of it and soon I could see some of the enemy routing; those less fortunate had either been killed or captured. Now that we had taken these guns, we had no fear about being shot at when it was time to retreat back to the castle, and the men were talking excitedly about a job well done.

'The job's only half done,' barked Captain Chisenhall. 'Captain Fox, take your men and work your way along their trenches to the mortar. Mr. Morrow will follow you with the drag.'

We did not encounter a great deal of resistance as we made our way down their trenches. Most of the enemy had retreated to the mortar and were sheltering behind the ramparts that protected it. As we got close to the earthworks they began to fire muskets at us. Ours were useless against their defences.

'First two ranks of pike to the fore,' ordered Captain Fox. As a full length pike would be unwieldy in close quarter fighting, the men had cut their pikes down to half size. They came forward and on Captain Fox's command they rushed at the earthworks.

They slowed down as they got close for there was a trench to cross. Picking their way around stakes rising out of the ground, they made it to the ramparts. Their half pikes served them well and they began to get the upper hand. Still it was savage fighting and it took them a quarter of an hour to break in. Once our men got into the enemy's earthworks their morale broke and those who could fled.

Now we had to work quickly if we were to capture the mortar. In order to have an easier route to drag it away, I ordered the servants to fill part of the trench in with earth. While they were doing that, I took a couple of them up to the mortar with some ropes.

'Look, we can fasten the ropes to these rings,' I said pointing to a pair of large iron hoops on each side of the mortar's mounting. 'Thread it through to the other side and then we should be able to lift it onto the drag.'

Close by I could hear our men firing their muskets at the enemy who were trying to advance and recapture the mortar. I looked to see what was going on and saw George reloading. I smiled, grateful he was with us.

Some of our soldiers had also joined in to level the ditch and we were now able to bring the drag across to the mortar. We brought it in through the entrance at the rear of the earthworks which meant the enemy had a good view of it. Once they worked out what we were doing they would renew their attack, so we worked fast. I put half a dozen men on each side of the two ropes, and on my command they pulled with all their strength.

The mortar lifted, but only a couple of inches off the ground. 'Another man on each rope,' I shouted as I grabbed the end of the nearest rope. 'Lift again on my count of three.'

This time we raised the mortar high enough. 'Forward to the drag,' I rasped. We moved it towards the drag, our legs, arms and backs straining under the weight, and when we had it centred I called for it to be lowered. Everyone had been waiting for this command and with a great clatter the mortar was more dropped than lowered. We all straightened ourselves and I gratefully sucked in mouthfuls of the cool morning air.

'Give us some covering fire,' I called to Captain Fox as we prepared to move the drag. Once we had got outside the earthworks we were exposed, but fortunately the firing from our men was so intense that the return fire was nothing more than a trickle. I helped pull the drag until we had crossed the ditch; then I broke off to assess the situation with Captain Fox.

'If we can keep them at bay, your men will get the mortar back to the castle,' said Captain Fox, straining the upper half of his body to see what the enemy were doing.

'I want a go at capturing their other guns,' I shouted above the roar of battle, so our men would hear and take encouragement from me.

'You can take a score of my men. Do not dally for they will soon be upon you,' warned Captain Fox.

I looked around my new company and saw that George was one of them. 'Get the men advancing towards the other guns,' I said to him, pointing in the direction they were to take. 'I will bring up the men with the drags.'

To avoid the enemy's fire, George and his men jumped down into the trench and moved along this towards the guns. We could not follow him for the drags could not be manoeuvred along the trench, and we kept as low as we could as we worked our way along to the guns. One of our men was hit by a musket ball and as he crumpled forward we all stopped. I could see from the rapidly spreading red stain in the side of his shirt that it was a serious wound.

'You two,' I yelled at the two nearest men. 'Take him back to the castle.'

One of the drag teams was now down three men, so I called one over from the other team and also pitched in to help. We made it down to join George at the guns without any other casualties.

George was looking at the guns and scowling. 'They'll be a lot heavier than the mortar, and we've still got the ditch to fill in before we can move them. And look over there,' he said inclining his head. 'The rebels are getting ready to counter attack.'

I followed his gaze and could see a large group of Parliamentarians being drawn up into order by their officers. I assessed at least fifty pikemen in the centre with a score of musketeers on each flank. There was no way George would be able to hold them off with his twenty men.

'We'll spike the guns,' I shouted. We set to this task while George fanned his men out in front to shield us. George instructed half of his men to fire a volley. When they were halfway through reloading, he ordered the second group to fire.

My hands were shaking as I hammered a spike down the vent of one of the cannons. I knew every moment we stayed here put the men into more danger. We were exposed, out numbered and a long way from the castle.

I looked up to see the enemy had now advanced half way to us. George had his musket poised to fire, but seemed to be waiting to get a better shot at his target. Then he span backwards as a bullet ripped into his leg. He steadied himself and fired, bringing down one of their officers. Another bullet hit him in the chest and he slumped forward onto his knees. I could sense the men around him were about to flee. I ran over and leant him against my knee. 'Fall back,' I called out. Looking into the eyes of the first soldier as he ran past me I yelled,

'Help me with George.' But the man's eyes were staring wildly ahead and he did not stop.

I felt something warm and wet on my knee. It was George's blood, seeping out from his wound. I pulled my knee away and steadied him with my arms. George turned his head to look at me, and I felt guilty for worrying about a bit of blood on my clothes.

'It's bad,' George rasped, taking short panting breaths. 'I'll not make it back.'

'We'll carry you,' I replied, looking around for someone to help me.

'No,' he panted. 'They'll capture you and I'm a dead 'un anyway. Here take my fowling piece, I don't want them to get it. Load me a musket and give me your pistol. I'll hold them up while you get away.'

I tried to lift him, but he was heavy and did not try to get up. He grimaced in pain and I knew he was right; even if I got him back to the castle, there was nothing we could do for him.

One of the musketeers had stopped to help George. 'Is your musket loaded?' I asked.

'Primed and ready to fire,' he replied.

'Give it to George and your match. Put your musket rest into the ground over there and lean it back to George so he has support to fire.'

I did not know what to say to George as we prepared to leave him.

'Do me one thing,' he said. 'Parley with the rebels for my body. I do not want the Puritans to toss me into a ditch. I think her ladyship will find a corner in the castle for me. That will be fitting.'

'Yes, George I'll do that for you,' I replied, my words barely audible.

The rebels were getting closer. I stood up to leave and took the pistol out of my belt. I put it on the ground beside George. I looked into his eyes one more time. His eyes were already turning glassy, but he shrugged himself and returned my look.

Muskets were now being fired at us and I turned. The urge to stay with George was great, so I forced myself to run. Behind me I heard George fire the musket. I turned back to look and saw him raise the pistol as a group of rebels closed in on him. His shot took one of them down, but then they were all around him. I saw a sword raised high in the air, and as it came down I turned away and continued to run. I stumbled on, my eyes stinging wet, blurring my vision. I lifted a hand to my face and wiped my eyes dry.

I reached the safety of the castle courtyard and mingled with jubilant soldiers gathered around the mortar. They kicked the mortar with their feet and slapped each other on the back. Some stood on the mortar to the cheers of their fellows. It was as if they had spent the day drinking ale. I felt no joy and broke off from them. I wanted to see Charlotte and tell her of George's last request.

She was coming out of the Eagle Tower with Major Farmer to congratulate us. She almost skipped over to us, so great was her joy. 'So this is the beast that so troubled us,' she said smiling.

'Ay, this is it,' replied Major Farmer. 'Doesn't look so dangerous now, does it?' Turning towards me he continued, 'and here's the laddie we have to thank both for the plan to capture it and its execution. Three cheers for Paul,' he shouted.

The soldiers took up the cry and the first loud cheer rang out. Some of them decided to hoist me onto their shoulders, and they did so as the second cheer rang out. They paraded me about in front of the mortar and then dropped me to the ground, laughing and cheering all the time.

Still I could not share their joy. The image of George looking into my eyes when he told me to leave him, kept coming back to me. Then the harrowing picture of the sword coming down to take his life. I approached Charlotte and Major Farmer. They both looked jubilant as they watched the carousing soldiers.

Charlotte sensed I was distressed. 'Paul, what troubles you?' she asked.

'My Lady, George Brereton the gamekeeper was killed during the sortie. Although mortally wounded he continued to fire on the rebels until they overcame him.'

'That is sad news,' replied Charlotte. 'Does he have a family?'

'No wife my Lady, but I think he does have a mother near Blackburn. His dying wish was that his body would not be allowed to rot in a ditch, but we would recover it and give him a proper burial.'

'Then that is what we must do,' answered Charlotte. 'I will have to appeal to Rigby, though I doubt it is in his nature to be gracious in defeat.'

'We captured some prisoners,' I replied. 'Perhaps we can exchange them for George's body?'

'Yes, I suspect he will agree. Have a messenger sent out under a flag of truce. If we recover George's body, I will have Chaplain Rutter say a thanksgiving for the capture of this mortar. In fact Mr.

Rutter will be the best messenger. His religion might not be as puritan as Rigby's, but Rigby should listen to a man of God.'

Mr. Rutter was summoned and asked to go and bargain for George's body. Although he wore minister's surplice and stole over his cassock he took a white flag with him as well in case the rebels thought he was a fair target to shoot at.

We watched him from the battlements as he made his way over to the enemy lines. They watched him approach, but did not take any hostile action against him. After half an hour there was movement amongst the Parliamentarians and a group of them assembled near to where I had last seen George. A body was put onto a stretcher and a group of soldiers bore it up to the castle; Mr. Rutter walked solemnly in front of them. They stopped about one hundred yards from the walls and set down their load. Mr. Rutter continued on alone up to the gates. Keeping a careful eye on the rebels in case they tried to rush the gates we opened them to Mr. Rutter.

Once inside he quickly recounted what he had agreed with the rebels.

'We are to give up the five prisoners we took during the last engagement,' he revealed. 'In return they will give us George Brereton's body. '

'Agreed,' said Major Farmer. 'Have the prisoners brought here. Mr. Rutter please tell the rebels they are to bring George's body up to the gate and then retire. When we open the gates to retrieve his body we will allow the prisoners to go free. If they try to surprise us with an attack we'll shoot the prisoners before they get back to their friends.'

And that was how it was done. There was no attempt to attack us and we brought George's body back inside the gates. Mr. Rutter celebrated a thanksgiving to our Lord for our success in capturing the mortar. I also gave my own thanks to our Lord for the recovery of George's body. The next day we laid his body to rest in a small graveyard at the back of the Eagle Tower.

***

'Do you have to leave us again?' Louise asked anxiously the next morning.

I had spent most of the night worrying about breaking the news to her. 'You'll put yourself in danger again,' she continued, taking hold of my hand.

As I looked into her imploring eyes I felt conflicting loyalties. 'Yes, but we might be able to break the siege. If I go to James, and tell him how Rigby is a poor soldier and how we have captured the mortar, he might be able to persuade Lord Byron to provide a relief force.'

She let go of my hand and walked over to where my sword lay in its scabbard. She picked up the sword and walked back over to me. Holding it out to me she said, 'Go safely and remember you have a family here that need you. If you can break the siege then I will take the children to Knowsley. Charlotte has already given her permission.'

I took the sword from her and lay it down on the bed. I reached out my arms and held her tight to me. I took strength as she returned the embrace. We stood like that for a long while, and it took a great effort for me to eventually let go. We kissed and then reluctantly I took up my sword and buckled it on.

Moving towards the door I said, 'I will not be leaving until it is dark. First of all I have to memorize some messages to take to James. Then I will see the children and tell them I am going away again. The boys have got used to having me around and it will be a wrench to leave them and Alice.'

With a final look towards Louise I went out of the room. I sought out Charlotte and together with Major Farmer we agreed on the verbal message I was going to carry to James. My mind kept wandering back to Louise and the children. What if I was killed or captured? This time there was no sortie planned to cover my escape. I watched Charlotte's mouth moving, but I was no longer taking in the words.

'Paul, are you listening to us?' Charlotte's voice was growing louder and this brought me back with them.

'Eh, sorry, yes. Carry on.'

'We were saying, perhaps the best way to persuade Lord Byron to come to our aid is to appeal to his vanity. Tell him there is glory to be had here. If he comes with even a thousand men he will either scare Rigby away or defeat him soundly. Either way we will let him have the victory and the honour.'

I smiled as I saw some hope in this plan. 'I do not know the character of Lord Byron, so I cannot say if this will tempt him of out Chester,' I began cautiously. 'But the idea has merit and we must do all we can to press home our advantage.'

'Make sure you convince James to tell Lord Byron it will be his name that will be known as the saviour of Lathom,' insisted Charlotte.

Major Farmer interrupted her. 'But that honour is yours Madame, for the heroic defence you have conducted and for the way you have shamed Rigby.'

'I seek no glory for myself, just an end to the siege,' replied Charlotte looking down at the table as she did so. 'Gentlemen are we agreed? Paul is to tell James to offer the honour to Lord Byron if he will come and rout the rebels.'

'Aye, agreed,' muttered Major Farmer.

***

With my mood a little brighter, I went to see my children. First of all I sought out Alice who was with her mother learning how to embroider.

'How clever you are,' I said as I looked at the delicate red flower she was working on.

'It's for you Dada. Keep you safe.'

She put down the material when I asked her to come with me while we found her brothers. Henry and Charles were playing a game of chase with the other boys who lived in the castle. I called them over and asked them to walk with me.

Standing between them I put an arm around Henry on one side and Alice and Charles on the other. 'I have to go away again for a while,' I told them conspiratorially. 'I won't be gone for long, and if I succeed then you won't be prisoners here any longer.'

'But what if they capture you Dada?' asked Henry, stopping and turning to look into my eyes. Since the death of George he had been quiet and withdrawn. I had also noticed he had stopped playing games of fighting; he seemed to know now that war was not a game.

'They'll not capture me,' I said, hoping they would not see through my bluff. 'See you can't catch me,' I said as I let go of them and danced around, keeping just out of their reach as they rushed after me. Then I gathered them into me and held them there, thinking how they trusted me completely and believed all that I said. I prayed to the Lord that I did not let this trust down.

I caught sight of William Kay who was walking up to me, smiling as he approached.

'I've an idea how we can make your escape easier,' he began, his eyes alight with excitement. 'You know how we have fixed matches to trees and lit them in the night to vex the rebels?'

'Yes, I remember, but their guards are doubled now,' I replied. As I spoke the dread in my stomach came back.

'Exactly,' answered William, smiling again. 'But one of the horses of the castle troop is ill and no longer fit to be a trooper's mount. My idea is to fix the tapers to the horse, light them and then set it off towards the enemy lines. They'll think the devil has come amongst them,' he said laughing.

'And while they are praying for their mortal souls, I will be stealing out of another gate.'

The children looked up at me seeking more reassurance. 'This is how I will escape,' I said to them. 'It'll be all right, you'll see.' I said these words as much to steady myself as to reassure them, but thanks to William's plan my mood was a lot brighter.

That night I made the best preparations I could for my flight. I put on black breeches and a dark shirt with a black doublet on top. I blacked up my face with soot from the fire. In order to be nimble and silent as I moved, I limited myself to just a sword, two pistols and a waterskin.

Outside in the courtyard, William and several of his troopers were waiting. They had attached unlit matches to the horse's leatherwork and were waiting for me. Seeing me approach, William ordered one of the men to go over to a brazier and light a taper.

'Well Paul, are you ready?' said William. 'Get yourself over to the sally gate while we light these matches and set the horse out of the gatehouse. We'll give him such a kick, he won't stop galloping until he reaches their trenches.'

'I'll wait for the commotion and then I'll be on my way,' I replied.

'God speed,' answered William, patting me heartily on the back.

Thanks to the diversion created by the poor horse, I was able to slip away unobserved from Lathom. I walked for several miles in the darkness to one of the tenant farms and picked up a mount for my journey to Chester.

***

Our plan did not work. James and I spoke with Lord Byron and for a moment it seemed as if the temptation of honour and glory would move him to lead an army out of Chester. We watched the conflict in his face as he balanced between furthering his name and following the orders of the King.

'I won't disobey my orders,' he shouted as he banged his hand down on the table to end discussion. 'It grieves me I cannot go to the defence of a lady in her hour of need, but my first duty is to my King.'

So we kicked our heels in Chester. James sent out to his followers, asking them to come to him with men and any weapons they could bring. Some came, most stayed at home.

May blossom was on the trees, but it did not lift our mood. Then one day we received some heartening news. A rider had galloped into Chester that morning sent by Prince Rupert. Rupert was in Shrewsbury and making his way north. James was overjoyed.

'See, Rupert will come to aid his kin,' said James. 'I wrote to him a month ago and urged him to come north and capture Liverpool. It is a thorn in our side. From the shelter of its port, the Parliamentarian ships harass our supplies from Ireland.'

'When he enters Lancashire, the rebels may lift their siege of Lathom,' I replied, the optimism stirring in my voice.

'I hope not,' answered James with an ironic smile. 'I told him it would be easier to attack Liverpool while the rebel forces are engaged in the siege of Lathom.'

'In truth, Liverpool is the strategic prize, my lord, but Lathom has more value to us,' I said thinking of my family cooped up inside the castle.

'Well let us pray to our Lord that Rupert can capture both,' replied James. 'Come let us gather my men together and prepare to ride out. We'll go south to meet Rupert.'

It took the rest of the morning to get the earl's troop of sixty men ready to ride. James was impatient to get going, pacing up and down like a mouser waiting for scraps from the kitchen.

'Where can Rupert cross the Mersey? That will be the key to this,' he said to me. 'Warrington is in the hands of the rebels. Rupert will have to go east to find a crossing point.'

'East takes him away from Liverpool and Lathom,' I replied.

'I know, I know,' said James making a fist with one hand and banging it into the palm of the other. 'Have some scouts sent out to probe along the Mersey; to Lymm, to Cheadle, as far east as Stockport if necessary, but find me an unguarded crossing point for Rupert. We have to get across this river.'

***

The earl's troop of horse clattered out of the city gate, shod hooves sparking on the cobbles. Following James's order a small scouting party was sent north-east up to the Mersey. The rest of us rode south in search of Rupert.

We met up with Rupert's advance guard near to Nantwich, where Lord Byron's forces had suffered a defeat in January to Sir Thomas Fairfax. There was an awkward moment while we faced each other, uncertain whether we had encountered friend or foe. Once the commander of the advance guard was assured of our identity we were immediately taken to see Prince Rupert.

Passing through ranks of marching men we came into the heart of the army. James pointed to a group of officers on horseback and laughed when he saw one of Rupert's famous dogs cavorting around the horses. It was not difficult to see which of the well attired riders Rupert was. His companions matched him in the quality of their clothes, mounts and horse furniture, but Rupert's renowned good looks set him apart. His flowing dark locks and dark eyes were set off by his pale complexion. He was clean shaven which accentuated his slightly feminine mouth.

Rupert hailed us as we approached. 'Well met my Lord Derby. What news from Chester?'

'We hold much of Cheshire, but nothing in Lancashire apart from Lathom House and Greenhalgh Castle.'

'Yes, my noble cousin Charlotte defies the might of Parliament,' replied Rupert. 'Well we are come to your aid now. We'll clear any rebels who stand in our way and then we'll go to the relief of your lady.'

James straightened himself in his saddle. 'I am most grateful my Lord Prince. I have felt so powerless mulling around my house in Chester, deprived of even a hundred men by Lord Byron.'

'Come let us ride together,' answered Rupert. 'Tell me more about the state of Lord Byron's Irish troops. I am eager to know if they are good for a fight.'

Rupert's words took me back to my first encounter with him; when he was a boy at James's and Charlotte's wedding. I smiled to myself recalling how my legs had born the bruises from his wooden sword. Here he was fulfilling his destiny as a soldier.

'I cannot vouch for their quality,' James replied. 'They've not left Chester very often, and when they have they've been beaten.'

'Could the blame lie with the general and not with the men?' Rupert asked.

'I cannot say, for I have not been present at Lord Byron's battles,' answered James cautiously. Despite his family tie to Rupert I could see he did not want to be drawn into criticising the King's commander in Cheshire.

Rupert shifted uneasily in his saddle, realizing he had put James into a difficult position. 'Don't worry,' he smiled. 'There'll be plenty of fighting ahead. I'll lick them into shape.'

That night we rested in a small village; Rupert and his staff getting the best lodgings. We were invited to dine with him at the inn he had taken over. The place was chaotic when we entered; armed gentlemen of Rupert's retinue crammed into every space available. Serving girls were carrying food to the tables where Rupert and his officers sat; one received a smack on the backside as she passed too close to the carousing men. In the midst of this was Rupert's white poodle, scampering around and begging for food.

A space was made for us at Rupert's table, not without some resentful glances at me from some already there.

'My Lord Derby,' asked Rupert. 'I hear of great deeds at Lathom. Are the rumours true or just stories we tell to fuddle our enemies?'

'No, the stories are all true,' James replied. 'It is Paul here who must take the credit for a lot of the successes we have had at Lathom.'

I felt my cheeks flush crimson as the group's attention turned towards me.

'So it was you who captured the mortar from under the enemy's noses?' queried Rupert.

'I thought of the plan my Lord, but it was executed with the help of the captains and soldiers of the garrison. We all played our part,' I replied with sadness as I remembered that George's role had cost him his life.

'Just what I need around me,' Rupert commented. 'An intelligent captain who can show initiative. Not like the dolts I have here,' he said laughing.

The 'dolts' answered his teasing with laughter. Most of them were young like Rupert himself, still dazed by the glamour of war. This was a close group of men who would die for their prince. I hoped someone could bring this war to an end before too many of them had to answer death's call.

***

Two days later we were preparing to set out for Cheadle, probing for a crossing point. William Kay, the officer of James scouting troop was being escorted into camp.

'This man says he is one of your officers,' said the captain of the guard who had brought him in. Will you vouch for him, my Lord Derby?'

'Indeed I will,' James replied. 'William, have you found somewhere we can cross the Mersey,' asked James.

'We rode as far as Stockport before we found a bridge that was poorly guarded. The small party of rebels there are lax, and won't be able to stop us.'

'Excellent, we must go and tell Prince Rupert at once.'

Nobody barred our route to Stockport. Whether it was down to the ineptitude or over confidence of our enemy, he had not put out any pickets south of the river. On a warm, hazy May afternoon we came within sight of the church towers of the town. Rupert who was leading the advance guard drew rein and addressed us all. Instead of a note of caution, there was a hint of impatience as he spoke.

'We wait for the first regiments of foot to catch up with us; then we attack. Have a messenger sent back to tell the foot to make haste. Tonight we will rest in Stockport.'

Rupert's prophesy proved to be true. When the Parliamentarian defenders of the bridge saw the massed ranks of two foot regiments and Rupert's cavalry coming towards them, they fired a few musket shots in defiance and then retreated back through the town. Rupert spurred his horse to give chase. The excitement gripped the rest of us and we thundered across the open ground to the bridge. The narrowness of the bridge slowed us down, but as we reached the other side we broke out again. We were like a storm river momentarily held back by a dam, before cascading free.

We chased the fleeing men up narrow cobbled streets. Initially they turned to face us and tried to knock us from our horses with their muskets. A few succeeded and we rode in to rescue our fellows. Swords slashed down onto the foot soldiers and they began to panic. Some asked for quarter and it was given. Others continued to flee and these were often cut down from behind. The battle rage left me and I felt sick. Rupert's companions did not seem to grant anyone quarter. I knew many of them had served with him in the wars on the continent.

We had heard stories of terrible atrocities in these wars and there were rumours that similar infamy had occurred in other parts of the kingdom during this war. I remembered how we had burnt Lancaster two years earlier, but there we had allowed the people to flee, not butcher them in the streets.

My mouth was dry. I rested my horse and took a drink of small beer from my drinking skin. James rode over, followed by Sir Thomas Tyldesley who had rejoined us after serving with Prince Rupert.

'Another sad business, Paul,' said James shaking his head as he looked at the bodies of the Parliamentarian foot strewn around the streets.

'It is necessary, my lord,' interrupted Sir Thomas. 'These are the same rogues who would have your wife and your children cast out of Lathom, to await some dreadful fate.'

'I know that, but I can't stomach killing them when they have no chance to escape,' said James furrowing his brow.

'Steel yourself,' replied Sir Thomas. 'This is war, and to survive it you need to think like a common soldier does. They are the enemy and you need to kill them or you will be killed.' As he spoke, Sir Thomas wiped his bloody sword on a rag of cloth which he then discarded onto the ground. James and I had no such task to perform; our swords were as pristine as when we had drawn them as we charged towards the bridge. We sheathed our swords and rode on in silence.

Our next destination was Lathom and with Rupert pushing the foot hard, we made it there in two days. To our surprise Rigby has already lifted the siege, no doubt warned of Rupert's approach.

As we rode up to the castle, Rupert laughed. 'In the words of my uncle, the birds have flown,' he smirked. His companions all laughed out loud too. Sir Richard Crane the commander of Rupert's Lifeguard replied, 'we are the hunters who will bring them to ground, my lord.'

James and I were both overjoyed by the flight of the rebels. It meant that Charlotte, Louise and our children were safe. James spurred his horse into a gallop and I followed him. Our horses' hooves churned up a cloud of dust as we raced to the gate. We were recognized by the guard on the tower, and the drawbridge was lowered as we galloped up. We trotted across the bridge and into the inner courtyard, the clatter of our horses' shoes echoing around the walls.

Charlotte and Louise were there to meet us. James vaulted from his horse and ran to meet Charlotte. After the strains of the siege she now dropped her guard and raced towards him, her arms outstretched.

Gone was her usual austere demeanour and oblivious to all onlookers, she launched herself into his embrace and buried her face into his shoulder.

I also dismounted and embraced Louise. Although we had not been parted for long, I still felt a great sense of relief, for my wife and children were safe. I said a short silent prayer of thanks as I held Louise to me.

Hearing more horses come up behind, I turned to see Rupert and the gentlemen of his lifeguard ride up. He smiled warmly as he saw Charlotte and spoke to her.

'My cousin, I see I find you in good health and the vanquisher of our enemies.'

'We owe our freedom to you, Rupert,' she replied. 'When Rigby heard of your approach, he turned tail and fled.'

'Happy to fight a woman, eh Derby, but runs away when the men come back,' said Rupert laughing as he turned to James. 'Seems he picked the wrong woman.'

'Indeed he did,' said James who was looking proudly at his wife.

Chapter 24 – *Bolton 1644*

"Thy Servant hath found grace in Thy sight tthat hast magnified Thy mercy in saving of my life." Genesis xix. 19.

James wasn't expecting to suffer a defeat before Bolton as he had done the year before. I was riding with him and a small escort to Hoghton Tower where we expected to collect some reinforcements under the command of Roger Hoghton.

'They'll not be able to stop Rupert's army,' he said confidently. 'Once we capture Bolton we can turn and seize the rest of the county.'

'But what are Rupert's orders from the King,' I asked. 'Is it his plan to recapture Lancashire or does the King want Rupert to lead his army to the relief of York?'

James slowed his horse, allowing the other men to pass us and we dropped back out of earshot.

'Rupert confided in me that he has orders from the King to go to York,' said James in a whisper. 'But first he wants to settle our county and recapture Liverpool.'

'And he thinks he can do this while still obeying his uncle?' I replied. I must have sounded incredulous for James turned to me.

'Rupert appears rash and impetuous, but he is still a fine soldier. I have faith in his abilities and you should too. His presence in our county is bringing more men back to our banners. Look how many men came back yesterday, and today we will get even more from Hoghton.'

'True, we grow in strength all the time. May, God help us to use it to our advantage and defeat our enemies, and bring peace to the county.'

'Amen to that,' replied James.

***

May blossom was still on the trees and the morning was warm and light as Rupert drew up his army before Bolton. The town was protected by a crude mud wall and our men laughed at it as they marched towards the town. Perhaps realising his cavalry would be of no use inside Bolton, Rigby sent them out into the open to annoy their foot. I was riding with James and a troop of Rupert's horse. James saw the enemy cavalry advancing to our front and spurred his horse into a gallop, hardly waiting to see if anyone was following. I urged my mount to follow, and when I caught up with James I could see his face set resolute in grim determination. Released from months of inactivity and anxiety, he was going to take his frustration out on anyone who dared to stand in his way.

Rupert's horse were veterans and we broke the enemy line in the first charge. Some of them fell where we hit them, others deprived of their wits by our assault stood motionless on their horses. Others turned and fled back to the walls of the town. These we chased. James caught up with the cornet of the enemy troop and slew him, grabbing the colours from his hand as he fell. He whirled the enemy's standard above his head to show them they were beaten and to encourage our own men. Our foot came up to the mud wall which did not detain them for long. Soon they were opening the gates and men and beast both streamed into the town.

What happened next has been described as a massacre by those who suffered that day. It is true that many Parliamentarians died in the bitter fighting amongst the streets and gardens of the town, but for my part I did not see senseless and indiscriminate killing. Quarter was given to those who asked for it. What shames me to this day came towards the end of the fighting when we had control of most of Bolton, and were looking to see if Rigby was amongst the captured or slain.

The fury of the battle had died down; no longer could I hear the clash of steel on steel. Instead there were the groans of the dying and the wounded. Women had come out of their houses to look for loved ones and to tend to their injured. The sun, sinking in the sky was a ball of red anger. Word came that a group of the enemy had taken refuge in the church on the market square. They would only surrender to the Earl of Derby.

'Perhaps it's Rigby,' said James, and he set of brusquely towards the market place.

I followed him, my sword still drawn. As we entered the square I could see our soldiers ringing the church, but keeping a wary distance. James walked up to the church door and shouted, 'You asked for the Earl of Derby. Here I am. Are you ready to surrender?'

For several anxious heartbeats we all waited. I was worried that they had lured James here to take a shot at him. Then we heard the church door being opened. Three men came out into the porch. They put down their pistols and unbuckled their sword belts which they also lay on the ground. One of them walked towards us. I could not believe what I saw. It was Bootle.

His face bore a disarming smile and his hands were out in front of him, palms upward. 'James,' he implored, 'I want to surrender to you because you will protect me. Nobody has had fair treatment from Rupert's men.'

'And why should I treat you fair? Did you not desert my house? Did you not assault my wife in my home?' The emotion in James's voice rose higher as he spoke.

Bootle was edging closer all the time, his arms still out in supplication. 'I will bow down on my knees before you in surrender.' As he spoke he knelt down in front of James. He remained like that for a while. James dropped his guard and moved towards Bootle as if about to raise him up. Bootle's hand slipped down to his boot, and as he stood up I saw his intention.

'Knife,' I screamed in alarm. For a heartbeat everything seemed to stand still. Bootle sneered, his eyes narrowing as he stood up and raised the knife high, ready to strike. James's face was one of utter shock. Instinctively, I leapt forward and thrust my sword into Bootle's side. The knife fell with a clatter on the cobbles and Bootle turned his face sideways to me. I saw the life draining from his eyes as he looked at me in accusation. My hand could no longer grip the sword and it slipped out of my fingers onto the floor, like an echo of Bootle's own blade.

He fell to his knees and rasped, 'Paul, still the lap dog of the Stanley's?' Even in his dying moments his expression was one of hostility and loathing. An image of him as a smiling youth came to my mind, confusing my senses. I could not feel any hatred for him.

'Forgive me,' I said. I knelt down beside him and cradled his head on my lap. His eyes were glassy and staring at the sky. Despite all he had done, I hoped that he had found peace.

I looked up. James was by my side, his face one of compassion. 'Thank you Paul, you saved my life. I had not expected him to try to kill me.'

'Me neither,' I whispered in reply. 'His hatred of us killed the man we used to know.'

I still cradled Bootle's head, though he no longer needed comfort. 'Come away,' said James. 'He has gone now. May our Lord God show him mercy.' James beckoned some soldiers over to take Bootle's body away. Gently I lay his head down on the ground, the words of the burial rite coming to my mind, 'earth to earth, ashes to ashes, dust to dust'.

Chapter 25 – *Marston Moor 1644*

James and I rode up to Lathom, passing the remnants of the enemy siege camp. The discarded pots, broken weapons and empty trenches reminded me of the danger my family had been in. While we could not expect to be safe anywhere during a war, I was relieved that their forthcoming move to Knowsley would put them out of immediate danger.

Rupert had now turned his attention to Liverpool, the only port on the west coast in Parliament's hands. He did not want this stronghold left to his rear when he went to the relief of York. On his march to besiege the town, James and I had been excused by Rupert to go to Lathom and see to our families. The castle was to be put under the charge of one of Rupert's men. Rupert had insisted his cousin be spared any further hardship at Lathom and James had agreed. No one had yet thought to tell Charlotte, and I tried to imagine the conversation James would have with her.

I smiled inwardly to myself, recalling the campfire chatter of some of the soldiers the night before. James had stayed to talk to Rupert, and as I was coming back alone to my tent I overheard a group of James's men discussing the recent siege. One soldier had summed up Charlotte's talents perfectly with the words, 'while the master was away she pulled on his breeches and fought as well as he would have done'. The others all laughed. Before the war most of them were wary of her, perceiving her as dour and unfriendly. Now they all had a great affection for her and were proud to have fought with her.

I looked over at James. His face was furrowed; perhaps he was searching for the words to convince Charlotte to leave Lathom. He caught my eye and began to speak.

'Charlotte will not like these orders coming from Rupert. She still thinks of him as her young cousin, not as a man.'

'Tell her it will be safer for your children to be at Knowsley,' I replied. 'The rebels might be beaten around here for now, but they have plenty of armies in the rest of the country. Who knows what will happen? Knowsley is a house, not a castle. No one will expect Charlotte to defend it. If the rebels come back they might seize the estate, but surely they will allow her to live safely in her own home?'

'You are right. Now that I am here she will see it as her duty to protect the children, and Knowsley is the best place for that. Excellent, excellent,' he said clapping his horse's head and smiling.

***

I was awake long before Louise, sleeping peacefully at my side. We had a comfortable room in Knowsley, Charlotte having reluctantly accepted the fact that she should leave Lathom. My mind raced and I lay listening to the birds and thinking of the day ahead. Sleep had been easy the past few weeks, but yesterday James had received a summons to join Rupert at Skipton, where he had a rendezvous with the Northern horse under Lord Goring. Today we would set off to meet Rupert and ride with him to York. The men who had been besieging Liverpool were to rejoin the main army, and I expected to see Sir Thomas Tyldesley again.

York was like a honey pot to our enemies, and was now besieged by three armies. Lord Fairfax's Yorkshire army and the Scottish Covenanters had now been joined by the Earl of Manchester's army. The presence of this army in the Trent valley earlier in the month had prevented Rupert from marching to York from the south. He had said he had happily accepted this misfortune as it meant he had to come through Lancashire to approach York from the west. Louise stirred beside me and I reflected that this had given Rupert the opportunity to come to the aid of Charlotte.

***

Soldiers and horses crammed the road into Skipton. A woman following the army scolded two young boys for getting themselves wet in a ditch. An artilleryman swore as one of the wheels of his saker stuck fast in a muddy pot hole. He gripped the wheel and grunting he put his weight behind it, causing it to jerk forward. He pulled his hands away quickly and staggered. His companions laughed and he cursed again.

Up ahead I caught sight of Sir Tomas Tyldesley and I eased my way through the soldiers to pull up alongside him. He turned as he heard me approach.

'Ah, Paul it is good to see you again,' he said, his eyes smiling from beneath his hat.

'And it is good to see you as well,' I replied, realizing I had been a little apprehensive that he might not return from Liverpool. He had been the commander of the town when it had fallen into Parliament's hands the year before, and I suspected he might expose himself to unnecessary danger in order to win it back. 'So Liverpool held out for a good few weeks, then? I bet that chaffed at Rupert?'

'Oh, yes it did,' Sir Thomas replied. 'But, all's well now. We took the town in a night attack. Lord Molyneux's brother, Caryll led the assault and I was in the vanguard with him. The rebels must have decided they could no longer hold the town for they had already embarked on their ships when we entered.'

'So you took the town easily no doubt?' I enquired with a tone of hope in my voice.

'No, the townsfolk still opposed us and it was a street to street battle. Eventually we overcame them, but not before a lot of the traitors were lying in the gutters. We captured so many that the tower was not sufficient to hold them and we had to imprison the rest in a church.'

I tried to put the image of these prisoners out of my mind. I consoled myself with the thought that Louise and my children had been spared such a fate at Lathom. I had to think like Sir Thomas; there was no place for sympathy for our enemies.

'Rupert's gathering quite an army together,' Sir Thomas continued. 'I hope he will be strong enough to challenge the rebels in open battle. We've had years of skirmishing in the North. One big battle could settle it all.'

'Enough to end the war, do you think?' I replied.

Sir Thomas turned in his saddle and thought for a few moments before replying. 'I don't see the King parleying with the rebels until he has defeated them. He does not want to accept their terms. Defeating these three rebel armies will give him a good position to impose his will. We must do all we can to bring about the victory, that could end this war.'

And what if we were defeated, I thought to myself. I could not see the King surrendering. He was too intractable for that. No if we lost, the war would continue as long as the King could gather enough men together for an army. We had to win to restore peace to the kingdom.

Sir Thomas interrupted my thoughts. 'Rupert is looking for volunteers to lead scouting parties and find an unguarded route into York. I'm going to lead one. Do you want to join me?'

'Yes, I do. It will be good to be doing something again. Lets' hope we can bring the enemy to battle and defeat them.'

***

We rode slowly and quietly, approaching Boroughbridge from the shelter of a wood. Through the trees we could see the reflection of the sun on the river. More importantly we could not see any reflection from breastplate or helmet that would give away the presence of the enemy. Sir Thomas surveyed the scene in front of us with obvious delight.

'Looks like we've found our way across the Ure. Paul, take ten men and cross the bridge. Ride to the far side and then report back telling me what you've seen. Keep a watchful eye open for the rebels. I can't believe there aren't any hereabouts.'

We clattered across the bridge, the noise of our horses panicking a pair of swans who took to the air, whooping out their alarm. Something else had already warned the villagers, for the road past their houses was deserted. I reflected on our good fortune so far, and hoped there weren't any enemy pickets out in the woods on the far bank watching us. We had left Skipton several days before and come by way of Harrogate. At Knaresborough we had found the enemy who blocked our route to York. After some probing of their lines and interrogation of prisoners, Rupert believed the enemy had deployed an army on Marston Moor, barring the western route into the city. He put out a screen of cavalry under Lord Byron and turned the rest of the army north, making rapidly for Boroughbridge. James, riding with Lord Molyneux and the horse he had furnished at the start of the war, had declared this to be an inspired move by Rupert as it would allow him to outflank the rebels.

What made Rupert's plan hazardous was the need to cross three rivers before we could get to York. All the rebels needed to do was to defend one of the bridges in strength and our plan risked being undone.

I put my arm up to stop the men once we had reached the edge of the wood on the far bank. In the distance a group of men on foot with a couple of wagons was moving away from us in the direction of York.

'A foraging party, no doubt,' said the sergeant of the troop next to me. He was a portly man, fond of food and ale, and always keen to lead our own men out foraging.

'Ride back and tell Sir Thomas that it is safe to come over, and if he's a mind we can have a free supper,' I instructed the sergeant.

We rested our horses and waited, watching the enemy amble away in the distance. Waiting for Sir Thomas to ride up, I formed a plan in my mind to capture the supply wagons, Once he was alongside me I outlined my idea.

'The rebels are on foot, so won't be able to outrun us. See this hedgerow on our right?' I asked Sir Thomas. He nodded, listening intently. 'If we send a column the other side of the hedge, they can ride alongside it until the bend in the road.' Sir Thomas followed my arm as I indicated the turn in the road. 'They should be at the bend before the rebels. We ride up behind and close the trap.'

'Your plan has merit,' replied Sir Thomas. 'You can lead the flanking column. I will bring up the rest of the horse.'

I ordered a couple of the men to swing open the wooden gate into the field and we passed through two by two. Seeing the men bunched up I thought it a good opportunity to remind them how to keep close order in battle. I called out, 'remember lads, boot to boot like this when we charge.'

We cantered through the field, the horses' hooves drumming on the dry earth. We were about two hundred yards away when the enemy heard us. They began to form up, taking shelter behind the wagons. But then they must have seen Sir Thomas bringing up the rest of the regiment, and they could see it was an uneven fight.

I stopped the men about one hundred yards short and then sent two troops of them behind the enemy. A man called out from beyond the wagons, 'Parley; we do not want to fight.' He had a harsh Scottish accent.

'Put down your weapons and come out where we can see you. You won't be harmed,' I replied. I took a troop forward up to the hedge, bordering the road. We drew rein when we reached a gate.

I could hear the enemy soldiers disputing what to do, but then a few of them walked out from behind the wagons. To a man they wore grey cloth uniforms; a couple had blue bonnets and one had an old cabasset helmet. I considered they would be useful for intelligence and instructed a couple of the men to search them for arms and bind their hands.

Seeing that their fellows were not being cut down, the others tentatively came out from behind their shelter. I approached their leader, a barrel of a man, his broad shoulders accentuated by a gorget around his neck. He looked at me with fierce, proud eyes, fingering a thick beard with one hand, the other holding the pommel of a broadsword still fastened to his belt.

'Arthur Baillie, of the Buccleuth regiment of foot. I ask for quarter and for fair treatment for all of my men. I will surrender my sword as a sign of my good faith.'

'Quarter is granted,' I replied.

The Scotsman unbuckled his broadsword and walked towards me with it resting flat in the palms of his hands. 'To whom do I give my sword?' he asked.

'I am Paul Morrow, secretary to the Earl of Derby, and serving in Sir Thomas Tyldesley's regiment of horse.'

'You have surprised us in seems. We had heard that Rupert's thunderbolt of terror was approaching from Knaresborough. He truly moves like the devil if he now comes at us from the north.'

'We are just a scouting party,' I lied. I did not want him to know that we were the vanguard of Rupert's army. He might be a prisoner now, but he was intelligently probing for information that would be useful if he could escape.

Our conversation was interrupted as Sir Thomas rode up.

'Well done, Paul. Prisoners and some good forage by the look of it. We might be tired tonight, but at least we'll eat well. On now, to the river Swale. Let's hope we don't find more of these Scots there.'

Again we were fortunate. The speed of Rupert's march had caught the enemy completely off guard. It seemed they waited transfixed on Marston Moor for his army to appear from behind Lord Byron's horse. We reached the river Swale at Thornton Bridge and again the river crossing was unguarded.

'I'm going to take the regiment across and seize that ridge over there,' said Sir Thomas pointing to the high ground on the far side of the river. 'Take ten men and ride back hard to Prince Rupert and tell him we have secured the crossing.'

Ride hard we did. Rupert's ambitious plan was to be close to York by nightfall. We had already covered about fifteen miles on horseback. The foot, encumbered with their weapons and baggage had a hard day's marching and it was important they knew where they could cross the Swale without delay.

We passed through the dragoons who were covering the advance of Rupert's army, our red bands around our hats marking us out as friend not foe. As I rode up to Prince Rupert I could see him in conversation with James and Lord Goring. James saw me and signalled to come over.

'What news from Sir Thomas?' Rupert asked. 'Good news, my lord. He has led the vanguard through Boroughbridge and across the Swale. He now waits on the far bank guarding the passage.'

Rupert smiled. 'Two of the three rivers taken. All we need to do now is secure a crossing across the Ouse and we can reach York. Ride back to Sir Thomas with new orders. Once the foot begin crossing the Swale he is to continue on, looking for a crossing place on the Ouse. We shall rest the foot tonight within striking distance of York.'

On the ride back to Sir Thomas I went over the capture of the Scottish foraging party in my mind. Something was wrong about the scene, but I could not work out what was out of place. Then it struck me. I had heard a couple of the wagon drivers speak and they had sounded like Yorkshire men. Now they might have been from Lord Fairfax's army, but perhaps they were neuters pressed into service by the Scots.

Sir Thomas was still on the ridge when I got back. The first regiment of foot had crossed the bridge and was moving up to join Sir Thomas's horse. One or two of the young recruits were struggling with their shouldered pikes as they moved up the slope. I reflected that most of the Lancashire men were raw and they had needed the three days drilling and weapons practice Rupert had given them at Skipton. I could see Sir Thomas was questioning the Scottish captain, but by the stern look on his face he wasn't getting any answers.

'Sir Thomas, where are the other prisoners?' I asked.

'Over there,' he replied indicating where prisoners sat. They had split into two groups, the larger group all wearing the same grey uniform with bandoliers strung across their chests, the smaller group sitting apart and looking like farm labourers not soldiers.

I walked over to the labourers. They looked apprehensive; the soldiers just looked resigned.

'Are you good subjects of his Majesty, lads?' I asked as I approached them.

They eyed me warily. 'It's all right, we're not going to torture you,' I said. One of two of the soldiers shifted uneasily as I said this.

'Perhaps if you see an image of your King, you will affirm your allegiance,' I said as I took some coins out of my money pouch. 'Look a sovereign with the head of King Charles on one side. It's yours if you can tell me where we can cross the Ouse.'

One or two of them now eyed me with greed. 'For two sovereigns I can take you to a crossing place,' said one of them.

'Are there any soldiers there?' I asked.

'Yes, some dragoons from East Anglia, lording it over the local people. You'll do us a favour if you chase them away.'

Sir Thomas appeared behind me. 'Right, order the regiment to move again,' he shouted. 'Get this man a horse, and tie a rope to its saddle. We don't want him trying to escape.'

On the ride the man was reluctant to speak to us, no doubt fearing if he revealed what he knew too easily then he would not get his reward.

'Tell us when we are close and I will send you to the rear out of harm's way,' I said to him. 'I do not expect you to fight for us.'

'Will I still get my money?' he asked. 'The land around York has been striped bare, first by Newcastle's men and then by the Parliament, and now by the Scots. This money will help feed my family through the coming winter.'

'You'll get your money, as long as you play us true,' I replied, feeling sorry for the man. 'Now, tell me where are you leading us?'

'To Poppleton,' he answered. 'They have a bridge of boats strung out across the river.'

'And is it well guarded?' I queried.

'Some dragoons as I said before. They have some sentries out, but most of them are camped on the far side of the Ouse.'

'How many are there on this side of the river,' Sir Thomas probed.

'I'm a country man, not a soldier,' he replied. 'But I don't think I saw more than three men when we passed by this morning.'

'We should be able to rush them,' said Sir Thomas. 'Paul, we'll lead the charge.'

***

We were hidden from sight in a small wood a few hundred yards short of the river. I could see the Ouse up ahead and stretching across it was the strangest bridge I'd ever seen. A row of boats lashed together with rough hewn planking running over the top. I was with Sir Thomas in a small scouting party, for he did not want to give away our presence by bringing up the whole regiment. My horse, grateful for this lull tried to nuzzle on the ground for some grass, but I pulled his head back and he snorted in disgust.

'Just as he said,' whispered Sir Thomas. 'A small group on this side, a few more on the far bank, and the rest of the dragoons encamped over there up on the ridge. The bridge won't support more than half a dozen horses at a time, so we're going to do this carefully.' Beckoning one of the sergeants over he continued, 'ride back to Captain Hoghton and tell him to watch for us to cross to the other side. Once he sees us there he is to bring the whole regiment across six at a time, and await further orders. The rest of you, remove your hat bands. Let's not make it too easy for them to identify us as the King's men.' As the man turned to leave, Sir Thomas repeated, 'remember no more than six at a time.'

The sergeant rode off and we prepared to charge. With half the troop, I was to deal with the men at this side of the bridge, while Sir Thomas was to continue to the other side and secure it.

We drew our swords, edging our horses to the edge of the wood and then broke cover. Once in the open we spurred our horses on and by the time the dragoons saw us we were bearing down on them at a gallop. Two of them got a shot off from their firelocks while a third rang on a bell hung up on a pole. He rattled the bell for all he was worth. The dull, metallic clanging toned out, rousing the men on the far bank. To my left one of the men had been hit by a musket ball, and he slumped back in the saddle.

We were upon them before they could reload. One of the dragoons went down, slashed on the side of the neck by one of our troopers as he passed. I was aiming for the dragoon who tolled the bell. As I went by one of the sentries, he struck out at me with his firelock and it caught me on the side. It rattled off my backplate, winding me.

The third dragoon had ceased tolling the bell and had armed himself with a half pike which he thrust out at me to meet my charge. With spur from one foot and a tug on the reins, I steered my horse around him and thrust back and down with my sword as I passed him. I felt contact and slowed my horse in order to pull him around. I turned to see the dragoon pulling out a pistol, but then he was floored as one of our troopers beat him on the arse with the flat of his blade as he rode past.

He dropped the pistol and remained on his knees as I rode back. I noticed a gash on the side of his arm where I had caught him with my sword.

'Surrender?' I asked as I approached.

'Aye, I do,' he replied as he hugged his wounded arm. A couple of the troopers seized him. I looked over to the far side to see how Sir Thomas fared.

He had dealt with the dragoons over there, and the second and third ranks of his half troop had now crossed over. I heard the rest of the regiment approaching behind me and rested as the first rank passed over the bridge. Over on the ridge there were signs of frantic activity as the rebel dragoons stirred themselves. A few isolated musket shots were aimed at our men on the far bank, but then their sergeants barked out orders, quietening their fire.

Sir Thomas was getting the men to spread out in two lines on the far bank and forming them up ready for a charge. The dragoons were mounting their small, shabby ponies. Dragoons of any army weren't expected to fight as cavalry. They were little more than musketeers mounted on beasts the rest of the army had rejected. The only advantage the enemy had was that they had the higher ground on top of the ridge. We would have to charge up the slope, slowing us down. If they had a good commander he would use the slope and charge down it just as we were beginning to ease up.

We were now able to cross the river and I led my men across. I instructed them to take their place in the second line and I rode up to Sir Thomas to be with him in the front rank when we charged. Sir Thomas was reloading a pistol as I approached. He spat the ball into the barrel and then rammed home the wadding to keep it in place. After putting the pistol into the saddle holster, he drew his sword and held it high above his head.

'Are we ready lads?' he shouted, looking along the line for confirmation. One or two of the troopers nodded and I pulled the face bar of my lobster tail helmet down in front of my nose.

'Forward,' ordered Sir Thomas as he brought his sword down to signal the advance.

We trotted, and then cantered towards the enemy who remained immobile on the higher ground. At the base of the ridge, Sir Thomas issued the order to charge. The excitement spread along the line, and my horse tossed his head as he was allowed to gallop. Still the enemy waited. One or two pistol shots rang out from above, but too few to do any real damage. And still the enemy waited. Like King Canute on the beach they waited as the tide came towards them. But we would do more than wet their feet. We would break them and scatter them to the four winds. Too late the dragoon commander issued the order to counter charge. We hit them as they had started their horses forward. We hit them hard.

I slashed out at the enemy immediately in front of me. I no longer looked into their faces, but watched their sword arms. Having the advantage of the higher ground, he sliced down at me. I parried, and then I was past him and into their second rank. My next opponent seemed motionless and I cut a deep gash into his left arm as I passed. Then the charge was spent and I turned my horse back into the confused mêlée. I was alongside a dragoon, our mounts jostling shoulder to shoulder as we fought. Our swords were locked; neither of us could get an advantage. With my other arm I pushed his sword arm away and quickly slashed down with my sword, catching him on the thigh, cutting through the buffcoat to the flesh below. In reply he thrust down at my head. The blow hit the side of my helmet with a great clang and my head spun. I aimed another blow which crashed onto the pommel of his sword and then passed down to his wrist, biting through the glove. He dropped his sword and spurred his horse to get away. With my head still ringing I let him go and took a look around me.

Our charge had broken them. One or two still fought on, but most were dead, wounded or had fled. I rode over to Sir Thomas who was also surveying the carnage.

'The bridge is won,' he said.

I nodded and instantly regretted it, for the pain raced to the base of my neck. Tentatively I removed my lobster pot and looked at the dent in the side.

'You'll live,' laughed Sir Thomas. 'I can't send you back with a message to Prince Rupert. You'll probably pass out on the way. Wet a cloth and hold it on the base of your neck; that'll help.'

***

We were to spend the night in the dragoons' camp on the ridge, defending this crossing to York. The rest of the army had reached the Forest of Galtres, where they settled down, tired after a long day's march. But before we could rest, Sir Thomas and I were to accompany James, Prince Rupert and his senior officers to meet with Newcastle to discuss plans.

Except Rupert did not want to meet with Newcastle.

'I hold a commission from my uncle that is superior to the one held by Newcastle,' said Rupert as he conferred with his officers in the kitchen of a farm house. He paced the room, nervous energy betrayed by the clenching and unclenching of his fists behind his back. 'I won't ride into York to attend upon Newcastle. He can come to me. If he won't, I will send him my orders.'

Lord Goring was silent. Although he was the commander of the horse of Newcastle's Northern Army, he was also a fiery cavalry commander in the mould of Rupert. It seemed he did not want to give any counsel to Rupert.

James broke the silence. 'Your Highness, I will go and speak with Newcastle. Although in the last few years he has left my counties vulnerable to our enemies, your help has restored our fortunes in Lancashire. I will ask him to come and confer with you.'

'James, how fortunate you and Prince Rupert should come to my aid,' said Newcastle with a courtier's smile, his voice as sweet as honey.

'The irony is not lost on me,' replied James abruptly.

'But where is the Prince,' Newcastle continued, fingering the red whiskers of his beard to a point as he spoke. 'I had hoped to discuss strategy with him and Lord Eythin here.' Lord Eythin, Newcastle's councillor in war, a professional soldier with experience in the European wars, looked up from some papers he had been reading.

'His Highness is still attending to his army,' replied James. 'He has the infantry in the Forest of Galtres and has summoned Lord Byron to rejoin us from Knaresborough. At this moment he is sending out scouts to check that the enemy is still on Marston Moor.'

'And what of Rupert's plans after that? Does he intend to offer battle, or wait on the actions of the enemy?' enquired Lord Eythin.

'I confess I do not know if he wants to offer battle,' answered James. 'His immediate concern is to confer with you to learn the state of your army.'

'My army has endured a siege of three months,' replied Newcastle. 'The men complain of want of food and of pay. They are in a mind to plunder the enemy's siege line now Rupert has drawn them away.'

'Will you come and meet with the Prince?' asked James.

'What is the hurry?' Newcastle retorted. 'I will send him a deputation to offer all the necessary formalities that the Prince is due.'

'But what if the enemy prepare to attack?' James interjected, gripping the edge of the table. 'Will you bring your men out of the city to fight?'

Newcastle studied his fingernails a few moments before replying. 'I don't think the enemy want to fight. Rupert has broken their siege. Fairfax will be worried that Rupert will strike into the West Riding.'

'What about the Scots?' asked James.

'Leven is a prudent commander,' said Lord Eythin. 'I know him from the wars in Europe. Rupert has out manoeuvred him. He will want to secure his line of march back to Scotland. He won't want to fight.'

'I say we give the rebels a few days to disagree amongst themselves and disperse. We can then unite our armies and attack them one by one,' said Newcastle. 'Here take this letter back to Prince Rupert.'

I wondered if Newcastle's reluctance to meet with Rupert was due to the fact that if he spoke with him he would feel bound to accept the Prince's orders. If he avoided him, he had more chance to retain an independent command. I could sense the meeting was coming to an end. Newcastle was sending for men to go and convey his thanks to Rupert. James took his leave and we returned to Rupert.

***

'Intolerable,' spat Rupert. 'He shirks his duty to the King and his responsibility to fight.'

'Newcastle is expecting about three thousand men under Colonel Clavering to join him in a few days,' answered James.

'My uncle is hard pressed in the South,' stressed Rupert. 'He faces two armies alone. We do not have the leisure to wait to see if these three armies will go their separate ways. Besides, Meldrum is bringing more rebel forces from Manchester, so we need to strike now.'

'Here is a letter from the marquis,' said James.

'A letter, a letter,' echoed Rupert. 'I have one from the King which orders me to defeat these rebel armies. What more is there to be said?' retorted the Prince. He took the letter and read it through. His revelation about the King's letter had stunned us.

'Ah,' he said looking up from the letter. 'The marquis will be obedient to my commands,' he revealed, looking around the room at us all. 'Tomorrow we shall seek the enemy and offer battle. Lord

Goring, take my order to Newcastle. He is to have his foot ready to march at four o'clock in the morning. He is to meet me on Marston Moor. Tomorrow, with God's help we will defeat these rebels.'

***

'Where the devil are they?' Rupert asked as he paced up and down. It was after nine o'clock and his army was deploying onto Marston Moor. There was still no sight of Newcastle and his men.

I looked over to the right wing of our army, knowing Sir Thomas and Lord Molyneux were deploying the Lancashire horse behind Lord Byron's cavalry. James had been offered the command of these regiments he had raised, but he declined saying he had no experience of leading such a large body, and that he preferred to fight alongside the Prince. I wondered if he followed the lead of Newcastle, who left the soldiering to his professional generals, preferring instead to command a small group of gentlemen volunteers. We were in the centre with the foot, Rupert's lifeguard and the horse of Lord Widdrington. Over to our left, Lord Goring was deploying the Northern Horse.

I looked back over to York. The Minster was just visible in the distance, but there was no sign of Newcastle's Whitecoats and the other troops of the garrison. Rupert needed the four thousand infantry to join him before he could offer battle. But Rupert's scouts had reported that the enemy was marching away and their retreat was being covered by their horse. Maybe there would be no battle.

Again I looked over towards York. 'Look,' I shouted. 'A carriage and some gentlemen on horse.'

We watched as they rode closer. It was a grandee's coach, painted in livery and I assumed it to be Newcastle's. I wondered if this was the same carriage that Newcastle had loaned to Lady Fairfax after his soldiers had captured her the previous year, allowing her to return home to her husband.

Once the coach had drawn level with us we waited for Newcastle to alight. A servant opened the door and down stepped the marquis. I was surprised to see he was not in armour, but sported ordinary clothes.

Rupert too noticed Newcastle's attire, but did not betray any disappointment when he spoke. 'My Lord, I wish you had come sooner with your forces, but I hope we shall yet have a glorious day.'

'Your Highness,' said Newcastle with a shallow bow. 'I am afraid my men are tardy. Some regiments would not march until we had settled their arrears of pay. Those that did march early have stopped to plunder the enemy siege lines.'

'How soon will they be here?' Rupert asked.

'I really cannot say.'

'You can't say, sir,' retorted Rupert. 'I mean to engage the enemy now, but I can't do it without your foot.'

Lord Eythin who was part of the escort spoke out. 'Sir, your forwardness lost us the day in Germany, where you were taken prisoner. Perhaps we should me more cautious today.'

The Prince looked about to scold Lord Eythin, but instead bit his lip and took a deep breath.

Newcastle stumbled into the silence, 'Your Highness, I advocate we wait. I suspect the enemy will divide if we leave them be. Combined they possess more men than we do, but if we let them divide they will weaken.'

'I have a letter from his Majesty with an absolute command to fight the enemy, which according to my duty I am honour bound to perform.' Rupert spoke with a calm but steely tone, challenging any man there to dispute his order.

It was quiet again for a few moments. Then Newcastle again spoke into the silence. 'I am ready and willing to obey his Majesty in all things and will accept this command as if his Majesty were here himself.'

'But my lord,' said Lord Eythin. 'I thought we had resolved to wait for the arrival of Clavering's men before giving battle?'

'I will not shun a fight,' replied Newcastle. 'I have no other ambition than to live and die a loyal subject to his Majesty. Lord Eythin, return immediately to York and hurry the foot along. If you can get them here soon enough, we will have a battle today.'

Lord Eythin flashed a look at Rupert, but said nothing. He turned and left the room.

***

But as the day wore on there was still no sign of Newcastle's Whitecoats. On the ridge above us we could see more and more enemy colours as regiment after regiment arrived back. Their colours bobbed up and down as the regiments were manoeuvred around into a battle order. Rupert was becoming agitated as he sensed his chance to attack the rebels was slipping away. Our nervousness infected our horses, and the beasts fretted and whinnied as we waited. I was sent by James to check on the deployment of Lord Molyneux's horse and was grateful as it gave me something to do.

Lord Molyneux was in conversation with Sir Thomas Tyldesley as I approached.

'How do you like it, Paul?' Sir Thomas asked, nodding in the direction of the enemy forces arranged on the ridge opposite us. 'You'd better be ready for a fight as it looks like we're going to get one.'

As he spoke artillery boomed out from the enemy lines. Some of our guns answered and soon smoke was billowing around, covering the moor like a sea har.

'Who's that fool out there?' asked Lord Molyneux, indicating a lone rider who was out in front of the enemy, calling them to fight him in a duel.

'I don't know, but if he's not careful one of those puritans will take his head off,' replied Sir Thomas.

The lone rider continued his progress up and down their lines, but nobody came forward and he turned and trotted back to rejoin us.

More enemy cannon boomed out and one ball struck the rider. It knocked him off his horse which scattered in panic. A couple of our troopers rode out to him. They dismounted and tried to lift him from the ground. I could see his body was limp and one of the troopers shook his head. They began to drag him back towards us. Stopping in front of us they removed his helmet.

My stomach churned. Instantly I recognized him. 'It's Roger Hoghton,' I blurted out.

'May God have mercy on his soul,' replied Lord Molyneux, of a similar age to the dead man. 'Take his body to York. Others might die and lie on this field today, but he at least will have a proper burial.'

I rode back to inform James of Roger's death, feeling numb. I recalled Roger's part in the capture of Preston the year before and remembered how his sense for adventure was always getting him into trouble as a boy. He died true to his spirit. I seemed to have lost the awareness of my surroundings, and without knowing how I had got there, I found myself back at Rupert's headquarters. I came out of my musing, realizing it had begun to rain. Rain was the scourge of the musketeers for it damped their powder and could put out their matches. If they were not able to fire their weapons they were little better than clubmen. Gradually the sound of the cannon began to die down as the artillerymen looked to keep their own powder dry.

After I had told James of Roger's death, the two of us sat silent for a few moments.

'Do you hear that?' James asked.

I listened and thought I was dreaming for I could hear psalms being sung. 'Yes,' I replied. 'Where is it coming from?' I asked.

'It is coming from up there,' answered James. 'It seems our enemy are calling upon the support of the Lord.'

It was an eerie sound, so incongruous on a battlefield.

'I've heard of their zeal,' said James. 'The rumours are that the Puritan commander of their cavalry, Cromwell has instilled a deep religious fire in their bellies. They fight like the Israelites, believing they have God on their side.'

As we listened to the psalms we were aware of another sound, gradually getting louder. It was the sound of drums beating out the march. Coming from the direction of York, it could only mean one thing.

'It's the Lambs,' shouted an officer who had just ridden up. The Lambs was a name Newcastle affectionately gave his soldiers on account of the unbleached linen they wore as a uniform.

'Is it still Rupert's intention to attack today?' I asked James.

'No,' he replied. 'Now that all the enemy's regiments have returned, Rupert can see that he is outnumbered. He tells me he is staying here to invite the enemy to attack us. Look how he has strengthened his position with musketeers alongside the horse to fire upon the enemy as they approach. That is why he has deployed his own foot regiment and Byron's foot in a forward position on the left flank of Byron's horse. They are there to fire a volley into the side of the enemy cavalry and so disrupt their charge.'

'What if they don't attack us?' I asked.

'It's likely they've used up the water and the local forage as they have already spent a day on this moor. They'll either have to attack or retreat to find new provisions.'

'And if they retreat then Rupert will attack them?' I asked, half sensing the answer.

'Yes, he will go after them if they retreat and hope to catch them unprepared.'

***

But it was us who were caught unprepared. Towards six of the clock I accompanied James who had been called to another council with Rupert.

Newcastle and Lord Eythin were already there, seated on some stools. 'It seems the foe will not attack today,' said Rupert. 'Gentlemen, sup with me and we will agree our plans for tomorrow.'

Plans were duly drawn up for the army to spend the night on the moor and await the enemy's movements. It was Rupert's fear the enemy would slip away in the night, so orders were issued to both wings of horse to each keep a regiment saddled and ready throughout the night. The rest of the army was ordered to stand down.

All across the moor, weary pikemen put down their weapons and prepared for their supper. Boys were sent to fetch water and firewood, and happily ran off on this task, grateful that some form of normality had returned. The cavalry dismounted from their horses and sat down, bridles in their hands. Pipes were lit as the men chatted and joked amongst themselves, glad to have been spared from battle.

At the end of our meal, Newcastle who had not eaten much rose to his feet.

'I'll return to my carriage to smoke my pipe,' he said. 'Send for me if the enemy move away. I shall enjoy the hunt.'

'Gladly,' replied Rupert, laughing. 'I hope we shall have a good day's sport tomorrow.' With a hound's excitement for a hunt, Rupert's dog, Boy bounced up and looked at his master expectantly. 'Not this time for you my friend,' said Rupert as he patted him.

A clap of thunder overhead caused me to look up at the sky, checking for more signs of rain. I looked across to Tockwith on the edge of our right flank and saw angry black rain clouds, swirling on the wind. A gust of wind hit me, bringing an earthy smell with it. Forks of lightening lit up the sky, followed by more claps of thunder, mimicking the sound of cannon. The storm clouds arrived on the wind and cast rain down upon us. Another clap of thunder echoed out, but then I knew this was different. It was the sound of cannon.

'Look they are coming towards us,' shouted one of Rupert's officers. We all looked out at the enemy positions. Their infantry were running towards us, aiming to cover the ground as quickly as possible. On both wings their horse began to move forward in unison.

'To arms,' cried Rupert. 'Gentlemen, get back to your regiments and meet the enemy.'

We all ran to our horses and mounted. James and I rode with Rupert to his lifeguard. We watched awe struck as all across the field the enemy came forward and pushed our musketeers back from the ditch. The sudden downpour had put out many of the men's matches, and only a few of them managed to fire at the onrushing army. Rupert mounted alongside us was also watching, but with a keener eye, looking for where we were at our weakest.

'It is on our right that we will be hard pressed,' said Rupert. 'The ditch is not so great an obstacle to their horse and they have cleared away some of the hedges. If Byron can buy some time, we will support the second rank.'

'Lord, if we forget you this day, do not forget us,' exclaimed James as we spurred our horses forward.

As we rode over to the right wing we could see Lord Byron charging with his regiment to hit the centre of the enemy horse as they reformed after crossing the ditch. It was a brave act, for his regiment was soon swallowed up as the greater number of the enemy came round his flanks. It was desperate hand to hand fighting, but after a few minutes the weight of numbers told and Byron's regiment broke off and sought safety. He had however granted us a few precious moments. The rest of the horse were now back in the saddle and awaiting orders.

We had come up to Rupert's own regiment of horse and he called them forward into battle. Rupert led the line and wheeled his regiment into the flank of the enemy cavalry as they recovered after the initial charge. We hit them hard, but they did not break. They were like a rock. We were like waves, crashing down upon them, but being forced round them as they stood firm.

I was beside James and Rupert who were both striking down the enemy in their path. The Prince's dog was snapping at the legs of the enemy horses and weaving in and out to avoid their kicks. One of their troopers aimed a blow and cut the dog open at the neck. Boy turned and looked up with questioning eyes to his master and then slumped down. Rupert snarled and made for the killer of his dog. He was in a rage and struck down with tremendous force on the man's helmet. The blade bit down through the steel and into the man's skull. We pressed forward again and Boy was left behind on the ground.

The enemy knew they were fighting Rupert and they renewed their attacks against him. If they could kill or capture him they might shorten the battle. By his skill as a swordsman and through the savagery of his attack, Rupert had forced open a gap in the enemy into which about half a dozen of us followed.

The enemy seemed to be giving way and I felt elated. The battle rage was upon me and I hacked and sliced at anyone in my way. Then as with the tide, our energy was eventually spent, but the rock stood firm. We now seemed surrounded. The enemy had fed in more men and Rupert saw the danger.

'Fall back,' he shouted and he turned his horse round. 'Fight your way free.'

As I turned my head looking for a way out, I saw an enemy trooper riding towards Rupert who was now facing the other way. I spurred my horse to intercept him, allowing Rupert to break free. This man was fresh while I was fatigued. He beat me back, but I prevented his killer blows from reaching me. Another trooper rode up and seized the bridle of my horse.

'Yield,' he shouted. 'Yield and you will be spared.'

I could not fight the two of them, and with my horse motionless it would only be a matter of time before one of them got past my parrying.

'I yield,' I cried, half expecting one of them to run me through. No blow came and I lowered my sword.

'Got ourselves a nice lord here,' said the first assailant as he took my sword from me. Cromwell will be pleased.'

Exhausted I slumped in my saddle. A lord, why did they mistake me for a lord? Then I realized. I was mounted on a fine horse and wearing expensive armour. A suit of armour James had given me when he purchased a new set before the war against the Scots. This armour had saved my life many times in battle and now it saved me once more.

'Come with me,' said my captor who still held my horse's bridle. His voice was gruff with an accent I did not recognise. Not Yorkshire; if he fought for Cromwell then he was probably from the Fens. He led me away from the fighting. I tried to see what was happening, but it was all confusion. We approached a formed body of cavalry in dull grey cloth, on small, scraggy beasts. They were armed with lances and as we passed they were ordered to advance. Scots, by the sound of the voices. These new men could turn the fight behind me, as Rupert did not have any more men in reserve, Molyneux's horse having also joined the fight as we rode in. That's if Rupert was still alive. I did not know if he had got away. He might be dead or captured like me. What of James? The last time I had seen him he had been fighting to break out of the enemy's clutches. He too might be dead, or lying wounded on the field.

My captors took me to a piece of high ground that offered a good view of the field. It looked as if it was a command post, but the commanders were all away at the battle.

'Take yer helmet off,' one of them ordered.

Wearily I removed my helmet, taking a lungful of air as I did so. This restored me a little and I glared back at the two men.

'Who are you then?' asked the man who had seized my horse.

'My name is Paul Morrow. I serve the Earl of Derby.'

'Not a lord? What are we going to do, Isaac? Cromwell won't be pleased that we deserted our posts for 'im.'

'Let me think,' replied Isaac who removed his lobster pot to scratch an itch on his scalp. 'Serves the Earl of Derby he says, and we captured him helping Devil Rupert. He could still be useful to us. Let's keep hold of him.'

'Still, what about Cromwell?' replied my captor.

'Go back to the fight if you want to,' retorted Isaac. 'But hurry about it. Look, those Scots have tipped the balance. Rupert's men are retreating and some are running.'

I looked to see if it was true and to my horror it was. All across the engagement our men were peeling off and retreating. I watched, surprised that the enemy did not follow them. Instead they stood still, perhaps exhausted after the fighting. Or was it iron discipline? These two troopers who had captured me were obviously afraid of Cromwell. With a chill, I realized he would now be able to turn his horse against our foot in the centre of the field.

My timid captor spoke again. 'You keep hold of the prisoner. I'm going back to the fight.' Without looking back he spurred on his horse and rode back to his resting regiment.

'Don't think you can get away from me,' Isaac warned, withdrawing a pistol from its saddle holster. 'You're not so useful to us now alive, so I'll shoot you if you try to get away.'

Horrified, I watched as Cromwell wheeled his cavalry into our foot in the centre. Now they were the tide, but they were relentless and nothing could stand in their way. Our foot had held their own against the rebel infantry, but could not stand when hit in the flank by cavalry. All our regiments broke under this onslaught; all except one, Newcastle's Lambs. They held firm and kept up a steady fire as the enemy tried to close. It was getting dark now and wisps of smoke from their muskets billowed in the air.

Like hounds after a cornered stag, the enemy circled and crept closer and closer. I watched aghast as the firing of the Lambs whittled away. Soon I could not see their white coats; such was the mass of the enemy in front of them. Then the hounds were upon them, snarling and biting, bringing the Lambs to the ground.

The field belonged to the enemy. To the right it looked as if Goring's horse had won their battle, but he had not been able to intervene in the centre as decisively as Cromwell. The day was lost, and in the gathering darkness our men fled the field, making for the safety of York. The rebels pursued them relentlessly, killing, wounding and capturing hundreds.

I felt the despair of defeat. My right arm ached from sword play and my body twinged from bruises beneath my armour. For their part the rebels were elated with victory. Darkness fell, and in my despair I lost sense of time. They moved me back to an area where a large group of prisoners were sitting and lying on the floor. The wounded moaned, and as it got colder some of them fell silent. I stumbled around, but could not find anyone I knew.

The sun was starting to rise over Long Marston village when Isaac came back for me. A party of their horse rode up.

'Who's this, Isaac?' asked one of their front rank, a cloth stained with dried blood around his neck.

'One of Derby's men, my Lord General,' replied Isaac.

A little warily the lord general turned his head round to me, sucking a breath through his teeth as he did so.

'He looks like a gentleman. Just what I need. I want to tour the field and see who has fallen.' Fixing me by the eye he continued, 'you, Sir can come with me and identify who is dead from your side. I had hoped to kill or capture Rupert, but I think he has escaped.'

This must be Cromwell who Isaac was so afraid of. I hoped he would treat me fairly as I had been granted quarter.

I rode in solemn silence alongside Cromwell and his escort. Thousands of our men lay dead or wounded, strewn across the ground where they had fallen. Pitiful cries for water escaped the lips of the injured. Most looked away as we rode up; those with less serious wounds tried to crawl out of our path. Then we came across a mound where there were no wounded. All of the men here were slain. They were Newcastle's men, blood now staining their white coats. In death they wore the colour some said Newcastle had wanted for them, but he had clad them instead in cheaper white cloth.

Here Cromwell rested his horse as he surveyed the scene. 'I will bring them down like lambs to the slaughter, like rams with he goats,' he recited. He looked at me. 'Do you know my meaning?'

I hesitated for a while, for although I knew why he quoted the Bible in this way, I did not agree with him. After several moments I replied. 'You believe that in order for true godliness to be restored to the Kingdom, all who support superstition and idolatry must first of all be laid low.'

'Indeed,' he replied. 'And we are God's instrument in this. All Papists who have corrupted the King must be rooted out and destroyed. Once this has been done the King will seek the council of his Parliament once more.'

I remained silent. I did not think it prudent to reply that a good number of the 'Parliament' had joined the King's own Parliament at Oxford. Neither did I want to challenge his theology.

Cromwell pulled on his horse's reins and the animal turned its head in the direction his master wanted to go. As yet I had only identified some of the junior officers from Molyneux's and Tyldesley's regiments. We rode on and came across a lone woman who was obviously agitated. To my surprise Cromwell looked genuinely concerned at her discomfort.

'Why do you weep,' he asked. The woman looked up at us and I recognized her as Mary Townley, from Townley Hall near Burnley.

'I'm looking for my husband, she sobbed. 'I fear he has been summoned up to the Lord before his time.'

'This is no place for you,' replied Cromwell kindly. 'This battlefield is a hideous sight, and worse still you could come to harm. While most of my men are God fearing, I cannot speak for all men on this field. Who knows what some of them will do if they come across a lone woman.'

'But I must find my husband,' she retorted. 'I have been told that he fell in the battle. Perhaps he is only wounded.'

'My Lady,' I interrupted. 'I am afraid your worst fears are true. I have seen the body of Colonel Townley. Here, let me take you to him,' I said looking to Cromwell for permission.

Cromwell nodded. 'Get yourself up behind this gentleman on his horse. Once you have found your husband you both have my leave to quit this field. We have enough prisoners, one less won't make any difference in the exchanges.'

Mary climbed up behind me and I expressed my thanks to Cromwell.

'Isaac, you go with them to see they are not troubled by any of our men out chasing the enemy,' ordered Cromwell.

I led the way over to the place where I had seen Colonel Townley's body. I felt Mary's breath on my cheek; it was irregular as she choked back tears. I pitied her but could find no words of comfort. I wondered what James would have said if he were here, for he usually had the right word in moments like this.

I stopped my horse when we arrived at the body. Mary gasped and jumped down to him. She lifted his head and cradled it in her arms, brushing the hair back from his face. His eyes were wide and glassy, and she gently pulled each eye lid down with her finger.

She took a deep breath and drew herself up. 'We must take his body to York for burial,' she said resolutely.

My own emotions were mixed. All I wanted to do was leave this field as quickly as possible, but I could not refuse her. I looked around and saw a horse munching on some grass, his owner probably dead. I dismounted and asking Mary to hold my horse, I went to fetch it. Between us we lifted Colonel Townley's body and slumped it across the horse. Isaac watched us impassively, keeping his thoughts to himself and not offering any help.

The three of us partly rode, partly walked back to York. Several times enemy patrols challenged us, but Isaac's gruff response with the password of the day sent them away. Once in sight of the white towers of the Minster, Isaac turned his horse and trotted away without a word to us.

We rode on, gaining entry into the city without hindrance. All discipline appeared to have broken down and there were no guards on the city gate. I took Mary to the church next to the Minster. Leaving our burden at the door we entered, the cool church air smelling unusually sweet. Scented candles flickered in the draught from the door, and I saw several bodies laid out in the nave for interment. I left Mary as she explained to the vicar that she had brought one more for burial. I needed to find James.

Chapter 26 – *York and the Isle of Man, 1644*

The horse bearing Colonel Townley's body stood obediently outside the church. With a pang of guilt I passed by, telling myself his wife would find help.

The streets were still thronged with soldiers; they had probably been too scared to sleep with the enemy closing in upon York. I came across a group of officers arguing with an innkeeper about rooms he had let out to somebody else.

I caught the attention of one of them and asked him if he knew if the Earl of Derby and Prince Rupert had made it off the moor.

'Rupert lives, that I know,' he replied. 'He is back in his lodgings. I don't know about the Earl.'

I hurried to Rupert's quarters and was almost knocked over by a group of his aides who were leaving the building. I recognised one of them and asked him did he know if James was alive.

'Praise God he is. You'll find him inside.'

James looked up as I entered and smiled. He looked tired, but had no visible wounds. 'So Paul you are safe too. It was all so confused yesterday. I feared you dead when we could not find you last night.'

'I was detained by Cromwell who hoped I would find Rupert's body on the moor for him.'

'Rupert is safe you know.'

I nodded and James continued. 'It seems Cromwell and his cavalry won them the battle. Rupert calls Cromwell's men the Ironsides. We just couldn't break them. So tell me, did you escape?'

'No. We came across Lady Townley searching for her dead husband. Cromwell let me go to escort her and the body to York.'

'A man of compassion then.'

'So it would seem. And a man of great conviction. His soldiers seemed almost scared of him, or at least in awe of him.'

'Compassion and conviction. Strange partners, but then this war has brought forth many strange things,' said James.

After a pause I continued, 'What do we do now?'

'The North is lost. Newcastle is dismayed at the loss of his Whitecoats. He says he is taking a ship and going into exile. Rupert is taking as many horse as he can gather back into Lancashire. He wants me to go back and garrison Lathom, but he advises I cross over to the Isle of Man with Charlotte.'

I was pleased by this news, as Louise and our children would go with Charlotte as I would attend James.

'Do you have a horse Paul? We are leaving within the half hour.'

'No, I lost my horse in the battle.'

'Come outside. One of the troopers will find you a mount. We have to get back to Lancashire and salvage as much as we can. The longer we stay here, the more men will desert.'

***

The next months were the nadir of our fortunes. After a brief pause at Lathom we crossed over to the Isle of Man. It seemed every day brought more bad news. York surrendered two weeks after Marston Moor. Liverpool fell in November. Only Lathom and Greenhalgh Castle remained in our hands in Lancashire.

'I think our cause is lost Paul,' said James. 'My conscience has been troubled these last few weeks, but I have now come to a decision. I will write to Sir John Meldrum to enter into negotiations to find a peace for my county. I know Parliament's Propositions for Peace named me as one who shall receive no pardon either for life or estate, but I will work through my kinsmen, Earls Pembroke and Salisbury to settle this. I'm sure we can find an accommodation.'

I was struck dumb by this confession. Although I had been thinking that the war was lost, I had not expected James to parley for a peace. He was safe on the Isle and was sheltering several other lords and gentlemen.

'It is Katherine and Amelia I am most concerned about. They are kept prisoners in Knowsley, and I fear I won't see them again.'

So this was what most worried James. I understood his concern, having spent a lot of time away from my own children while they were in danger.

'Paul, you have to agree this is the best course.'

'Yes, my Lord. I think it is. Just think; we could be celebrating the peace at Christmas.'

***

Christmas came, and snow furred the ground like a cloak of ermine. Still we did not have peace. Sir John Meldrum had written to James, arranging a safe passage across to London. Then a new letter arrived from Sir John, explaining that Parliament found the terms offered to James to be too lenient. Most of all they wanted him to surrender the Isle of Man.

'I can't do it,' said James once he'd read the letter. 'To surrender the Isle would be to turn over dozens of men to Parliament, and while I can bargain for myself I cannot negotiate for them. I will hold this island and offer sanctuary to any who are pursued by Parliament.'

Chapter 27 – *Isle of Man, 1647*

'The gentlemen need something to raise their spirits,' said James one evening after supper. 'They are cooped up in the castle most of the time and the town doesn't offer them many distractions.'

I looked around the hall and saw some of them were drunk, as they had been the past few nights. In the first years of our exile they had ridden and drilled, but after years of inactivity they had become increasingly despondent. 'We should have a hunt,' I replied.

'No, that won't be enough. I'm thinking about a horse race along the beach at Derbyhaven. If I offer a piece of plate as a prize to the winner, that'll give them some competition. I'll announce that the race is to be held in a week.'

The mood was totally different for the next week. The gentlemen practiced riding the course on the beach. They bought and traded horses. They drank less and gambled less, saving their money to bet on the race.

'Will you ride, my Lord?' I asked James a few days before the race was to be run.

'No, I won't. I am putting up the prize. It's not right that I should try to win it. Paul, I want you to ride for me.'

'My Lord, that will be a great honour, but I am unprepared.'

'Choose whichever horse you want from my stable. I'll not have my rider disadvantaged.'

***

The smell of dung and sweat greeted me as I entered the stables. Grooms were excitedly brushing down the horses, happy they had a part to play in the forthcoming spectacle.

'Good morning Mr. Morris. Are you wanting to take out a horse?' asked the senior groom.

'Yes, I've to practice for the race. Can I take out Hector?'

'A good choice, young, but not too skittish. He'll last the course.'

I rode him over to Derbyhaven and allowed him a short rest before attempting the course, marked out with posts at the start and finish. The distance was short, but the sand was softer than turf which made it hard going. I turned back at the end and rode over to a small group who had watched my ride. I pulled up my horse and recognized William Christian in midst of the riders.

'I find it hard to ride a race alone,' he said. 'Would you like to go again, with us to race against?'

'Yes, I would. That'll be a better test.'

'And a small wager will make us all try harder. Say, a pound from everyone; the winner gets it all?'

Although usually not one for gambling, I agreed to this as I wanted a practice race.

At the start line William Christian asked one of his companions to start us. That still left six to run. We all handed a coin over to the starter.

'Take off your hat and drop it to start us of,' said Christian.

We all got ready at the starting post, my horse pulling against the reins. The starter dropped his hat and we set off, the other horses all slightly ahead of me. Hector soon made up the ground on them and with about a quarter of the course still to go, I pulled out in front. Christian was the closest to me and I heard him shouting at his horse to catch up. Seeing the finishing post, I spurred Hector on and we passed the post in first position.

'Well ridden. He is a fine animal,' said William Christian as the starter handed six pounds over to me. I was delighted and I muttered my thanks, thinking this had been a good morning.

***

There was a holiday mood on the day of the race. People from Castletown walked the couple of miles to Derbyhaven, carrying picnics to share after the race. Baker's boys ran in amongst them, trying to sell rolls and pies. Louise and our children had set off with Charlotte earlier in the morning. I rode with James, who carried the piece of plate in a saddlebag.

I saw William Christian at the starting line. His horse edged back and forth, strong muscles evident at the top of its silky black legs. The other riders from our practice race were there too, and when we were called over to the line they put themselves to either side of me. James was going to start the race and he raised his hand for silence.

'Lords and gentlemen. I shall fire a pistol into the air as the signal to start. You are to race from this line in the sand to the finish post down there. Anyone who starts before the pistol is disqualified.' A pistol was handed to him, which he pointed into the air. 'Make ready.'

I tensed my legs, ready to kick them into Hector's flanks and watched James's finger on the trigger of the pistol. He fired and shouted at us to start. Hector leaped off as I spurred him. The noise of hooves drumming up the sand reminded me of the charge at Marston Moor, and I had a brief image of Rupert in my mind. We had made a good start and there were just a few horses in front of me. Two of these were William Christian's friends and I was sure they had started before the signal. No matter, they would be disqualified. These two riders stayed in front of me and two more of Christian's friends rode close to my horse's flanks. Hector was trying to push on, but I could not get him past these horses. Then I saw a chance, a gap to my left. I steered Hector into it and kicked him on. I was out of the trap and gaining on the three riders at the front. I in the last fifty yards I passed two of them, but could only watch in disappointment as William Christian crossed the line in front.

William Christian had plotted this victory. No matter if his men were disqualified; their purpose was to block me. I did not take it badly. In fact it was probably a better outcome for James for Christian to win rather than me. There could be no talk of favouritism to the household.

Chapter 28 – *Isle of Man, 1648*

'Carlisle has been seized for the King.' James had called me into his solar and was pacing the room as he spoke. 'Things have been stirring since the King signed the Engagement with the Scots last Christmas. First there were riots in London and Norwich, and now Sir Philip Musgrave has taken Carlisle. Berwick has also declared for the King. The Scots will have free passage into England to support Charles. It might have taken four years, but it is just as Newcastle said before Marston Moor, the Parliament and the Scots will fall out given time.'

'Can the Scots defeat Parliament's armies?' I asked.

'I don't know. It will depend upon how much support the King gets in England and indeed Wales. I've received messages asking me to raise Lancashire for the King and support the march of the Scots down into England.'

'Will you do it?'

'I don't know. My duty is to my King, but I'm not sure I can support a man who starts a new war. He has had two years to make a peace with Parliament and he has not taken it. I fear he will keep fighting until either he wins or he is dead. You know that after the battle at Naseby was lost, he personally wanted to fight inviting certain death.'

I was glad to hear these words from James. I did not want him to put our lives into danger again for a man I considered intransigent. I had seen the most committed Royalists slip away from the Isle. Sir Marmaduke Langdale had left a few months earlier, and here was the news he had seized Berwick for the King. I had been on edge every day, wondering if James was going to return to Lancashire.

'If the King cannot win back his kingdom or if he is killed in battle, then won't we need a new prince to restore the kingdom?'

'I would support his son, Charles for he has had no part in all this.'

'But does it have to be his son? Machiavelli writes of constitutional principalities where the nobles select one of their own to become prince.'

'Paul, what are you saying?'

'You are a noble man with a strong lineage. Could you not be that man?'

'Where would that lead?' replied James. 'To perpetual war as each lord tries to win the throne. You know I'm not a politician. I don't want that.'

'But couldn't one of the nobility find accommodation with his peers?'

'It is past all that now. The nobility is divided and there is no single man we would all follow. Besides, the army is strong and led by men who are not from the nobility.'

'What if a new Caesar were to come out of the army and take the throne?' I asked. ''Would you support such a man?'

'Not while a legitimate prince still lives, and Charles has three living sons. I would oppose such a general. No, I will wait until the Scots have marched down into England, and see how strong they are and how much support the King has in England. If it looks as if the King will win, I will cross over to Lancashire and declare for him. In the meantime I will put out that I'm raising men on the Isle and preparing for a crossing. I will bide my time.'

***

And so we stayed on the island despite several requests to cross over to England. James sent each messenger away with placatory words, but each one left more exasperated than the last. The war did not start well for the King, with Thomas Fairfax defeating the Royalists in Kent. Then in July the Scots army crossed into England and more messengers came to tease James out of the Isle of Man. Still he would not cross over. It was tense as we waited for news. We knew the Scots were in Lancashire and trying to join up with forces in Wales being raised by Lord Byron. Then in late August, some bedraggled Royalists landed on the Isle bringing news of a defeat for the Scots. Cromwell had marched north and joined with the forces of General Lambert. He had then attacked the rear of the Engager army and defeated Sir Marmaduke Langdale, before dealing with the main body of the Scots army in the course of the next few days. The Scots were dispersed and defeated. This new war was petering out as Cromwell dealt with isolated Royalist strongholds. More fleeing Royalists came over to the Isle and James gave shelter to Lord Byron and Sir Philip Musgrave.

'It has been a sorry business,' said James.

'One that you did well to avoid,' replied Paul.

'Yes, I was troubled by it, but I think my decision not to fight was the right one. What worries me know is that the Parliament has lost patience.'

'How do you mean?'

'Look how Fairfax had Sir Charles Lucas shot after he surrendered Colchester. I think they are increasingly frustrated. These are dangerous times. I am glad we have the safety of the Isle and its castles.'

Chapter 29 – *Isle of Man, 1649*

"Our holy and beautiful house, where our Fathers praised Thee, is burnt with fire, and all our pleasant things are laid waste." - Isaiah lxiv. 11.

'The King is on trial for his life,' James said gravely. It was the middle of January. Our spirits had been lifted a little with feasting at Christmas, but now the weather was cold and we had a long wait until the comfort of spring. A ship had landed at Derbyhaven that morning, bringing messages from England.

'How can this be?' I replied.

'The army has purged Parliament of all but its own supporters and set up a court to try the King. What's more they have appointed John Bradshaw as the court's Lord-President.'

'What, Bradshaw from Congleton?' I asked, scarcely able to believe what James was telling me. This was the man who had been on the fringes of James's life until the civil war, when he had conducted a vicious campaign against Charlotte at Lathom.

'The very same. Nobody else would do it. Who would want to sentence their own King?'

'He has always been ambitious,' I replied. 'Remember how he tried to get the chamberlain's office at Chester.'

'He might be the man to do the army's bidding and sentence Charles to death. No murder in a dark corner of a castle for them. They want as much legitimacy as they can get. That's why they are trying him.'

'How can they try him, he is the King?'

'He is accused of "maliciously making war on the Parliament and people of England". They are going to find him guilty, or why would they hold the trial? The House of Lords wanted nothing to do with it, so the Commons have declared they can pass laws without the Lords or the King.'

'But by what right can they kill him?'

'Are you familiar with the idea of blood guilt? It means if the magistrate does not punish someone guilty of spilling innocent blood, then God will punish them and the nation. The minority of forty or so in Parliament believe Charles is responsible for the bloodshed of the past seven years. The sorry state of the kingdom will get even worse if

God punishes the nation. They are the magistrates and as they see it, it's up to them to punish the King.'

***

James proved to be right. At the end of January, Charles was found guilty by the High Court of Justice and declared guilty by Bradshaw. To our great dismay he was beheaded outside his own Banqueting House at Whitehall. I had not seen James so low since the death of Earl William, not even when he had heard the news that Lathom had been razed to the ground after surrendering in 1646. Bradshaw's hand was behind that act too. We heard he had been the one who ordered the wainscots be sold off, and the boards to be taken from the house and sent to the garrison at Liverpool. I too had taken the news badly; thinking of Earl William's wonderful library with the volumes of rare books and the manuscripts of his plays. It had rivalled Thomas Bodley's library in Oxford and now it was all ash.

'I have to make my peace with them. My estates are in ruin. Lathom is demolished. Paul, I want you to go over to England and seek out Lord General Fairfax. He seems to have turned away from the regicides, but he is still the commander of the army. I hope he will allow me to compound for my estates.'

'Can you trust Fairfax?'

'Apart from the deaths of Sir Charles Lucas and Sir George Lisle at Colchester he has always appeared to be just. He stayed away from the trial of the King, so I don't think he wanted him dead. He knows the North, so will have a good idea of the value of my estates.'

'Very well, my Lord. I will cross over. Do you have any thoughts about how much you will have to pay?'

'I can't begin to work that out. I have no choice but to hear what they say. Come back as quickly as you can.'

***

'How much?' asked James.

'Fifteen and a half thousand pounds,' I repeated. 'Well, to be precise £15,572 16s 5d,' I said consulting my notebook.

'By God's blood, they mean the end of me. I'll be in debt to the moneylenders until my dying day. But you said Lord Fairfax had put in a good word for me with the Committee for Compounding.'

'Indeed he did, my lord, but I suspect there are others behind this, who work against Lord Fairfax.'

'Ireton, perhaps. I have received a letter from him to surrender the island without delay.'

'Amongst others. I suspect Bradshaw's hand is behind this. He is in high esteem with the regicides for sentencing the King.'

A look of anger flashed across James's face and he replied in a voice as cold and hard as the steel of my sword. 'Get some paper and write down my reply.'

I wrote out James's reply as he dictated it, and thanks to a moneylender in Lombard Street still have a copy of it to this day. He said these words in anger and to a degree they sealed his fate. I think he had expected to be given a small figure to compound. He still thought his lineage carried weight, when in fact it merely disadvantaged him. The very sort of functionary who sat in James's house in Canon row, penning every sort of rule and regulation under the name of the "Derby House Committee", was not going to be impressed by James's rank and titles. Indeed perhaps they still feared him. With King Charles dead and his sons in exile in the United Provinces, James himself had a strong claim to the throne. I see now why they did not want him to compound. James's reply to General Iteton became well known for it was printed and circulated in London. I can almost recall his words without reference to the printed copy.

Castletown, July 12, 1649.

> *Sir-I received your letter with indignation and scorn, and return you this answer :-That I cannot but wonder whence you should gather any hopes from me that I should, like you, prove treacherous to my sovereign, since you can-not but be sensible of my former actings in his late Majesty's service; from which principles of loyalty I am no whit departed. I scorn your proffers, disdain your favour, and abhor your treason, and am so far from delivering up this Island to your advantage that I will keep it to the utmost of my power and your destruction. Take this for your final answer, and forbear any further solicitations, for if you trouble me with any more messages on this occasion I will burn the paper and hang the bearer. This is the immutable*

resolution, and shall be the undoubted practice of him who accounts it his chiefest glory to be His Majesty's most loyal and obedient servant,

DERBY.

As if to thrust the knife deeper into James, the very next day he received a certificate of safe passage to cross over to England to raise money to pay his compounding fine. Over the course of the next few weeks his anger cooled and in the middle of August I was sent to London as his agent with instructions to pay the fine. First of all I had to approach various moneylenders in Lombard Street to obtain credit. They knew James's dire straits; indeed it was one of them who gave me a copy of James's reply to Ireton. They asked for higher rates of interest than had been expected and it took over a week of bargaining before I could guarantee sufficient funds to pay the fine. I went to Goldsmith's Hall with sufficient letters of credit to pay the fine, but when I presented myself before a clerk of the committee I was refused and told that James would not be allowed to compound.

Chapter 30 – *Isle of Man, 1650*

"I have forsaken my House; I have left mine heritage; I have given the dearly beloved of my soule to the hand of Enemies. My heritage is now to me like a Lion in the forest; it cries out against me." Jeremiah xii. 7, 8. Private Devotions of James Stanley.

James had enemies everywhere, and in England they moved against his daughters. In May Katherine and Amelia were seized and taken from Knowsley to be held in Liverpool, together with their guardian John Greenhalgh. James was incensed at this act, and coming after his failure to compound, it moved him to a more extreme path. When he learnt that Charles Stuart had signed a treaty with the Scottish Covenanters, he began to prepare earnestly to cross over to England in support of the uncrowned King of England. James did this in spite of Charles's cold blooded sacrifice of the Marquis of Montrose, leaving him to be executed by the Covenanters.

The defence of the Isle of Man was still important to James and he was anxious to see the fort at Derby Point, as there had been rumours of a large force of Parliamentarian ships being sent to capture the island. The fort was on Michael's Isle and had been built by Earl William's grandfather as part of the kingdom's coastal defences against the French, necessitated by old King Henry's campaigns against them.

A small party was assembled in Castle Rushen, consisting of James, Colonel Snead, Mr. Richard Weston and myself. We arrived as the tide was going out and spurred our horses across the sand where William Christian had won the Derby plate, reached the Isle and rode past the small church of St. Michael before spying the fort. We were greeted by the captain of the small garrison who had watched our progress across the bay. He had used the time from first seeing us to turn out all his men, and they were assembled in the courtyard inside the fort. One remained as a lookout on top of the wall.

The captain reported they had not seen a ship for three weeks, and that one had been Captain Bartlet's sailing back to Derbyhaven from a patrol around the south of the island. James told him to double the guard at night time as he was concerned that if any Parliamentarian ships came, then they would try to use the cover of night to evade the fort and its guns. Next he informed the captain that he was going to meet with Captain Bartlet on his frigate the Elizabeth with the intention of trying out the usefulness of the fort against enemy ships. The fort was not to fire on the Elizabeth, but it was to track the ship's course and the captain was told to use his quarter hour glass and record how long the ship was in range of the guns.

We took a small fishing boat rowed by two Manxmen, to carry us out to the Elizabeth at anchor in the bay.

'Good morning my Lord and welcome aboard' greeted Captain Bartlet.

'Good morning to you, captain. Are you ready for today's work?'

'Indeed I am my Lord and the crew are all ready too. I've taken on some local fishermen as some of my regular crew have a sickness, and I didn't want them near you, nor your gentlemen.'

'Most considerate. Let us be under way as quickly as you can make it. And do you have powder for your guns and shot too? I want to make some noise to harden the boys at the fort. Most of them have not been shot at before and I want to know if they can follow their captain's orders not to return fire.'

'Indeed I do and I have some canister shot too, so we can splash the water before their eyes'. Cast away and let's catch the last of this tide.'

Looking across the bay we could see the fort, though it looked very small from so far away, and I could not make out the guns on the wall. We sailed across the bay and drew parallel to the fort, making a steady pace under sail.

'Captain, time now to wake up the boys in the fort. Aim short and wide, I don't want to bring the place down' said James.

'Right lads, load the two guns on the port side and the guns aft with canister and don't fire until I've set them'.

Once he had set the guns, the captain waited for the ship to settle, not wishing the guns to get extra trajectory, which could bring the fort into range. He fired the first gun, and as we heard the report and saw the smoke he walked to the second and fired it immediately. We waited for what seemed an age, but was in fact just a few breaths and then we saw the shot fall short and to the sea side of the fort.

'Nicely done, let's trust they remember not to fire back,' said James. 'Now continue a bit further into the bay and then signal for the fishermen to take us back to Michael's Isle.'

Back on the fishermen's boat we were making our way back to the Isle when we heard another shot from Captain Bartlet's ship. I presumed it was another ruse being played against the men in Derby

Fort, but this thought was knocked from my mind as the boat lurched and Mr. Weston crashed into me. Men were crying out, Mr. Weston was screaming aloud. One of the fishermen had slumped over and looked dead. There were holes in the side of the boat and pieces of iron sticking out of its timbers. I pushed Mr. Weston back, supporting his head as I did so.

'It was a shot from the Elizabeth' I exclaimed. 'Mr. Weston are you all right, sir?' I felt him heavy, as if he had no strength to hold up his own body. He did not reply and blood was tricking from the corner of his mouth.

'He has taken a wound in the back and Colonel Snead has one as well,' said James. 'The fisherman is dead.'

No more shots came and there was obvious commotion on board the Elizabeth. I took one of the oars and James took the other. We rowed without a further word to Michael's Isle. Mr. Weston was groaning in a low constant tone and he was clearly finding it difficult to breathe. We carried him to the fort, but before we could see to his wounds he fell silent.

'My dear friend. May the God of mercy hear my prayers for your salvation. The Lord killeth and maketh alive; He brings down to the grave and brings up.' With that he looked to me and asked. 'I have enemies all around. It does not seem as if I am safe even here.'

Chapter 31 – *Worcester, September 1651*

We crossed over to England in James's two frigates, bringing three hundred assorted men; some gentlemen in exile and some Manx soldiers. Summer was coming to a close and the farmers were hurriedly gathering in their crops, almost as if they wanted to get them safely in before the arrival of war.

I rode alongside James on the way to Warrington, where we were to meet with Major-General Massey; King Charles already having passed through Lancashire on his way south. James was wearing his George and Star of the Order of the Garter, King Charles having made him one of the twenty-four Knights Companion on St. George's Day. James planned to raise as many Lancashire followers as he could, before following after the King's army. I looked around the men closest to James. Sir Thomas Tyldesley was in the group and as eager for a fight as he had ever been. He was not the only Catholic in the troop and I reflected this would not be popular with King Charles's Scottish allies, Presbyterian to a man.

We reached Warrington late in the afternoon and went immediately to see Major-General Massey. He was leant over a table studying a map, flanked by his aides and two dourly dressed Presbyterian ministers. He did not look up as we entered.

'Where is Cromwell?' asked Massey.

'Reports say he is coming down the east coast via Newcastle,' replied one of the aides.

'Then where is Lambert?'

'We don't know. He was in Scotland with Cromwell, but we have not learnt whether he marched down with Cromwell or not.'

Massey looked up and continued. 'Then he could be behind us. Ah, my Lord Derby, very good to see you. Give me some good news. How many men have you brought?'

'Three hundred cavalry all brought over from the Isle of Man.'

'Zounds, is that all you can bring us?' said Massey.

'I will raise more in my county. Already men have gone out calling loyal supporters to a muster at Preston. I expect to raise a thousand more.'

'You must take the Covenant and there are to be no papists amongst your men,' said one of the drably dressed ministers.

'Come sir' replied James. 'This is not a time to pry into a man's conscience, Catholic or Presbyterian. If he is a loyal and dutiful subject of the King and will fight for his cause, then I will have him under my banner.'

'Your latitude is well known,' replied Massy. 'But having papists in our ranks may stop English Presbyterians from joining the King.'

'These papists, as you call them fought for the late King. Did not some of the Presbyterians fight for the Parliament against us?'

'You know damn well they did, including me. But things have changed. It is a question of numbers. How many Catholics follow you? Ten, twenty? I doubt no more than that. We could have hundreds of Presbyterians join us, but they won't want to fight alongside papists. Come now, take the Covenant and send away Tyldesley and the others.'

'Oh, if it were that easy,' replied James. 'Is an oath taken without sincerity worth anything at all? On such terms the late King would neither have lost his kingdom, nor his life. He remained true to his beliefs and I to mine. I will not shun a loyal follower on the grounds of his religion.'

'Then I fear you can be of no service to us or his Majesty,' replied the minister.

'You won't sway my course. I will still have a muster at Preston and march south with the men I have. If I perish I perish, but if my master suffers, the blood of another prince and all the ensuing miseries of the nation will lie at your door.'

Massey and the ministers looked at him blankly.

'Come Paul, we are not wanted here.'

***

Massey's words seemed to ring true. Only three hundred men joined James at Preston, most of them poorly armed. We found government broadsheets in the town, which portrayed Charles as a puppet King of the Scots, and reminded everyone of the destruction in Lancashire wrought by the Scottish army in 1648. With a sense of foreboding we rode south, spending the night near Ormskirk. A ride past the ruins of Lathom House, jagged remains of the walls littering the ground, dampened our spirits even more. With intelligence that the Parliamentarian Colonel Lilburne was nearby, we set of for Wigan, a town with strong royalist sympathies.

As usual I was riding with James in the middle of our men. We were on the outskirts of Wigan and had just entered a lane that would take us into the town. Without warning, musket fire opened up from the hedges stopping our men at once. James kicked his horse forward to assess the situation. Once we were close to the front we could make out troops of dragoons riding towards us.

'We'll have to fight our way through,' said James. 'I'll try to break through with half our men. Sir Thomas you take the others and follow after me.'

It was not a large battle like Marston Moor, but it seemed just as bloody. I charged with James and on our first attempt he had a horse shot from under him. I rallied the men and we found him another mount. Again we charged and again James was unhorsed. On the third charge Lord Witherington was cut down in the fighting. James was unhorsed again. I grabbed Lord Witherington's horse and James mounted up once more. I saw he had several dents in his armour and many gashes in his beaver hat. Looking behind we could see that Sir Thomas was not able to break through and was surrounded by the enemy. Many of our men were dead or wounded; some were surrounded and being asked to surrender.

'We've got to escape,' shouted James above the din of battle, to a handful of us still able to fight. 'Through there,' he said pointing. 'Make for the town and we may lose them there.'

Several of us broke free from the Parliamentarian troopers and hacked our way through another line of them. We galloped down the lane into Wigan, not knowing where we were going, but seeking to escape our pursuers. Reaching the market place we reigned in to assess our progress. Only four of us remained.

'Look there,' said James. Nearby, I could see an open door. 'We'll hide in there and see if we can get away tonight.'

'You go, we'll draw them off,' I replied.

'Meet at Lathom tomorrow at dawn,' said James as he dismounted. 'If I'm not there, go south to the King.'

I grabbed the reins of his horse and we set off again. Glancing back across the market place I saw the door closing behind James.

***

Lilburne had his men scouring the lanes around Wigan, and it was with great difficulty we reached Lathom, arriving a few hours after sunset. To see the place in ruins filled me with a deep melancholy, made worse by the fact that I did not expect to see James again. About half a mile from the house, we found one of the outbuildings practically intact. Holes in the roof and blackened timbers, pointed to an unsuccessful attempt to burn it down. We took the horses inside and settled down to wait, sharing what little water and food we had.

I took the last watch before dawn. I had not been able to sleep earlier, and now my thoughts continued to trouble me. I saw men with no limbs. I turned over a dead body and looked upon the face of Sir Thomas, eyes gashed out and blood gurgling from his mouth. A noise startled me, and I jolted awake.

'Paul,' I listened again. 'Paul, are you there?'

Sword in hand, I edged to the door. 'James, is that you?'

'Yes, by God's grace it is. Are you going to let me in then?'

I opened the door and saw James was alone. 'Bring your horse in.'

I stood aside as James led the animal in. I noticed how he leant against the horse for support. Dried blood was visible at the top of his arm. 'You're wounded,' I said in alarm.

'Yes, lots of sword wounds to my arms. But if I'd not had the steel cap under my beaver, then I wouldn't be here.'

'How did you get away?'

'Remember the house I went into? Well, the lady knew who I was and led me out to her garden. She told me I could hide in the piggery. I waited for several hours, only disturbed by an inquisitive pig. Once I heard sounds of a cavalry troop in the lane nearby, but no-one came to find me. When it was dark the lady's son led me to the edge of the town, where they had a horse waiting for me. I thanked them, giving them some gold crowns in payment for the horse. I made it to Lathom and have been searching for you this last hour.'

My joy at seeing James again could not abate my melancholy. 'Did you see Sir Thomas get away?' I asked.

'Last I saw he was leading another charge. I fear he has been taken, or worse.'

'What are we to do now?'

'We must join the King,' said James.

'But there are only four of us. What can we do?'

'We must rally as many as we can. I'll call on several families on our way south. I'm sure I will find some loyal to His Majesty. First I must rest.'

Before James could rest I looked at his wounds. One of the cuts on his left arm was quite deep; blood was still slowly seeping out. The flow did not stop until I tied a piece of linen tightly around the arm.

He was exhausted after the escape, so we decided to rest through the day and travel by night. That way we hoped to avoid the patrols that would be out looking for us.

Again we took turns on guard, but no dragoons came near. Once darkness fell we set off south. James knew the area better than anyone, and we had no trouble keeping to the route. We travelled like this for three days, heading for Shrewsbury. Twice I left the others and went into a village or small town to buy some food. Fortunately, I did not run into any patrols, and did not arouse any suspicion.

Arriving near Shrewsbury, James led us to a secluded house in the country called Boscobel. He knew it to be the home of a catholic family, the Giffards; and we sheltered there for two days. James rested, but could not wait until his wounds were fully recovered, for we knew that Parliament's armies were closing in on King Charles in Worcester. After a half day's ride we entered the city and James immediately sought out the King.

'My Lord Derby, I am so pleased to see you,' said the King to James once we had found him at the mayor's residence. 'I am counting on you to have brought more troops, for we face a battle with Cromwell.'

'I fear to disappoint you, your Majesty, but I was defeated at Wigan and only just escaped with my life. I have Paul, my most loyal servant with me, but only a handful in all.'

'Well, your presence and loyalty gives me heart. I cannot expect you to fight in this battle, for I see you have been badly wounded. You must stay by my side and give me counsel.'

'As your Majesty commands,' replied James.

'Now go and find some quarters. My generals tell me Cromwell's army is massing outside the city. They expect him to attack tomorrow.'

***

And so he did. It was one year to the day that Cromwell had defeated the Scottish army at Dunbar, but none of us voiced this thought. We spent the morning with Charles and his commanders on the roof of Worcester Cathedral's bell tower, watching the Parliamentarian army deploy for battle. I felt strangely detached from the scene below, like a Greek god on Mount Olympus watching the heroes at Troy. But I no longer had any pretensions about heroes. It suited me fine being up in the tower. Why should I risk my life fighting with a Scottish army who would make us all Presbyterians? I was only here because James was. He was only here because Charles was. Charles was here because he would do anything to get the throne back.

To the south they were expected to force a crossing of the Teme. Major General Montgomery was to oppose this with infantry, including veteran highlanders. To the east of the city a large enemy force was assembled on Red Hill and around Perry Wood. These were expected to approach the city and to try to gain entry. The river Severn split the enemy's force into two, giving Charles the opportunity to concentrate on one force at a time. Lieutenant-General Leslie commanded the Scottish cavalry, held in reserve to the north of the city.

During the hour before midday, our men at Powick Bridge had repulsed the attempts by the enemy to cross the river. Charles was pacing nervously on the lead roof of the tower. In turn we became increasingly agitated as we watched the battle unfold below us. Just before one o'clock in the afternoon, we saw some boats being towed up the Severn.

'It seems they intend to cross over from the east of the river into Powick meadows,' said Charles. 'We must be ready to lead out the cavalry to support the infantry. Gentlemen, make sure your servants have your horses ready down below.'

'Look there, your Majesty,' said James who had his spy glass to his eye. 'Beyond the meadows, to the east of Powick Bridge.'

'I see them. They are sending boats across the Teme. They need to be stopped, before they establish a foothold.'

We watched in silence for a few moments. The enemy troops got ashore and held their ground. Behind them more boats came across and in about half an hour they had a pontoon bridge in place. Soon afterwards more of the enemy were seen on our side of the Teme, to the west of Powick Bridge. They must have forded the river above the bridge.

'Gentlemen, now is our time. We must stop them outflanking the men at Powick Bridge. Get to your horses. We must push them back across the river.'

James moved slowly down the stairs and we were amongst the last to mount up. We followed the cavalry column out of the city, down to the river.

Charles led a succession of charges against the enemy. He could not force them back across the river, but prevented them advancing any further. Then we saw a messenger ride up to Charles and point over to the Severn. I looked over to our eastern flank and saw that a force of enemy foot and horse had crossed the river and were attacking Powick Bridge from that side.

After about half an hour, our men began to retreat from Powick Bridge and Charles ordered us all back behind the city walls. We rode back, leaving the foot to their fate.

'Look how their eastern wing is exposed,' said Charles from the Cathedral Tower once more. 'The Duke of Hamilton will lead an attack on Perry Wood. I will attack Red Hill. Send a message to Leslie. He is to support us.'

With artillery support from Fort Royal, our small force of horse rode forward to support the infantry. Charles was to the fore, encouraging the men into the fight. Our move out of the defences of the city seemed to have surprised the enemy and initially we pushed them back up Red Hill. Then it became a slow drawn infantry fight, columns of pike bristling against each other. This went on for a few hours, with neither side gaining an advantage. Expectantly we waited for Leslie's horse to arrive and launch into the flank of the enemy, as Cromwell had done so ruthlessly at Marston Moor.

'There,' I shouted to James as we watched the foot contest it out. 'They are bringing their horse back across the Severn. It will be our flank that is turned.'

'Charles will be captured out here,' said James. 'We have to get him back into the city.'

We rode up to Charles who was still directing the assault up the hill.

'Your Majesty,' said James. 'I fear we will soon be outflanked by their horse.'

Charles looked across to where the enemy cavalry were forming up after crossing the river. 'Where is Leslie? We could have seen them off by now with his support. Dam him, this is his fault.'

'Shall I go and get him?' James asked.

'No, it is too late. Sound the retreat,' said Charles as he turned his horse about.

Initially our men retired in good order. Then they realized they would be cut off by the enemy horse, before the safety of the walls.

The retreat became a rout. We galloped back with the King, wondering why Leslie had not brought his horse in support.

Charles regrouped his regiment of horse and sent his officers to rally men to the walls. Later, artillery fire began to descend on the city. One of Charles's officers rode up.

'They've stormed Fort Royal and have turned the guns on the city.'

Night was closing in and the flashes of the canon looked a devilish sight in the dusk. Panic soon broke out with the news that Parliamentarian troops had stormed into the city. Men began to melt away down the burning streets, hoping to escape to the north. John Greenhalgh knew the situation was dire, and he seized the royal standard from its pole and wrapped it around his body. Charles called to us for one last charge.

I followed James forward and then looked around. Less than ten men were with the King.

'It is hopeless, Your Majesty' said James. 'Would you go to your death? Come away, you must escape before we are overrun.'

'Dam him,' was all Charles said as he allowed James to lead his horse away. I was not sure if he meant Cromwell or Leslie.'

***

North was the only way open to us, so we headed for Kidderminster. Here we halted and took stock. It felt as if it was the first time I had drawn breath since fleeing Worcester. Charles Giffard was close by and James called him over.

'Charles, I think His Majesty will need somewhere to hide. Can you shelter him in your home as you did me?'

'Of course, my lord.'

'It will be more dangerous than hiding me. You could be killed if you are caught.'

Charles nodded assent. 'I'll do it.'

'I will speak with him in private,' replied James. 'The fewer people who know about this the better.'

James and I now rode over to the King. He was a few paces away from his servants and staring into the distance. The servants were whispering amongst themselves, but it seemed none of them knew what to say to Charles.

'Your Majesty,' said James. 'I think we should separate from the rest. I will take you to a place of safety, where you can spend the night.'

'What, a place of safety you say. I doubt there is anywhere safe for me now.'

'There are still men ready to protect you. We must get you to France. But first we need to put a few more miles between us and Cromwell. Order the others to spread out in several directions and try to lead their patrols away. I will escort you.'

***

The onward journey to Boscobel was harrowing. Whenever we reached a village or crossroads, we had to stop and send a few men ahead to scout. We saw several patrols in the distance, but these seemed to be following the other fugitives. Eventually we arrived at Boscobel.

'Your Majesty, this is where you can hide,' said James. 'It will be safer if you are alone, so I will leave you in the care of Charles Giffard. He sheltered me here before the battle and can be trusted. What's more, he is a catholic and knows how to get men safely through England to France.'

'Lord Derby, your service to me will not be forgotten. I pray you reach safety too.'

***

The story of the King's escape to France has been told many times and I will not repeat it here. We were not to be so fortunate. Having formed up with some of the other fugitives, we had nearly reached Nantwich without being apprehended. Here we came across some Scottish foot who had made it this far.

'If we stay with them, they will slow us down,' I warned James.

'Our horses are tired. We can't go much faster than them anyway. We'll stay with them today.'

Less than an hour later we approached the River Weaver to the south of Nantwich. We rode as the vanguard, but found the bridge guarded by enemy troops. We made one unsuccessful attempt to rout them, but they stood firm. We rode off and the Scottish foot took another road for Nantwich.

'We'll never get away to safety,' James said to me. We were sheltering in a field behind a hedge. 'They seem to have all the routes through Cheshire blocked. The men and horses are tired and we are no match for any formed unit of Parliament.'

'Perhaps if we split up?' I replied. The two of us could get to the coast and find a ship for the Isle of Man.'

'And leave these poor fellows behind? I won't abandon these men. I'm responsible for them.'

The plod of a horse on the other side of the hedge stopped our discussion. I peered through the hedge and saw a single horseman.

'No, I know what I must do,' said James. 'Surrender to them.' Having said this he rode right up to the hedge and shouted. 'Sir, are you an officer, able to grant quarter to soldiers captured in battle?'

'Yes, I am. I'm a captain in Parliament's army. Do you surrender to me?'

'Yes, I do and I offer the surrender of these other gentlemen.'

I took a deep breath and exhaled slowly. So this was how it ended. After being at war for nearly nine years, James surrendered to a single soldier.

Chapter 32 – *Chester, September 1651*

"So ye shall not pollute the land wherein ye are: for blood it defileth the land: and the land cannot be cleansed of the blood that is shed therein, but by the blood of him that shed it." Numbers XXXV.33

They were treating us tolerably well in Chester Castle. James hoped to secure our liberty by surrendering the Isle of Man. He was having daily negotiations with Colonel Duckenfield, the governor of Chester. Duckenfield had even agreed to release James's former chaplain, Humfrey Baggarley. Baggarley would take letters to Charlotte, who had received no communication from James since we had landed in Lancashire.

Duckenfield would not give James any news about the King, which led him to believe that Charles was still at liberty. We prayed for the King's safety and that he would get over to France.

One week and a day after the defeat at Worcester, we were admitted in to see Duckenfield. He looked up from a document he had been reading. 'Ah, Stanley. I have orders from London. You are to be tried by a court-martial.'

'How can this be? I was given quarter on surrendering to Captain Edge. It is against the laws of war to charge me now.'

'You are to be charged with: traitorously bearing arms for Charles Stuart against the Parliament, for fortifying Lathom House against Parliament and for holding the Isle of Man against Parliament. You are to be tried for your life.'

James's shoulders slumped and he was silent for a few moments before replying. 'But what if I surrender the Isle of Man and go into exile. Won't that be enough?'

'That is for the court-martial to decide,' Duckenfield replied. 'You may have a lawyer to prepare your defence. I expect the trial to start in a couple of weeks.'

***

An unexpected visitor was waiting for James back at his chamber. It was his son, Charles. James had not seen him for over a year for they had become estranged over Charles's marriage. He had chosen as his bride Mademoiselle de Rupa, one of the maids of Elizabeth, Queen of Bohemia. This match was not approved of by James and Charlotte, and I had been asked to draw up a new will by James. Charles was only to receive five pounds.

'Father,' said Charles. 'I had to come to see you. Are you hurt?'

'I have no serious wounds, but I fear for my life. They are going to try me for treason for aiding the King.'

Charles can over and hugged his father. 'But why, didn't you surrender?'

'Yes, I did, but I do not think that will save me.'

'I'll go to London to seek a pardon. Who do we approach, Parliament or Cromwell?'

'All my crimes seem to be against the Parliament, so it is to them I must appeal. We'll draft out an appeal together with Paul, and you must take it to London.'

Two days later the appeal was ready and Charles set off for London. I had been told by Duckenfield there would be no charges against me and that I was free to leave. I chose to stay with James.

***

When James learnt the names of the men who would comprise the court-martial he seemed to lose the last traces of hope. None of the men were from Lancashire, where James might have counted on some vestiges of loyalty to his family. They were all Cheshire and Shropshire men and included Henry Bradshaw, an elder of John Bradshaw, James's intractable enemy.

'It's clear; they intend to find me guilty. Bradshaw is behind this. For his treachery as judge at the trial of King Charles, he has been rewarded with power. He's now using it to settle his vendetta. What's more, I hear a rumour that I'm to be tried for the death of Bootle at Bolton.'

'But James they cannot try you for the death of Bootle. He died at my hand. I will confess to killing him and then they'll have to try me.'

'Paul, it would make no difference. It is not about who killed Bootle. They mean to kill me. The death of Bootle is just pretence; they would find another. Your offer is noble, but I cannot allow you to do this.' Looking at me directly in the eye he continued, 'Let's not give the executioner two necks. Do you understand?'

A shiver went through me and as I replied the words caught in my throat. I had to cough before I could get them out. 'James, I will never forget this. You will take my killing of Bootle as your own. You will die and I will live.'

***

And that is how the trial went. James was found guilty of treason. Although there was no specific charge concerning the death of Bootle, when we learnt that the execution was to take place at Bolton, we understood.

Charles had returned from London, unsuccessful in his attempt to secure a pardon. However, he had thought to hire horses at relay posts on the London road, in case another journey was needed. James now sent him back with a petition each for Cromwell and Speaker Lenthall at the House of Commons. These were sent on October 11th, the execution was set for October 15th.

Chapter 33 – *Bolton, October 1651*

"But the goat, on which the lot fell to be the scapegoat, shall be presented alive before the Lord, to make an atonement with him, and to let him go for a scapegoat into the wilderness." Leviticus xvi. 10.

We were in James's cell with the chaplain, Greenhalgh, when the door burst open.

'Who are you?' asked James.

'Lieutenant Smith,' the man replied. He did not remove his hat and stood insolently before James. 'You are to be ready to leave for Bolton by six o'clock tomorrow morning.'

'Well, I thank God I am readier to die than for my journey. Commend me to Colonel Duckenfield, and tell him by that time I will be ready for both.'

'Do you know of any friend or servant,' replied Smith, 'Who will do that thing at Bolton?'

'What! Would you have one of my own friends cut off my head?'

'It would be easier for you if you did.'

'If those men that want my head can't find one to do it, then let it stay where it is. I thank God that my life has not been so bad that I should be instrumental in ending it.'

Smith went out and called Greenhalgh to go with him.

'See how they are ashamed of what they do, Paul.'

'I would do it for you, if it spared you pain,' I replied.

'You came to my father as a servant. Since then you have been more than that. You have been a true and faithful friend, but I could not have you do this. No, they must find their own executioner, and if he needs to take two or three blows, then it is God's will.'

Greenhalgh came back into the room. 'Smith asked me to talk to you again, but I refused,' he said.

'Thank you.' Turning back to me he continued. 'Paul, there is one final thing you can do for me. Go and buy as many gold rings as you can in the town. I want to send them to my family and friends. I don't have much to give any more, but this will show my love to all of them.'

Patting a tear away from the edge of my eye, I left the room. James's two eldest daughters, Katherine and Amelia were on their way to see him.

'How is father?' Katherine asked.

'He is bearing up remarkably well. His faith supports him.'

***

I came back later after supper. Katherine and Amelia had gone. I was surprised to see Sir Timothy Featherstone in James's cell. A bottle of wine was on the table between them. Sir Timothy had also been found guilty of treason, and was sentenced to die a week after James.

James greeted me warmly, 'Paul, come join us. Colonel Duckenfield has permitted me the company Sir Timothy. Here take a cup.'

James handed me the wine and I drank in silence.

James raised his cup to Sir Timothy. 'Be of good comfort. I go willingly before you. God has strengthened me, and you will hear I submitted both as a Christian and a soldier, to be both a comfort and an example to you.'

'I know it will be,' Sir Timothy replied.

'Now I shall make my final toasts to family and friends,' said James. 'Paul, fetch more cups.'

'To Charlotte, my loving wife: to my children, Katherine, Amelia, Mall, Ned and Billy. And to Charles, our differences behind us.' We all raised our cups and drank.

'A toast also to my loyal friend, Paul.' After a few moments he continued, 'Do you have the rings?'

'In my purse my Lord.'

'Give them to me. I'll wrap them up in the letters I've written for my family. God will look after them.'

***

I awoke the next morning thinking my head was jammed into a helmet. I touched my temples and realized it was a bad head from too much drink the night before. James had talked long into the night, almost afraid of sleep. I hurriedly got dressed and ran to his cell.

James was receiving the sacrament from Greenhalgh. Once they had finished and Greenhalgh had left the room, James spoke to me.

'Tomorrow, once they have done with me, you must take these letters to Charlotte and my children. Greenhalgh will take my body to Ormskirk for burial. When you see Charlotte you must convince her not to resist any more. The best hope for her and our children is to surrender up the Isle of Man to Duckenfield. He is already making preparations to sail across, so you won't have long to get over.'

'You know your wife James. Do you think she will surrender?'

'She has to, or you must see to it that she does not fight. She might see this as a betrayal, but remember you are doing this for me. If you have to, you must surrender the Isle to Parliament. Promise me that, Paul.'

'I promise.'

***

Outside in the castle courtyard Sir Timothy and several other gentlemen were waiting. Sir Timothy kissed James's hand and wept.

'God bless you,' said James. 'I hope my blood will satisfy them, and you will soon be free. But if their cruelty isn't abated, then I know God will be with you. He will give you courage to endure the ordeal.'

Orders were given for the men escorting James to mount up. I looked at the beast they had for James, a Galloway pony. James wasn't going to be able to run away from them. The escort was a full troop of cavalry. Perhaps Duckenfield feared some of James's friends would try to rescue him.

Duckenfield himself was there. 'It's time,' he said. 'Lieutenant Smith will take you to Bolton.'

The party set out with Katherine and Amelia following in a coach. At Hoole, just outside of Chester, James asked the escort to stop.

'I don't want my daughters to come to Bolton. Let me say my farewell to them here.'

He dismounted and went over to their coach. I watched them kneel and pray together. Then he kissed them both. The two girls were crying. He asked them to get back aboard. After a final embrace with James, they walked hand in hand back to the coach. James remounted his horse. I could not look at his face, but saw tears splash onto the neck of his horse.

We rode in silence for most of the day, until we came to Leigh.

'Lieutenant Smith,' James asked. 'Can I have your leave to go to the church here? I'd like to visit a friend's grave.'

'Would that be Tydesley's?' asked Smith. He straightened in his saddle. 'No, you can't. I've to get you locked up for the night. And I'll take the precaution of locking up your chaplain and servant too.'

***

With a guard accompanying me, I was allowed to go and get some supper for James and his group. I exchanged a few small coins for bread and a cheese. The inn keeper wouldn't take any payment for a pitcher of beer, and said he would pray for the earl that night.

I came back to the room where James was confined with Greenhalgh and Humfrey Baggarley.

'I remember a conversation I had with Archdeacon Rutter,' said James. 'I told him I did not fear death in battle, but it would be different if I had to die on the scaffold. You can tell him from me, when you see him next, that with God's help, I will lay my head upon the block, as willingly as if it were a pillow.'

'The Almighty will be by your side,' replied Greenhalgh.

I tried to dismiss the image of a scaffold from my mind. The inn keeper had told me timbers from Lathom House had been taken to Bolton, to be used for the scaffold. Even now I was appalled by the vindictiveness of James's enemies.

'Paul, I see you have been able to find us something to eat,' said James. 'I will imitate my Saviour and have a final supper. I am heartened, for I know none of you will betray me.' After he said this, his gaze rested upon me for a few moments. An unspoken pact went between us.

A little while later James said he would try to rest. As he lay down on his side, with a hand under his face, he said, 'Look at me, like a tomb in a church. Tomorrow, I will really be one.'

***

I had a fitful sleep that night. I awoke from a dream in which I was walking up to the scaffold, two drummer boys beating a slow march. I came to and realized that it was someone knocking at the door.

Baggarley went over and opened it. Charles came in, looking for his father.

'Is there news of a pardon?' he asked.

'No, Charles,' replied James. 'Or if there is, then they haven't told me.'

'When I left London, they were going to present your petition to the Commons on the 14th.'

'But that was only yesterday,' I said. 'How can they expect to get the pardon here in time?'

'They don't,' said James. 'It would be just like them to pardon me when it's too late. I hope they don't, for that will be too much for Charlotte. She won't be able to live with that knowledge. No, I must get ready. Paul, get me my clean shirt.'

James washed from a bowl of water while I retrieved the shirt.

'This shirt will be my winding sheet. See that I am buried in it.'

Momentarily mute, I acknowledged this with a nod.

Attaching his Order of the Garter to his cloak he said to Charles, 'After today, please take this back to the King, and tell him it is returned to him from a grateful servant. Now, Mr. Greenhalgh, please read the Decalogue to us.'

At the end of every commandment we all echoed James's "amen". Then Mr. Greenhalgh gave James the Sacrement.

Outside I could hear orders being given for the soldiers to fall in.

'Now gentlemen, it will soon be the hour,' said James. 'I will pray alone now.'

About a quarter of an hour later, Lieutenant Smith came in to fetch us. Outside the horses of the cavalry troop were fidgeting with impatience, their breath suspended in the air. A company of foot were being formed into line, the noise of pikes bouncing off the cobbles.

My senses were heightened, as if it were my last day on earth, not James's. Eggshell blue sky poked around the roofs of the black and white buildings. I heard the chatter of the crowd that had gathered, excited yet apprehensive.

To mount our horses we would have to stand in the filthy drainage channel in the middle of the street. 'Wait here,' I said to James. I walked over and took our horses by the reins and moved them to stand on dry cobbles. Better to have mud on my boots than James's.

We mounted and waited for Lieutenant Smith to give the order to move. A cry of 'God save the Earl of Derby,' came from the depth of the crowd. This was followed by a murmur of approval from others.

The crowd was silenced by Lieutenant Smith barking out the order to set off.

Once out of Leigh our horses scrunched through golden brown leaves on the road.

'I am like these leaves,' said James. 'As a mortal man my life is at an end. But with the grace of our Saviour I will live on, like the tree.'

As we came into Bolton another crowd gathered and followed us up to the Market Cross. Some of them were weeping. They ran alongside and again we heard the cry, 'God save the Earl of Derby.'

'I'm glad to see they don't hate me,' said James. 'I had feared they would hold me responsible for the deaths during the storming of Bolton.'

I remembered one particular death that day in 1644, that of Bootle. Even now I did not feel safe publicly admitting that I had killed him. Despite what James had said, I still felt James was suffering because of me. Perhaps he hoped that his death would be an end to the killing. A lesson from Leviticus read by James's chaplain came into my mind. It was about the scapegoat, the symbolic bearer of the sins of the people. James was to be such a scapegoat. I could not speak these thoughts out loud and instead I reassured him.

'The people have never hated you, James. The only people happy today are Bradshaw and his friends.'

The sound of hammers on the market place indicated that the scaffold was not yet complete. As we drew up alongside it, Lieutenant Smith spoke, 'It's not ready yet. You may have until 3 o'clock to prepare yourself.'

'I will not stand here and watch these men erect my scaffold,' replied James. 'Can I go to the church?'

'No, we have a room for you in the inn. You will have privacy there.'

***

The innkeeper led us upstairs to a room which overlooked the market place. 'It's the largest room I have,' he said.

'It is fine,' replied James. 'Can you bring us something to drink? I don't know about my friends, but I'm parched.'

After the innkeeper had brought us refreshments, James raised a cup one last time to us. 'So many of my family and friends are not here, but I am thankful to be with my son Charles and some of my most loyal friends. You have all served me well. I could not have asked for more. You all know what you have to do when I am dead. Now, I would like some time alone in prayer.'

We left the room and went downstairs to wait. My mind was not still enough for prayer and I paced up and down. The hammering of the men outside echoed in my head.

Shortly before 3 o'clock, Lieutenant Smith came back in. 'I have come for him,' he said.

'I'll see if he is ready for you,' I replied.

Keeping Smith standing on the stairs, I knocked on the door of the upstairs room.

'Come,' replied James.

I went in followed by Smith, Charles, Humfrey and Mr. Greenhalgh.

'I see by your faces that it is time. Don't worry. I am at peace with our Lord. I don't fear death. My only worry is what will happen to my wife and children. I have prayed to God, asking Him to be a husband and a father to them. I know that He will do this.'

Charles embraced his father. 'I have failed you. I couldn't get a pardon.'

'Charles, you have never failed me. Now you must be strong and do all you can to honour the Stanley name.' Turning to Smith he continued, 'I'm ready.'

Smith turned and led us outside. A group of soldiers was waiting to escort James through the crowd. As we walked up to the scaffold, people on either side reached out and tried to touch James. One of them received a jab from the bottom of a soldier's pike. The crowd got noisier and the soldiers drew closer together. Our progress got slower. Finally we arrived at the foot of the steps to the scaffold. Smith stood aside, reluctant to mount the steps, and waited for James to climb up. We followed him onto the platform.

James took a deep breath and took his speech out of his coat. He turned to face the crowd. 'I am content to die in this town, where some say I slew a great many people. I know I'm not a man of blood, as some have falsely slandered me. There will be some here who will remember my mercy and care in saving many lives that day.' Some in the crowd murmured their assent.

'As for my crime of assisting the King, I do not consider it a crime to obey my master's commands. The Lord bless and preserve him.' 'Bless and preserve him,' echoed a few brave people.

'I always fought for peace. I wanted neither estate nor honour. I am condemned to die by his Majesty's enemies, by new and unknown laws. May the Lord send us our King again. May the Lord send us our religion again. I die for God, the King and the laws. I am not ashamed of my life, nor afraid of my death.' The crowd started to press forward, pushing against the soldiers.

One of the soldiers shouted, 'We have no King, and we'll have no Lords.' He drew his sword and slashed out at a woman in front of him. She screamed as a red slash seeped through the arm of her dress. The crowd surged forward, knocking some of the soldiers against the scaffold.

Wide eyed, Lieutenant Smith shouted for the troops to clear the street. The company of horse rode into the crowd, reigning blows to left and right.

James called out to Smith. 'Stop your men. Do you think I will escape?'

Smith did not reply. Gradually the violence subsided. James spoke to me. 'Paul, they'll not let me finish. Here take my speech and papers. Keep them safe.' He looked to the executioner, only his mouth and eyes visible behind the mask. Putting his hand into his coat-pocket he said, 'Take these coins. They are all I have. Do your job well.' James removed his coat and then spoke to the headsman again. 'I think your coat will hinder you in your work. Please remove it.'

James's voice still carried authority and the executioner removed his shag coat. A woman in the crowd cried out for him to ask James's forgiveness. The headsman remained silent.

James looked at the block and spoke again. 'Can we move it to point to the church? I want to be facing God's sanctuary.' The headsman repositioned the block and stood back waiting for James.

'When I am upon the block,' said James. 'I will lift up my hands as a signal for you to do your work.' He knelt down and prayed silently, ending with the Lord's Prayer spoken aloud. Several of us on the platform recited it along with him.

He stood up and addressed the crowd again. 'The Lord be with you all. Pray for me. The Lord bless my wife and children, and the Lord bless us all.'

Then he knelt at the block, and leaned forward so his neck made contact with the rough wood. He stretched out his arms and said, 'Blessed be God's glorious name for ever and ever. Amen. Let all the whole earth be filled with His glory. Amen.'

Then he lifted up his hands and tensed for the blow. The headsman did not see the signal and stood with his axe resting on the floor. James rose again and said, 'Why don't you do your work? I will lay down again in peace. And I hope I shall enjoy everlasting peace.'

He set himself down again, with his neck upon the block. Stretching out his arms, he said again, 'Blessed be God's glorious name for ever and ever. Amen. Let all the whole earth be filled with His glory. Amen.' He lifted up his hands and the executioner raised the axe.

On the echo of 'Amen' from the crowd, the axe swung down, taking James's head in a single blow.

Chapter 34 – *The Isle of Man, October 22, 1651*

Pausing on a hill overlooking Douglas, Paul prepared his thoughts for the meeting with William Christian. He suspected that as Christian was a native of the Isle, he might be willing to surrender to avoid any deaths amongst the Manxmen. He had some authority, as James had appointed him as governor during his absence. Paul nudged his horse's flank with his right heel to set her on again, hoping he would be able to get to see Christian without any delay. Parliament's fleet could arrive off the Island any day now. It was best he knew where everyone stood, before he was holed up in Castle Rushen.

When he arrived at the castle in Douglas, he asked to see the governor. The news was disappointing. 'Gone up to Ramsey, he has,' replied the sergeant on the gate.

'When will he be back?'

'Said he'd be back tomorrow. But with the Isle in such a panic, he could be gone longer.'

Becoming increasingly anxious, Paul rode north to Ramsey. He pushed his horse hard for the last few miles. Why would Christian come up to Ramsey? It had no great fortress, but it did have a sheltered bay. An undefended bay, ideal for the enemy fleet to land an army in safety. James had strengthened the defences at Peel and Castle Rushen and repaired the fort at Derbyhaven, but with limited resources he had overlooked the North of the Isle. Christian would know this. Perhaps he was seeing what he could do, even at this late hour to muster some form of defence at Ramsey.

He could see the bay now, but there was no sign of anyone preparing defences. Paul found Christian in the upstairs room of an inn in the centre of Ramsey. He was talking in Manx to a small group of men gathered around him. They looked up suspiciously as Paul approached.

'What do you want?' asked Christian.

'A word about the defences of the Isle. I'm Paul Morrow. You may remember our horse race, a few years ago?'

'Aye, I know who you are. Had enough fighting across there and come to tell us what to do, have you?'

'No, it's not that. I just want a private word about Castle Rushen.'

Christian looked at Paul for a few moments, before continuing. 'Lads, go downstairs and get something to eat. Tell the innkeeper to bring up two of his pies. Oh, and a jug of beer, we've got something to discuss.'

Paul waited for the men to leave the room. 'Did James leave you any instructions about what to do if he was killed?'

'Not especially, no. Why do you want to know?'

'It's just that, as governor, you have a responsibility for the protection of people here.'

'Right enough, but what's it to do with you?'

'I have an order from James to see that no harm comes to the people on the Isle. He knew it was pointless to fight on.'

'What are you saying exactly?' replied Christian, moving in a little closer to Paul.

'That we should not prevent Colonel Duckenfield from landing his troops on the Isle, and we should negotiate with him for the best terms we can get for Charlotte.'

'Charlotte, what concern is she now?' asked Christian.

'She is the one person who can prevent a bloodless end to all this. And, she wants to fight.'

'What can she do? She does not control the Isle, I do.'

'But she has Castle Rushen and a hundred men in there. If she fights, people will die. And the Isle will be worse off after she is beaten. Do you want their military rule here?'

Christian looked at Paul for a few moments. 'I can see to it that Duckenfield lands on the Isle without a shot being fired, but how can I stop her from fighting?'

'You leave it to me,' replied Paul. 'Just get them ashore and down to Castle Rushen and I'll do the rest.'

Chapter 35 – *The Isle of Man, October 25, 1651*

Henry threw the ball to Paul who watched its flight, a small shape against the dark rain clouds. He caught it and drew back his arm to throw it to Charles. He stopped in mid throw, his action blunted by the sombre chime of the alarm bell.

'Ships out at sea,' cried the watch. 'Looks to be more than a dozen of them.'

Paul dropped the ball and ran up the tower, his boys following. Panting at the top of the stairs, he looked out at the ships. Too many to count to be sure of the exact number, but they looked to be more than a score. This had to be the Parliamentarian fleet. Henry and Charles were counting out loud. The watchman swore quietly.

More people came up onto the walls, and for nearly an hour they watched mesmerised as the ships made their way across the bay in the direction of Derbyhaven. With the fort guarding the entrance to the bay, Paul doubted they would attempt a landing there.

This was it then. They had arrived. Not since Marston Moor had Paul felt so conscious of his own mortality. Once again he thought about what might happen to his family if the castle were stormed. Now he was even more convinced about his course of action.

He went up to see Charlotte, hoping her resolve had been broken by the enemy's arrival.

'Paul, you must ride over to Derbyhaven and make sure they don't land there. The fort is well armed, but I'm worried about the men's loyalty.'

It was as if she was testing him. Could she have guessed his intention? Paul agreed to go and set out immediately.

***

The enemy ships were coming into view as Paul climbed the steps of Derby Fort's gun platform. He could smell fear in the sweat of the gunners and their captain, as they watched the enemy ships come into range. Had Providence given him the opportunity to allow the Parliamentarian fleet to land unopposed? Would they believe him if he said he had an order from Charlotte not to open fire?

Paul decided they would not fall for a simple trick. No, better to prevent the ships from using the bay, but avoid causing them any damage.

'Captain, if you engage them in a battle, then they will pound this fort to rubble. A shot across the bows may persuade them to continue on and land somewhere else. That way we do our duty and live.'

'A sensible course,' replied the captain. 'I'm not willing to die for the Lady Derby. You'll tell her we fought them off?'

'Aye, I will, if the plan works. Let's hope they aren't expecting the fort to be armed, and will leave us alone when they know we're here.'

'We'll shoot before they reach the bay. Get ready to fire, boys. Aim well in front of the lead ship. Whatever you do, don't hit her!'

The gun crew made ready to fire, the captain standing with a lit taper. The lead ship was getting close to the gun's line of fire.

'Prepare to fire,' the captain shouted. The gunners moved away from the gun, not wanting to be hit when it recoiled. The captain put the taper into the firing hole and we all waited for it to catch. A few moments later the gun belched into life, sending gulls screeching away to safety.

Paul watched the bow of the ship. Heartbeats later a splash in front of her indicated that the aim had been good. He tensed, waiting for a deadly reply from the ships. His mouth felt dry as he watched the gunners reload. Slowly the ships continued their course, not deviating into the bay. They weren't going to land at Derbyhaven.

Chapter 36 – *The Isle of Man, October 27, 1651*

Paul was looking down at the main gate from the walls of Castle Rushen. It was well guarded and the men were alert. He did not see that as a possible way in for the Parliamentarians. No doubt they would bring heavy guns in close to batter the walls. After that it would be a messy struggle inside the castle. There would be many deaths and Paul feared for his family's safety. To have survived nine years of war to be killed now when their cause was lost, was hard for Paul to contemplate. He was more convinced than ever he needed to betray the castle.

Turning away from the gate he started a circuit of the walls, looking for any point of weakness in the defences. Half an hour later and feeling increasingly despondent he arrived at a small tower on the eastern side of the outer wall. He looked down at the moat, protecting the base of the wall from cannon fire. Then he noticed a sally port at the bottom of the tower. If he could get this open it would give the Parliamentarians access to the inner bailey, bypassing the gatehouse. Paul went down the spiral staircase to the dark depths of the tower. His eyes got accustomed to the darkness, aided by light coming in from a small gap down one side of the door. He tried the door. It was locked and secured with three heavy bolts. The bolts were not a problem, but where would he find the key?

Furtively, he made his way back up the steps and out of the tower. The key was probably kept in the guardroom in the gatehouse. He walked across the bailey, feeling as if he was being watched all the way. The guards in the gatehouse were chatting and smoking clay pipes. Paul had tried the tobacco pipes, but it was not something he enjoyed and the smoke in the air made him cough as he approached them.

'Sovereign isle,' he said giving them the password of the day.

'Yes friend, what can we do for you?' asked one of the guards.

'I want to make a tour of all the sally ports to check we can use them. Who knows if we can get them all open when the fighting starts.'

'Got a lass in the town have you? Can't let a siege get in the way of your love life.' The other guards laughed and Paul felt his cheeks colour.

'No lads. It's just that I've spoken to governor Musgrave and he agrees the enemy will deploy their guns outside the walls. It may be useful to make a sally out to spike them.' Paul knew his lie was unlikely to be found out, as these men would not bother Musgrave about this.

'Right it is then. Bill you go with the gentleman and check the doors. Here, you'll need the keys for the west and east towers. Make sure you bring the keys back mind, or it'll be my balls that swing if you lose them.'

To hide his intentions, Paul suggested they went to the west side first. This time he took a torch down with him. The sally port on the west side was very similar to the one he had seen earlier. Bill drew back the bolts and fumbled on a large key ring to find the right key for the door. Letters were painted on the keys, and Bill was looking for a "s" for the sally port in the curtain wall, outside the West Tower. After separating the keys he found the correct one and opened the lock. He put both hands on the handle and pulled the door back. A couple of spiders ran out as their webs were broken by the opening door.

Blinking in the light Paul said, 'That's good. See how we can pull a small boat through the door to get onto the moat. Let's get over to the east side and check we have the key for that one.'

Across on the eastern side Paul asked if he could open the door. Bill handed him the keys in return for the torch Paul had been carrying. Paul located the key and turned the lock, before pulling back the bars and drawing back the door. Again he was momentarily blinded by the light. Outside the door were a small platform and some steps leading down to the water.

'You can go. I want a look around the tower,' said Paul. 'I'll bring the keys back to the gatehouse when I've finished.'

Bill looked at him for a few moments. Paul felt blood echoing in his head. Eventually Bill replied. 'Right enough. I'll get round to the kitchens to see what I can scrounge, before the sergeant misses me.'

Paul waited a few minutes for Bill to get away and then bolted the door, withdrawing the key without turning the lock. His heart pounded as he made his way back out to the bailey. He was risking a lot by doing this, and doubted whether his reputation would save him if Charlotte found out he was trying to betray her.

Chapter 37 – *The Isle of Man, October 28, 1651*

'She's beginning to change her mind,' said Louise to Paul. 'She is now talking about seeking terms that will give her the means to care for her daughters.'

'Does Charlotte now intend to surrender?' Paul asked.

'I think so. She wants a safe passage to go to Holland or France.'

'And what about us? Has she spared a thought for her servants and the soldiers in the castle?'

'I don't know. Come, let's go and speak to her,' said Louise.

'Have your thoughts changed, my Lady?' Paul asked.

'My wish to fight for my husband's name has not diminished, but I see I have to make terms while I am at my strongest. Once they start a siege, and indeed if they take the castle, they will not offer any clemency.'

'So what will you ask for?'

'That I am allowed to take my children over to England and that my daughters, Katherine and Amelia are released. That James's will is honoured and I am given what is mine to live on and bring up our children. I will also ask that my servants and chaplains are allowed to go over to England if they wish.'

'What about Sir Philip and the other gentlemen who are here?'

'I'll ask that they are also given liberty, and that they are allowed to compound for their estates.'

'What about our children?' asked Louise.

'Don't worry, they will be safe,' replied Charlotte.

'What if they do not agree to these terms?' continued Louise.

'Then I shall continue to fight. Winter is almost upon us and I'm sure they won't stomach a long siege. After a few months in the cold, they'll grant these terms.'

'No, you're wrong,' replied Paul. 'They'll bring up their guns, and this time we can't expect any relief. There won't be another Rupert to come to our aid. When the end comes many of us will die, including our children.'

Louise looked in horror at Paul as he expressed in words what she feared most of all.

Chapter 38 – *Isle of Man, October 29, 1651*

"Madam - I presume to return this answer to your Ladyship's Letter sent to me by Mr. Broyden, that I have earnestly solicited the Council of State, and my Lord General, to commiserate the condition of the late Earl of Derby, and his Family; but they have since commanded me hither, for the reducing of this Island; and therefore, according to the trust reposed in me, I shall by the help of God, endeavour to lose no time in gaining such holds as are yet defended by your Ladyship, against those I serve, and hope to manage the same as becomes a Soldier and a Christian: and I really believe, there is no way left for your Family, of avoiding utter ruin, but by a present surrendering the castles of Rushen and Peel to the State of England; the delaying whereof, will render me unable to approve my self, Your Ladyship's servant,

ROB. DUCKDNFIELD.

Castle Town Octob. 29, 1651."

'So, he and Cromwell commiserate with me for James's death,' said Charlotte, putting down the letter. 'Why didn't Cromwell save him then?'

'I don't know, my Lady,' replied Paul. 'Perhaps Cromwell couldn't control James's enemies. Or he may have wanted James dead. Whatever. You must now look to save yourself and your family.'

'I'm sending Mr. Broom out to them. He will take my terms for surrender.'

'Do you still try to seek terms?'

'Yes, the terms we discussed yesterday. If they don't grant them to me, then I will hold the castle against them. I won't surrender meekly.'

Chapter 39 – *Isle of Man, October 30, 1651*

'Where is Broom? Surely he has their answer by now?' Charlotte was pacing around the presence chamber, watched by Paul and Sir Philip Musgrave.

'Perhaps it is a good sign,' said Sir Philip. 'That they are considering your terms?'

'Or they have strung him up for insolence,' Charlotte retorted. 'Leave me now. Send word when Broom returns.'

***

Paul paced around the castle. Charlotte was unpredictable. She was likely to bring about the deaths of all the people he loved. He was not going to allow the death of his family. In his mind, he rehearsed the plan to betray Charlotte. He was going to have to wait until Duckenfield had lined his men and guns outside Castle Rushen. Until then he had to bide his time.

***

Paul was called back to the Presence Chamber. Broom was standing in front of Charlotte, his head bowed.

'What do you mean, they haven't sent an answer to my letter?' said Charlotte.

'All they said was, "go back and tell her she will see our answer tomorrow." They were marching here when they sent me back. And bringing their siege guns.'

'Sir Philip, call the garrison out,' said Charlotte. 'Get them on the walls. I want them to know that I'll fight.'

***

Paul watched from the walls as the Parliament's army deployed around the castle. With grudging admiration, he observed their neat drill and orderliness. What worried him most were the siege guns, grouped together menacingly. A few hours close bombardment from them would bring the walls of the castle down.

Chapter 40 – *Isle of Man, October 31, 1651*

Paul had been tormented in his sleep. He had been dreaming about James's execution. James's dead body was lying on the platform. Blood was spurting everywhere. His fleet were slipping in the warm crimson tide. He was struggling over to pick up James's head. He was pushing the blood matted hair aside to clean his Lord's face, expecting to look into the dead man's eyes.

Paul screamed himself awake. It was not James's face he saw on the scaffold. It was Louise's.

'What is it?' asked Louise coming awake instantly.

'A nightmare,' Paul replied. 'But one that shows me what I must do.'

Paul got out of bed to get dressed. 'Remember how I said I'd made a promise to James?'

'That you'd stop Charlotte from fighting?'

'Yes, but as I've not been able to persuade her, I'm going to have to surrender the castle to Duckenfield. Get the children up. I want to see them.'

'Don't put yourself in danger,' said Louise. 'Charlotte will come round. I'll talk to her again today.'

'It's too late for that. She has had her chance. Today they will start firing, and then we might all die. Please go and get the children.'

Louise walked through to the children's room. 'Time to get up! Come and see your father.'

Paul looked at the sleepy faces of his children as they filed into the room. If he died, then at least they might survive. However, he could not tell them what he was going to do. He could not risk them with such a secret.

'Stay with your mother today. There may be some fighting. But if you all stay in here with her, then you won't come to any harm. Do you all promise me?'

'We promise,' said Alice and Charles. Henry did not reply.

'And that includes you too, Henry,' said Paul.

'But aren't I old enough to fight?'

'You don't want to fight. Trust me,' said Paul. 'We've had more than enough of wars. And too many good men have died. I'll not see my own son die needlessly.'

'But what about you?' Henry asked.

'Don't worry about me. I'll be alright. I'll be back here before you know it.' Paul hugged Louise. The silence between them revealed more than any words. He buckled on his sword belt, ruffled Alice's hair, and with a last look at them all, he left the room.

***

Confusion abounded in the castle. None of the captains were given orders, and the soldiers were trying to decide what to do. Some of them had obediently taken to the walls. Others loitered in the bailey, smoking their pipes.

'Get away from that powder,' Paul shouted at them. 'Do you want to blow us all up?'

Looking at the barrels stored at the bottom of the wall, the men shuffled away.

Paul climbed up to the wall of the east tower, cold air on his face. Cautiously he peered out over the stone. Enemy sentries were watching the castle, and larger siege guns were being manhandled into position. The breath from the struggling soldiers was forming little clouds in front of their faces. He would be putting himself at risk by opening the sally port. Paul wondered if he would need to do anything to attract their attention, or it might all be a waste of time. He exposed a little more of his body above the parapet. No shots came. Venturing further he made himself visible to the sentries outside the castle. Again he waited, tensing his body for the impact of a shot. Again he was relieved when none came. One of the soldiers had stopped marching and seemed to be looking at Paul.

Paul glanced around to see if anyone in the castle was watching. Nobody seemed to be interested in what he was doing. He put his arm over the wall and pointed to the door of the sally port. The Parliamentarian sentry looked down at the door, and then back at Paul. He nodded, and then called for some more soldiers to join him.

This was his chance. Slowly, Paul made his way down to the dark base of the tower. His sword clattered against the side of the wall. He reached over to the door and began to draw back the first bolt.

'Stop!' called a voice from behind him. He turned around to see the sergeant from the gatehouse pointing a pistol at him. 'I saw you up on the wall and wondered what you were up to. Bolt that door again, and then come over here.'

'What good will it do to oppose them?' asked Paul. 'Surely you don't want to die?'

'I don't intend to. But I'll get a reward from Lady Derby for turning you in.'

'I doubt she has even a sovereign to give you. These wars have ruined the Stanleys.'

'Oh, I'm sure she has some silver hidden away.'

'I'm going to carry on undoing these bolts. Shoot me if you want to.'

In the semi-darkness, Paul waited for the flash from the pistol. He heard the click of the firing mechanism and ducked down.

'God's blood,' shouted the sergeant. The pistol had not fired.

Paul leapt up and drew his rapier. The years of sword drill meant there could only be one outcome. Thinking only of his family, he ran the sergeant through with brutal force, the sword only being stopped by the stone wall behind.

'Dear God, forgive me,' said Paul as the sergeant slumped to the ground.

He turned back to the door and unbolted it. Pulling it open, he looked out to see a group of soldiers paddling over in a boat. The nightmare was over. Paul had kept his final promise to James and saved both their families.